Moon's Web

Praise for *Moon's Web*

"The writing team of C. T. Adams and Cathy Clamp work to-gether beautifully to write an engrossing story that will have you reading long into the night. Once you start *Moon's Web,* you won't be able to put it down until the last page is turned. Fast paced with a dash of humor and romance thrown in, this book has something for everyone."　　　*—Romance Junkies*

"C. T. Adams and Cathy Clamp have outdone the wonderful job they did with *Hunter's Moon*! The action begins on the very first page and doesn't let up throughout the story. This is definitely a book you don't want to miss reading!"
—ParaNormal Romance Reviews

"Ms. Clamp and Ms. Adams pull no punches with this story. Readers will love the world created in this series, and espe-cially enjoy the complex society made up of shape shifters of every kind imaginable."　　　*—Love Romances*

"These aren't your average characters. They're gritty and of-ten brutal. To them, death is a natural act, especially when it comes at their hands. But the authors have made them com-plex and three-dimensional, inviting readers to care for and love them. It's rare when a second book surpasses the first, but *Moon's Web* explodes onto the scene, earning a Perfect 10. If you're a fan of Laurell K. Hamilton or Kelley Arm-strong, *Moon's Web* is definitely a book for you!"
—Romance Reviews Today

Moon's Web

CATHY L. CLAMP
and C. T. ADAMS

tor romance

A TOM DOHERTY ASSOCIATES BOOK
NEW YORK

MOON'S WEB

Edited by Anna Genoese

A Tor Book
Published by Tom Doherty Associates, LLC
175 Fifth Avenue
New York, NY 10010

Tor® is a registered trademark of Tom Doherty Associates, LLC.

ISBN 0-7394-5711-X

Printed in the United States of America

Acknowledgments

EVERY BOOK IS a team effort, and more than just we two as co-authors. Above all, this book is dedicated to Cathy's wonderful husband, Don, and Cie's terrific son, James. We'd like to thank our families and friends for their input, suggestions and support. But none of this would be possible without the people behind the scenes, so we'd like to take the time to thank our amazing agent, Merrilee Heifetz and her associate, Ginger Clark, as well as our talented editor Anna Genoese, plus the marketing team, copy editors, publicists and artists at Tor who turned this book from a mere idea into a compelling read. And, as always, we'd like to thank Laurell, Darla, and so many other authors we've met who have helped with our success. You all know who you are! Thanks, everyone!

Moon's Web

Chapter 1

THE SCENT OF snow on the wind raised the hairs on my skin like distant lightning. I lifted my nose into the icy breeze that rushed past me through the open window of the bus. The moon was hidden behind a thin barrier of clouds, but I *felt* it. Its weight pressed me with a sensuous, almost sexual, insistence. It reached for the wolf beneath my skin. I started at the realization that all sound had stopped in the bus. Just moments ago it had been a party on wheels with liquor flowing freely among the poker and dice games. Now, as the bus reached the edge of the park near Wolf Lake, the others began to snuffle and writhe. A woman's high-pitched whine made me shiver.

A deep voice like liquid velvet reached my ears. "Soon, my wolves. Very soon I will let the moon take you."

I glanced to the front of the bus. Nikoli Molotov's eyes glowed yellow, revealing the effort he was expending. He had told me he would use the Sazi magic inside him to keep the pack members from turning to their animal shapes until we were well within the state park. But the thin shell of magic could barely contain the power that welled up inside of me. I felt like an overripe fruit, threatening to burst through my own skin.

This was my first full moon since moving to Chicago. There are few actual wooded areas here, and none that aren't accessible to the public. Still, I was told that the lakes and the parks can be sealed with magic so that no humans would want to enter while the pack hunts the animals native to the park. I'd never been hunting with a pack. Until recently, I'd only known of one werewolf besides myself—the one who'd turned me.

Who'd have believed that there were real werewolves among us in modern society? I certainly hadn't. I'd spent my first Sazi year in partial denial. I sealed myself away each month so I could turn into a wolf at will in the privacy of a hotel suite. I hadn't tried to find others like me. I hadn't wanted to. Until I met Sue, I had pretended—had hoped—that this disease would just go away.

The hissing of the air brakes interrupted my thoughts. The whines and whimpers around me brought a deep-throated growl from my throat. The magic roiling through the close confines of the bus was stifling. You could walk on the tension. The scent of musk and fur was overpoweringly sweet. It was hard to breathe. My muscles were twitching in earnest now. At the front of the bus, Nikoli smiled.

"Come, my wolves," he whispered. "It is time. Join the hunt." He exited the bus. We followed in his wake. I scanned the area with my vision pink-hazed from blood. I fought not to howl. Shuddering, I pulled the clothes from my body, reveling in the feel of the wind against my over-heated skin. My eyes moved constantly, watching the others—my pack.

Some of the men had to turn their eyes away from the lithe nude forms of the women in the group, but I felt nothing for them. My mate was elsewhere. I glanced past the sign identifying the William W. Powers State Conservation Area. In the distance, I smelled the sharp hot and sour soup scent of abject fear. I quickly wiped a small line of spittle from the side of my mouth. I tried to appear composed but it was a lie.

"So, how does this wor—?" I began, when Nikoli interrupted.

"Let the hunt begin!" he boomed and released the magical shield protecting me. The moon's force struck like a sharp blade, shattering my control and sending me to my knees. I screamed in pain as a thousand pinpoints of light and magic erupted from my skin. Fur raced over my body and twisted my limbs. A full-grown, hungry wolf leapt out from inside me. I couldn't have stopped it if I wanted to.

I didn't want to.

The world suddenly shifted. Color disappeared, giving way to a thousand shades of grey and black. I stood on four feet, basking in the finger of moonlight that pried its way through the cloud cover. Beside me were over a dozen snarling wolves. I'd met one or two of them as humans. I couldn't tell who they were as wolves by sight, but my nose knew. Human or wolf, their scent was the same. I scanned the group for the leader of the pack. He wasn't hard to find. I felt my eyes go wide.

Nikoli had transformed into a huge black timber wolf. He easily stood three foot high at the shoulder. The only white on him was two spots on his knees. They glared like headlights in the darkness beneath the amber lights in his eyes. I realized that I didn't own a gun big enough to defend myself had I met him in the woods as a human. Not a comforting thought.

A single howl rent the night, quickly joined by other voices. The sounds were deep and throaty, not at all the high-pitched yelp of a coyote.

I felt the lips pull back from my fangs in a smile. Until I'd mated, my nights as a wolf had been lost to me. My thoughts inhuman, memories nonexistent. The difference is phenomenal. Now wolf or man—I'm *me*. That's thanks to Sue. I could feel fragments of her warmth and anticipation in the back of my mind. I knew she would be enjoying every minute of this new experience. The thought of the hunt was getting my mate turned on.

I like that in a woman.

She had believed in and accepted the mating bond even

before I did. The sex had been incredible from the start. Not surprising since we can feel each other's pleasure through the bond. Still, I had struggled and fought the tie between us. I hadn't wanted to give up what I believed was my identity. But when she was dying of a gunshot wound, I made my choice. I accepted the bond, accepted the fact that we are truly a part of one another—just in time to have them cut me off from her for weeks while she's been healing in Colorado. It's a struggle now to share our thoughts, and I can't sense what she's doing at all. I hate it. I miss her. I want her home with me.

One of the wolves spoke. It's still weird hearing human speech coming from a furred muzzle. "Where's dragon lady tonight, Nikoli?"

A decidedly evil chuckle erupted from the black wolf. His eyes turned and locked on mine. "Our lovely Asri did not trust herself to ride on the bus and attend the pack meeting around our newest acquisition."

Now, what the hell did that mean?

"Which brings me to business," he continued. "Let us all please welcome our newest member of the pack. Anton, please step forward."

I sighed. I had tried repeatedly to get my new pack leader, a former member of Czar Nicholas II's court, to call me Tony. That's me, Tony Giodone, former high-end assassin, catering to both the paying public and the mob. I'm good enough to have never been caught. But a stupid mistake on my last job caused me to go underground and assume a new—or more precisely—a *former* identity. Here in Chicago, I'm Joe Giambrocco. But Nikoli keeps Russianizing everything. I finally decided that Anton was better than Yosef if I was going to be stuck with a Russian name.

I stepped forward and the other wolves parted like water to let me pass, reforming in a circle around me and Nikoli. I stopped a few inches short of his muzzle and looked up into his face. He towered over me. His yellow eyes narrowed, as he watched me coldly. I stood steady, giving no sign of fear, despite the muscles rippling under his sleek black fur.

"You are Sazi," he said. "Blood of my blood. But to be of my pack, you must swear fealty to me and mine. You must give of yourself so that the others will recognize you as brother."

This was starting to make me nervous. It's one thing to be part of a club, but another thing entirely to swear some sort of blood oath.

I felt my eyes narrow, "Just what are you asking me to do?"

Nikoli smiled, baring fangs. His scent changed, but I couldn't pinpoint what he was feeling. I'd have to go by his words alone.

"I rule here. You will accept my authority over you. Yes?"

I had no problem with that. "I accept your authority as the pack leader. Yes."

"Excellent." I had just turned to leave when I froze completely. I literally couldn't move. I felt a flash of panic in the back of my mind that wasn't mine. Sue knew something I didn't, but it was a struggle to keep connected with her. The magic that flooded my body and mind was overwhelming. It was a pounding ache with sharp edges.

Nikoli stalked toward me. His lips had pulled back even further to reveal pink gums.

"Then know my *power*, whelp." He came at me in a rush of fangs and fur. I could do nothing to defend myself. He bowled me over and his teeth found my neck. A flash of pain seared my mind as his fangs broke through skin and I was thrown bodily to the ground. But the pain washed away as quickly as it began. My mind was floating suddenly as a wave of magic filled me. I could hear his voice in my mind. It was as thick and sweet as honey.

"You are pack of my pack, young one," said the voice. I knew I was bleeding, but I couldn't seem to feel it. I could hear Sue trying to call to me. It was a struggle to hear her.

The liquid baritone continued. "You will live for me, through me, and we all will live for you. We will protect you and you will always be fed. Be now one with the Sazi, Anton."

I came to myself with a dozen noses sniffing my head. I abruptly remembered part of my training on Carmine and Linda's island after Sue's near-death. One of the Sazi psychiatrists explained that the packs only functioned in the modern world because one person can control the individual wolves.

"If individual wolves were autonomous," Dr. Betty had said, "The world would quickly learn of us. Close to the moon, most lesser wolves can't control themselves when prey is near. humans were once prey to our kind. Now if we were to attack them, it would be war. The humans would slaughter us. People always destroy that which they fear. Only by having a leader strong enough not to be affected by the moon can the natural instincts of the wolves be restricted to proper prey. We insist that lesser wolves remain with a pack so that the pack leader can maintain control."

It made perfect sense. But I hate the others thinking that I am a "lesser wolf." I knew I was going to have a hard time going from being on the highest rung of the food chain to just slightly above dirt. I also disliked that I had to struggle even harder to reach Sue when Nikoli was in my head. I promised myself that I wouldn't be a lesser wolf for *long*.

I stood shakily. It was unnerving to see Nikoli's face painted with my blood, and the other wolves tentatively licking at it.

"Now, my pack, let us begin the hunt!" He turned, launching himself into the woods in a blur of speed. I found myself following behind him with the rest of the pack before I even realized I was moving. It was like being in a slipstream behind a semi. Where he moved we followed.

We ran silently over the carefully tended grass toward the trees of the park. My senses were sharper than I could ever remember. I heard a small mouse scurry under the leaves as we approached. Birds ducked their heads and hunkered down in their nests. Even the great horned owl flew higher into the trees. We were a force of nature to be reckoned with as we moved through the woods. A panicked pounding of hooves sounded to the left. Nikoli turned fluidly toward it. I felt my body move left in a silent command that required no words. An image flashed in my head. The pack would split and cut off the prey. I was to surge forward and overshoot the deer the pack herded toward me.

My feet barely touched the leaves and fallen logs of the deeper woods. I skirted rocks I couldn't see in the darkness and followed unknown paths effortlessly. My body seemed to know this place. Or perhaps it was Nikoli who knew the way.

A small clearing appeared. This is where the feast would take place. The pack would push the deer to me and I would take the lead animal down. The rest of the pack would attend to the other two. There were three deer. I could smell them now and hear the breaking of branches in their frantic flight for survival. But they would not escape. I would see to that.

I waited patiently as the thundering hooves grew louder. Just a few moments more. I crouched on a fire-blackened log to spring from above as moonlight surged power through my veins. The power fed my hunger. The hunger intensified the power and then rolled back on itself, like a snake swallowing its own tail.

"Tony!" The voice was a shout in my head. I struggled to keep my mind on the prey. "Tony, Bobby's here with me. We're back in Chicago. He has to see you right away. He needs your help. It's urgent."

The words had no meaning to my animal mind. I knew Sue's voice. I was glad. It was good that my mate would be here for the kill. So close. Just a few moments more.

Sue seemed to understand that I couldn't think. She tried to make it simpler. "It's Bobby, Tony. The snake from the island."

An image came to my mind. A python. We'd hunted together for birds. But there was no time to respond. With a crack of breaking branches the first russet form bounded out of cover. The scents of musk and fear were nearly overpowering.

I leapt with all my might and grabbed the lead deer by the throat. It turned and screamed as the other two animals tried to get around our battle. But it was too late. The pack had them. I rode the stag to the ground, twisting quickly to avoid taking a head shot with its hooves. It struggled to right itself but my teeth dug in deeper. Hot salty wetness filled my mouth. It was the finest thing I'd ever tasted in my life. I could feel Sue's pleasure in the background as she too forgot where she was or what she wanted to say. There was nothing beyond the moment. Time slowed until everything had a crystalline sharpness and didn't start again until the deer's eyes stared blankly into space.

Blood lust took me. I gorged myself on the still warm flesh and sweet metallic taste of blood. I was ravenous, insatiable. Never before had my hunger been so great. Snarls and growls erupted behind me. One of the others tried to push me away from the kill, but I bared bloody fangs before turning back to the feast.

I heard the soft pad of footsteps as my pack leader moved behind me.

"No, Alena. Let him be. It is his first kill with the pack. You enjoyed the same luxury." I felt Nikoli's hot breath right next to my ear as I tore and swallowed as fast as I could.

"But be very clear, young one. This will be the only time you will ever feed above your station." He moved his face so that our eyes were almost touching. His lips pulled back in a toothy snarl. The magic he raked across my skin made me gasp with pain.

"If you ever again attempt to feed before I have had my fill, it will be my great pleasure to sate my hunger with *your* flesh."

Chapter 2

A SHARP PAIN in my side woke me. *"Prosypát'sia, Anton. Ee-dyóht snyeg. Mwee noozh-nah rabótat! Prosypát'sia!"*

Huh? I shook my head to clear my senses and tried to make sense of the words. The smells of burned coffee, burned steel, and fur chased away contented dreams of sweat-soaked skin and the scent of meat. A rush of air warned me before a booted foot found my body for a second kick. I rolled sideways and reached out my hands in a blinding flash. I grabbed the boot, pulled and twisted hard. I was rewarded with a surprised sound and a grunt as my assailant hit the ground. I was on my feet over him before my eyes were fully open.

It was just past dawn. The moon's glow had faded to a near memory as the rising sun painted the clouds an angry red that looked warmer than it felt. The lightly blowing snow raised the hairs on my naked skin. Falling flakes melted as they touched me. A part of my brain knew that I should be cold, but the snow swirling around me felt incredibly good. My nostrils flared to the icy wind. I could still smell the deer; still remember the moment when it became mine. The intensity of the memory made me shiver. My assailant started to roll over and spit out snow. He smelled like pack.

I recognized him slightly from the hunt but we hadn't

been introduced. His scent was birch bark and some sort of moss. I looked around. The bus was gone, and along with it the rest of the pack. They'd apparently left me and this other man alone in the woods, miles from home. Gee, what pals.

As he rose to a sitting position, he growled and struck out again with a kick. A weak flow of Sazi magic pressed against me. My answering growl came without warning. It was a deep-throated, angry sound. I avoided his blow easily and landed a heel right to his bearded chin. There was a satisfying echo as the back of his head smacked against the frozen ground from the blow. Then I planted my bare foot on his throat and pressed.

"Stohp!" he shouted as well as he was able with compressed vocal cords. That word I understood. I was fairly sure what he'd been saying before was in Russian, but couldn't be sure.

"Who are you?" I asked. I watched the bulk of his body carefully. If he intended to continue fighting the first clues would be visible in his body. And he might fight. Both his eyes and scent were angry. Blood trickled from his nose to disappear into the black hair on his lip.

He tensed and began to struggle, but I was ready for him. I pressed more weight onto the neck, grabbed the fist he'd raised to hit me between the legs and twisted sharply. Bones and tendons stretched nearly to breaking. After a moment he gave up. His scent changed to a sharp hot and sour soup mingled with mildew. Afraid and amazed. I seem to have that effect on a lot of people.

"Men-yah zah-voot Yurgi Kroutikhin," he whispered hoarsely.

I shook my head in annoyance. "I really hope you speak English, buddy. Otherwise, I'm going to be forced to put you out until I figure out what's going on." My muscles tensed. I had to struggle not to end this as my instinct was urging me to. He was pack. Intellectually I knew it would be a bad idea to hurt him. But I *wanted* to.

"I am called Yurgi Kroutikhin," came the heavily accented words in a wheeze.

"Nice to meet you, Yurgi," I put a little extra twist on the arm. His gasp of pain, and the resulting scent of Worcestershire sauce pleased me more than I'd like to admit. My voice was harsh as I asked, "Why the hell were you kicking me?"

He coughed and tried to draw air so I eased up on the foot a fraction. Only a little, though. I didn't want him to get any ideas.

"I was trying to wake you, Anton. It began to snow. We must finish work and return before midday."

I gritted my teeth. "First, I'm *Tony,* not Anton. I tolerate Nikoli calling me that because he's the boss. You don't get to. Next, the only thing I intend to do before midday is get dressed and get the hell back to town so I can have mindbending sex with my wife."

His eyes grew wide and the ammonia scent of his panic struck me like a blow. "No, no! We must *khoronit* the deer. It is our duty."

"Do *what* to the deer?"

His free hand twirled as he tried to find the English word. He snapped his fingers in frustration. "Khoronit. Uh . . . dig into the earth and . . ." he moved his hand in an imitation of pushing and patting.

"Bury?" I asked.

Relief flooded his face. "Yes! Bury. We two must bury the deer bones and skin. It is the Omega's duty. I am fortunate that you are also now, Tooney. We will be quick, like rabbits, yes?"

"Where are my clothes?"

He pointed with his free hand to a small bundle lying on the pine needles under a tree. "Yurgi, I'm going to let you loose now so I can get dressed. If you make one move toward me I'll kill you. You understand *'kill'*, right?"

A clove-pride scent dusted my nose, mingled with the soured milk of disbelief. "I am Sazi. I will heal."

I shook my head with a slight smile and cold eyes. "Heart and then head, Yurgi. *Kill.* I've done it before so no tricks." It had taken me a long time to understand that death comes hard to the Sazi. I hit one in the chest with two barrels of a shotgun, only to have her get up and be waiting at my car. But a bullet or a sharp branch through the heart and another through the head before the first one can heal will put a Sazi down permanently. Permanent is my business, after all. Or was. "No." I corrected myself silently. My identity may have changed, but *I* was still the same man: deer or humans; for money or hunger. I am an assassin.

A flood of memory found Sue at the back of my mind. Shit, that's right! I had to get back home ASAP. Bobby was waiting for me. I tried to reach my mate in my head, but I had to struggle to get through to her. It was incredibly frustrating. *I'll be home soon, Sue.* I knew she heard, but didn't respond. I was annoyed—mostly with myself, but also with Nikoli. I hadn't planned on being out all night.

Yurgi's breathing had increased as I was lost in thought. His nostrils flared briefly as he scented the air. He gasped with what little oxygen I allowed him. "You do not lie! But no, you would not do this!" he exclaimed. The sour milk scent mingled with ammonia and vinegary disapproval. Nasty combination. "We are pack. Nikoli would never allow you to kill me, even with my lowly station."

"We're all alone out here, Yurgi. Nikoli would never find out. I'm really good at keeping secrets. Now, I'm going to let go. Just stay there until I reach my clothes. *Capisce?*"

I released Yurgi and he remained where he was. When I reached my clothes he raised to sit and laughed bitterly. "You are a very foolish *shchenók*, Tooney."

I hurriedly put on my thick black turtleneck and socks. "It's T-o-ny. And what's a *shchenók*?"

A small smile stretched his beard. "A puppy. A cub. One who is naive. You have much to learn of our pack leader . . . T-o-ny."

"Yeah?" I finished zipping my jeans and slid my feet

into sturdy black boots. "Well, maybe I'll ask him when I see him." I turned, found my bearings and started walking through the trees toward the road. I turned my head slightly to see Yurgi's startled face. "Good luck *khoronit*-ing the deer."

When I reached the road, I listened carefully for any human movement. Fortunately, it was a Sunday morning in miserable weather. The hush was broken only by small animals scurrying under the snow. But I'd fed well last night and wasn't hungry enough to chase them down.

I started off at a fast jog. When I was confident there was no one around to see, I increased the speed to Sazi level. I've been told that some Sazi can use their magic to create illusions and make the humans see whatever they want them to. Since I have neither the skill or knowledge I'm stuck avoiding people or pretending to be a normal human.

Normal. It had been a while, but I still remembered being human. So far the only *good* thing I'd found about being Sazi was my mating to Sue. So, while a part of me knew that I should have stayed to help Yurgi, I chose to go home. Whatever crisis Bobby was dealing with had to be more important than burying deer bones. And the thought of seeing Sue again beat them both.

Just thinking about seeing Sue again made me willing to risk another burst of speed. She's been in Boulder for almost two months now attending classes with Dr. Perdue—Betty—the Sazi psychiatrist. It takes a little work to help someone adapt reality to include the fantastic. Let's face it, werewolves aren't supposed to exist. I haven't seen or touched Sue for seven weeks. The thought of her summer forest scent mingled with sweat and desire raced through me. My body tightened with a hunger that had nothing to do with food.

I caught the pungent fishy scent of Lake Michigan. I made up my mind to avoid the major interstates. There'd be too much traffic and I couldn't move as fast. I hit 55th Street and headed west toward Canaryville. It's a great, albeit humorous, name for the area near wolf pack headquarters. Our apartment is in an exclusively Sazi neighborhood right near the old stockyards. The pervasive smell of old death keeps out the average tourists. For those remaining humans who venture too close, a general pallor of unease awaits. Something way down deep in the DNA makes humans recognize predators and stay away from them. It makes it easy for the Sazi to live and work right out in the open.

Eyes followed my movements as I neared the neighborhood. Residents are openly hostile to visitors. I wasn't known by sight yet so people stood silently until my scent reached them. Once they knew I was pack they continued with shoveling, jogging, and other morning chores.

I was nearly home when I was stopped cold in my tracks. An invisible hand had closed around me until I couldn't move.

Come home, Anton. The deep voice resonated in my head while pinpricks of power danced over my skin. It tugged at me, trying to pull me toward the honey-sweet sound. I wanted to feel more of the fire, the magic, that coursed through me. But it seemed wrong. I shook my head as I tried to think clearly. I looked up at the decaying brick building and tried to get a fix on what the hell was happening. I scanned the windows looking for . . . something.

Outwardly the place looked to be a wreck: heavily barred windows, layers of graffiti that had been carefully commissioned and painted by local gangs. But the gangs don't come here uninvited. This territory is Nikoli's. The gang members know they wouldn't survive a turf war. But again, the visuals keep out the curious. No one outside of the pack will ever see the beautiful, comfortable apartments housed inside.

My hand trembled as I struggled to force it forward to touch the doorknob.

Now, Anton!

Sweat painted my brow. Why couldn't I reach the latch? My muscles ached with the attempt.

Tony? Sue's voice was a small, tentative sound in the back of my mind. *Tony, who is tha—OW!* A sharp pain that wasn't mine coursed through my left calf and flooded my body with adrenaline. It sliced through the mental fist holding me. I bolted upstairs.

"Sue?" I called as I kicked in the front door of the apartment. Bobby Mbutu was kneeling next to Sue. His dark fingers were prying the mouth of a child about six from Sue's leg as she stood stock-still with gritted teeth. Sue smelled as tired and frustrated as I had ever known. Why hadn't I noticed it in my head? I *should* have known!

Bobby looked up calmly as the door exploded inward.

"Forget your key, Giambrocco?"

I didn't answer right away. I was taking in the scene in front of me. A young girl was playing with Sue's most treasured possession—a battered plastic doll with red nylon hair and a green dress. A second older girl watched a blaring television. Bobby was using his other hand to hold a dark-haired boy of about eleven by the collar.

"What in the hell is going on?" I called over the din.

Sue shrugged her shoulders and then gave a sigh of relief as Bobby finally used his magic to lift her assailant into the air and open his mouth. She reached down to rub her calf. Her hand came away with spittle covering it.

"Babysitting," she yelled over the commercial as she limped toward the kitchen to clean her hand and leg.

Bobby continued to hold the child frozen in the air. He shook his head with annoyance as he watched Sue hobble from the room.

"Enough!"

With a tiny motion of his hand, all of the blinds in the living room snapped shut simultaneously. The television turned off and the other three children became living statues in the sudden silence. They slowly turned toward my dark-skinned South African friend with wide eyes. His energy wasn't the encompassing wave that Nikoli's had been. This was pinpoint precision.

It was a scene right out of a B-grade horror movie. The limp forms of children slowly skimmed the carpet in whatever pose they were when the magic hit. Their eyes began to move frantically in fear when they realized that it wasn't a game. Bobby's eyes were cold. He stopped the children right in front of him and removed his contact lenses. His pupils became reptilian slits in a red iris. The longer he stared at them, the more anxious they became. It calmed me down a bit. I guess the kid had done something more stupid than I thought. I would have just spanked him. I couldn't imagine what Bobby might do.

Sue came out of the kitchen, still favoring that leg. I wanted to reach for her and bury my face in her shoulder-length auburn hair. She used to have honey-blonde curls, but we'd both made a change to match our new identities. It's odd. I can't seem to remember my life before I met her, but we've only known each other four months.

I stared at her as though seeing her for the first time. Sue isn't gorgeous, but she's pretty. Her heart-shaped face compliments a well-curved body. She'd dropped some weight after a recent coma, when we could only feed her through tubes. I was guessing she was a size twelve now, but I'd thought that when I'd first met her, so I could be wrong. Still, she was looking damn good and I let my eyes reflect the thought. She caught me watching and blushed. I still think it's cute when she does that.

I breathed in her scent as she walked toward me. Rain-kissed plants and warm rich earth from a forest in summer mingled with the baked cinnamon smell of love. I would never get enough of her scent. It coursed through me like a drug, nearly shutting out coherent thought.

"Sue, let me see your leg." The words cut through the cloud of scent like a knife. Bobby's voice was the sharp command of a cop. Of course, Bobby *is* a cop. He's part of

Wolven, the law enforcement branch of the Sazi. Call him double-o python. All agents of the organization have a license to kill. They're the nastiest of the nasty of each of the Sazi species. It's their duty to *permanently* remove from the gene pool any were-animals who break felony human laws or any of the big Sazi laws. Can't have a shape-shifter locked up in jail during a full moon. The humans would find out we exist. That is the ultimate rule of the Sazi. Keep our existence secret from the humans.

Sue hesitated for just a second, while we stared at each other lustfully. But at the sound of Bobby's impatient hiss, she limped over and raised her leg to rest on the cushion next to him.

"Relax." He moved his face closer to her leg. "This won't hurt."

"Hey!" I exclaimed as he suddenly licked the wound. He held up a hand in a sharp motion to stop me moving forward. I trusted Bobby but it was unnerving to see his tongue darting out and touching each indentation. When he reached the last tiny tooth print, he stuck out his tongue and waved it in the air over the wound. His whole upper body began moving fluidly from side to side like he was in a trance. After a few tense seconds he stopped, opened his eyes and glanced up. He spotted the charm bracelet that Sue always wears and touched it lightly with his fingers. I saw a small wisp of smoke as the silver scorched his skin.

He gave a satisfied nod. I could've sworn I saw a flicker of relief, but it was gone in a fraction of a second. "Sue, Tony, you should both hear this, too." He gestured in the general direction of a puffy brown leather recliner. I took the seat and Sue perched on the arm beside me. I reached up and slid a gentle finger along her arm. It made her shudder and close her eyes. Her hands balled tightly into fists to fight the need. When the scent of her desire reached my nose, it was all I could do to pull back my hand and return my attention to Bobby.

Bobby did a fine job of ignoring our little struggle. He

kept his gaze locked on the blond biter. "Denis, we need to have a serious talk." He released the child from the magic and the boy dropped an inch or so to the carpeted floor. Tears were rolling down his terrified face. The air in the apartment was filled with the stench of ammonia emi- nating from the children. I could feel Sue's discomfort for the boy. I couldn't share her sympathy for him. I'd have gotten my teeth knocked out if I bit a stranger when I was that age.

The longer Bobby made him wait, the more terrified Denis became. He was like a cornered rabbit. His eyes moved rap- idly from side to side and his body actually twitched from the tension. Bobby watched the boy with those strange red eyes, his expression utterly neutral. Even his natural scent of sweet musty jungle vines showed no sign of discomfort or anger.

"There's no use running, Denis," he warned. "I know your scent, the taste of you. I could find you anywhere you'd go." Denis backed up until his spine was against the wall. He curled into near-fetal position and began to suck his thumb. His hazel eyes were wide and showing too much white. Bobby released the other children. They dropped gently to the carpet but didn't move so much as a hair. Only their shal- low breathing told me they weren't statues. They didn't want to turn Bobby's attention on them for any reason. I couldn't blame them.

"What are you?" the boy asked in a whisper before tuck- ing his thumb back between his lips.

"You're lucky, Denis," Bobby said in a stern voice. "I'm a python—a very special member of Wolven." The two older children looked at Bobby with new panic plain on their faces. The dark-haired teen opened her mouth in a silent 'o'. A second wash of ammonia-laced hot and sour soup filled the air. Wolven is the Sazi equivalent of the bo- geyman, and not just to children. Knowing that the cops had a license to kill—and wouldn't hesitate to use it—was enough to instill fear in most anyone.

The kids hadn't known who Bobby was. They all

flinched when he stood to his full 6'2" and reached down one nearly blue-black hand to touch Denis's head.

"I'm the chemist for Wolven. You're lucky I was here instead of one of the other agents. I can use my tongue to detect and analyze any organic or man-made chemical on earth—even the tiniest little bit—and know what it is instantly." He glanced at me and Sue.

"When I used my tongue where you bit Mrs. Giambrocco, I didn't find any traces of blood. That's why you're lucky, Denis." He raised the boy's face to meet his gaze. "Most Wolven agents wouldn't have taken the time to check. You all know that biting and scratching is absolutely the worst thing in the world you can do, don't you!" The blank stares from the kids weren't just because they were frozen in place. They actually seemed confused.

Bobby's face grew suspicious. "You don't scratch and bite each other at *home,* do you? Your parents have forbidden that, like riding with a stranger, or crossing the street without looking—right?"

Denis shook his head until his hair raised a breeze. The thumb popped out of his mouth. "Mama doesn't care if we bite each other. She said that's what wolves *do.*"

I'd seen that tight, angry expression on Bobby before. Someone was going to get hurt, now or later. I might be forced to step in, but I hoped not. I didn't have to, because he calmed down quickly when Denis recoiled so sharply from the anger that he nearly bumped into the wall. Bobby sighed.

"I know that Mrs. Giambrocco made you mad when she wouldn't let you change the TV channel, Denis. But you need to understand that she's human—and you're not. If you bite or scratch a human and they aren't wearing silver, they will become Sazi like us."

"But that's *good,* isn't it? Mama says we're better than humans."

The hell you say! A growl rose from my chest before I could stop it. The children's fearful eyes turned from

Bobby to me. They huddled together in a quivering group, not knowing who to trust.

Bobby shook his head. "No, Denis. We're *different,* not better. Let me explain how our law works, kids. Gather 'round." Three of the children moved tentatively forward to sit down cross-legged in a semi-circle just out of Bobby's reach. The older boy took Denis's hand and had to tug a little to move him closer. Now that I looked, there was a strong resemblance.

"Sonya, Vera, Alek—and Denis." Bobby looked at each one of them slowly and strongly as he spoke their names. He needn't have bothered. He had their full attention. "It is against the law to scratch, bite or injure a human so that they bleed. The magic that makes us Sazi can get into their body through the blood. Most humans who are attacked will die when the animal inside tries to come out to greet the moon."

Bobby pointed at me. "Mr. Giambrocco was attacked by one of us. He is lucky to have lived. If he hadn't already been a predator in the human world, he wouldn't have survived. He was a hunter, so it was easier for him to be like us."

The two older children looked at me with a new level of respect. They suddenly liked me more. I tipped my head in acknowledgment. Nice to know it has value in both worlds.

"Sonya," he continued to the girl of about six, "If Denis had drawn blood on Mrs. Giambrocco, what would have happened?"

She wasn't as impressed by Bobby or me as her older counterparts. Innocence has its advantages.

"His *aht-yets* and *maht* would have spanked him?" she asked tentatively. Her voice was a soft alto. I could tell it would end up a really sexy contralto by the time she was a teen. Sue elbowed me in the ribs without the kids noticing. I stifled my amusement. It wasn't the time.

From Sue's mind, I heard Sonya's Russian as father and mother. Hmm. Didn't know she spoke other languages.

Bobby gave a negative shake of his head. "Vera?"

The dark-haired teen glanced at Denis before turning her eyes back to Bobby. Her strong soprano voice was confident and a little too predatory. She smelled amused at the child's mistake. She smirked as she spoke.

"The *Alpha* would punish him." The Alpha—as in the pack leader, Nikoli.

The children around her gasped and Denis lip started to tremble again. Hot and sour soup filled the air again and made my jaw clench. I needed a steak. And soon.

"I don't want to go to the Alpha's dragon!" he wailed. "It'll *eat* me!" Alek looked at Bobby with wide eyes and hugged Denis to him protectively.

That was the second time someone mentioned a dragon. It made me more than a little curious. I couldn't wait to meet this enforcer of Nikoli's.

Bobby sighed deeply. He shook his head again. "Your parents have been careless in your schooling. Neither answer is correct. You need to understand that it's not your parents, not your pack leader, but *Wolven* who would punish you for attacking a human." The older children gasped a second time but the younger boy and girl just looked blank.

He looked around at all of them and then to us. "If Denis had drawn blood, *even if* Mrs. Giambrocco was wearing silver and wouldn't have turned," he said, pointing a shaking finger at each child in turn, "I would have found you guilty of *grave damage* and I would have killed you. Right here and right now, without anyone's permission. Biting or scratching is as bad, or even *worse* than telling the humans the Sazi exist. There is *no* excuse that is good enough for attacking a human short of defending your life or your family's life! And even then, you may die if the investigator decides it wasn't justified."

He waited until he knew that the words had full effect. I admit I was a little surprised. The children were apparently *very* surprised by scent of shock that rose from them.

The wolf who turned me, Babs, only got knocked around a little. Well okay. She got knocked around *a lot*. Of course, I was trying to kill her at the time so she could claim self-defense. Denis had no such excuse.

Bobby was continuing on with the children hanging on every terrifying word. The stench of ammonia would take a full day to air from the apartment. It was making my eyes water.

"Do you understand, kids? It is *Wolven* that enforces the laws of all Sazis. Your parents can punish you for violating the decisions they've made for your family. The pack leader governs the *pack* and enforces its rules. But if you don't follow the laws of *all* of our kind—the principles we live by to protect us from being discovered by the humans—then your parents or your pack leader must call *me*. It's why you must always be careful to not harm anything but proper prey. You must NEVER let your temper, your fear, or even your *pride* make you do something as foolish as Denis did today. Every human that joins our society increases our risk of discovery. Every single bloodletting can let a human in."

I watched Denis carefully. His eyes were wide, his breathing was fast. He was still terrified, but overriding the scent of ammonia was the soured milk smell of disbelief.

Vera tipped her head toward him to catch his scent. Her nostrils flared delicately as she inhaled. "Denis, you *have* to believe him if he doesn't smell like black pepper. Trust your nose."

The boy tentatively moved forward and sniffed the air around Bobby, who waited with reptilian patience until he was done.

"Denis, even for biting, I *should* punish you. You have caused Mrs. Giambrocco damage."

Sonya furrowed her small brow and asked an innocent question in that so-adult voice. "She'll heal, won't she?"

Ah, yes. The standard line of the Sazi. Enough that it's practically a joke to me. They're just so damned *casual* about it. A shrug of the shoulder at a broken bone or a crippling wound with the words "You'll heal." And they will. In almost a blink of an eye.

Bobby shook his head. "You should know better than that." His voice was stern, "Aren't there other family members who don't change with the moon?"

"Well, yes," Sonya admitted, "But Mama doesn't like for us to talk to *them.*"

I fought down another growl. Bobby just looked disgusted. "Fine, Sonya. But the rest of you *should* know. That bite will leave a mark and a bruise that will last more than a week."

The jaws of the two younger children dropped simultaneously and the air filled with the mildew smell of their amazement. Even the older two turned to look at us curiously. The dusty scent of Sue's embarrassment reached me. I knew exactly how she felt. It hadn't been that long ago that I was a human—and I still thought and felt like one. In this place *we* were the freaks. Oddities to be put on display to help children to learn the foreign world of humans.

I'm still amazed by it all—that their perspective of time is so incredibly different. The Sazi live their whole lives with the sure knowledge that nothing will actually *hurt* for more than a day. They will live for decades longer than a normal human lifespan. The strongest Alphas can live for centuries.

Denis actually looked shaken, not just scared. He turned to Sue with an expression of horror.

"I didn't know I *damaged* you. I know what that means. I'm really, really sorry." Tears welled up until his eyes glittered like polished gems. He finally understood what he'd done and knew there would be consequences.

He took a shuddering breath and squared his small shoulders. He was going to be a man about it. Attaboy. He stood up and turned to Bobby. "What will happen to me?"

Sorrow overwhelmed my nose—thick and foggy and laced with worry. I guess they didn't teach Sue everything in her classes in Colorado.

I heard her tentative whisper in my mind. *Would he really kill a child, Tony?*

I shrugged my shoulders. The law can be harsh in the world of predators. I just didn't know. I've seen Bobby do things that would make other people blanch, though. *It's a question of order over chaos, Sweetheart. The boy could endanger all of the Sazi. Bobby might have no choice.*

She closed her eyes to concentrate on hearing my reply. She stiffened for a moment as the words sunk home. Then she nodded her head numbly and bit on her lower lip. She looked about as uncomfortable as when we first met. The brief flash of our first meeting made me wonder about my old friend, Jocko. I hadn't seen him since I "died" four months ago.

"Well, at least you understand *that* concept." continued Bobby, bringing me out of my daze, "Fortunately, you're young, Denis, and *obviously* haven't been trained properly. No harm was done—this time. But I have to know what you've learned today, little ones."

Denis looked up and the cool air of hope filled the room. His words were very serious and grown-up. "Never, ever bite a human."

"Never bite *anyone*," replied Bobby. "A Sazi would have torn your throat out."

Denis nodded quickly. "Never bite." He thought for a moment and added, "Or scratch."

Bobby nodded and looked at the others. "And the rest of you?"

"Humans are just as good as us?" said Sonya with her head cocked and brows raised. She sounded a bit doubtful about it. When Bobby nodded, she continued with more confidence. "We're only different."

"Alek?"

Alek had apparently realized how little they knew and was annoyed. He shook his head and let out a frustrated sound. His hands had closed into fists.

"Tell our parents to find us a new teacher 'cause otherwise we're going to end up dragon food or worse," he snarled. A small smile turned my lips at nearly the same time as Bobby's.

"And you, Vera?" Bobby asked as his lid blinked up again over the red iris.

The teen couldn't seem to take her eyes off Bobby. With every upside down blink of his reptilian orbs, she flinched.

"Never do anything to make our parents or Alpha have to call *you.*"

This time Bobby smiled, showing broad white teeth that didn't seem the least bit menacing. But both Vera and I knew better.

"Very good. Now, Vera, why don't you call your mother to come get the lot of you. I think the Giambroccos have had enough excitement for today, hmm?"

Vera quickly went to the phone and called home. I glanced at Sue and then fought through the layers of haze in my brain to think a question into her head. *What happened here? Who left these kids with you?*

Her brow furrowed for a second and she closed her eyes. Then she shrugged and responded the same way. *They just showed up on the doorstep. The car pulled away from the curb before I could see who it was. But I couldn't just leave them in the snow. They knew my name and said I was supposed to watch them. They hadn't even had dinner yet, Tony. I couldn't just leave them outside.*

Great. That probably meant that all the steaks in the freezer were gone. I needed to eat. It had been too damned long since I'd gorged on that deer—especially with the scent of fear so heavy on the air. I wasn't going to ask for more details until they were gone, but I was *going* to find out who dropped a bunch of werewolf kids at my house to stay the night.

Chapter 3

I LET BOBBY handle gathering the children's belongings and getting them ready to leave while I went and said a proper hello to my wife.

Sue was standing in the bedroom, glancing around for anything the kids might have missed when I entered and shut the door behind me. She started at the sound and turned around suddenly.

"Oh! You startled m—."

Her voice fell off. I let all the intense feelings I'd been tamping down show in my eyes. She was looking *really* good. I stopped right in front of her and reached up one hand to brush back a few strands of hair that had covered one eye. My fingers traced slowly down the line of her jaw. I watched her shiver in the soft light. The need to touch her was impossible to ignore. Electricity tingled my skin, teased along my hand and flowed up my arm. Her eyes were suddenly wide and panicked. A light hot and sour soup smell rose and blended with her summer forest scent. The same desire and hunger that I felt burned right under the surface.

"But what about the kids? They're just outside."

My hand slid behind her head and I pulled her toward me slowly. My words were a whisper as I watched her shudder with pleasure. "That's why I shut the door. Welcome home."

I tilted my head and pulled her mouth to mine. A moan escaped me as the teasing tingles became raw need. My arms wound around her and pulled her tight against me. Electricity became fire as we fed at each other's mouth. Blue light danced just behind my eyelids and I knew that my eyes were glowing. Our tongues tangled while magic began to swirl around us. It filled the room as I tore my mouth from hers and moved it to her neck. My hands slid under her shirt to caress her curves. I licked the scent from her skin and rolled it on my tongue. I showered her neck with little kisses and nips that left her legs shaky.

Her voice was breathless. "Oh, God! I'd almost forgotten how good this feels. I've missed you so much!" Her arms tightened and her fingers dug into my shoulders.

I couldn't answer. I couldn't even think enough to form words. There was only light and heat and that intoxicating scent that was driving me wild. I shook my head, trying to clear it. I didn't want to get so wrapped up that we ended up having sex and missed the parents arriving. I planned to have a little chat with them. The pain in her leg was washing away in the pleasure of my touch, but I knew it would be back. Nobody hurts my mate without a price.

Her fingertips reached up and smoothed through my hair, raising another series of shudders in me.

"We'd better stop now." I said, but I didn't want to. I pulled back and looked into those drowning deep green eyes and kissed her once more, softly. We stood like that for a moment, our lips just barely touching, the knowledge of what lay ahead hanging in the air.

A car horn honked outside. That, and the sudden scampering sounds in the living room, shattered the crystalline moment.

"Why don't you lie down, Sue. It's been a long night. I'll be back in a few minutes to tuck you in." My eyes reflected the humor in my voice. I pulled away from her and stepped to the door. Her responding chuckle was throaty and warm.

"I'd like very much to be *tucked*. Hurry back." She walked toward me again with a sultry sway. She reached out and traced an electrifying pattern on the back of my hand and I had to shake my head again and take a deep breath to convince myself to leave. Better change subjects or I would drown in the need.

"When did you learn to speak Russian?" It had been nagging at me.

She stepped back and sat down on the bed. "I only know a few words. Lucas thought I should learn a bit—mother, father, sister, brother and some household things, because quite a few of the pack members are immigrants. And I had plenty of time to study. I learned some food words and what letters go where in the alphabet. That's about all."

I pursed my lips. "Great. You'll have to teach me. Apparently, my new counterpart doesn't speak very good English."

She nodded and stretched out on the bed invitingly and closed her eyes. I started to move toward her. I wanted to touch her skin, kiss her mouth, cup her breas—

No! Control, Tony. Keep it together! I had other things to do. Taking a deep breath, I walked out of the bedroom, down the short hallway, and found Bobby standing by the front door. I was still a little hot and bothered, but the icy breeze from the open door cooled me down a bit. I started past him to talk to the driver of the car as the kids were finishing gathering their things. Bobby stopped me with a sharp look. Fine, I'd wait until the children had said their good-byes. They each apologized to me in quiet voices and solemnly shook hands with Bobby. They thanked him for sparing Denis. Both the apologies and appreciation were genuine. The horn honked a second time. Steam rose in clouds from their mouths as they ran down the walk and greeted their family with hugs tight enough to crush. Bobby and I watched through the closed storm door. With a start, I recognized the woman as the one called Alena before she disappeared behind the foggy layer of ice that formed on the glass.

I started forward once more. No, damn it! They were going to get a piece of my mind.

Bobby's grip on my bicep stopped me cold. "Don't do it. They were only following instructions. They won't understand why you're upset."

"Who the hell would give them instructions to leave a bunch of kids with a complete stranger?" I snarled.

"Only Nikoli would know where you live and that Sue was home," said Bobby ominously. He waited to see my reaction. His eyes were angry but I didn't think it was because of Sue having to babysit.

There was something wrong with that scenario but I couldn't decide what. In a second it hit me between the eyes.

I frowned. "Wait a minute. I didn't even know you'd arrived until the middle of the hunt. Alena was on the bus with us. How would she know to bring the kids here *before* we left?"

Bobby's brows raised. He'd apparently been thinking the same thing. "Exactly."

"I think I'll go have a chat with my pack leader," I said with fire in my voice.

"I'm going with you."

"Like hell you are! This is my problem, Bobbo."

His eyes were cold and deadly. "I almost had to kill a child tonight, Giodone. I wouldn't have enjoyed it much. Nikoli is going to get a piece of my mind about his lack of training of our young. And he'll be damned lucky if I don't turn him over to the council for damages."

His arms closed over his chest and the burning coffee of his anger rose from him in a cloud.

"I also don't like being spied on. He had to have bugged something or someone to know we were in town."

I nodded my head. Good enough. I grabbed my coat and had just turned to tell Sue what was happening when the pain hit.

"Christ Almighty!" I screamed. I dropped to my knees and put fists to my temples with gritted teeth but it didn't help stop the ice pick of pain being driven into my brain. Bobby bent down to check on me until he heard a scream and a crash from the bedroom. He leapt to his feet and sprinted down the hallway. I didn't know where it had come from but the migraine was even making my eyeballs pound. At least I made it to the bathroom before I vomited. The sudden movement caused a new wave of violent pain and nausea. I didn't dare turn on the light. It was as bright as the mid-day sun in the windowless room.

I glanced in the darkened mirror and didn't like what I saw. My steel blue eyes were squinted almost shut, and my face was pale and drawn beneath recently dyed brown hair. Death warmed twice would be an improvement.

I heard Bobby whispering to Sue down the hallway. My hearing had sensitized to the point that his soft murmuring was like standing next to the big speakers at a rock concert. I grabbed a pair of pillows from the couch and covered my ears. Sue was suddenly gone from my mind. I couldn't hear her; couldn't feel her. But every time I tried to stand to get to her I lost balance and got dry heaves. Sparkles danced across my vision and continued even after I shut my eyes tight.

I've had a couple of migraines before. Not often, thank God. You usually have a few minutes of warning before the pain really hits. This was like nothing I'd ever felt before. I told myself I could get through this. I knew I could.

Bobby came out from the bedroom looking grim. He seemed to know to speak in a whisper. I hesitantly removed the pillows from my ears.

"We need to get a healer in here. Both of you are in bad shape. All I can tell is that it's something magical. You stay here with Sue. I'll go get the pack healer. It's not something a human doctor can handle."

I stood up and fought through the pain to stare at Bobby with a tight expression. The sparkles were still there but I could stand without falling. I'd spent my life in the mob. I'd been beaten, shot, cut, and had my throat torn out. I could get through a headache. As Dad used to say, "Headaches are all in your mind."

Still, I winced as my own voice reached my ears. "I still have a score to settle with Nikoli, Bobby. I'm going with you."

Bobby looked at me with exasperation. He's tried to talk me out of stupid things before and hasn't succeeded yet. "You're in no condition, Giodone. It would be better for you to stay here with your wife."

"Probably." I said as I reached for my coat once more. I shot him a look of annoyance that cut through the pain. "And don't call me that."

He started visibly. This was the second time he'd called me by my old name. He's smart enough to know better. The only thing I could think of was that the thing with the kid had toasted him more than I'd originally thought. He's not normally so careless. I certainly couldn't afford him to be. There's still an APB out for me. One slip of the tongue and some wanna-be snitch might place an inconvenient call to my old nemesis on the homicide squad.

Bobby's scent turned to cloves with the sharp tang of worry. His face went blank and he nodded. His scent faded as well as the snake in him took over. He was back to his professional self. My vision was still dark edged and fuzzy but I could see. I rummaged around in the drawer next to the door and found a pair of wrap-around dark sunglasses. That helped a bit with the sparkles.

Next, I went to the darkened bedroom. Sue was out like a light. Apparently Bobby had used his Sazi magic to put her under. I wasn't thrilled with the idea of him doing it, but I didn't want her to endure this kind of pain unnecessarily. If I'd let him, he'd probably have done the same for me.

I went to the closet and pulled out a pair of shooter's foam earplugs and stuck them in my ears. It helped, but only a lit-tle. The screaming of the refrigerator compressor dulled but I knew that voices would still be uncomfortable. I tried not to think about the noise of weekday traffic.

I reached back into the closet to retrieve one of my guns. Bobby eyebrows rose a good inch as he watched me strap on my inner pants holster.

"You're going to go armed into your own pack den?" He sounded bemused. Sunny oranges glided over his worry.

"You showed me the key, Bobby. Heart and then head." My voice was flat and burned metal chased away the citrus. I flipped open the cylinder of the Taurus three inch snub nose .38. Five .999 fine silver bullets filled the chambers. I swung it shut sharply and turned to him with a grim expres-sion. "I've been practicing ever since you left the island. I used a bunch of paper targets Carmine left at the house and figured the proportionate distances with a measuring tape. My speed has improved over sixty percent at fifty yards."

He raised his brows and let out a low whistle. "It wasn't too shabby to begin with. Were they confirmed lethal zone hits?"

I didn't even dignify *that* with a reply. I just shot him a withering glance.

He shook his head again, almost sadly. "*Truly* a shame you're a three-day. But just remember—I can't allow you to kill unless it's in self defense. I'll put you down without a second thought."

I stopped and stared at him, trying to catch his scent. He looked away first and walked out of the room. The black pepper gave away the lie. I knew he would do it—but not easily.

I holstered the revolver and untucked my sweater to hide it. Then I pulled out the box of hand-loads. I grabbed an-other ten rounds, quickly removing each bullet from the box by the casing. I swore lightly when one silver bullet scorched my hand as I dropped the bullets in my pocket. At least I'd had the sense to reinforce the pockets of all my pants with thick canvas. My scarred thighs were living testament to being careless, and once was enough.

I stepped out into the lighted living room and swung on my winter coat. I was dressed all in black and the heavy bomber jacket completed the outfit. I was as ready to see Nikoli as I was going to get. Bobby was waiting by the door, still looking like this was a bad idea. I stared at him through the mirrored sunglasses, even though I knew he couldn't see my eyes.

"They think I'm the lowest dog on the totem, Bobby. I've been called 'puppy' and 'whelp' and been told to bury bones. I'm nobody's *pet*. They're about to learn that this yearling has teeth."

Chapter 4

THE VOLKDOM HOTEL was built in a by-gone age when visitors flocked to the stockyards for livestock auctions. The name is a rough phonetic of the Russian words, "Wolf House." Shiny new fire escapes that had been installed to meet Fire Code requirements had been grafted onto a brick building that had obviously seen better days.

It was a six-block walk from the apartment to the lair. I stared at the building from across the street as we waited for traffic to clear. Bobby stomped and waved his arms wildly as he tried to keep his blood moving. He glanced at my open jacket and cursed lightly.

"At least have the decency to *look* cold, Giambrocco." He huddled further inside the heavy down jacket and stomped his feet again. I didn't have to be able to smell him to know he was annoyed.

"It's not exactly frigid, Bobby. It's only about twenty degrees out here." I'd been in worse. Hell, I've had to lie in wait for marks in blizzards for hours. At least the sun shone in the icy blue sky. Mind you, it didn't warm the air any and the reflection off the snow made my head feel like the inside of a kettle drum.

"Damn mammal," he muttered as he clumsily pulled down the furred flaps of his cap with thickly gloved hands. The adjustment only added a square inch more protection.

"Well, why the hell are you in Chicago if you can't stand a little snow?" I never had found out what Bobby wanted that was so important.

"I go where I'm assigned. I've been assigned to get *you.*" That little bombshell caused me to miss the opening in traffic. I turned without asking, the question trembling on my lips, and walked toward the intersection. Bobby followed grudgingly. Snakes don't like to move much in the cold. But we might as well go across with the light if we hoped to get to the hotel today.

"Care to tell me why?" I asked as I pressed the button on the light pole. I tried to make the question casual, but he knew better.

He shook his head once. "I need to talk to Nikoli first. Just don't do anything stupid and get yourself killed before we have a chance to chat."

That was all right with me, since I had some things to discuss with the pack leader myself. The walk had done nothing to cool my fury with Nikoli for taking advantage of my mate. Still, Bobby's words brought something to the surface that had been bugging me since the kids left.

"Y'know, Bobby, I admit that I'm still figuring things out, but if you have to go through Nikoli before you tell me anything, why didn't you go there first?"

"I drove Sue back from Boulder. We didn't get to your place until after the bus was ready to leave and then the kids arrived. I could have followed, but I knew that Sue would have a hard time babysitting without another one of *us* there."

I picked up on his phrasing, as a couple walked past on the sidewalk. They were human. "Okay, but that raises another question—Denis is like *us* so why wasn't he on the bus with me?"

He nodded without looking at me, keeping a careful eye on the flow of traffic. He kept his voice low and quiet, even though the humans had passed. "It's a fair question. All of the kids have *potential,* but not all of them will ever turn.

Normally, a child has to reach puberty before the talent manifests. And it's generally a few months after that before they join the game. It's very unusual for a child of Denis's age to already have talent. It's only happened a few times. He'll definitely be a big dog. If Alek or Sonya had *done the deed*. I probably would have just pulled them off and scolded them. But as soon as we develop the talent, it's transmittable. Sonya will be on the bus soon, and since we *know* that she and Denis have both shown talent, the two of them have to be punished as if they'd already been to the first game."

Interesting how he phrased the words so that I would understand his meaning exactly, but no one overhearing would be able to interpret. Dr. Betty had already told me that *game* is a euphemism for *hunting*. He left me standing on the corner nodding as he sprinted through a sudden opening in traffic.

I darted across the street after him, skidding to an abrupt halt in front of the hotel. I stared at the polished dark wood of the doors as a wave of . . . something coursed through me. Though the doors were closed I could faintly smell the scents of musk and fur. But it was more than that. It smelled, *felt* like . . . home. A small smile played across my lips and I felt the furrows in my brow soften. Total acceptance waited behind those doors. I'd been here multiple times in the past month but never felt this way before. I belonged here. Bobby noticed the change, as well.

"Remember why we're here, Joe." Not even Tony anymore. He'd learned his lesson.

I reached for the polished brass door handle. It was a struggle to remember why I was here—why I was angry. As I pulled the door open my nostrils flared, saturating my nose once more with cinnamon-laced fur as we stepped inside.

For a hotel that's never had a single customer, Nikoli keeps up all the outward appearances. All the better to write off on his taxes. Bobby tensed beside me as we passed through the "doormen" posted on either side of the entrance. Several pack members stood and moved toward us. His tongue began to flick in and out of his mouth, licking his lip over and over as he scented the air around him.

Welcome home, Anton. said a honeyed baritone in my head. *Remove the snake and be one with us.*

I shook my head and blinked my eyes. Why was there a snake in our lair? I couldn't remember. But he knew he was outnumbered. I couldn't smell his fear over the musk of the others, but he had to be afraid. I backed away from him to join my brothers and narrowed my eyes. A low growl rumbled my chest. My hand started to move to the small of my back. Of course I would remove the snake. He didn't belong in our home. That only made sense.

The snake looked at me sharply and let out a frustrated sigh. I felt a veil of magic disappear from the back of my mind. My mate woke in a flash of pain that cleared my brain. An aching throb began in my calf and the sharp edges of the migraine that the snake—that *Bobby* had eased—rushed back in all its glory.

Damn it! I'd been tricked. It pissed me off. It shouldn't be that easy to get inside my mind. I shook my head and fought off the images of safety, pack and home. They were a lie. I was here for a reason and I would be damned if I was going to be hypnotized by Nikoli's voice and magic. I pulled my Taurus and pointed it at Bobby. He froze and looked at me strangely. I raised my brows a fraction. He took the hint. As I pulled the trigger he dropped and rolled. The bullet passed over where his shoulder had been.

A tall man called Sergei dropped to the floor from a mid-air pounce with a scream. Blood poured from a wound in his arm. The flesh had charred edges. Sergei kept staring at the wound, expecting it to heal. It didn't. That's the nice part about silver. It's worth a few calloused fingers. It turns the Sazi into just normal folk.

The other men caught the scent. One of them tried to lash out at us with magic, keeping his distance, but I fired a shot just an inch above his head. We weren't here to kill people. He didn't know that though, so he ducked. It threw off his aim enough that his attack only caught me in the shoulder. The invisible missile dropped me to one knee and my shoulder went numb. I raised the revolver and scanned the group. Bongo drums were playing in my skull and it was hard to focus. I offered Bobby a hand up without taking my eyes from my pack mates.

"All of you—*back off now* or you'll be joining Sergei." Brave words, but truthfully, I was a little worried. There were five of them, and I only had three bullets left. I didn't know if I could reload before they pounced on us. I could only hope that Bobby would be able to hold them off if it came to that.

Bobby and I stood back to back in the circle of growling wolves—human in form, but still wolves. And they were *pissed*. The room was awash with the scents of burning metal, burning water, and jalapeño peppers, hot and strong. One lone patch of hot and sour soup rose from Sergei.

"Thought I'd lost you there for a minute," Bobby said softly as we danced around in the ring of angry, growling men.

"You did," I acknowledged with squinted eyes. "Wish you would have found another way to break the spell, though. My head's ready to explode."

"Deal with it. I can't afford to protect you right now. I told you I need you alive. The same goes for me."

I could feel Sue's agony in the background and knew that she needed help. I tried to put her out of my mind but I just couldn't. My mate was in pain.

"Let's just get the healer and get back, Bobbo. I can deal with Nikoli another time. Sue's really hurting."

He gave a little bark of laughter. "Yeah right, Tony. Like we're going to make it out of here *without* seeing him. Look, I'll take care of the wolves. You just find Nikoli for me."

None of the wolves had made a move yet, but I could feel each of them twitching as they watched Sergei writhing on the floor. I struggled against a growing pain in my chest from seeing my pack mate hurting. I shook my head again as my gun started to waver. No! I was not going to give in.

"You'll heal," I said to him with bitter amusement. "Eventually."

I kept the gun out and we backed through the lobby. The double doors to the conference room were closed, but my nose told me that Nikoli was behind them with two other wolves. In one fluid move I spun and kicked them open while Bobby used his magic to freeze the pack members in the lobby. The guards inside started forward in a liquid blur that wasn't even *close* to being too fast for my eyes. When they saw my weapon, they stopped short and glanced to the back of the room for instructions.

Nikoli Molotov sat in a high-backed, black leather chair on a slightly elevated platform. A table near his right elbow held three computers. Each screen showed different data but all the words were in Russian. To his left, another table was laden with liquor and platters of food. Something on one of the plates smelled really strange. Sort of a musty fish smell, like moldy lutefisk. It's a stretch to believe that cod soaked in lye can mold, but it was the best description I could think of.

Nikoli turned toward us as we entered. The chair creaked under his weight as he leaned back to glare at us. He steepled his fingers over his buttoned vest then gestured abruptly for the guard to back off. Gone was the relatively benign man from the bus last night. Nikoli sat in his lair, bathed in his own power and rage. It made me think of something Paul Keating once said. "He is simply a shiver looking for a spine to run up."

Nikoli has classic Russian features that American kids were taught to fear in the fifties. His square face has a high forehead framed with wild black hair that must take a gallon of gel to tame. His eyes are close together and seem small under heavy black brows. He appears full of malice even when he smiles. A thick muscular body and full beard complete the malevolent image he strives to project. He's a powerful, double-dealing meglomaniac who is always thinking one step ahead of everyone else. He's also well-spoken, intelligent and utterly dangerous.

I admired and respected those qualities, but I was not about to back down.

I took a deep breath, trying to get a "read" as to what he was feeling. Unfortunately, his natural scent is like hot Hungarian paprika, which is part of the pepper family. He always smells of deceit and anger, even when he's happy and being totally honest. I'll probably never trust him, but that doesn't mean I can't work with him. Assuming, of course, Bobby and I got out of this alive.

Nikoli gestured for the guards to leave. Since he and all the other pack leaders hold their positions with pure power, I was fairly sure he didn't need the guards anyway. Still, I wasn't sorry to see them go.

As soon as the door swung closed Nikoli spoke directly into my mind.

You surprise me, Anton. I would not have thought you would bring a stranger—especially a snake*—into our home.* The pain in my head increased until each word seared through my brain.

Power like fire raged across my skin, bending me nearly double. It took more effort than I would've liked, but I fought until I stood straight.

"Bobby is a friend. He's always welcome in *my* home." I intentionally said the words out loud. Head talking with my mate was one thing. I didn't particularly want that kind of a bond with Nikoli.

I could feel Bobby's magic flow across my mind once more as he heard the effort it took me to speak. It made it easier to think through the pain—easier to block out Nikoli's smooth baritone.

When Nikoli couldn't reach my mind, he spoke with annoyance. "Agent Mbutu is not welcome in my territory. He should leave before I tear him to pieces."

Bobby stepped forward and I could feel, could *see*, a blaze of power emanate from him. The light was too bright even for the sunglasses. I had to close my eyes and fight down a wave of nausea.

"Wolven travels where it's needed, Nikoli. We answer to no pack, as you well know. While you may not *like* me, you would like my replacement even less. But I'm sure that Fiona *will* attend to my duties if she must."

Nikoli sat up straighter on his throne. I saw a brief flicker of what might have been fear in his eyes. A cautious breath confirmed it.

"You know how curious she is," Bobby continued in a voice that betrayed no emotion. "She might not be willing to investigate *only* the issues in my current case."

It was a thinly veiled threat, and a good one. From what I heard about Fiona Monier on the island she's a particularly nasty cougar who takes the concept of law and order *very* seriously. Bobby tends to let white-collar crime slide unless it's so blatant that it would be obvious to the human authorities. Something told me his boss wouldn't. Nikoli makes most of his money on the bare fringes of the law. He might not be able to afford the kind of full-blown investigation Ms. Monier would conduct.

I watched my pack leader take a deep breath and glare at Bobby. Nikoli's method of calming himself reminded me of my old boss, Carmine Leone. He let his arms go limp and moved his head from side to side briefly, easing the tension. The scent of ozone struggled to ride over the burnt coffee anger. As best as I can figure it, ozone is the expulsion of adrenaline, sort of like blowing off steam. Yet, it was all twined around that paprika-like smell, so I didn't know whether it was all a lie.

"Very well, Agent Mbutu. But first you must excuse Anton and I while we tend to a minor disciplinary matter. I'm sure you understand. It is *not* a matter that involves Wolven so it does not concern you. I will give you my undivided attention as soon as we are finished. You may wait in the next room. My wolves will not disturb you there."

From the corner of my eye, I saw Bobby flinch but I

didn't know why. He wears Wolven's special cologne. It makes it nearly impossible to tell what he's feeling. But his next words made the situation crystal clear.

"Normally I would do as you ask," said Bobby with an annoyed glance at me. "You're correct that Wolven doesn't concern itself with pack discipline. But Tony is part of the reason I'm here. I need him conscious and well enough to travel. For that reason alone, I must remain."

Nikoli growled deep in his chest. Burned metal and boiling coffee scorched the air—strong enough to make me cough. "Give me proof of this."

Bobby motioned toward the adjacent room Nikoli had pointed out earlier. Somehow I just knew it would be soundproof, even to my sensitive wolf ears.

Nikoli stood in a fluid motion that seemed impossible for someone of his bulk and gestured for Bobby to follow.

I tried to speak, to say that I ought to be involved in any decision about any discipline I'd earned, but no sound came from my mouth. Bobby's doing, no doubt.

He hissed at me as he passed by to follow Nikoli. "So help me, *Anton,* if you say one word to make this worse, I'll finish what he starts!" His magic constricted my throat enough to make me believe it. The door closed behind him before he saw fit to remove the magic.

I wasn't surprised I was in for it. Even if I hadn't shot Sergei there was that thing in the woods with Yurgi. I wondered how he made out burying the bones. I hadn't seen him since we'd gotten to the hotel. I'd take a beating if I had to, but before I did I was going to make damned sure to let Nikoli know that Sue's servitude isn't part of the bargain. I'd leave the pack and be a lone wolf before I let that happen. We'd just gotten her *out* of that kind of mess.

I used the time while Bobby and Nikoli conferred to get a handle on the pain in my head. I reached out to Sue with my mind. For a brief flash I saw through her eyes, felt the agony she was experiencing. She couldn't even think clearly enough to form words.

Work through the pain, I tried to soothe her with my voice, using every bit of my will to make her writhing body relax. *You've been through worse. Just stay still and it won't hurt as much.*

But she couldn't. It was just too much.

I took deep long breaths and added her pain to mine. I started kicking myself immediately for the impulsive action. The intensified wave of mind-numbing pain dropped me to one knee. My teeth gritted and my eyeballs threatened to explode. But I knew I would adjust to the new level of pain soon. That's the trick with torture. Adjust to each level so the only part that affects you is the new injury. I'd been told the mind is capable of adjusting to nearly anything if the injury isn't life-threatening. I hoped I wouldn't have to prove that theory today.

I had regained my footing and was meditating when the door to the adjoining room opened. Bobby walked to the far side of the large room and sat down. Nikoli returned to his chair and eased into it, all the while staring at me oddly.

"So, Anton," he began and steepled his fingers once more. The pinpricks were back, but they were closer to razor sharp daggers. I hissed through gritted teeth and concentrated on trying to breathe. "Let us begin this session with your failings as a pack member."

My anger cut through the net of pain. I managed to stand straight again. I won't deny it was an effort. "No, let's begin with *your* failings as an Alpha."

His eyes turned to blazes of amber light and his gums moved back to bare teeth. "The training of our young is not the concern of one such as you."

Ah. So Bobby had already brought that up.

"I could care less how the kids are trained, unless it affects me directly—like today. I can deal with my leg hurting, but you had no business telling Alena to drop those kids at my house. My wife is not some sort of pack babysitter."

Nikoli cocked his head as though I'd done something interesting. When he spoke he sounded the slightest bit confused. "All Sazi serve the pack as I think best. It is our law."

I shook my head slightly, trying to see Nikoli through the sparkles in my vision that had intensified when I'd taken on Sue's pain. "Not acceptable. Sue's not a member of this pack. She's human and not subject to your rule."

Nikoli didn't smell angry anymore. He had slipped into "instructor" mode. He shook his head lightly.

"Jessica is your wife. That *makes* her subject to my rule." The rest of the pack knows Sue as Jessica. It's part of the identity thing. Someday, I might make the transition, too.

Nikoli continued smoothly. "That is non-negotiable. Family members work in pack businesses. It is the way with our world. Only *pack* employers can possibly understand the odd duties that are required by the moon phases and plan a work schedule so that a business is not unmanned at key times." His voice was sarcastic when he continued. "But I agree that minding our young may be beyond her *capabilities*."

It was meant as an insult but it was the truth. From what I'd seen the kids were little demons.

His words were still sharp, but his scent was closer to greed. "Does your wife have any *other* useful skills?"

Sue and I hadn't discussed her going back to work but I remembered from our first night together that she'd said she missed her job. She won a bunch of money in the lottery and instead of working she became a slave to her family's needs.

I would like a job, came the whispered thought into my mind. She'd been listening the whole time. I was pleased that taking some of her pain had helped her cope. *I was a bookkeeper. A good one.*

"Do you have any businesses that are in need of a bookkeeper? That was her career before I met her."

"Strangely enough," he said with pursed lips and a rising scent of mildew. "I have need of someone to review the books of one of my businesses. I will send a car to get her and interview her for the post."

I shook my head. "Not today. That's the other reason we're here. I guess you have a pack healer? There's something wrong with her—with us. We've got a migraine that Bobby says is somehow magical."

Nikoli looked at Bobby sharply. "You said the young one did not draw blood!"

Bobby shook his head. "He did not, Alpha. Of that I'm certain. But the timing *does* seem odd. The pain is definitely magical. I have little healing skill. I am a chemist. I would request that your honored mother, the Duchess, assist your newest wolf's wife."

The formality of the words sounded odd to me. It reminded me of how a serf used to talk to the lord of the manor back in the middle ages. I didn't like it much, but I kept my mouth shut.

Nikoli was soothed by the formal request. He nodded his head thoughtfully as a *patrone* would in the mob. "My mother's gifts are more directly related to the future of our pack, but she does have some healing abilities. She should be able to help if the illness is not a human medical problem. I will have her attend to Jessica." He raised his voice and looked at the door. "*Serg*—"

He stopped abruptly and stared at me with anger growing in his amber eyes. Boiling coffee drifted on the breeze from the overhead fans once more. "Ah, yes. That's right. Sergei is somewhat *indisposed* at the moment, so he cannot drive my mother. He seems to be having a *silver bullet* removed from his arm." Nikoli's eyes had narrowed to glowing slits.

I can take a lead. Nikoli liked formal—I'd be formal. "I was defending our honored Wolven guest. I'm not as magically powerful as Sergei, so I've adapted my skills to my needs." Not perfect, but the best I could do. I waited to see how Nikoli would respond.

There was a long pause and a flood of scents too complex to sort. "Sergei was admittedly outside his bounds in attacking a member of Wolven who did not first offer a threat." Nikoli said the words grudgingly. But then his tone changed to outright fury. "But bringing silver bullets into our midst is an affront to us all!" He slammed a fist down onto the arm of his chair and let out a snarl that would send a full-grown bear up a tree. I fought an involuntary shudder, but held my ground.

I gave him a dark smile that was a little forced, mostly from the pain that had intensified when he'd raised his voice. "It's not an affront, it's a threat. A threat has no teeth unless your opponent knows you're willing to follow through. You can't expect me to be some sort of pack *omega* if I'm capable of more than that. I thought this culture valued power and ingenuity."

I know what an Omega wolf is in the wild and I'm *not* willing to be one.

Burned coffee flared in a blast of scent. "You spit the word *Omega* as though it has no value, and yet it is one of our most honored positions."

"I don't see being the pack whipping dog as an honor. Sorry."

He nodded his head and the sweet cloying scent of dark glee filled the room. He was ready to pounce on that statement.

"Ah, but you are the newest member, Anton. You *are* the Omega until you earn another position through proper combat. You *are* the 'whipping dog,' as you phrase it. You knew that."

"No. I didn't." My words were cold and flat. *"You* didn't tell me. That idiot historian of yours didn't tell me. Hell, I've learned less from her than the kids have. *How* would I know? I've been here all of two weeks."

Nikoli glanced at Bobby with shock that approached anger. "Santiago said he would be trained in our ways before he reached Chicago!"

Bobby stared at me open-mouthed. "You had the books, Tony. I saw Betty give you our historical records before we left the island."

I furrowed my brow, trying to remember. I shook my head. "Dr. Perdue gave me a couple of novels to read. You remember—you were there. She said, 'here's something to read if you get bored.' I didn't *get* bored. Besides, I don't like fantasy novels. The covers looked like sword and sorcerer stuff. I like mysteries and thrillers." The shock I was feeling rose to my voice. "It would never have occurred to me that you would actually put the history of your people in *print!* Are you nuts?"

I glanced back to see Nikoli nodding in agreement, but there was something under the surface that made his eyes glitter darkly. "Very well. I will see that you are properly trained. You seem to have made a few logical conclusions, which I will give you some credit for. Each pack position has benefits—and responsibilities. One of the primary duties of the Omega is to help maintain our secrecy among the humans. The only way to do that is to eliminate the signs of our hunt to passersby. As payment for this duty, the pack provides food, shelter and protection to the Omega."

I didn't want or need *protection*, as I'd just proven to Sergei. I am *not* burying bones. I glared soundlessly at Nikoli. He glared back, as though he could hear my thoughts. Without taking his eyes from mine, he snapped his fingers.

From the corner of my eye, I saw movement in a shadow in the corner of the room. A petite, beautiful Oriental woman stepped into the light. Where had she come from?

She stepped onto the platform and stood near Nikoli. She rested a tiny hand on his shoulder and stared at me coldly. Her slightly almond-shaped eyes were perfectly proportioned beneath penciled brows in an oval face. Her features and coloring put her origins somewhere south of China. Straight black hair framed the face and softened the broad nose and thin lips. I tried to place her nationality. Maybe Thailand?

Nikoli gestured to the woman with a small smile and a scent that was somewhere close to lust. "This is Asri. She is my enforcer. *Her* duty in the pack is to punish those who have broken our rules. Anton, you disobeyed a direct order today. Regardless of whether you know our history, I instructed you to bury the remains of our hunt and you failed to do so. You went so far as to attack our Omega. Normally, I would allow Asri to seriously injure you for your infractions. However, Agent Mbutu says it is in the best interest of all of the Sazi for you to remain conscious. So, my lovely Asri, make sure you leave enough of him to speak and travel."

The woman nodded once and stepped forward with eyes only for me. Fine. I'd take it like a man. Right now, I was about on pain overload anyway. Maybe she'd knock me unconscious for awhile. That'd be nice.

I didn't move as she stalked closer. I realized with a start that it was the *Asri* that smelled like moldy fish. She'd been in the room the whole time. I hadn't seen or heard her. A testament to how much pain I was already in.

"Still," Nikoli mulled. Asri instantly froze when he spoke. "You've impressed me today, Anton. You managed to break through when I called you home. You have endured the pain I have inflicted on you and remain standing even yet. You defeated Yurgi in the woods—although, admittedly, that isn't much of a challenge. But you also injured Sergei when he was in attack mode. That earns you a certain prize. Hmm, what should that prize be?"

Actually, his scent *was* a vague combination of oranges and cloves. I wasn't sure if it was a good thing to impress him or not. But call me cynical, I would've bet the bank he already had just the perfect *prize* in mind.

I heard Bobby clear his throat. Nikoli turned to him in a sharp angry movement. "You have something to say, Agent Mbutu?" The words were polite but had edges like daggers.

Bobby rose but didn't step into the light. I still couldn't figure out what his scent was. "Actually, Tony *didn't* disobey a direct order, Alpha."

Coffee and jalepeños rose into the air and joined the hot metal scent emanating from Asri. She put a hand on her hip and shot Bobby an annoyed glare. She obviously wanted to start in on me. I was happy to have Bobby talk for as long as he wanted. The look in her eyes was a lot hungrier than I would like.

"Explain, snake."

I turned to glance at Bobby, as well. His voice was calm and his face was a mask. He blinked his eyes and continued.

"You told Yurgi to tell Tony to help him bury the remains. We have just learned that he didn't understand that instructions through the pack members are the same as those directly from you. Yurgi attacked Tony. He defended himself. In the process, he defeated Yurgi. *Strictly speaking*, Alpha, after Tony defeated Yurgi, he was no longer an Omega. Even without realizing it, he was successful in a dominance challenge. Tony only disobeyed the order of a subordinate wolf, which is no crime."

I was wondering how the hell Bobby knew exactly what happened in the woods. I understand how Nikoli would know, since Yurgi should have made it back by now.

"A point well taken, Agent," conceded Nikoli. But the scent of dark glee oozing through the room belied his words. "The agents of Wolven must deal with the letter of the law and it is good that you consider these things. However, I am Alpha of this pack and it is the *spirit* of the law that I must consider. Anton understood that he disobeyed and, in fact, is this very minute expecting that he will be punished for his actions." He looked at me and his amber eyes could bore through stone. "You're willing to 'take what I dish out,' isn't that right, Anton? Please do not lie and make me angrier."

I think my face showed the surprise I was feeling. *Could* he read my thoughts?

"Fine. Yeah, I thought it might bite me in the ass. But Bobby said his matter was urgent. I know Bobby. I didn't know Yurgi. Bobby's 'urgent.' won out over Yurgi's 'urgent.' Is that what you want to hear?"

Nikoli raised his nose into the air. Then he looked searchingly in Bobby's direction. The mildew scent of curiosity overrode the smell of scorched coffee. "You told him your matter was urgent?"

Bobby's voice remained calm. "I told his wife to tell him it was urgent. Yes."

"Tell me, Asri. Do they lie?" The words were mild, but there was a note of dark amusement in his voice. It was a rhetorical question. He wanted to see what she would say. I got the impression that he didn't really value her opinion much. I watched her jaw tighten. Her anger bit at my nose. I couldn't blame her. She tapped long red fingernails rhythmically over the fabric of her blue jeans in annoyance.

Her voice was throaty but musical. There was no trace of accent. The words were carefully chosen and harsh. "No, Nikoli, I do not believe they lie."

Her eyes remained locked on mine and she easily transferred her anger for the pack leader to me. "Yet, the commands of an Alpha should not be so easily dismissed when something easier or more convenient appears."

"Hmm," Nikoli mused. "What is your opinion, Wolven? Should Anton be punished for his actions?"

Bobby's answer was succinct. "Yes."

I wasn't surprised, but I was annoyed. Nikoli *was* surprised. His brows raised high on his forehead. "Indeed? Why?"

Bobby stepped forward into the light. "Tony has always been a predator. He opens his mouth when he shouldn't. He does what he wants without regard to anyone else's needs. He's been able to get away with it in the human world because he was just that good. He never had to learn diplomacy because he simply eliminated any opposition. But negotiation is a critical skill in our world. Sazi are not easily eliminated and we all must *always* consider the whole of the Sazi people."

He'd been staring at Asri while he spoke. He barely tore his eyes from her long enough to give me a look that would cut stone. "Occasionally, Tony needs to get his teeth bashed in to get it through his thick skull that some rules can't be skirted. If you don't teach him control now, someday I'll be forced to kill him. He's a loose cannon."

I glared at Bobby. He wasn't wrong, but that didn't mean I liked it.

"But," he continued, "He has value, or Lucas wouldn't have convinced the Chief Justice to rescind the council's execution order and send him here."

That widened my eyes. Who *is* this Lucas and why did he keep doing things for me? I was wanted for murder. My number would be up if I got arrested. I already knew Lucas is the Alpha in Boulder, where Sue had been being trained. He's on the Sazi council. But why the interest in me? I didn't know his plan, and it made me nervous.

Nikoli laughed suddenly, startling us all. His roar of mirth filled the room and bitter oranges filled my nose. The sound stopped as abruptly as it began. He leaned back in his chair and studied the three of us.

"So you are asking me to somehow be strong, but merciful. Teach him our Sazi ways, but make allowances for his human skills and human wife. Bash in his head, but . . ." He held up one finger and continued with thick sarcasm painting his voice, "Not so much that he's not in perfect health when he leaves."

Worked for me.

He waved the words away with a dismissive gesture. "Bah! You ask too much, Wolven."

A look passed between Bobby and Asri. They each fought to hide a small smile.

"I suppose you're right, Alpha." Bobby responded.

Nikoli stood and walked toward us. His heavy black boots echoed on the platform until he reached the carpet. His eyes, which had faded to black during Bobby's discourse, began to glow softly. The amber light intensified with each step. I think it was *my* spine he was crawling up today.

"Anton, here is my decision: You have caused damage to my pack members and my authority. I will forgive damaging Yurgi because he attacked first. You defended yourself and defeated him. You are no longer Omega. You injured Sergei. He disobeyed my direct order that you and Mbutu not be attacked before you reached me. I will forgive you this also because you *chose* to injure, rather than kill. You will *not* take Sergei's place in the pack because it was not a proper combat. You did not answer my mental call, which no one before has withstood. I do not know how that was possible. It merits further study. However, it is already being discussed among the pack, and could undermine my authority. I cannot allow my authority to be questioned, so it is that for which you will be punished today. Asri is my enforcer. She will punish you. But. . . ."

He put his hands behind his back and leaned in toward me. The thick scent of mildew rose and blended with the deer blood still on his breath. "I am interested in testing your skills. You will be allowed to defend yourself. You will not be allowed your gun but I have a knife you may use. Asri is alphic so she may change forms at will. *You* will remain in this form." He looked at Bobby with a smirk. "Agent, I would ask that you remove your magic shield from Anton. I will do the same. I might also suggest you step back."

Bobby nodded and both he and the Alpha made a small gesture. Suddenly the pain in my head and body was only half what it had been. It was still intense, mind you, but I was able to relax my jaw for the first time in an hour. It seemed odd, but I had no time to dwell on it.

Asri smiled darkly, but her scent was the warm dryer air of gratitude. "Seldom am I offered such an honor. I am often called upon to punish, but the wolf must stand silent and endure my touch. It is hardly a challenge."

Nikoli turned and regarded her with furrowed brows. "I thought I was challenge enough, Asri."

She bowed her head. "In battle and in bed, yes." She licked her lips again. "But he still smells human, Nikoli. I have not tasted human flesh for so *very* long. Humans fight so much harder because their fragile lives are so fleeting." She bowed again. "I am honored, my Alpha."

Greeaat, I really needed a battle today with someone who craved human flesh. And just how old *was* she? I mean, Sazi laws had forbade killing humans for *centuries*. If she was that old, she was damned powerful. Not the kind of person I wanted to fight when I could barely see straight. The migraine was still hovering at the edge of my mind.

Bobby held out a hand expectantly. I grudgingly placed my Taurus in his outstretched palm. Nikoli reached down and pulled a wide push-knife from his boot. He tossed it to me right when I blinked and then turned away. I grabbed it out of the air when I saw it sail past my eyes. I cursed when the silver blade burned my hand. Oh sure. Silver is an affront when *I* have it . . .

A brilliant flash appeared in front of me while I was regarding my scorched palm. When I glanced up, Nikoli and Bobby had both retreated from the floor and I was now face to face with Asri's animal form. I didn't want to believe what I was seeing in front of me. I backed away instinctively. I had thought the term a euphemism but I knew now it wasn't. And I instantly knew where Asri was from.

Chapter 5

THREE STEPS BACK took me about two feet away but it wasn't enough. A forked yellow tongue flicked from between her scaly lips and touched my cheek. It smelled of rotting meat and old death. "You *taste* human, too." she said as the tongue retreated to her mouth.

She swished her tail so I could see the full length of her. Jeez! A normal sized Komodo Dragon is bad enough. They grow to about twelve feet. Asri was closer to twenty and her head stood to my thighs. That her tiny form could contain something that must weigh more than three hundred pounds amazed me. It also scared the shit out of me. I've visited Komodo. The dragons are nothing to be taken lightly. They're smart, fast and their bite is septic. That means if the dragon doesn't rip out your belly on the spot, you'll die from poisoning in a day or two. Then it'll just track you down at its leisure to feast on your corpse.

"I don't suppose you've got human teeth in there," I asked as I circled further from her. She followed my motions slowly and deliberately with short arms that ended in six-inch long claws sporting a stripe of the same brilliant red as her nails.

She smiled, showing curved teeth with jagged serrations. "What do you think?"

"I was afraid of that." One interesting fact about dragons—it's the *back* of their teeth that will shred your flesh to ribbons. I turned suddenly and sprinted to one side. I remember reading that dragons aren't too good at corners. I hoped not to give her enough running room to do serious damage.

"Stand still!" she said as we circled a third time.

"I thought you wanted a challenge," I taunted. Right about then, Nikoli turned up the overheads and the room was suddenly ablaze in light. I screamed as the light hit my already ravaged eyes. Asri took the opportunity to lunge forward. The sound of her feet on the carpet reminded me of machine gun fire about a block away. I moved out of the way, but not in time to avoid one set of claws raking down my arm.

"*Motherfu—!*" I drew in a sharp breath and instinctively clamped my other hand over the wound.

My biggest problem was that the damage was to my right arm, so now I was forced to use my burned left palm to hold the knife. I wiped the blood from it and winced as the raw wound scraped across the fabric.

Asri paused a moment to lap up the blood from the burgundy carpet as I moved to the side.

"Yum!" she said, licking her snout. "I can't wait to take a strip of hide."

Ah, Hell! That's right. I'd forgotten that's a standard Sazi punishment. They actually carve a strip of flesh from your body. Okay, I figured out my goal of the day. Keep all my skin attached.

My injured arm was almost useless now. I was going to need a healer myself pretty soon. Sadly, I was still fit to travel. I needed to find a way to end this quickly. I didn't know when someone would yell stop. How much damage would Nikoli think was enough? I did know there was no way I was going to actually defeat Asri. She was just toying with me. I needed an advantage. I looked up and around as

I sprinted around her again. The room was pretty empty with the exception of the few chairs against the wall where Bobby sat, and the tables on the platform by Nikoli.

Think, Giodone! The knife was no good. The push blade wasn't much more than three inches long. It probably wouldn't even make it through her armored scales.

I heard Sue's tired and pained voice in my mind. *I don't think dragons can see in the dark.*

That's right! It's why Nikoli turned up the lights. I looked up again and when I did, Asri struck. She moved forward in a blur and knocked me off my feet. I rolled hard to the side. Her teeth snapped in frustration as my stomach moved away from her strike.

With my good left arm, I heaved the knife upward as I stood and moved again. My aim was good, thanks in large part to years of practice in intentionally adverse conditions. The silver blade penetrated the ballast of the twin overhead fluorescent and shorted it out. It sparked and sputtered, sending blue fire to rain down on us. With a few choice swear words of his own—primarily in Russian, Nikoli reached over and started frantically clicking screens. In a moment, he had turned off the circuit through his computer, leaving only the light over his platform remaining.

"Nikoli!" the dragon exclaimed with annoyance.

He raised his hands in innocence. "He's allowed to defend, Asri. I will not burn down this hotel for your convenience. Perhaps he is more of a challenge than you thought. Even *I* did not expect *that*."

She hissed—an angry, vicious sound. Her massive head turned this way and that, searching for me in the dim room. Her tongue flicked out over and over as her head swayed from side to side. Just when she'd found me by scent, I would move. I stayed in the shadows of the corners. With the knife gone, I had little left in my arsenal.

Her tongue continued to flick out in rapid succession. Spittle dripped from her jaw in long strings. The forked yellow whip flashed as she walked through the light.

"You can't hide from me forever, Anton. I can smell your blood. You're over . . . HERE!" She moved with preternatural speed, knocking Bobby off his chair in the process. But I was already gone. I'd deliberately wiped blood on the carpet and then used the elastic of my inner pants holster as a tourniquet to stem the flow while she was searching the room.

Nikoli's eyes followed me carefully. A small smile played over his lips. He was enjoying the cat and mouse game. Asri still hovered near the chairs by Bobby. No good. I needed to be there.

Nikoli didn't stop me when I carefully reached onto the table next to him and removed a tray filled with fruit. His glowing amber eyes looked amused and he smelled of oranges and cookie spice. I darted to the other corner before Asri saw and tossed a large orange into the opposite corner of the room with the injured arm. There wasn't much feeling left because of the tourniquet, so I wouldn't be able to do that more than once or twice more. She didn't respond at all. Oh, that's right. A dragon's hearing sucks in the low and high ranges. I aimed the next piece of fruit at one of the overhead fixtures in the corner. The sharp clang of metal attracted her attention. Her head snapped around and she pounced on the fruit in a blur.

"Come out, little wolf," she called when she realized my trick. "It'll hurt a lot more if I have to keep chasing you."

I almost laughed but held back. I didn't really think the pain would be proportional to whether I delayed the capture.

She quickly moved to the corner and I ghosted her until I was behind Bobby. He glared at me, leaving the impression that he would *not* be a shield. I ignored him and carefully, oh so carefully, lifted a chair from the end of the row. His cocked head raised in understanding and he nodded slightly. I retraced my steps to my original corner. I heaved another piece of fruit but the arm wasn't working right. I nearly beaned Nikoli. He ducked and shot a look of annoyance in my direction. I'd bet that the oranges had been replaced by burning coffee.

"Finish this, Asri, or I will step in and *you* shall be punished."

That didn't occur to me. If it's Asri's job to punish me and I escape, what will he do to her? I felt worry and sorrow. I knew it wasn't mine.

Back off, Sue! I ordered, and shut down the connection temporarily. I couldn't worry about Asri right now. I was allowed to defend myself.

It didn't matter much, because Asri had found me. I'd waited too long and she was here. She stood on her hind legs to her full height. My head didn't even reach her throat.

"Enough of this, wolf cub! Take your punishment!"

"Not quite yet," I replied and raised my left hand. I slashed across her belly with the sharp metal tray. It stuck in between her ribs. She let out a grunt as blood began to flow. Rivulets swam and danced across the shiny silver. An eerie yellow light hummed around her and the wound sealed before my eyes, pushing out the tray. She stepped on it and hissed at me. I reached backward and found the chair. A quick swing caught her in the chest and she lost balance. I darted to the side and started to run, but she recovered faster than I expected and knocked me back into the corner. There would be no escape.

She quickly wrapped her arms and legs around me until I couldn't move. I could smell her fetid breath as she nuzzled my neck with her snout. She slid a slow tongue around my shoulders and ran it up and down my cheek.

"You've been quite an interesting opponent, little one," she said in a whisper low enough that even Nikoli and Bobby wouldn't be able to hear. "I'd welcome another challenge in better surroundings when you recover from today's injuries."

With those words, she started to bend me over backward to the floor. I twisted in her grasp but the sheer weight of her body was all the momentum she needed to complete the throw. She lay on me and methodically began to use all four sets of claws to rake down my back and legs. I couldn't stop the scream as my clothing and skin burst open in a wash of blood. Pain ripped at my mind and I felt Sue scream along with me through wave after wave of agony as Asri mauled my body. Bobby and Nikoli were both headed toward us when I mercifully blacked out.

Chapter 6

A JOLT SIDEWAYS awakened me from nightmares of pain and chasing prey that I couldn't catch. The sound of studded tires on squeaking snow warned me I was in a car before I even opened my eyes. The brakes protested slightly as the vehicle reduced from highway speed to a sliding stop on gravel. I was lying spread-eagle face down on nylon carpet. It smelled like other people and cleaning chemicals. The shampoo couldn't completely erase the underlying lap-dog urine. I opened my eyes cautiously without moving. I knew I was going to hurt when I moved.

The driver's door slammed and I was alone in the back of a rental passenger van. All of the rear passenger seats had been removed. A glance upward showed thick red twilight edging the tinted windows above the door latch. Hunger gnawed at my gut. I could smell fresh meat somewhere in the van, but I was really hoping it wasn't *mine*. That would seriously gross me out. I tentatively moved my hand to my face. The palm had healed from the knife burn. A second experiment with my other arm revealed slowly closing wounds from Asri's claws. I tentatively flexed and found I had reasonable range of motion and strength. Not as bad as I would have thought.

I was hoping Sue would be able to stand the pain of me rising to my knees when I realized she wasn't there. My heart began to trip like a jackhammer and worry flooded over me. I pressed my mind outward, searching for her frantically. I found a barrier that felt and smelled like fur and jungle. It's hard to describe something solid in your head. I couldn't tell what was beyond the barrier or why it was there. What the hell?

The scent of chapstick and aftershave flowed in an icy wave as the door opened. Ah, Bobby was my driver. I couldn't smell him directly but I knew it was him from the chapstick. He's worn it for years to heal the damage from constantly licking his lips to scent the air.

I hate that damn cologne Wolven uses. It masks an agent's natural scent, as well as anything they feel. He was again as I'd always known him—a mystery. It never used to bother me before I was Sazi.

"Where's Sue?" My mouth felt like it was stuffed with cotton and my voice was hoarse and cracked. An abrupt cough reminded me of the wounds on my back and sides. My head started to pound and I suddenly wasn't interested in being vertical anymore.

"You're finally awake. Good."

"Where's Sue?" I asked again with a dangerous edge.

"We had to cut you off from her." Bobby's voice was flat and as angry as I'd ever heard it. The sound was slightly muted by the thick woolen muffler wrapped repeatedly around his neck. "That fucking lizard almost killed you. It took both me and Nikoli to pull her off. Sue was in shock when the Duchess found her."

He turned and looked down at me from the driver's seat with fierceness in his eyes. "Another thing to keep in mind, Tony. Your mistakes can kill your mate."

We wouldn't go there. None of his business.

"Should we be driving this close to nightfall? I'm about ready to chew off my own arm. And where are we going?"

"Check the window, Tony. You're looking at the wrong horizon. Night's come and gone. You slept away the whole second night of the moon. Like I said, she almost killed you. But you're right about being hungry. You turned but didn't eat, so I have no doubt you're ravenous." He moved his head slightly back and to the left without taking his eyes from the road.

"There's some packages with raw beef back there that I bought for you. Sorry, no deer."

I found the packages in a paper bag near my shoulder. My head has always preferred rare to raw—anything to give the impression of humanity—but my stomach wouldn't listen to reason. I tore open the white butcher's paper and bit down hungrily into a thick, meaty rib roast. The first one disappeared in seconds. I tore and swallowed as fast as I could and tried not to be repulsed by how much I enjoyed the taste of bloody flesh.

"I thought you told her *well enough to travel*." I finally said, when my mouth was full of the same rich beef from the second package.

Bobby's voice lowered to an angry mutter. He moved his fingers expressively on the wheel as he shook his head. "Oh, I did. *I need him fit for travel,* I said. *Just rough him up a little,* I said. But *oh, no.* Let's give him to the dragon with no self-control who 'hasn't tasted human blood in a century,' instead. Yeah, let's let Bobby use all of *his* magic to heal him. *Great idea!*"

I managed to stop myself from licking the waxed paper clean of scraps. After I wiped my mouth and hands on some paper towel from the roll tucked under Bobby's seat, I folded the butcher paper and returned the bones and trash to the paper bag. The meat would curb my hunger for the moment. Every muscle in my back, butt and legs screamed at me as I rose to my knees. I was probably bleeding all over the back of the denim shirt and blue jeans I was wearing. Not a big concern, since I didn't recognize them. "I don't exactly feel healed, Bobbo. I think maybe your magic's broke."

He didn't turn his head. The slapping windshield wipers

told me that it was snowing. Bobby's always hated driving in snow. The heater was blasting hard enough that the air nearly burned my lungs as I inhaled.

"Oh shut up! You're as healed as I'm going to make you. You're not lying in a pool of blood, are you? Just getting you back from the edge of dying was plenty, thank you very much. I feel like a truck hit me."

I had crawled forward and managed to get my feet under me enough to slide one leg over the center console and onto the passenger seat. My hip lightly brushed Bobby's shoulder.

"Jesus! Watch what you're doing!" He kept his death grip on the steering wheel with both gloved hands. His multi-colored neck wrap slipped down a little.

"Well, why don't you pull over? I'll get out and go around."

"No time. We should have been there by now, as it is. *Damn* this snow!" He raised one fist toward the roof and then snapped it back down to clutch the wheel.

I checked my options as I stared down at the long route into the front seat. Well, hell. There was going to be no good way to do it. I held onto the tops of both of the head rests and carefully lifted my other leg over Bobby's soda. My boot sole got stuck briefly. Hmm. Didn't recognize the shoes, either. Guess they didn't dress me from my own closet. In freeing my boot, I nudged the gearshift into 'neutral.' I reached forward and used my heel to shift it back into drive. The back end slid the tiniest bit as the tires caught.

Bobby nearly panicked. "Stop it, Tony! I mean it!"

"Relax, Bobby. Even if you went off the road you wouldn't hurt anything. Maybe we'd get wherever we're going quicker if we were going more than twenty miles an hour. I never understood why you're afraid of winter driving. You're Sazi, stupid. 'You'll heal'—isn't that the line?"

He ignored me, other than a nasty glance my direction. I

had both of my feet down on the passenger side floor, but the rest of my body was half way in between. I gritted my teeth, closed my eyes and slid down the upholstery. White lights filled the back of my eyelids and pain seared through the wounds on my back. My breath was coming in little gasps, and I could feel wet warmth trickle down my spine as I finally sat down on the soft velour. We wouldn't get back the damage deposit. I blinked to get my vision to focus. I tried to leaned back, only to leap forward again as pain sliced across my back. Shit.

"Buckle up," Bobby ordered.

"Sorry. Ain't happening." I scooted forward on the seat and braced my hands over the glove compartment. I took a second to open it, and found what I hoped was there. Breath mints. If we were going "somewhere," I'd rather not smell like bloody meat.

"This is the best you're getting unless you feel inclined to heal me more." I said as I popped a mint into my mouth, closed the compartment, and braced my hands again.

"You'll heal on your own eventually. If I fixed you up, you wouldn't learn the lesson."

"Oh, I learned my lesson."

He spared me a glance and his tongue started to flick out of his mouth. "Oh, yeah? What was the lesson?"

I raised my brows and crunched down on the mint before swirling it around in my mouth. "Don't piss off the pack leader."

"Damn it, Tony. What am I going to do with you?" Bobby tightened his grip on the wheel as an SUV smoked by us in the left lane. Of course, anything over forty was "smoking" right now.

"Well, fine." I snapped. He was beginning to royally tick me off. "What lesson was I *supposed* to learn?"

He glanced at me with those fake human eyes and sighed. "You're supposed to learn that you're part of a community now, Tony. We're all in this together. Your actions have a direct effect on those around you. You need to figure out that you have to start playing by the rules."

I was getting sick of this b.s. I'd been told how to live my life—where I could live—what I could do, for just about long enough.

"Okay, ya know what, Bobby? Maybe I don't *like* your rules. I was doing just fine by myself. I didn't ask for this shape-shifter shit, but I adapted. I was living my life. Doing what I do. I'd figured it out. I wasn't endangering your precious *secret* any." I quavered my hands and made my eyes go wide. "Ooo, don't reveal the *secret*, kids." I shook my head and snorted. "Jeez, I mean—you teach your people that they're better than us poor lowly humans and then you hide like cockroaches when the light hits you. I just got the shit kicked out of me for not hiding a bunch of deer bones. Yeah, there's *superior* for you. If that's the attitude of all of the Sazi, then I don't want to play by your rules. I don't want to be part of your fucking *community*. We're not all in this together. 'Cause you know what? It *doesn't* take a village, Mr. Secret Agent. Not your definition of one."

I leaned back in the seat and let the pain be what it was going to be. The pain fed my anger and made it stronger.

"If you're going to lean back anyway, at least buckle up." The words were soft and thoughtful. Bobby deliberately kept his eyes on the road. I reached around and grabbed the belt and hissed as fabric abraided my skin. I stretched the belt across my chest and buckled it.

We drove in silence for some time. The wipers kept a steady beat against the falling snow. It was growing light enough to see. A road sign whizzed past. We were only forty miles from my old home town. I thought about asking Bobby why we were going there since I'm wanted for murder—and supposed to be dead—but didn't really feel like talking to him.

"Babs is missing. She's been kidnapped," he answered me as though he'd heard my thoughts.

"Why would I care?" I hated the woman ever since she turned me into a frigging animal. I tried to kill her four times but she kept healing. I finally got bored.

Bobby's voice was flat and annoyed. "Didn't figure you would. But *Carmine* cares. He's going to go looking for her."

"Bully for him." I crossed my arms over my chest and stared out the window. The snow was slowing and turning to tiny pellets of ice.

My peripheral vision caught Bobby's fingers doing a tap dance on the steering wheel. "We're here to stop him."

My voice was an angry hiss. "The hell you say! Why would we want to do that?"

"Linda was at home when Babs was taken. She said someone came in, threw Linda across the room, knocked Babs out and took her. We're looking for a Sazi."

"Did Linda *say* it was a Sazi?"

"For Christ's sake, Giambrocco! Get over being pissy and use your brain. Babs is a powerful alpha wolf. Who else *could* have knocked her out long enough to get her out of Carmine's fortress?"

"That still doesn't rule out a human, Bobby."

He gave me a withering look, so I continued. "Granted, I didn't manage to kill her, but I could have knocked her out any time I wanted to."

He shook his head in disbelief. "We heal too quick, Tony. You don't understand what you're saying. Alphas can't be knocked out."

"*Anyone* can be knocked out if you know what you're doing, Bobby. You just have to know your animal. They've got stuff on the black market that will put down an elephant. She wouldn't be out for long—just long enough to get her away. If Linda was unconscious, she wouldn't know."

"Then what, Tony? How do you keep down someone who can lift a car? Chains—nope. Steel cable? Only for a few minutes. You can use silver, but as a metal, it's not very strong. It burns our skin, but only until it breaks. No, it's one of ours."

"Fine," I replied with exasperation. "I don't know the bad guys of your world, Bobby. You tell me—who could have done it? And again, why do *we* care?"

"We're almost there. Get in back and keep your head down. There's still an all-points out on you."

I shook my head and unbuckled my belt. I started again to climb over the seat. My back and legs were a throbbing pain that wouldn't stop. Probably better that I wasn't connected to Sue right now. At least the migraine was gone. I was miserable, but I could *think*—clearly enough to know that this trip was just a bad idea.

"Yeah. My precise point. The one thing I've learned is to keep a low profile. This isn't helping. If you don't want Carmine to look for Babs, just go and tell him. It's not like I'll have any great influence over him that you wouldn't, Bobby. He's known you almost as long as he has me."

He shook his head and gritted his teeth. "I *told* Lucas you'd be like this." He dropped down the visor as the sun crested the horizon. "But he insisted."

"Yeah. And what about this 'Lucas' character? Who the hell is he and why is he so interested in me?"

"Lucas is one of the old ones, Tony. He's got his finger on the whole world. He works with the seers. Knows the past, the future—everything."

Oh, great. They've got psychics too. Figures. I snorted lightly. "But he doesn't know where Babs is. Some seer."

Traffic was heavier the closer we got to town. It was a work day. A little snow never stopped the town before, so ramps began to feed multitudes of cars onto the freeway. I could see Bobby flinch as people went zooming by on the right and left of our lane. Bobby quickly released the wheel long enough to flip on the right turn sign. Then he clutched it once more as he eased into the slow lane.

"Lucas isn't *one* of the seers, Tony. He just works with them. The reason we're going in is that they *don't* know where Babs is. That's the problem. We've checked up on known rogues but nobody knows anything."

"Rounded up all the usual suspects, huh? Fine. But that still doesn't explain why you don't want Carmine's help. He's got a lot of resources, you know. I know it's probably amazing to you since he's only a *human*, but he might actually be able to help."

"Knock off the sarcasm. Yes, I know that Carmine's connected. But we can't let him help. It's too dangerous."

A short bark of laughter erupted and pulled at the wounds on my neck. "Too dangerous for Carmine? Get real, Bobby! He's a mob boss. I wouldn't worry about him."

The turn signal began to click again as the van eased onto the exit that would take us to the center of town. Carmine lives in the 'burbs. I still didn't know where we were going. Bobby pulled into the nearest shopping center lot and stopped. He shifted into park and put on the emergency brake. Then he turned around in his seat so he could see me.

"Look, Tony. I'm going to level with you. I'll probably get my ass chewed, but so be it. The person took *Babs*. We don't have many Sazi with that much firepower. The few we have all had unshakable alibis. We're a little afraid that it's one of our agents gone rogue. Several have disappeared lately without the bodies being recovered. A rogue agent will turn Carmine into chopped liver if they don't eat him first. Linda would start a war with the Sazi to avenge him."

"If Babs is dead they might anyway. I mean, she's just their latest toy but she's *their* toy."

"Precisely. Carmine is too well known not to be noticed if he goes missing. He's too well known not to be noticed if he goes to war. And, if he or Linda bring in boys from other areas, too many people will find out about shape-shifters and the world will destroy us."

"This isn't the days of the Salem witch hunts, Bobby. I adapted to knowing about the Sazi. So would the rest of the world."

"Oh, yeah. We've adapted real well to different cultures since 9/11, haven't we? Ask your average Pakistani cab driver. Or some innocent Arab immigrant who's sitting in Gitmo for no reason—no charges, no accusations." Bobby's eyes were flashing and his voice was harsh. A snowplow noisily scraped by, carving a path around us.

"They can hold him forever that way with the new PA-TRIOT Act, you know. Maybe he did something. Maybe not. He might have been at the wrong place at the wrong time. But as long as he's deemed a 'security risk,' he'll sit there until they decide, in their infinite wisdom, to let him go or put him on trial. That's not just my vivid imagination, Tony. It's real. And forever's a long time to us."

Okay, he had me there. I've read some of the case files about the Act. I knew he wasn't kidding.

"Most of the Sazi are just like you, Tony. They didn't *ask* to be born like this. Those kids you met may be aggressive, but they're not *bad* kids. They don't deserve to be rounded up like anthrax-ridden cattle and destroyed just because people fear magic. And that's what would happen. You *know* it!"

I thought about it. A group of powerful people who can't be killed, who can mask themselves with illusion so you don't see them go wherever they want to. Wow. Talk about your *security risks*. Then I imagined the faces of those little kids and thought about what would happen if the troops arrived like they did in Florida with the Cuban kid. Shit. I'm not stupid and I'm not completely heartless. I threw up my hands and was annoyed when Bobby smiled.

"Fine." I snarled, "Maybe I'm willing to admit that one war at a time is all most people can deal with. But do you really think we're going to stop Carmine if he wants to go after Babs?"

"That's why *you're* going to offer to lead the hunt. Carmine and Linda will let you do your thing. You've always gotten results."

Well, I couldn't argue with that. I'm one of the best at what I do and Carmine knows it. "What if he wants the guy's head on a platter?" My mind switched into business mode.

Bobby's eyes were as cold as his namesake animal's. "We'll give it to him. Whoever it is can't be allowed to live. The execution order's already been issued."

My brows raised a bit. "For a kidnapping? When you don't even know the motive? Isn't that a little extreme?"

"Babs isn't the only one missing, Tony. We think we've got another Sazi serial killer on our hands. And one's more than enough."

Chapter 7

LINDA SPUN ME around before I could stop her, while I was still gasping for air. I caught the scent of tangy soured milk rise from her. Her eyes matched the surprise and worry.

I was standing on the landing overlooking Carmine Leone's underground war room. I'm not kidding about the "war" part. A number of men that I knew—and a few I didn't—moved with quick assurance cleaning and loading everything from rifles to shotguns to semi-auto pistols.

A map of the state was unfolded on a large table and was covered with colored push pins. The scent of Vic's Vapo-Rub assaulted my nose. It took me a moment to sort Joey the Snake from the crowd. I hadn't seen Joey since I landed in Chicago.

"Okay, Joey, you take your boys to Riverton. Try to keep a low profile but don't take 'I don't know' for an answer. *Capisce?*"

"You bet, Boss. And if we find anyone that knows any-thing, you want them back here, right?"

Carmine nodded with a cold light in his eyes. I'd seen that calm fury before. The person he questioned probably wouldn't leave standing.

Linda's voice cut through the din below. "God, Tony!

You're bleeding like a stuck pig. What sort of ringer have you been through?"

"I'll heal, Linda."

She summarily ignored me. That's Linda for you. "Carmine, we need some bandages up here. Tony's hurt."

Carmine looked up in shock. He was too far away to get the scent but the eyes were enough.

"Tony? How in the hell did you get in here? I've got more guards on this place than Carter's got little liver pills."

Bobby started down the stairs. "I brought him, Carmine. I told you I was bringing you a tracker. Who better?"

When my name was mentioned, the room fell silent. All eyes turned on me in disbelief. Sal dropped the pistol frame and cleaning rod in his hands. Louie looked like a statue with a Styrofoam coffee cup frozen near his lip, mid-sip. The last time I'd smelled that much mildew and soured milk, I had to scrub down my refrigerator with baking soda.

Joey was the first to recover. He headed toward me with a broad smile. I could see his hand was raised in his traditional greeting. I did not want him to slap me on the back. I put my hands out in front of me to ward him off.

"No way, Joey. Linda's right about the bleeding part. A handshake will do fine."

He stopped as he reached me and dropped the hand altogether. He went serious as he stared at me. I probably did look like shit. "Thought you were dead, man," he said with feeling.

"You were supposed to. That's how it works. Breathe a word of it and you *will* be." The tone was friendly, but I was serious. "That goes for the rest of you, too."

The remainder of the group suddenly lost interest in me and Bobby, with the exceptions of an occasional small smile or wink toward me. They went back to what they were doing as though we didn't exist, but the banter was a lot less tense. I had to admit I was flattered. I just hoped that nobody would end up getting an attack of the running mouth.

Joey nodded in acceptance and finally held out his hand. "Glad you're not. You're still the best and it looks like we're going to be needing you."

I took the hand and gave it a short shake. "Yeah. Well, I need to talk to Carmine about that."

Carmine hadn't greeted me yet because he was on the radio. He was chuckling when he turned around.

"A dog, Tony? A frigging *dog*?"

I had the good grace to blush. Bobby has an odd sense of humor when it comes to a disguise.

When we'd left the parking lot he had decided to take the plowed city streets over the interstate to get to the suburbs and Carmine's house. I had been trying to get Bobby to explain the comment about the "other" Sazi serial killer. He wouldn't budge except to say that Wolven had the situation under control. I got the impression that whoever the "other" serial killer was, he or she was well connected in world politics and was somehow blackmailing the Sazi Council to leave him or her alone.

It was on impulse that I suggested that Bobby turn on State Street. I wanted to drive by Nick's Tavern. The last time I was "alive," I'd left my car there. I knew logically that it wouldn't be there, but I wanted to look anyway. Bobby must have known what I had in mind. He took the turn anyway with a sigh. I wasn't too concerned. The windows of the rental were tinted pretty dark.

Something seemed odd about the block. It took me a moment to decide what was different.

"Where'd the upholstery shop go?" I asked the question out loud, even though I didn't expect Bobby to know.

"Torn down. The Fire Marshall made Jocko install an emergency exit after those nightclub fires back east. He tore down the other shops and put in a parking lot." Hmm. I hadn't known he owned the whole block. Live and learn.

Bobby was concentrating on the icy road, so he didn't notice the tan sedan that drove by going the other direction.

"Shit!" I exclaimed, and ducked my head as we reached the corner of the block. "That's Sommers."

Bobby nodded but didn't seem particularly concerned. "He's spending most of his free time at the bar. Thinks you'll *show up* here." His voice lowered to a sarcastic snarl. "Wonder what would make him think *that*?"

I ignored the dig. "Was that my car in back?"

He nodded. "Yeah. Carmine gave it to him to replace the Lincoln that got trashed at the airport when Leo grabbed Sue. You wouldn't want to see it now. He tore out the front seat."

"Ah, jeez." I exclaimed in disgust. Logically, I knew that Jocko's big frame—a massive 6'8"—wouldn't fit in my Mustang Fastback without removing the seat, but damn it, it was a classic.

Bobby turned the van down the alley that fronts the store. I peeked my head up and glanced through the van window as we passed. I couldn't stifle a strangled cough. The front window that had been covered by years of cigarette smoke haze and dirt was sparkling clean. Through the window I could see Jocko polishing the bar. When he turned, I got my second shock. He wore a *hairnet* around his waist-length black locks and his white apron was *clean*.

"God, Bobby! What did they *do* to him?" My voice held equal amounts of disgust and dismay.

"Sommers doesn't believe you're dead, Tony. He got a swarm of agencies to lean on Jocko so he'd squeal where you were. Of course, Jocko *doesn't* know, but that hasn't stopped the good Lieutenant from making his life hell."

I couldn't think of what to say. There really wasn't anything *to* say. I mean, it didn't change anything. I couldn't think of any decision I would alter had I known what would happen. Jocko has always lived under the knife. He knew he skirted a bunch of the health and zoning laws. I shouldn't feel responsible—but I did.

Another glance behind us cured any soul searching. I

dove to the floor and flattened against the carpet. I didn't have time to think about it right then. We'd picked up a tail.

"I see it," Bobby said when I swore and dived. "Just stay down and shut up."

The cruiser was following about five car lengths back. If I was a betting man—and I am—I'd bet that Bobby was on a list of "known accomplices" of me, Leo Scapolo and his boys. Since both of us were supposed to have died, Bobby's presence here would be noticed. It probably *had* been noticed by Sommers. So, I kept my body flat on the floor. Actually, it did feel better on my back that way.

"You know, if you'd teach me that illusion thing where they don't notice me, we could drive like normal people." I whispered the words, in case there was more than a police scanner in that cop car.

"Yeah, right. Like that's going to happen. Maybe if you agree to start playing by the rules you can have some of the toys, Joe. I don't give gasoline to firebugs."

I guess we just agreed not to even speak the old names. Yeah, probably safer.

"What happens when we get to Carmine's then? His boys are going to want to look in the back of the van. Everyone can be bought, Bobby. Leo Scapolo's old lieutenants in Las Vegas probably have a price on my head. And if they don't, Prezza's goons in New Jersey do."

"I said I've got it covered."

Oh, he had it *covered* all right. It turned out that the clothing I *thought* I was wearing was a freaking illusion and I was totally naked in the van. That same illusion made me look like a *dog* to all of Carmine's guards. Bastard! I had to get dressed in a rush before we entered the house, because I was so *not* going to be naked around my former boss and I am *not* a dog! I was very displeased with Bobby, although I had to admit to enjoying scaring the crap out of one of the guards by lunging and barking at him when he used the metal detector on me. Bobby convinced them that I had a couple of stray bullets in my "dog" body.

I was startled out of my memory as Carmine strode over to me with the weighty blur of a fast moving rhino. He bent down suddenly. He lifted the leg of my pants and let out an exasperated breath when he saw my derringer. He patted the back of my jeans. I let him. He found the Taurus. No problem. I wasn't trying to hide them. He let out a low growl that would do a Sazi proud.

"Jesus! You people are dangerous, Mbutu." He got back on the radio. "Mike. Hey, Mike."

"Yeah, Boss?" came the crackled reply. Hard to get a signal this far underground, even with the best equipment.

"The next time a *dog* don't pass the wand, you call me before you let it in."

I smiled in the silence.

"Uh, sure, Boss."

He waved to the assembled group. "Okay, everyone clear out. Go upstairs and blow off some steam for a while. Nobody leaves until I give the go." The men all looked at each other, not bothering to hide their annoyance.

Carmine glared at them. "You heard me. I gotta talk to these boys before we do anything else. So, go for a swim, bowl a few lines or help yourself to the pool tables. One drink apiece limit and leave the weapons. I still need you all in top shape. Get moving."

A few shrugged and a few rolled their eyes but they put down their guns and left. Bobby remained leaning with crossed arms against the wall. I just tried to stay standing.

Once they filed out the door, Linda latched the deadbolt and came downstairs. I hadn't noticed before how haggard she looked. Her shiny blonde hair hung limply and her normally flawless skin was drawn and grey. The smile she gave me didn't reach her eyes.

She sat down on the couch and Carmine started to join her when he stopped, grabbed a shotgun and tossed it my way fast enough it would have been nearly a blur to a human.

I reached out and snatched it from the air. I probably

failed miserably at hiding the stinging in my shoulders. He looked at me for a long moment and nodded.

He sat down next to Linda and patted her knee gently. "I hear you had a little run-in with your pack leader. You ever gonna learn how to shut up and do what you're told, Tony?"

I winced as I set the shotgun back on the table. "I'm working on it. Your enforcers didn't have teeth and claws."

Linda got a pained look when I said that. She'd seen Babs after Bobby knocked her around on the island. But she'd also seen Babs heal wounds that would have laid up a human in ICU for a month.

Carmine just pursed his lips and nodded. "So, Tony. Bobby tells me you want to go hunt down this person by yourself?"

I nodded. That's what Bobby and I had agreed to tell him. "You know me, Carmine. Other people are just cannon fodder. I work alone."

He kept nodding. I couldn't quite tell from his scent what he was thinking. The overwhelming wet mist of Linda's sorrow masked everything else in the room. But as I watched, her eyes became an icy blue storm. Linda's like that. She can push through pain with anger and keep moving. She gets dangerous when she's sad: the perfect gun moll. We'd been together for a time but it didn't work out. I don't like to share. Linda prefers frequent threesomes. Babs had been the latest in a string.

"You a cop now? Bobby's a cop. I don't want the law in this. They'd want to catch the person—put him on trial."

"And you want him brought back here to you." It wasn't a question. Carmine has his own version of justice. Not too different from what the Sazi use, really.

Carmine shocked me by shaking his head no. "All I want is the head. Nice, neat and recognizable."

He didn't smell like black pepper. He wasn't kidding. "You don't want to watch?"

"No, Tony. I've watched Babs train. She's tough. A real artist. Anyone who took her is out of our league. I won't risk the boys for trash like that. Swear to me that you'll bring me the head and I'll shut down the operation. You'll get your normal fee."

I stared at him for a long moment. I'd been listening to his voice, watching his movements. Carmine's *tells* were vibrating through the room. I settled my stance and crossed my arms over my chest. My voice was flat and non-negotiable. I needed to toss another chip on the table. "Not good enough."

His eyes narrowed and fury grew in his scent. Linda's sudden surprise widened her eyes, and her fingernails dug into her thighs. I could feel Bobby tense behind me. His voice was a little strangled when he spoke.

"Could I talk to you for a minute, Tony?"

I turned and cut him with a stony glare. "No, you can't." Then I turned back to look at Carmine. The only scent that Bobby would be able to get from me was calm and determination.

Carmine stared at me with that cold light in his brown eyes. His big hands were clenched into fists. "My money isn't good enough for you suddenly?"

"It's good—just not *enough*. This is a big job. You said so yourself. It'll cost extra."

Bobby's hand was reaching for me. I saw it in my peripheral vision. I sidestepped his grip, and kept my eyes on Carmine.

"What do you want?" Carmine's voice was carefully neutral. He was realizing that he might not have the better hand, after all. Bobby stopped moving when Carmine spoke. He went back to leaning against the wall, but he was *so* not happy—just a trigger pull away from being all over me.

I crossed my arms over my chest once more. There was fire in my voice and jalapeños in my scent. "You've got strings at City Hall. I want them pulled—*hard*. I want everyone off Jocko's back. You find a way to keep that damn Sommers the hell away from Nick's. Jocko guarded my things, helped me escape, and drove his car straight into the junkyard crusher for me. You gave him my ride. That's fine. But it's not *enough*. If he doesn't want to wash his windows, he shouldn't have to. And get rid of that damned hair net!"

Carmine's eyes had lightened in surprise and his mouth opened in shock when I mentioned the net.

Linda nodded her head in agreement. "Oh, God! He's right, Carmine. I forgot to tell you about that. When I went to pick up Tony's things, I saw it. Those assholes in County Health made him put all that beautiful hair in a *net*."

He turned his gaze to stare at Linda with a look of revulsion. Then he looked back to me. "He pours *drinks* for crissake!" he exploded suddenly. "They got him looking like a school lunchlady?"

I nodded, and he shook his head. Burning coffee rode the air. "No problem. Done. I'll call in a few markers—or more like, tear up a few. I'll get Sommers put back on a beat so fast his head'll spin."

"Just as long as his beat is across town. Do that, and I'm your man."

He raised one finger. I've never quite figured out how to define the scent when someone is hiding something. Sort of peppery, but sweet and thick. It's tough to describe but easy to spot. "Not quite yet."

The finger descended to level and pointed at Bobby. "First, magic man, you're going to heal him up."

Bobby moved away from the wall with a shake of his head. "I can't do that. That's up to his pack leader. I'm not allowed to interfere with pack discipline."

"His boss ain't here. You are. And you listen to me close, Mbutu. The *only* way I'm going to back off is if Tony is in charge. He can't even hold a fucking shotgun, for Christ's sake! How's he gonna take down this Sazi that can take Babs if he's not on top of his game? He's useless to me this way. So you patch him up or I call the boys back in and we go to war. Got it?"

Carmine and Bobby had a staring match that finally made even me and Linda uncomfortable. Bobby's eyes were narrowed slits. Carmine knew he had the upper hand. *I* certainly wasn't going to argue.

Bobby caved. "Fine. I'll get him back to his pack healer before we start out."

Carmine shook his big head. He stood up and walked over to Bobby. One finger raised up and he poked Bobby in the chest hard enough to actually rock him back for a second.

"Maybe you didn't hear me so good. I said *you* are going to heal him up. I saw what you did for Tony's girl at the airport. A one-minute miracle. Fine. I've got a minute to spare. I want it done before you leave here. *Then* I'll call off the boys. Joey has instructions that if I don't buzz the game room ten minutes from now, they're to turn this room into scrap metal with grenade launchers and *none* of us are going anywhere."

I watched Bobby's mouth open. His eyes widened in shock. It wasn't a surprise to me. Carmine always has a back-up plan. If he knew Bobby was coming, he absolutely would have some way to destroy the room to kill Bobby. None of the underground rooms are weight bearing. They can be destroyed and sealed over to hide the bodies. I'd just be unfortunate collateral damage. I presumed he'd have a convenient escape plan for him and Linda. Or not. Maybe Joey would end up in charge and they'd lay waste to the state finding Babs's kidnapper in retaliation.

Bobby let out a harsh breath of air. "Fine. Take off your shirt. You want to watch, Carmine? Fine, then watch."

I had just removed my shirt and turned to look at Bobby. Linda gasped when she saw my back. Even Carmine hissed through closed teeth. "Goddamn, Tony! Do those go all the way down?"

I glanced in the mirror. All of Carmine's high security rooms have mirrors. They aren't two-way or anything—

well, some of them are—but it's to keep people from sneaking up on you. It's hard to draw down on someone when everyone's always watching.

I finally saw what Asri had done to me. Yeah, they looked about as bad as they felt. The gashes on my back were obviously made by five toed claws. She had raked open the skin and muscle until the white of my ribs showed through in large patches. I was amazed that I hadn't lost any organs out the holes.

"To the ankles," I said. Seeing them had made them start to hurt again. Damn it. I'd almost forgotten they were there. The wounds throbbed in time to my heart. Amazing how the eyes and mind connect on shit like that.

Bobby began to load up his eyes with power. It's really weird to see a person's eyes glowing the first time. Of course, Carmine and Linda were a little more used to it because they'd been sleeping with Babs. Still, it's impressive. And more than a little scary.

He began to glow, softly at first but then brighter with each passing second. In another time, he would have been treated as a god. A wave of raw power began to soar through the room. It swirled around me like a whirlwind. The energy raised Linda's pale hair until the strands danced like gossamer around her.

The feeling of fur in the back of my mind disappeared. The room began to smell like a jungle. Even Linda caught the scent. She looked around with nostrils flared, seeking the source. Soon I couldn't focus and the room began to disintegrate. Thick vines began to flow in a bright muggy mist. Trees soared upward as high as I could see. The vines wrapped around me. They were warm and wiggly and tickled as they slithered over my bare skin. I suddenly knew that once there were many like Bobby. I saw his world in the jungle as it once was. Dark-hued people flowed in and out of their skins with the ease of breathing. I saw individual faces. People with histories and personalities and lives.

I saw the night the humans came. I watched the nets being thrown, the ropes drawn taut around the necks of siblings and cousins. I watched little kids being staked and stoned and cut apart. The trees that were home were burned to prevent the "disease" of being Sazi from spreading. Then it was gone. They were all gone. Bobby had seen only the aftermath but had "watched" it all in his mind as the cords of magic were cut, one by one. Hate and pain and sadness swept through me. Then that was gone, too.

I was back in Carmine's war room. I still breathed in Bobby's magic. I soaked in his power until I glowed like a nova. But I knew his pain and his weariness. My feet rose from the floor, held aloft by the sheer force of all of the Sazi that had come before and were yet to be. Light played over my skin like tiny rainbows and I got to watch the wounds on my arm knit back together as though in time-lapse. The skin of my back ached, tightened, itched and relaxed, all within seconds of each other.

When my feet finally touched the floor again, I knew I was healed. I also knew that Bobby was drained far beyond where he could afford to be. I'd have to thank him but not in front of the others.

Linda had her hand over her brows to shield the glare. Carmine hadn't moved. He sat like a statue as he watched in awe. The light finally faded from Bobby's eyes and he stumbled just the tiniest bit. He looked the same as normal, with the exception of tired lines set in his brow.

"Good enough?" he asked with an angry edge. I looked at my back in the mirror. It was once again smooth and flawless. I tentatively stretched my muscles and found them perfect. Better than perfect actually. I felt like I'd just got back from a visit to the chiropractor.

I spun around so he could inspect my back. Linda's reflected eyes were wide and her mouth remained open for some time. "Oh my God! That is amazing!"

"Good enough." It was all Carmine would say to acknowledge what had just happened. It was all that was necessary.

Chapter 8

BOBBY OFFERED CARMINE a few details, but not enough. Carmine wouldn't know where we were going, or how we were going to track the kidnapper. I insisted on seeing the room where they were taken.

"Have you moved anything?"

"No." Linda responded in an flat, annoyed voice. Her arms were crossed over her chest and she shot a glare at Carmine, who shrugged. Linda hates a messy house.

Linda unlatched the door and she and Bobby started down the hall. Carmine held me back with a firm hand. A quick call to the game room was made. I heard it ring twice and then it was picked up. No one spoke on the other end.

"We're good," said Carmine. Then the other end hung up. He turned to me and walked toward me.

"Tony, there's something you need to know." Carmine spoke quietly, his voice uncertain. I caught a whiff of the tart acidic smell of confusion and guilt. It's like bitters in tonic water.

I raised my brows to show I was paying attention.

"I didn't expect it to happen, Ton. But I love Babs. I want her found. This isn't a game to me."

My brows raised even further as I smelled the cinnamon apple pie spice that told me he wasn't kidding. He and Linda have an agreement. They both enjoy having a third person invited to bedroom games. But there are rules. Neither of them are supposed to get emotionally attached to the third. That's what keeps it from being cheating. As far as I'm concerned it's rationalization at its finest. But it's not my business.

Carmine's grip had tightened until his knuckles whitened. It would have been painful if I were still human. He released my arm, looking startled at his own display of emotion.

"I haven't told Linda, but we was trying to have kids, Tony. Me and Barbara. You know Linda's plumbing doesn't work." He took a deep breath. It was hard for him to admit this. "I had to tell you, so you'd understand. If Barbara would have asked, I'd have left Linda." He stared at me until I believed it.

Whoa. I did know Linda had some internal problems and they'd had to remove her uterus. But Carmine's crazy about Linda and kids had never been an issue. That he could fall hard enough for Babs to break them apart . . . I took a deep breath. Wow. The stakes had just raised. I let out a slow breath through pursed lips. At his next words I felt my eyes widen even further.

"And Tony? If she's . . . dead," The word was accompanied by a small choking sound. His eyes grew cold and wetness sparkled when he blinked. His scent became the fiery Jalapeño of hate. "I want you to promise me you'll make her murderer *hurt*."

I nodded my head, trying to think of something sufficient to satisfy Carmine's need for revenge if it came to it. I came up dry. I was suddenly hoping that I wouldn't only find Babs's *body*. Bobby's vision of war wouldn't even be a shadow of the real thing. Grenade launchers would only be the beginning.

"What's keeping you guys?" Bobby's voice echoed down the hall. I turned to the sound and when I turned back, Carmine was wiping his eyes quickly and shaking down his arms until he calmed. But this time no ozone scent of relief filled the air. He wouldn't relax until this was over—one way or another.

"You ready, Tony?" Carmine asked. "You ready to be my hunter again?" He clapped me on the back and I tensed, waiting for it to hurt. It didn't.

"Ready." I didn't mention that I had no clue how to hunt and take down something that made the preternatural cops nervous. I might be way out of my league. All I could do was try my best and hope that I'd come up with something along the way. I also knew that I'd rather face death from the kidnapper than to come back to Carmine and report failure.

"By the way, you want your stuff, or should we keep it here? You might need your tools for this job."

Ah, That's right, Linda said she'd picked up my stuff from Jocko. "Absolutely. You can keep the guns, though. Too many ballistic reports on them already. But I'll be needing the money to buy some new toys."

I leaned out into the hall to shout to Bobby and Linda. "Be with you in a minute. Got to get my stuff."

Bobby looked suspicious, but then shrugged and walked away with Linda. When I returned my gaze to Carmine, he had a puzzled expression. He walked toward the bar set into the far wall. "I had Mike clean out your place, but there isn't any cash, other than loose change. You can have all the rest back, if you want. Clothes, furniture—the works. The computer is toast. I had Ira overwrite the files and then reformat the drive."

I nodded. Standard procedure. Carmine couldn't afford any loose ends that might lead to him. "How'd you get everything past the cops? Didn't they have warrants?" I've been a little busy since I disappeared. I'd left everything behind and gave it all up for lost. Both because of the warrant, and because I was starting a new life in Chicago, courtesy of the Sazi.

He chuckled, but the sound was a little bitter. Scents blended and then split. I couldn't sort out what he was feeling. His voice was flat and unemotional when he spoke. "We arranged for there to be a body found that matched yours. We did it for all our guys, not theirs. We'd have done it for your lady, too, but the cops would've gotten DNA samples from the family as a matter of course."

I nodded. I wasn't surprised. He'd gone to a lot of bother, but he'd done it as much for his benefit as mine.

Carmine continued, "I don't know what Las Vegas and Atlantic City are doing to cover their tracks. All that was left for us afterwards was the clean-up." He paused, looking at me long enough that it made me a little nervous. "I suppose I should be pissed, and I assure you I *was* surprised. Fortunately, it worked out for the best. You left a will, Tony."

I froze in place at the words, and my heart skipped a beat. I had no doubt the shock showed on my face. Shit. I'd completely forgotten. I *had* drawn up a will years ago when Linda and I got engaged, long before she hooked up with Carmine. It named Linda as my sole heir. I'd never bothered to contact the lawyer to change it. Oh shit. How would *Carmine* react? I waited without even breathing. I felt my stomach unclench when the oranges scent of his amusement drifted to me.

Carmine changed the subject. He'd learned what he needed to know from my reaction. "I had Louis take over your security business. He needed to start going legit anyway. He's taking that kid—Scotty—under his wing."

That widened my eyes and allowed me to put our previous conversation out of my mind. "You'll need to keep a close eye on the kid." I warned. "Scotty is smart, but he's a psychopath. He *has* to kill to satisfy something inside." Being an assassin had allowed Scotty to avoid becoming a serial killer. He'd started his streak at six. One job a year after, and he was a full-fledged teenager with homicide on the brain. I *like* Louis. I didn't want to see him wind up on a slab. Scotty does close-in work. I wanted to make sure Louis wouldn't be getting a stiletto between the ribs.

"Don't worry, I'll be watching him. You know, the kid was pretty bummed when you turned up missing. He'd hoped to turn into a shooter. He might still. I'm having Joey work with him. And I already told the kid that if he so much as scratches the skin of one of my guys, it's open season."

I didn't say any more about it. Carmine's the boss for a reason. He's not stupid or careless. So long as Scotty was worth the trouble Carmine would use him. If the kid became a liability, it would be over.

Carmine shoved a couple of bottles aside to make room to slide a single finger down between the bar and the wall. At the press of a switch the panel next to the bar moved out a few inches and slid quietly to the side. The lights came on automatically as Carmine and I entered the room.

Carmine's outer war room contains all the tools for planning a war. The secret alcove we were in now stored his tools for *staging* a war. Wooden pegs line the walls in configurations that can change at a moment's notice. Every weapon currently on the market and a few prototypes hung in orderly rows. Waist-high cabinets hold multiple rounds of ammo for each of the

Carmine crossed the length of the room in four strides. He lifted the lid of a nondescript file storage box on the floor to reveal my own personal stash of weapons. I stared at them with lust. But no, they were known to the police. I didn't dare. Still, I couldn't resist the urge to draw one gun from the long leather holster. I'd bought this particular gun just before I'd been forced to disappear. But as I pulled the weapon from the custom holster I found myself frowning. This Thompson Encore looked *similar* to the one I'd had custom made, down to the black chrome finish, but it definitely wasn't the same gun. Carmine nodded as I stared at it and the scent of amusement and pride rose from him.

"Yeah, it's a different barrel. I figured you'd notice. We melted down the 6mm PPC that was on it. I got you one in that new load—.17 HRM. It's a sweet round. No mess at all. Goes in one side, doesn't come out the other. Can't beat it for close-in jobs. And if you miss, there aren't any ricochets. It just disintegrates when it hits something."

He wasn't telling me anything I didn't know. I'd been wanting to give that new round, plus the later version, the Mach 2, a try for awhile. I lifted the gun and sighted down the barrel through the Burris scope. Of course, everything was a blur. It's a 4X-16X-50mm ballistic scope. It's meant for long ranges, and the room was too short. "The scope will be too much for the .17," I commented, mostly to myself. "The round will only go about two hundred yards." Then I broke open the gun and looked down the barrel. I could tell that the factory oil had already been cleaned out.

"One hundred if you want decent accuracy," Carmine replied with a nod. Then he shook his head with just the slightest hint of annoyance. "Shame we couldn't save the other barrel, but the 6mm was tagged by Lieutenant Sommers. He found the shell casing in a drain in the garage where you took out Prezza's hitman last summer. He had you cold on that job. Not one of your better efforts, Tony. It's almost a good thing that Leo tried to kill you. You would have had to hightail it anyway. I know we were pressed for time on the job, but you left a witness alive, forgot the shell, and left a paper trail on the gun. Sloppy work."

I felt my jaw set. I couldn't disagree, but I had to at least defend myself. "I didn't *forget* the shell, Carmine, it rolled into a *sealed* drain. I would've needed a blowtorch or a crowbar to get it out. And as for the woman, I could have killed her, but I didn't think she would freak out that much when I offed the guy raping her."

Carmine shrugged. "Whatever. You know the saying,

Tony—'No good deed goes unpunished.' Still, you got the hitter. That's what counts. Prezza's been laying low since then. That's why I bought the new barrel. You earned it. Go ahead, take them all. They've been sanitized. New serial numbers—the works."

I snapped the Thompson closed and returned it to the holster. I placed it back in the file storage box with the other guns. "What about the package I left with Jocko? Did Linda and Mike get that, too?"

Carmine snorted and shook his head. He smelled of soured milk and black coffee. "Can't imagine why you stored it with him, but yeah, we've got it." He opened another cabinet and removed a carton that was about fifteen inches by thirty inches. It was an effort for him to lift it onto the counter for me to see. "They sell these at Kmart, you know. You don't need to hoard them."

I grinned at him as I stared at the heavy cardboard carton. "Had you fooled, huh? It's not what you think it is."

I glanced in the box and removed one of the smaller packages inside. Eight D-cell batteries were encased in their original half-box, but with different shrinkwrap—added after my modifications. I tore open the plastic with a fingernail and removed two of the batteries. I raised them to my nose and sniffed. Easy with my new senses to tell the difference, but even to a layman, it's pretty clear. I tossed one of the batteries to him and he caught it.

"Notice anything?" He turned it over in his hands, and then shrugged.

"Not a thing. It's a battery. So?"

"How about this one, then?" I tossed the second one and he caught it, as well. But the look on his face as he did was worth the effort.

"What the *hell?*" He tossed one up in the air with one hand and then did the same with the other. He looked closely at the second battery, turning it over more than once. "How come it's heavier?"

I pulled the knife from my pocket and slid it under the wrapping of the *fourth* battery in the pack, not the third. A quick slice revealed the secret.

"Jesus Christ!" exclaimed Carmine as the shiny gold caught the overhead lights. "Those are Krugerrands."

"Yep. Twenty of them per battery. Four in each pack of eight through the whole carton."

If he bothered with the math he'd know there was probably worth a mil and a quarter's worth. He reached out and pulled one of the gold coins from inside the metal wrap of the battery. The positive and negative terminals were barely glued onto light-weight aluminum spacers to get the perfect height. It had taken a lot of time to build them, but his face and scent made it worth the effort. "Why only four in each pack? You could fit a lot more."

I could see the gears in his head working. He'd be doing the same thing with some of his wealth pretty soon. I could just tell.

He handed back the two batteries and I put them back in their package. I took the coins out of the sliced battery and put them in my pocket. Then I crushed the shell in my fist until it was an unrecognizable lump of metal and dropped it in a nearby trash can. If he wanted to spend the time to figure out how I'd done it, he was welcome to. But the design for holding the coins, and cut gems, were *mine*.

"You'd notice the difference. The carton's heavy, but if it were too much heavier, people might get curious. Unless you have one eight-pack in one hand and one of these in the other, you can't tell because most people can't really remember how much a pack weighs. They just remember that it's heavy. Plus, you can pull out a couple of batteries and actually use them. It's not so obvious." I put the box of guns on top of the carton of batteries and lifted them smoothly.

Carmine shook his head and we exited the room. "Good thing Mike and Linda didn't know those were in there. You might be missing a few."

He had a point. Linda likes shiny things, and Mike's

youngest needs braces. Linda wouldn't consider it *stealing*—more of . . . a handling fee.

We headed down the hallway to where Bobby and Linda were waiting. Bobby stared at me with narrowed eyes as I passed him with the boxes. I didn't need to smell his scent to know he was curious. I didn't bother to enlighten him, just set the boxes on the floor of the hall.

The four of us entered the library together. There are three libraries in the house. Each holds different things. Babs had been taken from the "east" library. It's mostly mystery and science fiction with some scattered popular fiction. It's Linda's library. Carmine has two of his own rooms filled with books. One is strictly reference. That's the west library. Multiple versions of dictionaries, the-sauruses and maps. The north library is strictly historical novels, biographies and books about war and warriors. That's Carmine's choice of relaxing reading, although he will occasionally grab one of Linda's books on a whim.

The room was a mess. It was obvious that Babs put up a fight. I automatically glanced to the corner of the room. The security camera I'd installed was still hidden behind the seascape painting. That was useful information.

"What did the tapes show?" I asked Carmine as I walked toward the painting.

"Not a damn thing!" he exclaimed with fire in his voice. Hot jalapeños and burned coffee scorched the air. "All the tapes are missing."

Both Bobby and I looked at him sharply. "You didn't mention that the attacker had the run of the place, Carmine."

"Or that it might be an inside job," added Bobby.

"It was and it wasn't. Tell them, Linda."

We all turned to her and she described a scene where one of the guards, Sammy, appeared at the door of the library and told Babs that Carmine wanted her to come with him.

"But Barbara hadn't liked the look—or the smell—of him. She told me to run and get Carmine. She said he wasn't Sammy. But he *looked* like Sammy. Barbara seemed confused. She kept asking 'Who are you?' She circled the room opposite the intruder and kept telling me to get out and go get Carmine. But I couldn't move. I actually *couldn't*. My muscles wouldn't work. When they started to fight harder, I caught a book in the head and got knocked out."

Fear?—or was the intruder an Alpha who could hold a person motionless and change their appearance like Bobby had said?

I glanced at Carmine. "Why are you so sure that it *wasn't* Sammy?"

"I'm not *sure*. But Barbara said it wasn't, and it just seems out of character for him. What would he have to gain?"

I shrugged. "The usual—money, sex, hate. Any of them apply?"

It was Linda who answered. Her scent was fierce determination with coffee not quite burning. "Sammy liked Barbara, but he didn't lust after her. She could smell stuff like that. She always told me which people to watch out for. Sammy wasn't one of them."

Carmine nodded, his scent heavy with cloves. "It's true. If Barbara said it wasn't Sammy, I believe her. Her nose was amazing. We just don't have any leads other than what Linda saw."

Bobby was in full cop mode now. He settled his stance and addressed the big man like an equal. It startled Carmine a bit. When Bobby spoke it was with complete authority.

"Since we talked, I've been doing some checking. Sammy—if that's who it was—rented a car in Chicago day before yesterday. It was never turned back in. The cops found it this morning, abandoned on Highway 6 out by the ship canal. So, that's where we'll start once we leave here."

I began to scout the room, looking for anything useful. Books littered the carpet in a wide semi-circle that told me where the battle had been. I got down on my knees and slowly scanned the floor with my eyes.

I leaned down and put my nose against the carpet. Might as well use the new senses for good purpose. I took a deep sniff in the center of the circle of books. My brain didn't even get a chance to process the scent before I was violently sneezing with watering eyes.

"God! What the hell is that smell?" I choked when I could breathe again. I stood and backed away from the swath of carpet.

Bobby came forward and rubbed his hand along the carpet where I'd been and then put his hand to his face. His tongue flicked over his hand and then waved in the air. His eyes started to water a few seconds later and he bolted to the door where he spit repeatedly on the floor of the hallway. "I have no idea what that is. It's not any animal or chemical I've ever encountered. But it's . . ."

"Awful," I completed, and he nodded. "I don't think we'll have any trouble recognizing it again." I walked across the room and grabbed a tissue and blew my nose three times before I could clear out the smell. I tried to place the scent with *anything* I knew, but it eluded me. It was bitter and musky but so overpowering that it burned out my nose. Sort of like Bobby's cologne, in concentrated form.

Bobby took a Chapstick from his pocket and ran it over his lips and tongue for a moment and then rubbed his hand over the fabric of his jeans to remove the lingering odor. Carmine and Linda both went over and sniffed. Nothing. They just looked at each other and shrugged.

I snuffled and snorted a few more times. The smell lingered in my nose, but I could breathe again. I went back to the spot where I had been, keeping my face a safe distance from the carpet. Something had caught my eye during my sneezing fit. I leaned toward it. Tucked underneath one of the books was a wisp of white. I gingerly lifted the book and picked up the thread. It was incredibly soft and drooped over my finger like a thread of satin.

"What were you all wearing?" I asked Linda sharply. Out of my peripheral, I saw him glance at me. "Was Babs wearing silk?"

Linda shook her head, but the mildew gave away her curiosity. "Barbara was wearing shorts and a cotton T-shirt— that one of mine with baby wolves on it. She's always liked it. She wears lightweight stuff, even in the cold."

Yeah. She would. So do I when I'm alone. I was known for it even when I was fully human. Bobby had reached me and picked up the strand. He touched it to his tongue and then nodded. "Definitely silk. Raw, with no processing."

Linda's arms crossed as she struggled to remember. "Nope. No silk. Sammy was wearing a flannel shirt—red and black checkered, and suit slacks, and I had on a peach velour pullover with jeans. I don't think Sammy's pants were silk. The fabric wasn't shiny."

I shook my head. "Raw silk isn't. You know that. And you said it was only a minute before you got knocked out."

She shook her head in return and a hint of coffee burning joined the frustration. "I know cloth, Tony. It didn't move right for silk."

"Maybe some of the *threads* were silk?"

She shrugged, still angry. "Maybe. I don't know. It doesn't really matter, does it?"

I glanced at the thread on Bobby's finger. It was a clue, but it didn't really help us much. "Probably not," I admitted.

We spent some more time looking around, but didn't find anything else of importance. It wasn't long before we were heading back for Chicago. We exited the place in the same way we arrived, with me at Bobby's heel. The outside guards wouldn't know I'd been in the house. The inside guys wouldn't know anything about the dog. If pressed, Carmine would say that the dog kept the guards busy so I could sneak in. They wouldn't dare argue.

I was damned glad to get outside in the fresh air. It

helped remove the rest of that godawful smell from my nose. We made it out of the city before either of us spoke.

"So, what do you think?"

Bobby shook his head. "Not a clue. I don't like it. The missing tapes prove that the person had the run of the place, so maybe you're right. Maybe it *was* an inside job. The scent has me completely stymied. I'd expected to be able to tell whether it was a Sazi. I've got the best sense of smell in Wolven, so if I can't tell, it's useless to bring in anyone else to try.

"What about the fact that Babs told Linda to go get Carmine? Doesn't that say it *wasn't* Sammy?"

"Linda probably said something, made some comment to Babs or the attacker that made Babs realize that Linda was seeing Sammy. Or maybe that's what Babs saw, too. Maybe it was *Babs* that was hallucinating. It could lend credence to your theory about a drug. But if it was a Sazi illusion, they would have to compare notes to know for sure. Like if Joey and Marvin stood together and I only gave Marvin an illusion."

"You can *do* that?"

"It's not good practice. People often compare notes when they're confused or scared. Even when two human witnesses to a crime see different colors or makes of cars, they don't normally disagree on *whether* it's a car."

"So, a Sazi could've made Linda see almost anything? Then we're back to square one."

"Maybe. It's not a universal talent. It's a gift. Like your shooting talent. Most Sazi can't do it."

"But the rogue agents you're thinking of *can?*"

"Natasha can. She's a bengal tiger, but she's accounted for. She's not rogue. And, Babs knew her. So she would have said something to give it away to Linda."

"Babs was in Wolven?" I didn't exactly see her as the law and order type.

He waved away the implication. "No. Babs didn't make the cut. She was too aggressive, like Nikoli, but she knew a few of the agents. A lot of Alphas know each other—there aren't that many of us—and many *are* in Wolven, at least for a time. It's how we train Alphas to control their talent and teach them ethics. They get to see all the shit that can happen when you don't play by the rules and it tames them a bit. It's why I'd really like to get you involved. But you're not strong enough. You wouldn't survive the training."

"Don't underestimate me, Mbutu." I shot back. "You're just lucky I have no desire to be in Wolven. I'm not a cop. I'm what the cops chase. But I'd kick your ass."

"Yeah, well. It's not an issue anyway." He shrugged and I still couldn't tell his scent. I didn't know whether it was his cologne or the aftereffects of whatever that was back at the house. "But back to our suspect—Kalino is strong enough to make Babs and Linda both think he's Sammy. He's been missing about a year. But his illusion capability is limited to visual, so it might explain why Babs seemed confused by his scent. He's native Hawaiian so he's brown-skinned. Old time Hawaii, when there was still a king. Simple illusions, like facial features and size, are easier than skin coloration or gender. Sammy was dark, too."

"If they didn't know each other, what would his motive be?"

"Good question. Unless he just went over the edge and is taking out all the Alphas just for fun."

"Is that the problem with your *other* serial killer?"

Bobby made an exasperated noise. "No. And it's none of your business. We've got him handled."

Ah, it was a *him,* I dropped the subject for the time being. I can be patient as hell. But I would find out eventually.

We rode in silence for quite a while. I popped another trio of mints into my mouth and had to let out a slow breath when the burning hit.

We were rolling into Chicago when I asked "So, now what?" It was just after lunch. The moon pressed down on me behind the weight of the sun. The third day is never as bad, but I'd be turning again after dark.

"Now, I take you home and go and take my punishment from Nikoli. Just so you know, I ought to kick your ass for what you did at Carmine's. I ought to put you right back where you were when you got there. If I didn't need you on this case, you'd be laid out in the back."

I'd expected he'd be pissed about healing me, but *punishment?* "What punishment?"

"I *told* you—I'm not allowed to interfere with pack discipline. Because I did, Nikoli can cut me apart and *feed* me to that damn dragon if he wants and I'll have to take it." Bobby's eyes blazed with thinly veiled fury.

"What was I supposed to do?" I snarled. A part of me knew, and I was pissed it hadn't even occurred to me. I felt my eyes begin to glow. It wasn't a good time of the moon to get into an argument. For either of us. "It was Carmine's call. His demand, not mine."

"You could have stopped him. You could have done the same thing that Babs did on the island, Giambrocco. You could have said, 'Oh, no, Carmine. It's my screw up. I'll take the heat. I'll heal.' But you didn't. You had the chance to do the ethical thing and you failed. You didn't give a shit about the consequences to other people. One of these days you're going to figure it out, Tony. You better hope that someone still gives a shit about *you* when that happens. Which reminds me—what in the hell did you think you were you doing raising the stakes? You could have blown the whole deal!"

I rolled my eyes. "Don't they teach you *anything* in that agent training of yours?" I shot back. "You saw Carmine. He was ready for war. You think he normally stocks multiple grenade launchers?"

Bobby snorted and shook his head. "Don't be an ass, Tony. He was bluffing."

"The hell you say! I *saw* one of the shoulder-mount launchers in the gun room." Bobby stared at me long enough that he had to jerk the wheel to bring the van back into the proper lane. I continued on before he could get a word out of his dropped jaw.

"It wasn't the only one in the house, either. And, it's probably not the biggest thing he's bought. He would only *tell* you about mid-level stuff, not his top buy. *That's* the lie you were telling. You're getting too cocky, buddy. You're depending too much on those Sazi senses and not using your head. Fortunately for you, I know how Carmine thinks. I've played poker with him for years. If he sees a pair of kings on the table in front of me and I don't raise the bet, he'll think it's all I've got. He'll throw in everything, including the pink slip to his car, to force my hand— even if he's only got a high card. He has to try to make me fold. It's a control thing.

His voice took on a thoughtful edge. "So you needed to treat the job like it was as important as *he* believes?"

I nodded my head once slowly. "Precisely. If I accepted the same fee for a marital spat as this kidnapper he's stocking up on grenade launchers for, he *wouldn't stop.* He'd just send us off and then go hunting, too. Making him work for my fee is even better. Money's cheap, but the *effort* of him playing chess with city hall has real value. It's almost a shame that Jocko will never find out who's behind it."

Bobby sat in thoughtful silence. I glanced at his tired eyes and cracked, bleeding lips. He didn't even have enough juice left to heal himself. I was starting to regret how good I was feeling. I wasn't relishing the thought of seeing Bobby in the same shape as I had been in earlier. It might cost me his trust altogether, and I needed him if I hoped to catch the kidnapper.

How could I know Nikoli and his pet dragon would punish him? Consequences—the equal and opposite reaction. *"No good deed goes unpunished."* Shit. The more I thought about it, the angrier I got. Guilt is not a good emotion during the moon. The question burst from my mouth in a rush, startling him with the abrupt segue.

"How the hell was I supposed to *know* there would be consequences to helping me? *Goddamn* it, Bobby! You keep getting pissed that I break the rules when I don't even know what the rules *are*."

His surprise quickly gave way to rush of anger. "Fine, the next time you heard the words, 'I'm not allowed,' you'll know." I could've walked on the condescension in his voice. "Those words mean pain in our world, Tony. Pain like what Asri did, and worse. Learn it now. 'I'm not allowed' means *don't fucking do it!*"

He pulled the van to an abrupt stop in front of my apartment building.

I didn't climb out of the car right away. Instead, I took a deep breath. I couldn't feel Sue but I hoped her headache was over and she'd be okay. I needed to touch her, like a junkie needing a fix. Still, since I was in pretty good health, I threw myself in headfirst. I had to at least offer. I hoped he'd decline. I put an angry edge on my voice to cover the tiniest edge of fear. I could think of a lot of things I'd rather do.

"So, what?" I said through gritted teeth. "You want me to go to Nikoli and let him turn me back over to Asri? Would that make you happy?"

He glanced at me and his tongue flicked out, opening his healing lip once more. The drop of blood disappeared back into his mouth. He sighed. "It'd make me ecstatic. But now I can't let you. I gave my word to Carmine, and I really do need you whole for this hunt. You've got good eyes and ears and you're a hell of a shooter. My tongue's my best feature and isn't likely to be needed. They only sent me in because I know you. And, I'll heal the damage faster. You attack victims don't heal worth a damn." He reached across and pushed open my door.

"Go inside and see your wife. I'll be back in the morning . . . I hope."

I tapped my fingers on my jeans. I didn't look at him. I just stared out the window into the lightly falling snow. "For what it's worth, Bobby—I really didn't know. I did screw up and you could have left me that way."

The scent must have been strong to break through the cologne. The distinct scent of midnight in London drifted through the van. The misty, fog bank scent means sorrow. The scent surprised me. I expected anger or frustration.

"Yeah. I know. I've watched you take a lot of shit in your life and bear up under it. But you need to start using that brain of yours for something other than figuring out ways to punish yourself for being Sazi. It's not your fault, Tony."

I started visibly and turned to stare at him open-mouthed. What the hell was he talking about? I stepped out of the car and turned to ask him but he pulled away from the curb with the door hanging open. I watched the van swerve slightly on the snow about half a block down as he reached over, pushed the two storage boxes through the sliding door before both doors slammed shut.

Chapter 9

I STOOD ON the sidewalk in the snow, staring down the road long after the van disappeared. Bobby's got that same nasty habit as my old friend John-Boy. They psychoanalyze people against their will. Still, the words stuck. Was that what I've been doing? Do I intentionally piss people off so they'll beat the crap out of me? No. Of course it's not my fault I am what I've become. It's *Babs's* fault that I'm a frigging half-breed animal.

Ah, got it.

I shook my head and walked down to where he had pushed out the boxes of guns and gold. I needed to get them inside or the bottoms were liable to collapse from getting wet.

"Tony?" I turned to the voice and saw Sue standing in the doorway of the building, clutching a jacket around her shoulders. "Are you okay?"

I smiled to ease the worry on her face, picked up the boxes, and started back to the building. "I am now."

As I walked past her she stopped me with a hand on my shoulder. Her touch flowed through me like an ice pick, raising the hairs on my body and tightening my groin. Oh, my, it was good to see her. I was feeling plenty good enough to tuck her in now. I leaned in for a kiss.

"We have company," she said in a whisper before our lips touched. I furrowed my brow. Now what? With a sigh I followed her inside and up to the apartment. I set down the boxes in the hallway and followed Sue into the living room.

A slender old woman sat primly on the couch. Intense brown eyes looked out of a pale, wrinkled face. Snow white hair was pulled back into an elaborate bun. She wore a high-necked blouse with lace down the sleeves, tucked into a long black wool skirt. Sturdy, black leather boots with tiny buttons completed the antique portrait. On the coffee table in front of her was an ornate porcelain samovar—a Russian teapot, along with two tiny matching cups. They were white with pink roses and heavy gilding. It was an electric model, not as traditional as I would expect from a woman her age. Still, all that the scene needed was sepia tones. If she had an underlying scent, it was overpowered by the strong smell of tea oozing from the samovar.

Sue's voice was soft and nearly reverent. "Tony, this is the Duchess Olga Ivanevna. She's Nikoli's mother. Duchess, this is my husband, Joe Giambrocco."

The woman raised lightly-penciled brows. Her voice was heavily accented Russian, but the words were clear and concise. "Choose one or the other, young lady. If you call him *Tony* in your private life, introduce him as such. Many nicknames are allowed in human society. It will keep the curious at bay."

Sue's mouth dropped open in surprise. I merely nodded. It was a good thing to notice, and the reprimand was mild. I'd caught it, but hadn't been going to bring it up in front of company.

"A pleasure to meet you, Duchess. Is that a conferred title, or your name? I wasn't aware that there were any Russian royals unaccounted for." I've read a number of the books in Carmine's collection. One of them was on the Romanov family.

She smiled brightly, showing even white teeth. The smile took years from her face and I could see that she had once been a very beautiful woman. I wondered just how old a *Sazi* would have to be to show the years so visibly.

"That is a very personal question, and one that *most* have feared to ever ask me."

I smiled lightly, ignoring Sue's panicked look. "So I take it that you're not going to answer it."

"On the contrary," she replied. "Such a brazen challenge deserves a reply. You understand that in Russia, a title is born into, and the patronymic, or second name, is conferred upon adulthood, based on the father's name—*evna* for a girl, and *vich* for a man?"

I nodded and stepped into the room. I sat down in one of the kitchen chairs that Sue had placed opposite the couch.

"You can say that *Duchess* is an honorary title. When I was born, such a title did not exist."

She let the statement hang in the air with raised brows. She was waiting to see if I would figure it out. Her hands were loosely clasped together and her scent was calm but amused. Small wisps of steam rose from the teacup, pulling her scent up and away from me.

Sue spoke up. "But the Imperial Royal Family in Russia has existed for centuries. I've been reading about it in the books that Lucas gave me. It goes all the way back to—"

I saw Sue's eyes go wide as her voice froze from shock. A small smile played across the Duchess's face.

"The first person to name himself as *Tsar* was Ivan the Terrible in the sixteenth century." My voice was a challenge, but likewise filled with amazement.

"Is that so?" she asked craftily. I could feel Sue's sudden realization of Duchess's patronymic name.

"You can't *possibly* be that old!" The words matched the sudden and abject fear that knifed through me.

"No? Then perhaps it's your imagination. You young people believe you know all the answers, after all." Her smile was patient and amused. Her scent was a sunny citrus. She was enjoying this—a lot.

It took me a moment to get my feet under me, so to speak. But if she wanted a challenge, I was up for it. I don't have a photographic memory, but it's damned close. "Then why didn't you become Tsarina when your brother, Feodor I, died? Why did it take *fifteen years* to put another Romanov on the throne?"

She cocked her head and smiled sardonically. "So, you know your history. Very good. But you note that it was a *male* Romanov who ascended to the throne. It wasn't until two hundred years later that a *woman* came to rule Russia, after Peter decreed that the Tsar could choose his own successor."

"And that successor was his widow, Catherine."

"Very good, young wolf. In addition, I would *never* have taken the throne, because my mother was Sazi. I was an embarrassment to my father. He acknowledged only Feodor as his heir. But, blood is blood. He would not see me put to death. It would tell the world that the 'Tsar of all of the Russias' had made a mistake. Since that could not happen, I did not exist but, likewise, could not be killed."

I looked into the smiling face that had witnessed over four hundred years of history. I was having a hard time grasping the concept, even though Bobby had warned me. I just never thought I'd *meet* anyone that old. It was a struggle to think of something better to say than 'wow,' so I changed the subject.

"I believe we have you to thank for curing Sue's headache. What was the cause?"

I could feel that she was no longer in pain. I was pleased, since it would make our little "festivities" more enjoyable once our guest was gone.

The Duchess's face turned serious. "I wish I could accept your thanks, young one, but I have yet to determine the cause of your wife's misfortune."

Sue's forehead wrinkled, her scent echoed the confusion on her face. "But my head doesn't hurt anymore, and you used your magic on me. When you finished, the pain was gone."

"My magic did not ease the pain, Jessica. Of this I am certain. Nor do I know the cause of the distress. I have been reading your leaves to try to determine your future and see if there are any keys to the past."

"Reading her leaves?" The sudden insult on the Duchess's

face told me that my words had come out condescending.

"Do not scoff at what you do not understand! There are many gifts in the Sazi world that cannot be understood by the human mind. Seeing the future is but one of my talents."

"And what did the leaves say about me?" I tried to keep my voice neutral, but it was hard. Tasseography is a load of bunk.

Her voice was cold and could cut stone as she replied. "Perhaps we *should* see what your future holds. Your impertinence and brashness could have an impact on the future of our kind."

She opened a small satchel and removed a third delicately fluted cup. She placed it on the table before removing a small metal box. A fingernail popped a hatch on the side and she reached inside to pull out a few tea leaves. The scent of tea was strong and clean. It was high quality stuff. That's hard to find.

She sprinkled a few leaves into the new cup. "You understand that this is not zavarka for drinking."

"You can't read leaves from the infusion. I know that. Plus, I don't think you're supposed to drink proper tea from the *cup*. Isn't it the saucer you drink from?"

She smirked a bit. "Such a brilliant mind, but with so little intellect."

"Hey!" I exclaimed, but she ignored my outrage. I didn't like that slam at all. "I will not be insulted in my own home."

"You will be insulted where and when I feel it is necessary, young one. Now you will pick up the cup and swirl the leaves. It would be best to not make me force your actions. I *prefer* a clean reading."

But she was *willing* to do it the hard way. Yeah, I got the point. Her face was still calm, but I could see her eyes starting to glow. I needed to watch my step. Playing into Sazi hissy fits was *definitely* hazardous to my health.

I made my voice carefully neutral. I picked up the cup and started to move it until liquid inside picked up the leaves and spun them around in a vortex. "Fine. Tell me when to stop. Or am I supposed to drink the tea?"

The light in her eyes brightened. Soon they were twin amber suns that sucked me inside. I could hear her voice in my mind and my senses were suddenly wide open. The room was filled with colors I could hear and sounds that I could smell.

"There is no need." Her voice whispered and hissed on the air grown thick enough to touch. It pressed around me. It was getting hard to breathe. She reached out and touched my hand. I got my second shock.

I was standing in the woods. There was deep snow under the canopy of pines. I heard loud voices in the distance and saw the form of a young woman running across the frozen ground. She was huddled inside a thick fur wrap, seeming tiny in the vastness of the forest. Her eyes were wide and panicked and she turned often to look behind. Her breath came out in frosty gasps that filled the air. She favored one leg. I could smell blood flowing from a deep cut to her thigh. For a moment, the face stared right at me. Familiar hazel eyes looked out from a lovely heart-shaped face of about sixteen. A single wolf suddenly appeared in front of her, and then more joined, until the clearing was filled. She looked forward and then back, unsure of which way to run.

"Come with us, Lelya," said the lead wolf in a sweet, ringing alto. I knew it was Russian, but it sounded like English to my ears. "Leave the world of the humans behind and join us."

"He tried to kill me! My own father!" the girl sobbed.

"He fears you as he feared me. The fear attracted him, but it grew too much and he must destroy the fear if he hopes to rule. Shed your skin, my daughter. Let the moon free your true self."

The girl looked up just as the moon peeked

from behind a cloud. The voices were closer now. I could see a bright orange light bouncing in the distance. She looked behind once more and then threw off the cape of fur. The moonlight highlighted her auburn hair, turning it silver. The glow expanded to turn her whole body into a shining beacon. I had to shield my eyes from the white light that left patterns on my retinas.

The yelling crowd of people arrived just as the silver-tipped timber wolves, one bearing a scar down one leg, disappeared into the night. A large, barrel-chested man with a wide nose and permanent frown picked up the fur cape and glared after the retreating animals. Two men behind him, armed with swords and shields, started to press forward. He held up a hand and they stopped. His words were clipped and guttural.

"We will waste no more time here. She is gone and will not dare to return."

I came to myself with an abrupt shake of my head. If the Duchess noticed that I had gone missing, she didn't mention it. She was busy concentrating on the scene in front of her. I had to admit that even after what I'd just seen, it was impressive.

The porcelain teacup was still locked in my fist, but I didn't need to swirl the liquid anymore. The caramel colored fluid soared upward out of the cup like a tiny water spout, carrying the tea leaves into the air. When the water retreated, the leaves didn't. They continued to swirl in the air in front of my eyes, held aloft by the power of the Sazi magic that glowed in the Duchess's eyes.

"Stop," she said in a whisper, and the leaves obeyed instantly. They formed a shape that looked like an airplane, and then like a closed book. The leaves hovered, waiting for the next command.

"Show me more." I could barely hear the murmured words, but the bewitched bits of black and green heard her.

They once again began to spin until her next command to stop.

Another two shapes appeared. One was a double-sided axe with wide curved blades. The other was a modern pistol, a semi-auto.

Her eyes flared brighter still and the leaves spun a final time. A deer on its back legs with wide antlers jumped away from an eerily complete eye, followed by a series of wavy lines. Then the leaves dropped back into the cup. Not one missed to land on my pants.

Sue and I glanced at each other while the Duchess continued in a sort of a trance. "That's what they did for me, too," she said quietly. "I got a wolf, a boat, a rabbit, a head of lettuce—I think, and a dagger."

"And what do *they* mean? I only recognize a few of mine from an old article."

She shrugged. "That's where we were when you arrived. She hasn't told me yet what they mean."

I glanced back at the Duchess to find her staring intently at us. "Give me the cup," she said with an unknown emotion. There was too much strong tea smell coming from the samovar to figure out what her scent was.

I passed her the cup, but she grabbed my hand instead. I tensed, waiting for another picture show to start, but nothing happened except a strong electric shock that I felt sear through my body. I hissed through gritted teeth because it burned, cutting through bone and muscle. My heart fluttered and danced in my chest.

"Jessica, give me your other hand." Sue glanced at me nervously, but obeyed. I felt a flash of the same pain shoot through her. It tore through our bodies in a loop. I tried to let go of her hand, but it was like grasping a live wire. I couldn't make my fingers move. Sue's face was covered with sweat and her eyes were twitching from the burning sensation.

The Duchess's serene expression changed only slightly. I could see her eyeballs moving behind closed lids and her mouth was slightly open. Her chest rose and fell as her breath quickened. I was wondering whether she could let go either. Finally, I'd had enough.

"Stop!"

Her eyes shot open.

"It is not possible!" she exclaimed, and dropped both of our hands as though they had burned her, too. The pain disappeared the instant the connection broke. I stared at the Duchess. Her eyes had grown wide and slightly panicked. The scents of surprise and sour milk hit my nose in a flurry.

"Apparently, anything's possible with you people," I said angrily, rubbing my hand where it had begun to itch from the power surge. My fingers were still tingling. "Warn a guy before you do something like that again."

The Duchess looked at each of us in turn. I could feel Sue's nervousness and reached out to stroke a gentle finger down her arm. She shuddered and took a deep breath with closed eyes. But it cured the fear. When she opened her eyes again, she was calm.

"You two interest me," the Duchess finally said.

Good to know. "What do you find so fascinating?" I wasn't quite done being angry.

She pointed a long, bony finger at Sue. "You have no Sazi blood in you. You are fully human."

"Yeah. So?" I said strongly. "You're not going to start with that 'Sazis are better than humans,' are you? Because it's bullshit. I've been both, and I can assure you that I prefer human."

She looked at me curiously with furrowed brows. "Why would you think I believe such a thing, Anton? Humans *are* the superior species. Otherwise Sazi would control the world. We have many flaws—some of which you share."

"I may not know what *you* believe, but your teachers and pack members are teaching the *kids* that humans are inferior."

She leaned back into the couch cushions and regarded us with intense amber eyes. When she spoke she avoided the issue of the children. Instead, she said "It *should* not be possible for a Sazi male to have a double mating with a human. And yet you do share magic and thoughts. I felt it when we touched."

"Is that what the burning was—a touch? Wow. You need to tone down your magic, lady. You're dangerous. I don't know why you've got Nikoli ruling the pack. You're a lot stronger than he is."

Her brows raised and a lilt of amusement flowed through her voice. "You understand then why I say you interest me? You are the first person to recognize that I withhold my true power—even from my son. You are fully mated to a human. You have futures that both are bound to but are unique from each other. You are the person, but also two. It is very special. You hold in your hands great promise for our pack."

"So, those symbols meant something to you?"

She smiled, that baring of white teeth that fit so well with the oranges and hot tea. Her eyes glowed again.

"Jessica, you will soon have a visitor. A friend will need your help, but there will be danger involved. You must face this danger, but cautiously. Do not be reckless in your acceptance of the task. You will face jealousy and hate. You may mistake this for justification, but know that it is a lie and keep up your defenses. This is your mission alone, apart from your mate. He will have his own trials, but use his inner strength and judgment as your own. You must be strong of heart and body. Carry teeth and claws with you because you have none of your own."

"Whoa, whoa." I said, as bats started clawing in my gut. "What do you mean? Sue will be in danger but I can't help? The hell you say! No way. I'm not going to let her face danger without me." I'd only had her back for a day after coming so very close to losing her altogether. I wasn't letting her out of my sight ever again. I glanced at Sue, but her face was unreadable. Her scent was an odd mix that I couldn't sort through the aroma of black tea.

"You will have little choice, Anton. You, too, will be consumed by future events. Yours is an uncertain path. For the first time in your young life, you must avoid your impulsive nature. There are plans within plans. You must investigate that which you have been tasked. Be wary of the simple answer. There *are* no simple answers. Those you have trusted may fail you—not to intentionally harm you, but to fulfill their own destinies. When the truth finds you, others will not understand and only a few will follow. This is a time of growth, but you will must deal with it alone. Do not even trust the opinion of your mate, for she will use human values to judge. You must use the mind of a hunter. It is who you are."

A chill ran up my spine. A woman I'd just met had described me, and the job I'd been set on—but it had happened miles away. She couldn't possibly have known.

"You will be aided in your hunt by two new talents. You will have the ability to see what has been, as clearly as if you had participated. This is known to us as *hindsight*."

I couldn't help spitting out a laugh.

Her chin dropped and she stared at me coldly. "Do not mock me, or you will not learn the nature of your gift. It is a rare talent that I have never seen in one so young. Such a gift usually comes only to the truly introspective, which it is obvious you are not!"

Actually, I am very introspective, but this was just starting to get silly. "Yeah, I know. 'Hindsight is 20/20.' Cute joke."

Her back stiffened in outrage. "I *never* make light of seer gifts, Anton! You will *become* the memory. You will live it through the person who experienced it. You will hear it, feel it—smell what they smelled, see through their eyes. But lies can seem to be truth, so be cautious! As to your other gift, it eludes even my best efforts, but it is a gift of equal or greater value, so do not dismiss the value lightly, no more than you would stand without shielding in a room of enemies."

The force of her words made me wonder about the image of the girl in the woods. Had it been the Duchess?

"And, now I know the cause of your headaches, and will put a stop to it immediately." I gasped as I felt something like a clap of thunder with no sound. It roared through my head and exited through my heart. Sue felt it, too. She swayed and nearly fell to the floor. All the colors of the rainbow filled my mind in a burst of blinding light. The connection to Sue that had been so faint since she arrived here roared back to life. I could feel her heart beating, see through her eyes, hear her thoughts.

"What the hell did you do?"

"You are not alphic, Anton. You cannot be both pack *and* mate. The connection that bound you to our pack was diminishing your mating and causing you both to pine. That's what the pain was. Jessica will not survive if you remain with the pack. Since you are not yet strong enough to withstand Nikoli's magic, I have intervened. To survive with your mate, you must remain separate from the pack. But now that you have known a pack, that too may cause you pain. This will be your cross to bear. I am sorry. In time, you may grow stronger and be able to rejoin the mind and heart of the pack. You will be welcome if that comes to pass. Of course, you will remain here in Chicago with us and we will keep you fed. You will just not share the comforts of the group mind."

She stood abruptly and brushed off her dark skirt with sharp flicks of her hands. Her voice held icy cold anger when she spoke. "I will inform Nikoli that he may not reclaim your mind, Anton. My son should have sensed your bond. If he did, and ignored it . . ." She let the statement hang for a moment, and then continued, "In my time, to break a mating bond was a death sentence. While it is no longer so, it is dangerous to you and I will not allow it."

I winced as she said that name for the fourth time. "Any chance that someone in your family might call me *Tony?* 'Anton' is really getting on my nerves."

The anger fell away. Her smile flashed brightly and the scent of oranges filled the room. Her eyes sparkled with the same youth as I saw in the dream. "If you do something else to impress me, perhaps I will, Anton."

Is *that* all it took? Fine with me. "Okay, let me impress you. You lied to me, Lelya."

Her back straightened like a rod had been jammed down her shirt. Burning coffee, burned metal, and hot and sour soup assaulted my nose from the sudden outrage. "How *dare* you! I have assisted you, healed your mate, and you believe you may address me with familiarity *and* make accusations?"

I shook my head and smiled darkly. I wouldn't back down. She wanted impressed—she was going to get it.

Sue looked confused. Embarrassment heated her cheeks and then rose from her in a cloud of scent. She was about to open her mouth to reprimand me, but I spoke before she could. I guess she hadn't caught the little movie in my head or she wouldn't wonder about my statement. "You said your father never tried to kill you. You lied. You ran from his hunting party into the woods, bleeding from a silver knife wound to your thigh."

Her pale face went even whiter, eventually turning a dishwater grey. Her eyes were wide and tears sparkled at the corners. All that remained of the previous scents was fear. It was strong enough to make my jaw tighten. "*How* . . . my strongest shields were in place. How can that be?"

"Your mother found you and convinced you to accept your Sazi nature. You threw off a fur cloak and turned into a silver grey wolf before the lynching party arrived. But you *tried* to play human, didn't you, Lelya? You wanted to, but you were rejected. You still carry the scar. That's why you wear long skirts. That's why you let your son lead the pack. You don't even *hunt* with the pack to protect your secret. You are *ashamed* of your own kind. You hate that there is a wolf inside you."

Call *me* not introspective enough, will she—part of the last was supposition, but I could tell I hit the nail on the head. I hadn't seen her at the hunt, and Nikoli was a puppy compared to power. I'd felt them both.

Sue looked at me with something approaching awe. I could see it from the corner of my eye, but my gaze was locked on the Duchess. Surprise, disbelief and embarrassment rose from the older woman to join her own scent. They blended quite nicely. Sort of hot tea with milk on the stove. She took a deep breath, forcing herself to calm. She didn't speak until she'd reclaimed her usual serenity.

"You have more depth than I expected, *Tony*. You have great insight and gifts that should be explored. You *have* impressed me today. I would ask you not to reveal my secret, but that is not my choice. You may need to use the knowledge. I am not certain how you gained it, but few things happen without reason in our world. Perhaps it is time for curtains to be drawn on long-darkened rooms. It may be that my past will soon be known—or used against me. But you must not think of my wishes. You must think only of the hunt, because your task affects the future of all Sazi."

Her words took me by surprise. I was hunting a kidnapper, not taking a ring to a volcano. I cleared my throat as I tried to recover quickly.

"I wouldn't tell without a very good reason. I wouldn't risk losing your good graces. I get the feeling I'm going to need every friend I have for this job. And I kind of understand how you feel. I'm wasn't real enthusiastic about losing my humanity, either." I smiled at her, and she caught the look of dark humor. "I'm pretty good at keeping secrets. Plans within plans—remember, Duchess?"

She regarded me for a moment, and her scent was a blend of everything that I knew, and a bunch I didn't. She ended up smiling as she reached for a black shawl with brightly colored embroidered designs. She held her head high and regarded us both. Then she nodded.

"You two may call me Lelya. Yes—I believe I would like that. I look forward to speaking with you both more. Perhaps we can *all* learn things."

"Do you want help carrying your samovar to your car?"

She looked at it with affection and then shook her head.

"No. It is a gift to you. It is a fitting . . . how do you call it? . . . *housewarming* gift for you both. I only request to drop by for a cup of zavarka, and some conversation, from time to time."

Sue's whole face lit up. "Oh, I'd like that. I just got here and haven't had a chance to meet anyone yet."

"Then you will meet my granddaughter. She is close to your age, and human so far. Her name is Veronica, but we call her Nika."

Sue remained inside to clean up the cups. I offered Lelya my arm, and we descended the stairs to the snowy street. As soon as we got outside, I realized that her scent actually *was* tea, blended with sugar and cream. She didn't seem to need my help to walk. Her movements were smooth and youthful. As she closed the car door and started the engine of the shiny new Cadillac, I had to ask. I leaned in the window so that nobody else would hear the question. "So, Lelya, is this all an illusion? You seem pretty spry for your looks. Are you actually still that stunning girl of sixteen?"

Her laugh filled the car with sparkling sound. "That *will* remain my secret, young Tony. But thank you for the compliment. I wasn't considered *stunning* at the time. I was very ordinary."

"You will *never* be ordinary, Lelya." I made sure my eyes and my scent reflected the truth of the words.

A burst of tea became orange pekoe. "I see why you have survived this long, Tony. Human or Sazi—we are all quite vain."

My eyes were sparkling as I pulled back from the car. "The trick is to believe what you say." I paused for effect. "Isn't it, Lelya?"

Her laughter was ringing in my ears as the car pulled away from the curb.

Chapter 10

I CLIMBED UP the front stairs and felt my senses heighten for the first time in weeks. It was as if I'd had a head cold and could suddenly breathe. A blast of frigid air chased me in the front door. I was suddenly acutely . . . aware. Everything looked different. It was as though the chair, the lamp, every leaf on every plant, was somehow drawn in four dimensions. The scent of each item was visible in the air, rising above like tinted phantoms. The colors were as vivid as a Van Gogh. Was this the new talent Lelya had spoken of and, if so, what purpose did it serve?

My first stop would be the bathroom. The shower would wait, but I was definitely brushing my teeth and flossing. I wanted to greet my wife properly, and I figure wolf breath isn't the world's biggest turn-on. The cinnamon toothpaste glowed nearly florescent and the taste burned fire hot to my heightened senses, nearly bringing tears to my eyes.

I stepped out of the bathroom and walked through the house in awe, noting small changes Sue had made since she'd arrived. A brightly colored rag rug had been placed under the coffee table. The smoked-glass top both muted and electrified the colors. A vigorous wandering jew plant in full bloom billowed over a yellow ceramic pot on a stand in the corner. A trio of nesting dolls rested side by side on the mantle of the gas fireplace. Some scattered knickknacks perched on a small corner shelf unit. And Sue's purse hung over a chair back. They were little touches that turned the stark, newly-bought furniture into a home.

I stopped in front of a large painting on the wall. Something about it . . . I couldn't quite place why it seemed so familiar.

"Do you like it?" Sue was standing in the doorway to the kitchen with a smile on her face. The light jingling of her silver charm bracelet sounded like peals of chimes. Little rabbits and bells, plus one lone wolf. "I was pretty sure that it was the same print that I saw in your den. You said your dad gave it to you. It's a different frame, but I think it looks nice on that wall."

I looked again when she spoke. The mallard ducks exploded out of the water next to a fallen tree, and the fall sun shone brightly in a deep blue sky. The rich blues and greys of the water, plus the Ducks Unlimited emblem, should have given it away immediately. "It *is* the same one. Where did you get it?"

She moved into the room, and I could hear the gentle squeak of the floorboards as she walked. A pale green glow surrounded her. "In a gallery in Boulder. There wasn't much else to do but shop when I wasn't in classes or at appointments with Dr. Perdue. Lucas gave me some money for traveling, but I didn't need it all because Bobby drove me back. Good thing, too. The print cost most everything I had."

She stepped right in front of me and touched my arm. "But I know you had to give everything up when you came here to be with me. I wanted you to have something nice— something familiar."

"It is nice. Thank you." My voice was deep and sincere. She blushed and lowered her eyes and her hand at the same time. There it was again—that thoughtfulness she'd displayed when we'd first met. It reminded me why I *liked* her. The lust and need for her that I feel is something strange and supernatural, but her personality and humor attract me to her in a very human way.

I closed my eyes and inhaled. Her scent struck me like a brick to the head. Warm, ripe fruit, bursting in the sun; the clean, strong odor of newly turned soil; fresh, water drenched leaves, and flowers on the wind. The scent of a forest in summer. Heady—powerful enough to drown in. I brought a hand up and lightly ruffled the edge of the colored band around her, less than an inch from her skin.

Sue shuddered and goosebumps appeared on her skin. She raised her eyes to look at me in surprise. I caught a new scent. Pine trees, covered with ice; ozone-enriched air, scrubbed clean of all impurities, and the rich, musky scent of warm fur.

"That's you," she whispered. "You smell like the mountains just after a snow. It's cold and biting and wakes your senses. I'd never noticed. And I've never smelled flowers before. It's like a garden in the trees. Is that me?"

I nodded my head. "We haven't been together since we fully bonded. I think it's only the beginning of what's going to happen." I knew it was true the moment the words left my mouth.

She shook her head, and I could feel the brush of hair on my own neck as she did. The sensation was like a live wire attached to my groin. Once upon a time, the sensation had frightened me. But the shudder passing through me now had nothing to do with fear.

"That's not true," she said, and the slight scent of disbelief soured milk, rose from her. "We were bonded the whole time we were on the island with Carmine and Linda. It was never like *this*. I can see things, Tony—since you walked in the door just now. There are colors in the air. You're surrounded by a silver haze. I can *see* scents and . . ." A small edge of fear settled into her green eyes. Her words dropped to a whisper. "What's happening to us?"

My voice was a whisper as well, and I could feel my eyes start to glow. The sun was on the downswing, the moon waited in the wings. "*Magic's* happening, Sue. We *haven't* been together since the bonding."

My voice rose slightly and my tone was patient and

warm. "When we were on the island, Betty was acting like a shield between us because of your injuries. She said if you died, I would go with you without the shield. And, you wouldn't have been able to stand my changing with the hunt while you were recovering. She kept up the shield while you were in Boulder so you could go through training and therapy, and then I connected to the pack here in Chicago. When Lelya removed the connection, it became just the two of us."

Her voice was awestruck. "So this really *is* the first time we've been together. Will it get worse?"

I chuckled and reached up a hand to stroke her hair, appreciating the silky thickness and rich auburn color as it flowed through my fingers. She was frozen, unable to move through the sensation. She was feeling my hand on her scalp, and her hair *in* my hand—just like I was. It was an amazing feeling. "You say *worse* like it feels bad. It doesn't, does it?"

"I mean . . . I don't know what . . ."

I moved a fraction closer and fell into her deep green eyes. "Just kiss me, Sue. Let it all happen. Today we'll go places we've never been. Just think of it as our wedding night."

I pulled her against me and felt a jolt of electricity that nearly chased coherent thought from my brain. My mouth hovered over hers, waiting for her to make the first move. She gasped as my arms tightened around her and she reached up to seal our lips together. Power flowed and danced over our skin as we tasted each other.

My tongue explored her teeth, the roof of her mouth and under her tongue with almost frantic need. Her fingers reached up to slide through my hair. I groaned and traced my hands down the curves of her body. I lifted her hips until her legs wrapped around my waist as I moved back from the kiss. I couldn't resist the scent of her; that overpowering, seductive aroma. My nose soaked in the fragrance, stronger here along her neck, and I didn't fight the urge to press my lips to her neck. I pulled blood to the surface of her skin and then moved back to watch the red mark appear before I kissed her again.

I carried her down the hallway, her legs still twined around me, reveling in our mouths touching each other.

I set her down and stepped back for a moment. She was starting to remove her shirt when I stopped her.

"I've been waiting for this," I said in a husky voice. "Let me savor it. I want to undress you—slowly."

She dropped her hands to her side and stood motionless. Her eyes were dark and electric and her breath was coming in small pants. I stepped forward and touched her blouse, but not her skin. The tension was thick enough to walk on as I undid the first button. The second button was opened just as slowly. The white lace of her bra was peeking out and I wanted to see more.

Oops. First things first. I reached down and lifted one hand by the sleeve of the blouse, still staring at the swell of creamy skin hidden by the white lace. She reached up her hand to help me open the cuff, but I stopped her.

"Let me. You just stand there and keep looking beautiful."

She smiled at me, and it lit up her whole face. "You're the only one who's ever called me beautiful."

My glowing eyes caught her gaze. I found it sad that she was telling the truth. "Then the guys you've known have been fools."

Her scent was growing deeply musky. It made it hard to breathe. I opened the last of the buttons, and stared with lust at the long line of skin from her neck to her waistband. I wanted to touch her so bad it almost hurt, but I was enjoying making us both wait. I stepped behind her and nuzzled my nose in her hair, breathing in sweet flowers. She shivered as my warm breath tickled her skin.

I lifted the shirt from her shoulders and pulled it down. The cream-colored cotton slipped down her arms and landed on the floor at my feet. I moved away a little and looked at the long expanse of soft skin, broken only by a band of white elastic. I removed my shirt and the unlatched the buckle on my belt.

She gasped and shuddered as I unhooked her bra and then with slow, lingering movements, slid the straps down her arms.

My brow furrowed as I stared at her whole, perfect back. There should be a scar or a dimple where the bullet took her through the shoulder. I moved my thumb to lightly glide over the spot. She moaned expressively.

"The nerves are still a little sensitive there," she whispered. "It feels like little pins pricking me."

"There's no scar." My voice sounded deep and throaty with the slightest hint of a growl.

"Betty worked really hard to heal it so that it wouldn't leave a scar. It took weeks. But the wound was too well-known, being on the news and all. It had to be completely gone."

I nodded and let my fingers explore her skin. I put my hands on her waist and then slid them around to unsnap her blue jeans while I kissed her back.

I was easing down the zipper when she spoke with breathy urgency. "I'm not sure I can stand up much longer, Tony. My legs are all shaky."

I smiled. I liked having that effect on her. "We wouldn't want you to fall down."

I turned her around and caught her on the spin, bringing her against my chest tightly. She stared into my glowing blue eyes, unable and unwilling to move—to break the spell. I leaned forward, my lids fluttering closed as my lips traced her jaw. A small sound of pleasure spilled out of her mouth as I nibbled her earlobe, and then covered her neck with kisses. My tongue bathed her neck, taking her scent and leaving my own in its place. I slid a hand between us and completed unzipping her pants, accompanied by the sound of her moans.

Her fingers smoothed along my back as I slowly moved my hand up the side of her body. The silver bells and rabbits scorched along my skin, but healed as quickly as they burned. She had to keep on the bracelet. I knew that. One scratch without it and she might become Sazi.

But I'd forgotten the sensation of silver during sex. I'd never been much into pain before I became a wolf. I found I was liking it—a lot. My groin tightened with urgency as my hand stroked the smooth curve of her hip, the dip of her waist and then the fullness of her breast. I lingered there, feeling the weight of tissue between my fingers as I kneaded and teased. The texture of the skin changed as her nipple tightened in response. I moved my mouth to kiss her deeply and slowly as I fondled her.

My body was urging me on, turning the kiss fierce and hungry. I moved back from her breathlessly and fought for control with eyes closed. It would be too easy to have a quickie. This should be more special.

Sue wasn't helping matters any. She had leaned forward and was kissing a slow line down my chest and unzipping my pants. I could barely think, much less move. But I touched her shoulders as I felt my pants slide over my thighs.

"A little slower, okay? I'm going to be all over you in about ten seconds otherwise."

Her eyes were wide and nearly panicked. Her breath was coming in short gasps so that the words were filled with air. "I don't care if it's fast or slow, Tony. I just want you—I need to feel you inside me."

"But I have some new tricks to show you. I don't want to spoil it."

Her brows raised and she stood. Her voice was a little stronger as she regained control. "Tricks?"

I smiled lightly and then pushed her backward so she landed sitting on the bed. "Mmm-hmm. All sorts of *very* pleasant things."

I knelt down and untied the laces on her shoes and pulled them off. The pants easily slid over her legs and joined the sneakers on the floor. It was obvious now that she'd lost weight, but not so much that she still didn't have a nice hourglass figure. I find women who try to look like twigs annoying. Guys *like* curves.

She was down to just a pair of silken panties with a bare chest. I let my gaze wander over her nearly naked form. "Very nice. You look *incredible.*"

She smiled and gave a little laugh. "Nothing like a few weeks of being fed through tubes to help a girl diet. I will warn you, though—I'm a sucker for sweets. I might not stay this way. And speaking of looking good—you had a nice build before, but *wow.*"

I glanced down at my rock-hard pecs and thick biceps. I was also pretty proud of the six-pack I'd acquired. Betty and Bobby had told me that I could have a great physique if I worked at it. They'd said that the wolf blood maximizes body mass, so I gave it a try. All the better to start a new life with. It was years of results acquired with only a few weeks worth of effort. My favorite kind of exercise program.

I smiled in return as I took off my own shoes and socks and finished pulling off my pants. "Not much else to do on the island. I was a little crazy after they took you to Boulder and severed our tie. I got a few panic attacks. Running on the beach and working out in Carmine's gym in the cabin helped take off the edge."

"I was okay. They took good care of me."

I nodded and crawled up the bed to lie beside her. I pulled her into my arms and just held her for a moment. I breathed in her scent and let the warmth of her body seep into my skin. "I know. It was just a little hard. I missed you."

She was silent for a moment. I could tell from her thoughts that she wanted to say so much. *I'm here now. I'm yours.* She hugged me tight and my breath caught when the silver burned. It brought me back from the past to her very real, alive body.

"Speaking of being a little *hard,*" she teased, and moved her leg to press against the front of my briefs. "What sort of new tricks have you learned?"

I chuckled with my face buried in her hair. The press of

her body against me caused a rush of passion and fluttering of need to flow through me. She shivered as warm air teased her ear. "I think you're going to like this."

I moved up onto one elbow and took in the sight of her. The chestnut hair with hints of fire as the light caught it, her green eyes brimming with expectation and need, and the smooth expanse of skin with no hint of the trauma that had ravaged her chest—was it only a few weeks ago? I pulled on the power inside me, so close to the surface this near to the moon. I let it fill my arm my hand, my fingers—and then lowered the hand to touch her skin.

Her back arched immediately and her eyes went wide over a mouth that had opened to pull in a massive breath. Her hands scrambled on the bed, clutching at the spread. She couldn't speak, couldn't even think. I heard fragments of thought spinning through her head. *What is . . . How . . . Oh, God! Yes, more . . .*

After the initial shock, she managed to get in control enough to glance down at the patterns I was tracing on her skin. Her eyes blinked repeatedly as she tried to focus through the pleasure. "What *is* that?"

"I told you. It's *magic.*"

"It feels like there's a thousand fingers touching me, just behind where your hand moves. It's like something slithering over my skin that's connected to my stomach."

I smiled at her again and moved up the hand to slide along her jaw and tingle her lips. "I don't think it's connected to your *stomach,* Sue." I knew exactly where the feelings resonated. I could feel them too.

I moved my hand down—past her breasts, past her belly button, and along her hipbones to disappear between her legs. Her cries turned up the heat between my own legs. Her eyes closed, giving in to the rhythmic surges that caused wetness to fill my palm. The scent of her desire made my body tighten further and spasms racked my groin. The throbbing was insistent, needy. I fought again for control. I managed, but just barely.

My warm tongue found her throat and I bit down lightly. She groaned and grabbed my head to move it down. I obliged and licked a slow line to her breast as I moved my hand lightly over the silky cloth covering her crotch.

"God," she exclaimed. "That is *amazing!*"

"It gets better. Watch this." I pulled the power away from my hand and felt it crawl inside me, obeying an unspoken command. The magic resurfaced at the tip of my tongue. Each flick against her nipple caused gasps and cries. I moved in a steady line down her body, just lightly moving the magic along the hairs of her skin. Her legs spread as I lowered between them. I tried to pull down her panties as I reached the gentle mound of curly hair, but her open legs defeated me. My body was getting frustrated from being denied. I grabbed the pale blue nylon in both hands and ripped apart the narrow patch that fitted over both hips. She glanced at me in shock, but another surge of wetness told me she liked what I'd done. I pulled the cloth from her body with a light growl.

She was completely nude beneath me now, and I wanted nothing more than to be inside her, but instead I lowered my face to breathe in the deep musk between her legs. Magic swelled inside me and flowed out my pores. I distantly heard her scream in pleasure as my tongue opened her folds. The taste of her made me almost delirious with need. I found her small, erect center of pleasure, and moved it firmly and rapidly, letting my power fill her. Her back arched once more and I could smell, taste, feel as the climax ripped through her. Shooting waves of pleasure so great they were almost pain. I couldn't wait any more.

I pulled off my briefs in a sudden movement and was inside her before I could even think. Her arms reached for me as her body embraced me fully. I drew back and plunged into her again, feeling her spasming passage caress and tighten along my full length. I moved with her in unrestrained abandon, giving into the need. The smells were strong enough to drown in, so I allowed myself to be enraptured. My mouth found hers and we ate at each other, our jaws working in rhythm with the movement of our hips.

Her legs locked around me, pulling me in tighter, and changing the angle of my thrusts. There was no stopping now. The tension was reaching a peak. I could feel the climax gathering, hovering. I drove into her with raw force. She matched me move for move, and her nails bit into my back, ripping the skin in long lines. Every flash of pain sent searing pleasure through me. Just a moment longer. Just a mom—

Sue raised up to me with every nerve taut, her own orgasm near again. I reveled in the sheer sensual pleasure as I called out her name and we soared over the edge. My deep groan was in harmony with her breathless cry as she repeated my name over and over. Magic flowed through the room, soaring and pounding at our bodies as the climax claimed us. Once again, the whirlwind of pleasure began, spinning through Sue, into me, and back through her. I raised on my arms and gave a final scream that was filled with joy, pleasure and the weight of the moon on my back. We collapsed into an embrace, sated and happy.

Chapter 11

THE ROUND OF lovemaking was followed by two more, in rapid succession. It's one of the best things about the moon magic. It makes both of us almost insatiable. We spent the next couple of hours dozing in each other's arms, awaiting the rising of the moon. I hadn't been told that I *couldn't* stay at home on the third night of the moon, so I fully intended to.

A knock on the door shattered that illusion, plus the cozy sleep I was luxuriating in. I hoped that if I ignored the knocking, it would stop. But no such luck. The pounding increased, so I finally dragged my tired body out of bed. Sue was still asleep and probably would be for hours. I'd pretty much worn her out. I leaned over and moved her hair aside to give her a gentle kiss on the forehead before I pulled on my jeans and walked to answer the door, closing the bedroom door behind me.

I padded barefoot through the deep shadows of the living room. The sun had sunk low in the sky. I could feel the pull of the moon. Whoever was visiting would have to leave soon.

"Yeah, yeah, just a minute, damn it." I called as I reached the vibrating door. I opened it just as Bobby had raised his fist to pound again.

"What the hell took you so long?" he snarled as he

brushed past me. I shook my head in annoyance and started to shut the door when a firm hand stopped it. I turned to see Asri's raised brows and benign expression peering out of a fluffy hooded jacket. My jaw dropped open. What the hell was *she* doing here with Bobby? Did I get out of the frying pan just long enough to leap into the flames?

She brushed past me, as well. Her voice was a whisper that chilled my blood and stilled my breath. "Good to see you so *active*, Tony."

Asri untied the string at her neck with gloved hands as she entered the living room. She smelled like peppermint. She glanced around, noting every detail, while she slowly pulled the fur-edged hood off her head. Why didn't it surprise me it was *wolf* fur?

"Bobby, what the hell are you doing here?" I asked in a quiet voice. I didn't want to disturb Sue's sleep. I pointed at Asri with undisguised loathing. "And why did you bring that . . . *woman* with you?" She didn't even flinch at my tone. She just ignored me and continued to remove her gloves.

"It wasn't my idea. Trust me." Bobby's voice was just on the border of fury. He wouldn't even glance at her. "Nikoli insisted. She's my *guide* while I'm here." His voice was sarcastic and cold.

Uh huh. I knew what that meant. More like his *guard* while he's here. I guess I wasn't surprised. Carmine always did the same thing when a rival family would send a representative for discussions or was in town to visit. It's one of those *courtesies* that keep you alive.

Bobby's cologne had worn off completely. I could smell the thick jungle vines explode from his bulky down jacket as he unzipped it halfway. He smelled like peppermint, too, but then I saw the red and white swirled candy rolling around his mouth. Asri still smelled like moldy lutefisk under the mint. It was quickly becoming one of my least favorite smells. Burning coffee and jalapeños filled the air, replacing the warm musky scent of desire and sex.

"I hope we didn't interrupt anything." Asri's voice was

quiet and subdued. She'd noted the scent of our passion before Bobby did. Her tone was almost . . . *respectful*.

"It's been seven weeks since I've seen my wife. We've been getting reacquainted." Not that it was any of her business. The exchange made Bobby flick out his tongue. He finally glanced at my disheveled appearance—the bare feet and chest, tousled hair and sleepy eyes. He had the good grace to look a little embarrassed.

"Sorry. But we've got business. I hope you were done *reacquainting*, 'cause you need to get dressed."

"The moon's coming, Bobby. I'd planned to stay here and enjoy a few steaks and get some sleep."

"We've got to go to the airport and pick up my boss." Bobby was obviously annoyed, but I couldn't place the source. Was it that his superior was coming—maybe to get in the way or supervise him, or was it something more than that? Or less? He'd been pissy since he arrived.

"So? Go to the airport. What do you need me for?"

Asri spoke up from the couch where she'd primly seated herself. "Nikoli asked that you accompany us. Agent Mbutu and I will prevent you from changing until a more appropriate time."

"Did Nikoli give a *reason*?"

"He is not required to give a reason, Tony," Asri said seriously. "He is the Alpha. He asks and we obey."

Great. I was afraid of that.

I heard movement from down the hall, and looked up to see Sue enter the room, wearing the slightly rumpled shirt and jeans she'd had on earlier. I wondered if she had put on new through her hair and freshen her lipstick. The deep wine color made her eyes almost luminescent. She smelled of trees and flowers, and *me*.

"Oh, I thought I heard voices. Hello, Bobby." She glanced at the visitor on the couch, and paled. She stumbled against the half wall at the edge of the living room with wide eyes. I'd forgotten that she'd been present during our *discipline* session. She recognized Asri and was very,

very afraid. The scent of her terror made me fight down a growl.

Asri saw her reaction. Dry heat, mixed with thick dust rose in a cloud from the direction of the couch. Asri stood in a fluid movement and walked the short distance across the room to where Sue clutched the doorway. I reached out to intervene, when Bobby caught my arm and held me back.

"It's cool, man. Just listen," he whispered.

Asri stopped in front of Sue and dropped to both knees with head bowed. "Mrs. Giambrocco, I am Asri Kho. In my own language, I would tell you *Maaf*. It is our most sincere apology, for a great wrong."

I glanced at Sue. She was startled at the sight of the fearsome dragon who had kicked the crap out of me abasing herself. Frankly, so was I. Neither of us was quite sure what to say. A flurry of mixed scents rose to fill the room.

Asri continued to speak, her eyes firmly glued on the floor near Sue's sneakers. The dusty heat still flowed in a long line up from her body, turning the air golden. "I . . ." Her voice cracked and she had to start over. "I was unaware when I battled your great and powerful husband that he was mated. When I learned that you were human, and were forced to suffer the pain of punishment along with him, I was saddened and shamed. I would have refused the punishment had I known."

Sue's eyes were tearing up at hearing such a heartfelt apology. It was giving me a new dimension on Asri—not so cold-blooded, after all. While I knew the *great and powerful* crap was just that, it was intended as a compliment to Sue, not to me. I was fully aware that Asri wasn't crawling next to *my* shoes.

"I owe you a debt of honor. Our Alpha would not allow me to offer you damages, because you have no way to claim them, and the error was not mine—but his."

Really? Nikoli admitted a *mistake*? That seemed a little out of character. It made me wonder what Lelya said to him.

"But regardless, I feel deep regret, and ask for your forgiveness." She remained kneeling, not moving.

Sue looked down at the woman at her feet, huddled miserably, her shiny black hair brushing the floor. The tears were still in Sue's eyes, sparkling and rolling down her cheeks. She looked to me for guidance, but I had none to give. I shrugged and looked at Bobby. Apparently, he hadn't known quite what Asri was going to say, just that she was going to apologize.

He reached over and put his mouth close to my ear and cupped his hand to block the sound. "If you can reach Sue, just tell her to say *tidak apa-apa*. It's Indonesian for 'nothing,' or 'it's okay.' " He was speaking so quietly that his words were just barely audible to me.

Did you catch that? I thought to Sue. She nodded and wiped the tears from her left eye with the back of her hand. She squatted down and touched Asri's shoulder. Wide brown eyes raised to meet Sue's.

"It's okay, Asri. *Tidak apa-apa.* You didn't know." Then she added something new. She wasn't too bad at psychology herself. "I know now that you are a woman of honor, as well as a proud enforcer. I will not think less of you."

Very nicely rolled around to a compliment. Attagirl.

The surprise in Asri's face at Sue's use of her native tongue turned into an expressionless mask, but she closed her eyes and dropped her head briefly before she stood in a fluid movement.

"You are gracious and kind, Mrs. Giambrocco. It is too much after my actions, but I am grateful and, please—if I may ever serve you in a task within my power, you need only ask."

Sue was spared coming up with a reply because Bobby took that moment to clap his hands together sharply and then rub them briskly. "So, now that we're all friends again, can we *please* get our tails in gear and get moving?"

Asri regarded him as though he was a fly that had landed

on her food. She glanced at her watch and continued to take off her jacket. "We are not due for another hour yet. We will be very conspicuous if we leave now and are forced to wait. The authorities have come to look ill upon anyone of obvious foreign birth wandering the hallways. It is a small airport."

I pursed my lips briefly. Both O'Hare and Midway are pretty large and even a trio of Asian, African and Italian wouldn't stand out. "Where exactly are we going?"

Bobby glanced at me and likewise raised his brows. "I had *assumed* we were going to O'Hare." He turned to Asri.

Asri didn't answer. She finished removing her coat without even glancing his way. Sue started to reach for it and then realized that she didn't know where to hang it up. The layout was still too new to her. She pulled back her hand before Asri saw and moved over to stand by me. Asri carefully folded the jacket and put it on the couch cushion and sat down next to it. Bobby shook his head in annoyance at her deliberate casual motions and took off his coat in a huff.

We stood there in a growing well of silence. Sue cleared her throat uneasily. "It's going to be night soon. You're going to need some meat if you're going to be able to go hunting for another few hours. A woman named Pamela—I guess she's the wife of one of the other pack members—brought over some homemade bread and a small smoked turkey as a welcoming gift. Would you like some sandwiches?"

Asri raised her painted brows a touch. "I have never tried *smoked* turkey. If it is no trouble, I think it would benefit us all to eat."

Bobby threw up his hands, plopped down in the recliner and snarled sarcastically. "*Sure* Why not? Let's have a four course meal while we're at it."

I bit my lip to keep from making a smart-ass remark, but

Asri stared him down cooly. "I don't think we have that much time, Agent. But if you would prefer to go hungry, you are welcome to."

Sue hid a smile by turning and going into the kitchen. I figured I might as well help, rather than sit and listen to the pair of them bicker.

I opened the swinging door for Sue and followed her inside. I saw the bread in a basket on the kitchen counter and pulled a bread knife from the wooden block.

Sue opened the refrigerator and pulled out a tray with neatly sliced meat covered in plastic. "I went ahead and stripped the carcass so it would be easy to serve."

"Good idea," I commented and started to cut slices from the crusty loaf. My back was to her as she pulled dressings from the refrigerator. As I carried the sliced bread past the kitchen table, a scent caught my nose.

"No mustard for me, Sue. Just mayo on turkey." I was reaching into the pantry to grab some plastic wrap to cover the rest of the bread when she replied.

"I'm not putting any on," she said. "You don't like mustard. I don't think we even own a jar."

Odd. I could swear that I smell mustard. I turned around and saw that she was right. Only a jar of sandwich spread and some butter was on the counter.

"Isn't it cute the way Bobby and Asri are dancing around in there? Not like it's fooling anyone—it's pretty obvious they like each other." she asked in a small whisper with a smile.

I looked at her askance, while still trying to figure out where the mustard was coming from. "*Like* each other?" I whispered back. "They're about ready to *kill* each other."

She rolled her eyes. "Bobby's just acting like a first-grader, pulling her pigtails. It's *obvious* that he's attracted to her. He can barely take his eyes off her."

I moved close to her and helped build sandwiches. Even the thick smoky scent of the turkey couldn't erase that damn mustard. Where was it? "Well, she doesn't seem to be amused," I commented.

"That's not quite true," she mulled. "She's being really careful not to get too close to him. Sort of like the way you were with me at first."

I chuckled. "Oh, I don't know about that. I think we got *close* pretty early on."

She blushed lightly. "Well, yeah. But it's more like you were after. Skittish. Watch them yourself if you don't believe me."

I nodded, intending to do just that. It only took a few minutes to build some turkey and cheese sandwiches. I walked over to the table and lifted up a bowl of fruit to grab the tray underneath it. There it was again, the strong mustard smell. Something sparked my brain as I saw a small black object on the table behind the fruit bowl.

"Sue, is this your cell phone?" I asked, without touching it. It was face down.

She glanced at where I pointed. "Nope. Mine's in my purse. I thought it was yours."

The phone, plus the scent, added up and chilled my blood. We'd had a visitor. I picked up the phone and turned it over. A small sticky note was pasted on the front.

Call me when you're alone, Mr. G. That Chinese chick makes me nervous. 2410.

How long had he been in the house? Did he just arrive and drop off the phone, or had he been here while Sue and I were sleeping, or even longer? Dammit! I was getting careless. I couldn't believe that three of us with Sazi noses didn't notice a human hiding in the kitchen. Calling him would be easy, but it was obvious that whatever he wanted, he didn't want to talk about it with Bobby and Asri here.

"Are you okay, Tony? You feel like you've seen a ghost." Sue's face was concerned and she reached out to touch my arm. If she touched me, she'd know what I'd just realized, and I didn't want to panic her. I moved away from her touch casually and tucked the cell phone in my pocket.

"It is my cell phone. I guess I'd forgotten it in here."

Her eyes narrowed and her nostrils flared like a Sazi. "You're lying. What's going on?"

This wasn't going to work. I had to tell her. I couldn't afford to go to the airport and leave her alone. I leaned in her close to her. "When we leave here, I want you to go somewhere with lots of people. Maybe the mall. Take your cell phone and stay there until I call you." I extracted the phone from my pocket. "This is a little gift from a mutual friend. I don't know how he found us, or why he's here, but I don't want you alone."

"Mutual friend?" Her eyes widened.

I nodded grimly. "Scotty's in town and he's already been inside this house."

She almost dropped the sandwiches. I caught them in time. "What does he *want?*"

I shook my head and hefted the tray in one hand while dragging Sue to the farthest corner of the room. "I don't know. He wants me to call him when I'm alone. That won't be for awhile, so I need you to stay low. You know him, though, so you don't have to be too worried. Just keep your distance. It's me he wants—I think. But I don't want Bobby and Asri to know. Bobby would have my head for talking to him. I'm supposed to be dead."

Sue's scent was a jaw tightening fear that nearly made me attack a sandwich. I shook my head in annoyance and set the platter on the nearest counter and then turned my back on the sandwiches deliberately.

"What's with the fear, Sue? Scotty didn't bother you before. Not like this."

She turned from me and kept spreading mayonnaise on a slice of bread. "C'mon, Sue. Give. We can't walk into the next room like this. We can't afford for them to ask questions. You don't lie worth a damn." I wasn't all that worried about Scotty—he was nothing to me. But until I learned his plans, Sue could be in danger. While I had known Scotty for a few years, Sue had met him only six months ago. She'd been trying to find an assassin to perform an unusual task. Out of a deep and bottomless depression came the need to end it all. But she feared she would only have one chance to get away from her family and didn't think she could kill herself without messing it up. She believed that the money she'd won in the lottery would help with one final purchase, to find a killer to *kill her*. Scotty was recommended by someone. He had turned down the job—it would be too easy, no fun. I'd turned it down, too, but against my better judgment at the time, I'd agreed to listen to her story. I wound up liking her. A lot. With the help of my psychiatrist friend, John Corbin—John-Boy to me— we'd managed to get her to a point where she wanted to live. I planned to keep her that way.

After a series of bad surprises and worse enemies, I wound up on the dead rolls. Sue is 'missing and *presumed* dead.' While this might have nothing to do with Scotty's visit, I just didn't know.

"I can't help it, Tony," she whispered frantically. Her hand clutched my arm and I felt her nails in my skin. "He scares me."

"Since when?" I stared at her wide green eyes. They showed too much white and her nostrils were flared slightly. While a part of me wanted—no, *needed*—to protect her, I knew that she was better than this.

"I'd thought he was a messed up little kid until you told me he *likes* to kill. I saw the look in his eyes and all I've been able to think of since was that guy in that horror book who made "girl suits" from the skin of his victims."

I grabbed my fear by the throat and chained it to the floor of my mind. "Nah, Scotty's not like that. He's not into torture." I snapped my fingers. "His marks go down just like that. No pain. Just startled. Aren't you curious why he's here?" I asked her.

She nodded. Her whisper made the fear inside my head fight against the chains that bound it. "Do you think some-one else has hired him to come after me? Just after I finally decided I want to live?"

I shook my head. "No. He wouldn't accept the job for the same reason that he turned you down the first time. It wouldn't be any fun for him. You know him. You'd see him coming and he couldn't sneak up on you. Otherwise, why wouldn't he come into the apartment when I was out of town?" Scotty gets a high out of watching people die. He likes to see the lights go out personally."

Her eyes widened again, but this time in surprise. The hot and sour soup of her fear dissolved. "That's *right*. Then why *was* he here?"

The thick antifreeze scent of curiosity chased away the lingering fear scent. I raised a finger and tapped her nose gently. I smiled at her started expression. "Just hold onto that question when we go into the next room. You should also be curious about why Bobby and Asri are about to drag me to the airport to pick up Bobby's boss."

"They haven't explained why? I missed the first part of the conversation. What possible use could you be?"

I turned away from her and picked up the tray of sand-wiches. I could think of a thousand reasons why Nikoli might send me with Asri and Bobby. I was only worried about the one that I might *not* have thought of.

Chapter 12

NOBODY WAS MORE surprised than me when we exited Asri's silver Lexus in front of an airport in Gary, Indiana. Bobby stepped out of the car, once again bundled in his thick down coat, hat, gloves and garishly bright muffler.

He saw my small smile as he wound it again and again around his neck so he didn't trip over it. "Not a *word* about the scarf, Joe. My niece in Gabon knitted this for me."

"I thought you didn't have any relatives—that whole *last of my kind* stuff. And you still have *siblings* alive?"

He pulled the scarf down to reveal his mouth for an instant. "I have *human* relatives, stupid. Just not *Sazi* relatives. And she's my . . ." he counted his fingers. "Great-great-great-grand niece."

Asri came around to the back of the car, her hood drawn so closely around her face that she reminded me of the kid in the South Park cartoon.

Bobby's voice struggled through the layers of cloth and icy wind. "I didn't even know this airport was here."

"It's a way to get to Chicago quickly without notice," came Asri's likewise muffled voice. "It may be over the state line, but it's only about twenty-five minutes from downtown."

"Are you *certain* that the Wolven jet is scheduled to arrive tonight? I'd just as soon go back and sit on those heated seats in the car. Man, I've *got* to get me some of those."

Asri's face took on a sarcastic visage. "You weren't very interested when I first suggested it, Agent. I nearly had to tie you to it while you were trying to escape to the back seat."

I turned my face into the icy wind, feeling the fast-moving snow bite at my cheeks. A shiver ran down my spine and blended with the weight of the moon on my back. Both Bobby and Asri were preventing me from changing form. But they couldn't stop the scent of frost on the wind, or the pulse-pounding rush as power flowed over my skin, raising every hair on my body. It felt incredible to be outside, away from the oven of the car's interior. "I'm just glad you didn't stick *me* in that seat. How can you guys bundle up like that? This weather feels incredible."

"Damn mammal," came a chorus of reply. They looked at each other with a startled expression until I laughed. Bobby's deep chuckle and smile brought color to Asri's cheeks. They both quickly looked away. Combined with their almost panicked condition in the car, I was realizing that Sue was right about them.

Asri recovered quickest. She turned and walked toward the airport as the sound of jet engines began to fill the air. "Come—we are already late. We must hurry before he has a chance to depart."

He? I thought Bobby's boss was a *she*. I glanced at Bobby with raised brows, to find that he was similarly confused.

He muttered to me under his breath as we followed Asri's form, disappearing into the brightly lit snow. "I don't like this, Tony. Fiona should be the only one with access to the company jet. Who are we coming to meet?"

I shrugged my shoulders. "Don't look at me. I still don't know why *I'm* here at all."

Being the good enforcer, Asri held the door for us so that she could be at the rear of the group. Her voice was a hiss of air as I passed her. "You're fortunate that the bad weather delayed flights tonight, Tony. I was not pleased to spend the extra time at your house while your wife found a companion to *shop* with. You must begin to take your duties to the pack more seriously. I know you are lying to me about something. You should hope I do not find out *what.*"

I stopped to face her. The cold wind and snow poured into the building because my body was blocking open the door and preventing her from entering. "I explained that already. She doesn't know many people here and I didn't want her going out alone." That was the truth. Not while Scotty was on the loose.

Asri shook her head and sniffed haughtily. "The truth—but only *barely.* Your wife is an adult human in a human world. She has little to fear which shopping with *another* human would solve. You seem not to credit her with common sense or intellect. You will alienate her affections if you continue on this trend. She will leave you."

I snorted at the judgmental comment when she knew nothing of our relationship. I lobbed a bow shot of my own. "Big words coming from someone who puts up with Nikoli. Why don't *you* leave?"

Her face took on a look that said that she'd heard the same question many times. She leaned in until the scent of moldy lutefisk nearly made me gag. "My relationships—and my reasons for them—are none of your affair, young wolf." She released the door so that it hit me on the shoulder and slipped around me to enter the building.

Relationships? As in *plural*? Useful. Very useful. I allowed myself a small smile before I turned to join the reptile duo.

Minutes passed while Bobby and Asri checked with the desk to determine whether a private plane had arrived. We moved over to the Jet Center. After looking over the scene, Bobby decided that we should wait in the Pilot's Lounge. Asri was stunning in her portrayal of the confused step-daughter of our pilot. *But he doesn't know we're com-*

ing, she had sobbed. *What if he doesn't come into the passenger lounge?* Eventually, we were told we could wait in this room.

I followed along grudgingly. Nobody was telling me anything, and it was starting to annoy me. I spent a little time checking in with Sue in my head. It turned out that Pamela was *Yurgi's* wife. She was human and also worked in an office. She was delighted to have someone to shop with. Sue swore she was being extra careful and looking at every male teenager she encountered, just in case Scotty had changed his appearance.

A pilot was phoning for a taxi when we arrived. He was fine when we first arrived, but not after a few minutes. As he waited on hold he started getting really fidgety, glancing our direction and gnawing at his lower lip. The hot and sour soup scent of his fear roared through the room, hitting me like a brick between the eyes. I was suddenly *very* glad we'd eaten the sandwiches. Even so, it took all my willpower not to attack him, rip his throat out. I forced myself to sit down and closed my eyes to blot out the images, but I heard the bang of the receiver as he hung up the phone in a panic and bolted from the room. I couldn't blame the guy. I was feeling twitchy, and it showed. The moon was roaring over my skin, even through the snow, and I longed to race out into the cold to chase the quickly moving workers.

Once he was gone I rose and began to pace. Hunger burned through me and it was only Bobby and Asri's power that kept me in check. My skin itched and burned. I wanted to rip it off, tear it to shreds and let the fur escape.

The room we were in wasn't much to look at. A single couch sat next to a potted plant and a short row of chairs faced a small table holding the phone and a directory. The roaring of jet engines as they passed the building rose and fell painfully in my ears as I watched the activity outside. I was glad for my ear plugs.

One long window faced the runway, so it was easy to

watch for arriving planes. Fortunately, a pilot would be too busy following directions and driving the jet into the hanger to look in the lounge. There were no windows between the lounge and the hanger, so we would remain hidden until he stepped in the room.

My ears perked up when the sound of one jet didn't match the rest. I stared out the window, squinting into the swirling snow, and saw a small private jet quickly moving in for a landing. I whistled silently as it passed by. I'd seen one of the custom-made Maverick Leader jets only once before. They're pretty, but pricey—over two million a pop. Still, my friend swore by his.

I focused my eyes on the cockpit, barely lit by the instrument panel, as the wheels touched down and it glided to a stop on the wet pavement with a descending roar. A Latino man with salt and pepper hair was surrounded by thick band of blue-white . . . no, wait—I blinked and he was suddenly different. The face was still broad, but the sweep of the nose was different, the lips fuller. The hair was dark brown and wavy. This man was white with an "I-spend-all-my-time-in-the-sun" tan, and the band of color surrounding him was now thin and golden. What the hell? Had I only imagined the first image? The jet passed by me in seconds, leaving me little time to muse on it.

"Is that your guy?" I pointed to the jet. Bobby and Asri, who were once again trading whispered barbs at each other, stopped in mid-battle to look out the window.

Bobby nodded and quickly began to zip up his jacket and return his hat to his head. "That's the plane. Was a woman piloting it?"

"No," I replied, both shaking my head and furrowing my brow. "It was a man."

"What did he look like?" came the muffled words from behind the ever growing layer of knitted color.

I gave a short sniff of exhaled air, not quite a chuckle. "Good question." A *very* good question.

Asri spoke when her jacket was again secure. "The

storm is growing worse. The timing of this visit could be better. Tony will need to hunt soon and it will take time to reach a park."

Bobby glanced at her sharply. "Don't you mean that *we* will need to hunt?"

Asri's eyebrows raised. "I seldom hunt on the moon. Usually I swim."

I pursed my lips. I guess it never occurred to me that other species might treat the moon differently. Maybe dragons *need* to swim the way wolves need to hunt. I know they *can* swim. It hadn't occurred to me it might be necessary.

Bobby was equally surprised, and opened his mouth. But he didn't get a chance to ask his question, because the door to the lounge opened.

The man I saw last in the cockpit entered the room. He saw Bobby first, and a blue streak of muttered swearing caught my ear. His eyes flowed over Asri briefly, but spent a much longer moment looking at me. I've spent my whole adult life trying to remain unnoticed, so I'm acutely aware when someone *does*. It's all in the eyes, and his showed recognition. All of my senses went on full alert. His scent was like fresh cardboard coated with lemon oil. He was dressed in worn blue jeans and a denim shirt under a leather bomber jacket that is the twin of mine, except brown. He looked away when he caught me staring, and his face went to schooled blankness. I continued to study him, watching for any chink in the armor.

Bobby's mouth was still open, and his eyes had too much white. His jaw moved, but nothing came out.

"Bobby. You're looking well." The voice was as white bread, all-American as the face and perfectly matched his football quarterback body.

"But . . . but you're *dead!* For Christ sake, Greg—I saw you die!"

I didn't know anyone named Greg, but it was apparent that Bobby did. Asri was also studying the man. She seemed confused, which told me that she was expecting to

meet someone else. Her narrowed eyes relaxed and returned to normal. She was going to wait it out and see what
happened.

"No, Bobby, you didn't. You only *thought* you saw me
die."

Bobby's surprise turned to anger in the blink of an eye.
"*I know what I saw,* damn it! You ran back into the house
and it exploded. I know you're powerful, Greg, but *nobody*
could have walked away from that!" He took two steps toward the man and stared at him, his eyes flashing.

"Unless that person *planned* the explosion," came the
quiet reply. "It was the end of the road for me, Bobby. I'd
been in Wolven too long—made too many enemies. It was
time for me to die."

Bobby's face was contorted in fury. I was surprised
when he took a swing intended for Greg's face. The bigger
man caught Bobby's fist and held him effortlessly.

Ah ha. His eyes flashed for a moment when he got angry.
If I hadn't been watching so close I would have missed it. A
brief flash of blue-white flared from his pupils before it settled back to gold. The voice dropped a few notes past the
normal solid baritone, and betrayed his growing annoyance.

"Knock it off, Bobby. Other people have left the company and nobody ever cared. Why am I any different?"

"You *devastated* us, man! Fiona wouldn't talk to anyone
for nearly a *month.* Raphael quit the agency and has never
been the same. You self-righteous, self-centered son of a
bitch!"

Wow. I guess I didn't realize that they were close.
Bobby's never really been close to any of the guys since
I've known him. Now I knew why.

Greg shook his head—small, quick movements that ended
with a harsh release of breath. "You've got it all wrong, Bob.
Fiona knew. You think I walked away without my *pension?*
Why do you think Fiona does the payroll herself? I'm not the
only *dead* agent, you know. And as for Raphael—we both
know his leaving the company had nothing to do with my

death. He brought about his own downfall."

Bobby's arms were crossed tight over his chest. His initial fury of pain had gone cold. "Why now, Greg? Why show your face after all these years?"

The reply was sarcastic and biting. "I didn't intend to *show* my face, Bobby. *You* surprised *me,* remember? And—speaking of which . . ." He turned to Asri. "I don't know you. Who are you and why are you here?"

She stepped forward slightly and raised her face to meet his. "I am Asri Kho. I was sent here to welcome you to Chicago on behalf of Nikoli Molotov and drive you back to meet him."

A shadow of a smile passed over his face. "Fair enough. I *did* ask who and why. Perhaps I should have asked *how?* How did you come to be *here*—in Gary, Indiana—at this time—in a snowstorm? *How* are you here?"

She shrugged her shoulders, which drew a frown from Greg's face. "I'm afraid I know very little. I was instructed by Nikoli to pick up the pilot of the jet that just arrived. I didn't know who would be in it. You would have to ask Nikoli about the details."

Greg nodded his head briefly as his nostrils scented the air. I couldn't quite tell whether he'd spotted Asri's lie, but I could see it in her eyes. He pursed his lips and casually sat down on the stiff wooden chair at the table. He leaned back against the wall and crossed his arms. "Let's try that again. I think we should all sit down and have a chat before we go see Nikoli."

Bobby sat down on one of the chairs automatically. He was still angry, but the thick antifreeze of curiosity won out. Apparently Asri had been bullshitting us all evening.

I *couldn't* sit. I was too edgy, but I did at least lean against the wall near the towering ficus in the corner.

"I would prefer to stand," Asri said calmly.

The blinds on the window suddenly dropped and snapped shut, just like Bobby had done at my house. "And I would rather you *sit*." The word ended with a dagger edge and I watched Asri's face grow startled and her eyes change from defiant to nervous. I knew why. A blaze of light emanated from Greg. It surrounded her and began to compress. She slowly, but methodically began to sit on the couch. Her every muscle fought the action, but she was outclassed. He had finesse, I had to admit. Once seated and leaning back into the cushions, one of her legs crossed over the other and her fingers interlaced and hugged one knee. Only her face showed the fight she was putting up. Her teeth were gritted and sweat painted her brow. Her panic made her bold. A furiously bright glow of amber light struggled and strained against a wash of blue-white. I had to shut my eyes against the blaze. Bobby didn't even seem to notice the light, but he did notice the struggle. He looked a little uneasy, which surprised me.

"Now—once again, Ms. Kho. How did you know that I would be arriving tonight at this airport?"

She opened her mouth, but it took two tries for words to come out. "I . . . told you . . . I *don't know.*"

Greg sighed and shook his head briefly. The blaze of light intensified. The effect of his magic was startling. Asri began to sink into the couch, pressed into the springs by the sheer weight of Greg's power. Springs squeaked and then groaned. The vinyl stretched and started to rip.

Asri gasped. I could hear her heartbeat race. The scent of fear finally erupted from her intense pain showed on her face. The smell made my stomach growl. I wiped a line of spittle from the corner of my mouth. This was not the time for me to be smelling fear.

Bobby couldn't stand it anymore. He stood in a burst and advanced across the room. "Greg—*Stop it.* What the hell is wrong with you? This isn't *like* you."

"That's because it's *not* him, Bobby," I replied quietly from the corner. All eyes turned to me.

"What the hell are you talking about, Joe? You've never even *met* Greg Hamilton before. You were barely a kid when we worked together in Wolven."

Greg's eyes had narrowed as they stared at me, and once again I spotted the clear signal of recognition with just a hint of . . . something. Not quite fear. I shrugged and stared right back. I had finally figured out who he really was, but I didn't care if anyone else knew or not.

He forced his gaze from me and turned again to Asri. "Once last chance, Ms. Kho. Tell me what you know or I'll compress you into a puddle of tissue on the floor."

Asri's breath was coming in short, pained gasps. I couldn't say I was very sorry after what she'd done to me, but Bobby couldn't take it anymore.

"She doesn't know, Greg. Back off." He lashed out at Greg with his own magic, a whip of green energy. It didn't even dent the handsome football hero. Bobby's anger was torn from him when a second bolt of energy—this time fully blue-white—smashed Bobby against the wall. The scent of fear now erupted from a second source.

"Stay out of this, Bobby. This is a security issue. I told no one of my plan to come to Chicago tonight. If Nikoli Molotov has a spy in our organization, *I will find out!*" He turned a face seething with anger to Asri. "Now—*tell me!* How did Nikoli know about my plans?"

Asri's chest was compressed so that her voice was strained and hoarse. "I . . . *swear*. We did not expect *you*. It was Lucas Santiago who was to come tonight."

"And how did you know *that?*" Asri jumped as one of the springs under her broke with a sharp snap. She sunk even further down, her body bent nearly in two.

I put a hand up to shield the glare and narrowed my eyes so I could continue to watch the action. Greg noticed. But once again, he forced his attention back to Asri. But I knew he'd get back to me eventually.

"Tat . . . Tatiana Santiago told us. She . . . was arriving for a conference in the city. She called . . . the . . . Duchess and said her husband would be . . . joining her."

Greg released his magical hold on both Asri and Bobby so

suddenly that they both let out a small yelp. He turned to me.

"And what does that mean to you, Tony?" Yeah, I figured he knew my name. It was the blue-white light that gave him away.

"The Duchess is Russian royalty and as old as dirt. The name *Tatiana* is Russian, and is historically a royal name. My bet is that Tatiana and Lelya are kin and you hadn't considered that particular leak, had you, *Lucas?*"

His voice changed. It turned deeper and more polished. His scent turned to desert grass and something fruity. The closest I match it to was watermelon. Bobby and Asri both looked at each other in shock. "What gave me away?" he asked with a smile.

"Sue told me once that she met a white wolf with blue eyes. The wolf turned into a Latino man with black hair in a burst of blue-white light. I *thought* I saw that man as the plane landed. But after you got stressed when Bobby attacked you, your magic turned blue-white, and then *I knew.*"

He swore again. "You've got *second sight*. Damn it!" He turned to Bobby angrily. "Why wasn't that in your report, Agent?"

"Second sight? Is that what this seeing colored auras shit is?"

He shot me a suspicious look, but it quickly faded. "You didn't know? Hmm. It must be new then."

Bobby was trying to recover from the series of shocks. The first words out of his mouth weren't an answer. "You *can't* both be the same person. Lucas doesn't have illusion abilities. And you were the pack leader in Boulder when Greg was in Wolven."

"I have a *number* of abilities that I don't advertise, Agent Mbutu." Lucas's voice was filled with menace. I recognized that tone. It was both warning and threat. He blurred around the edges—that's the best I can describe it. I blinked and he was suddenly a different person. A medium-height Latino man stood in front of us where the football hero once was. His salt-and-pepper hair looked comfortable on him. He was dressed in a suit and tie, looking like the lawyer Sue told me he was. I could feel her burst of recognition and happiness in my head. Bobby and Asri were still struck dumb.

Asri was trying, without success, to extricate herself from the couch. Bobby finally had to reach over and offer his hand to get her out of the hole. I started when I saw a color shift as they touched. When Bobby's green met Asri's golden, the colors blended and the new gold-green started to crawl up both of their arms. They must have felt whatever I saw, because Bobby let go of Asri's hand abruptly, before she had her feet completely under her. She stumbled a bit on her first step and stared at her hand like it burned.

I shook my head and turned my attention back to Lucas to give them a chance to recover from whatever it was I saw.

"Sue says hi," I commented blithely as Greg—now Lucas—stared from me to the two, who were now both staring at their hands. Bobby clenched his hand into a fist and then opened it more than once. Asri was busy concentrating on rubbing her fingers together like she was trying to regain circulation. She looked a little panicked.

Lucas's brow furrowed but he didn't comment. He spoke to me as though Sue were standing in my place. He must understand the connection between us better than most. "Hello, Sue. I hope you're enjoying Chicago. Sorry I had to leave Boulder during your training but, as you can see . . ."

He spread his arms out with palms up. "I had business to take care of. I'd *hoped* to do it discreetly." He turned and put on a black overcoat that had magically appeared on the table next to him. "Apparently, I need to have a long chat with my wife about how to keep *secrets*."

I had to agree. People got killed for less in the Family. I would remember not to mention anything important to his wife.

He looked at Bobby and Asri. "Well? We might as well go. My cover's completely blown, thanks to you three."

I smirked. "What sort of cover could you possibly maintain by showing up as a dead man?"

He smirked in return. "Better than appearing in two places at once."

That made sense.

"The case is very sensitive, and none of your business." He ran a hand through his hair. "I'll come up with something creative to work it. I always do." Then he walked to me and held out his hand. "By the way, a pleasure to finally meet you, Tony. I look forward to getting to know you."

I held out my hand in return. Asri seemed particularly interested in our exchange. "I thought you already knew everything about me."

He smiled tiredly. "I used to know a lot more. But you keep changing the rules."

The moment our hands touched, a flare of magic hit me in the chest. I fell forward into a black pit.

When I looked up, there was an old, Native American woman in front of me. The room was all dark wood and muted light. Thick books lined shelves along the walls. A red leather wing chair edged with brass tacks made the woman's compact frame seem every more tiny.

"The meeting will be in Chicago next week."

"Chicago?" came the startled reply from my mouth, except that it wasn't mine. It was Lucas's voice that flowed from me. "But it's already scheduled for Paris. We can't change the plans of that many people with so little notice. And Nikoli doesn't have the facilities—or the security—to host a council meeting."

The lined dark face took on an ominous visage. "Then it would be advisable to make sure that his facilities—and his security—are upgraded, and quickly, because Chicago is where the meeting will be. Charles will make sure that everyone attends. And please inform our counterpart in the city that it will be a complete council meeting, with all groups fully represented. Her presence will be required."

"A complete meeting? What does that mean?" My brow furrowed, but terror struck my heart because I—or, more precisely, Lucas—knew what it meant and didn't want to consider it.

The old woman smiled. "Just what you think it does, my old friend. We will need four extra rooms in the hotel."

The woman faded from view, but not before she gave me a look that chilled my blood. It was as though she looked through the eyes of the person I was in the image and saw *me*—Tony.

"Tony? *Tony!* You okay, man?" Bobby was trying to help me up from my knees. Lucas released my hand while giving me a strange look.

"What was that all about, Tony?" Lucas asked.

I shook my head, trying to fight my way out of the vision. "I don't know. There was an office and an old woman . . ." Something made me stop there, not revealing anything that I heard. "I don't know. I can't . . . remember."

Asri gave me a panicked look and gasped. She clutched a hand around something that was under her shirt near her throat. When everyone stared at her, she released her hand self-consciously and pulled up her hood. "I agree with Mr. Hamil—with Mr. Sant—with our esteemed guest. We should go."

I felt the sky clear outside. The moon was shining. It sliced through the roof of the building and raised every hair on my body. The world turned pink, cut with shades of black and grey. I heard my voice deepen into a hungry growl. "I need to hunt. I can't stand much more of the moon. It's doing weird things to my head."

Lucas grabbed my chin and turned my face to meet his eyes. A snarl curled my lip. I fought the man who held me and snapped at his hand. This time, there was no connection when we touched, no flash of magic. He gave an annoyed shake of his head.

"His eyes are starting to bleed. No wonder he's blacking out. We need to get a move on. Bobby, you and Ms. Kho pull back your magic. I'll control him."

I felt the skin-ruffling scent of jungle and musty reptile disappear from my head, and warm fur, powerful and protective, take its place. Even with the effort he'd expended on Asri and Bobby, Lucas held the moon away without any visible sign.

It was only the second time I'd had the moon held at bay. Nikoli had tried to make sure that we arrived at the park before the moon was up. But now the bright orb that called to me, pulled at me, had been fully in the sky for more than an hour and I was paying the price for the delay. We hurried out of the Jet Center into the snowy night. But by the time we reached the Lexus, my leg had started to twitch so much that I almost ended up face down. I hissed through gritted teeth as I heard a sharp snap and felt a corresponding pain in my right thigh. The bone was trying to reform into a wolf leg, but the magic wouldn't let it. A second later, my arm did the same thing. I was expecting it, but it was still painful.

"Damn that hurts!" I exclaimed as my other leg went out enough that I had to lean against the wheel well. The snow had mostly stopped, but it was still slick enough that I couldn't afford to lose my balance. I felt Sue start in my mind, and wondered where she was while she was enduring the pain along with me. Some aspects of the mating are a pain in the ass—especially for her.

"What hurts?" asked Lucas with a furrowed brow.

"My bones are snapping like twigs. Can't you hear them? The moon's trying to change me, but your magic is holding it off, so the bones are breaking and reknitting in seconds. Gotta tell ya—it stings like blazes."

My arm broke at that moment, and I saw the three of them wince. Asri fumbled with the push button combination lock on her door. She finally had to take off her gloves to enter the code.

"I didn't realize that popping sound was your *bones*, Ton," Bobby mumbled. "That's got to smart."

Lucas's face looked odd. "Nobody's ever mentioned before that it hurts for me to hold off the moon until we reach our hunting grounds."

I winced again briefly as my hip popped. "You're the boss. Nobody *would*." An ankle went. I had to take a few deep breaths before I could speak again. It wasn't quite as bad as when Asri sliced me up, but I didn't know where the pain would be next, so it was more startling. "And you probably don't let the night get this far along, either."

"Still . . . it's not acceptable." I felt power flood over me. I lifted my hand. It glowed like a nova with blue-white light. The moon silenced completely and the resulting lack of pain surprised me. "That should take care of it. Bobby, you sit up front. I'll keep watch on Tony in back."

Both Asri and Bobby suddenly looked panicked. Bobby pulled down his muffler enough to yell, "NO!"

Lucas was taken aback. His voice lowered to a rumble. He was reminding me more and more of Carmine. "*What* did you say?"

Bobby's scent was clearly fear now, but the panic was there too, which told me that they were for different reasons. Asri escaped the confrontation by slipping into the driver's seat and starting the car. "I mean—I'll ride in back with Tony. I don't mind. You sit up front with Asri. The view's better."

Lucas's eyebrows rose until they disappeared under his dampening hair. He gave Bobby a searching look while Bobby fidgeted nervously. "The *view*. Fine. I'm shotgun. Let me know if you start to hear any more snapping. I presume we'll be on the road awhile."

They both started to open doors when I had to interrupt. No one else seemed to notice that I was shining like a beacon.

"Wait, wait. You're telling me that *none* of you—nobody

else in this whole city—is going to see me sparkling like a Christmas tree in the back of the car?"

"Second sight is a very rare talent, Tony," Lucas explained as he held open the front car door. "I can count the number of people in the world with it on one hand."

"So seeing people glow isn't something temporary? I thought it was just something that happened because Sue and I were finally together and it would fade."

Bobby spoke up with one leg already in the car. "It's only Sazi who glow with the sparkles. I'll see if I can get a friend who used to be in Wolven to explain it all to you. He says it's pretty useful. You'll get used to it."

"I'll get *used to it*. Gee, that's comforting."

He shrugged his shoulders and ducked inside the car. I heard his voice before he closed it. "At least you can eat a candy bar without tasting and categorizing the preservatives. Don't bitch."

I got in the door opposite Bobby and sat down in the back seat. The silence stretched and lengthened as we drove onto the snow-packed streets. There were only smells in the car—fear's hot and sour from Asri, and burned metal frustration plus hot coffee, not quite boiling, from Lucas. Bobby was so covered by winter wear that I had no clue of his emotions, but he was fidgety to the point of twitching.

Even through the glow that burned around me, I could feel the moon rip at my body. Thick fur itched just under my skin. I tried to think about something different. I found Sue at the back of my head, but she was hard to hear through Lucas's magic. I wanted to touch her but I knew that she was still at the mall with Pamela. I told her that Lucas was who we'd come to pick up but she already knew. She was busily finding a suitable gift for him. I didn't really think it was necessary, but she was adamant that a gift for a visiting dignitary was custom with the Sazi. The books had told her so. At least she had some money. I'd given her some of the gold coins from my pocket to trade in at a coin shop, but didn't have time to show them all to her. The cash would keep us in kibble for a few weeks if she didn't go nuts on a gift. The connection with Sue was strengthening as we talked, which was fine with me. It distracted me from the pounding power that was giving me a headache.

You need to read the books, Tony. I hope you didn't leave them on the island.

She growled when she learned that I did. She was startled when Pamela grabbed her arm and started to drag her to the food court. I guess she had growled out loud. Oops. Fortunately, her new friend was used to it and knew what she needed.

No sign of Scotty? I felt her negative response, but she was starting to feel the moon as well, and it was difficult for her to talk. *Keep an eye out if there's a pretzel stand. He lives on them.*

Our connection flared for a moment and I was in the mall with her, smelling cooking beef from a steak sandwich stand, seeing bright lights and laughing humans. The scent of the raw meat as it began to sizzle on the grill froze me in place. I could feel a small trickle of saliva slide from between Sue's lips, but it was too difficult to raise my hand to wipe it away. Movement from the corner of my eye returned me to the car. The air was finally oven-like enough for Bobby to start to remove his scarf. I spotted Lucas moving all of the vents so they blew on Asri. No wonder he'd wanted to sit in the back.

Bobby's hand moved in rotation as he unwound the wrap from his neck. Cartoon colors flashed in the light from the street lamps. I ducked his arm once as he continued to unwind. The next movement was even larger and his fist threatened to smash me in the face. I put up a hand to grab his arm just as I felt Sue bite into her thick, rare steak sandwich. I caught his wrist and felt a jolt as the car disappeared into a black nothingness that was becoming annoyingly familiar. Sue was likewise gone as I soared and dropped until my stomach lurched.

"I thought we were going to a sparring room," I

heard Bobby's voice say from the mouth that was now mine.

"We are," said Asri, who was still hidden in darkness in front of me. Lights flared and a stylish, modern apartment stretched in front of us. The room was warmer than the hotel had been and it felt good on my face, which was tight and slow from the cold.

"Then why are we here?"

Asri took off her jacket and limped slowly across the floor. She entered another room and turned on the light in there, as well.

I heard her voice from inside. "Well? Are you going to follow me or just stand there all day?"

Bobby walked forward cautiously. I could feel his nervousness and a tingling fear flow through every muscle. He stopped at the doorway and could only stare at Asri. She had stripped down to a tight sports bra and delicate black lace panties. Her slender body looked stiff and achy as she crawled on the bed and picked up a remote control.

It took Bobby three tries before he could speak. I could feel the panic in him, but couldn't figure out why. Asri was pretty cute under all those clothes. "Wha . . . um . . . what are you doing? We're here to fight."

Asri shot him a withering look. "Which we can hardly do if we both have the agility of desert tortoises." She lifted the remote and pressed a button. A panel above the bed opened and five spotlights turned the thick comforter red. She raised her face to the warm light, closed her eyes, and then leaned back onto the bed with a sigh.

Bobby's eyes lit up. "Heat lamps?"

"It's the only way I can stand to live in this miserable, ice-ridden town. You smell like a snake, so I presume you're also cold." She pointed to a darkened doorway, her eyes still closed. "You may change in the bath. My weight room and arena are downstairs. We will battle there when we are sufficiently warm."

"You have a private gym? Isn't there one in the hotel?"

Her laugh was a short bark of sound. "Certainly. But it would be hardly useful to train with those I punish, would it? They would learn my tactics."

Bobby entered the bath and shut the door. He removed his contacts and stripped to boxers, but hesitated in removing them. I knew that being nude wasn't much of a problem for him, so it seemed odd. But when I concentrated on feeling what Bobby was feeling, I understood why. He was attracted to Asri—very attracted and didn't want it to show.

He needn't have worried. He turned off the bathroom light and opened the door. A blinding flash of pain erupted in his face and he went down on his tail. He looked up in shock to see Asri standing over him, smiling. She dropped her raised fist to her side once more.

Her voice was filled with dark laughter. "Surely you didn't think I was going to play fair, did you, agent? I will wait for you in the arena. The stairs are in the living room." She turned and started to walk away. She easily leapt over the foot that Bobby tried to kick out to trip her. She spoke over her shoulder as she left. "And don't get blood on my towels."

Bobby raised a hand up to his face, and it came away smeared with blood. He stood slowly. I felt the ache in stiff muscles. Did he feel like this every time it got cold? No wonder he was so grumpy.

A quick glance in the mirror showed that his

split lip was already healed. He very deliberately wet one of the clean white towels and wiped off the blood. His face was smug in the mirror, but he was muttering. Apparently, I couldn't tell what a person was exactly thinking while I was in their head. I only got sights, sounds and sensations, plus a general impression of what was on their mind, which was plenty.

Speaking of sensations—the warmth from the heat lamps as they seeped into his body felt great. It wasn't long before small beads of sweat appeared on his skin. I could tell he was getting more and more irritated as he warmed. He knew that making her wait would get her mad, as well, which is exactly why he was doing it. Finally, he decided it was time to stop stalling, and he turned off the lights and went downstairs.

He could hear the drumbeats of Asri's animal feet as he walked down the stairs. Yes, better to change now and be able to surprise her. He stripped off the boxers and magic flowed over his skin. His arms moved to his sides and blended into his body. He lowered closer and closer to the floor, until his eyes were at ground level. The door at the bottom of the stairs was open and bright light glowed in the rectangle. Bobby remained in the shadows half a flight up—waiting.

When Asri passed by the next time during her shadow fight, he struck. I felt the stairs flow under my belly, and thousands of muscles contract and loosen to pull me forward in a blur of speed. The attack was well placed—had Asri been any other sort of animal. Bobby's mouth opened wide and his fangs tried to dig in to her armored scales. His head moved side to side quickly as he tried to grind his teeth into her hide.

But she was fast, as well. She was expecting a

snake, even though she didn't know the type. The strike was enough to knock her off balance, but she used the momentum to roll away. She came up on her feet on the other side of the room and turned to look at him. Now that he'd responded to her punch in the bedroom, he raised the front third of his body off the ground and brought his full thirty-three feet of length into the room.

While Asri's face remained cold and reptilian, her voice betrayed her surprise. "You are a regal python? I did not . . . I was not sure your kind truly existed." He continued to stare at her without blinking or speaking. She recovered and said haughtily, "I believe that my kind once ate the young of your kind for sustenance."

Bobby's tongue flicked out. The twin points gathered the scent of her sudden fear. It pleased him. "Seldom. Very seldom. But I can assure you that my young pythons once feasted on your kind's adults."

Nasty little slam there, and it was possible. Both the dragons and pythons are native to the far eastern islands. Bobby had always said he came from South Africa. Maybe he lied.

Asri's eyes narrowed dangerously, but Bobby only continued to stare. His tail began to make small flicking motions, as though he had a rattle. She wasted no time. In a blur of motion and sound that echoed off the high ceiling, she raced across the expanse of floor and rammed right into his body, where his chest would be if he was still human. At the last second, he moved aside smoothly and slapped his tail hard across her eyes.

"A little slow there, Kho. You'll have to do better if you want your strip of hide."

She hissed angrily and spun around. Then she stopped and regarded him for a moment. "Your attempt to get me angry enough to make mistakes won't work, Mbutu. Better men than you have tried."

"Ha! Wolves—hardly better. You've gotten soft fighting mammals. You need to learn how to fight a real opponent."

She pulled back her lips to reveal sharp, jagged teeth. "Do you have anyone in mind? I didn't know you'd brought a friend with you."

His mouth opened and I knew that he was showing off his teeth. "These are all the friends I need, lady."

I realized that the short gasps of hisses was her laughter in this form. "And your friends had little effect on my hide. But let's see how you fare against my bite!"

She followed up the words with action. She came forward and he let her. I realized he was curious to find out whether she could bite through his skin. Personally, I wouldn't ever be curious enough to sit there and watch her race forward with jaws dripping saliva, but he continued to wait. She struck just below his neck. Her jaws closed and started to grind and pull backwards. Bobby was pleased when it had no effect. But he used the opportunity to feign surprise. He slithered and whipped his body like Asri was hurting him. He bit down on the thinner skin near her neck and slid the tip of his tail under her belly. Before she realized what was happening, he had two full coils around her and her back legs were helpless.

She realized her mistake too late. She struggled furiously to escape his grip. He laughed lightly and continued to wrap himself around her.

"I guess I fared pretty well against your bite, Kho. But let's see how long you can hold your breath, shall we?"

Bobby's powerful muscles began to constrict Asri's ribs. I could smell her panic, but she smelled different, too. To Bobby's tongue, Asri didn't smell like moldy lutefisk. Her scent was complex and enticing. Jasmine and sea salt, with rich humus. It smelled far too much like home for his taste. He was having a hard time concentrating.

But Asri was concentrating just fine. In a brilliant defensive move, she suddenly turned human. Her smaller body size slid easily between his coils before he could react and squeeze down. She propelled her naked, sweat-soaked form across the room like a rocket, and then stood and assumed a martial arts stance.

"I can hold my breath for over three minutes, Mbutu, just for your information."

He also turned human in a burst of magic and laughed. "Perhaps this will be more of a challenge than either of us expected."

Blurs of sounds, scents and movement passed by me faster than I could follow. They spun and bounced and kicked and punched. But they seemed equally matched. Soon they were both sweating freely under the heat lamps, but Bobby was actually enjoying himself, and it seemed Asri was, too.

Asri's fatal mistake was doing a spin kick to his face. Being taller, he grabbed her leg before it connected and lifted her off the floor. She tried to recover by kicking out with the other leg, but he pushed forward and toppled her to the ground so that she was on her stomach on the thick mats.

What had never occurred to me was that Bobby might retain his fluid flexibility while human. Apparently, Asri didn't realize it either. She was startled, and then panicked, when each of Bobby's legs wrapped around her legs multiple times until she couldn't move them. Then he did the same with her arms.

"Bet you didn't know I could do this, huh?" he whispered in her ear once she was completely immobile. "It only lasts for a little while after I change. Then the bones harden. But I have plenty of time left to finish you off. Now . . ." he lengthened his neck and slid his mouth under her chin. "Submit!"

She shook her head, not speaking. Her heart was racing and she struggled mightily to free herself.

He bit down on her neck but then froze. The taste of her—my God! It was like nothing he'd ever experienced. He suddenly couldn't think. He could only feel the softness of her bronze body under his, the scent of her silken black hair as it flowed over his skin. Her struggles felt amazingly erotic.

"You smell . . . different," she whispered.

His body was suddenly aroused in ways he'd never felt before. "So do you."

He stretched his neck farther and brought it around so he could look into her eyes. The reptile slits in golden pupils reminded him of women long lost to him. He couldn't seem to help himself. He turned his face and brought his lips against hers. She opened her mouth to him and kissed him long and deep. He realized that his body was positioned over her so that if he moved even a little, he would be inside her. He desperately wanted to be inside her.

Okay, this was way more information than I needed! But I couldn't free myself of the scent of her body, the feeling of her struggles under me. It was beyond voyeurism. It was more like an orgy and I was being forced along for the ride.

Bobby moved back from the kiss. "You realize

that in both of our cultures, I could—I would be obligated—to take you, and mate with you, by right of conquest?"

Her voice was barely audible. "Yes."

Bobby's voice was stern. "But we are in a different time, and we are the last two of our kind. We may make our own rules. So I will tell you that I would very much like to be with you— here, now. But I will leave it up to you. Do you want me to finish? I can make you feel things that no mammal ever could. You know it."

She closed her eyes, and Bobby could smell her fear, but the desire, the hunger was stronger.

"Nikoli would kill us both, Mbutu . . ."

His voice was a whisper in her ear that made her whole body shudder. "I am Robart—only for your lips. I want you badly enough to taste it, Asri Kho. I have not been with a woman so close to my own species for nearly a hundred years. I am not willing to risk your wrath if I give in to my desires. But I can smell you. I know what you want. I know what you need. Say yes, Asri."

Her voice was close to panic. "He will kill us. I am his mistress, Robart, not just his enforcer."

Bobby's eyes widened, and then closed. His breath and heart both stilled for a moment. He hadn't known. He put his lips to her neck . . . one last time before he let her go.

But the taste made desire tighten his body. He slowly unwound one arm from hers and placed it close to her mouth.

"Tell me you can taste me and then ignore this feeling, Asri." He slid his sweated skin across her lips. It was as though an electric shock ran through her when she flicked her tongue from her mouth. Her heart jumped and pounded like a caged animal.

"It's like nothing I've ever . . . I . . . I can't . . . think, Robart."

"Nor can I. Right now, all I can do is feel." His voice lowered even further, to a hiss that raised the hair on her neck. "Some things are worth dying for, Asri." He put his lips to her throat, and then bit the skin lightly. She gasped and then whimpered. With a sudden movement that surprised him, she pushed backward quickly and he slipped inside her.

Their combined moan filled the room. Time stopped as they moved together. I could feel every thrust, hear her cries as he wrapped himself around her. She raised his weight until she was on her knees and then met every one of his movements until they were one body, one mind, one immense sensation.

Her cries as she climaxed hit him in the chest. I recognized the sensation, but it was new to him. He had hoped to hold out, to savor this experience, but his body wouldn't cooperate. When she went over, so did he. He thrust hard once, filling her, but it started another orgasm in her. His mind spun in a haze of pleasure as they climaxed together over and over, and the scent of the deepest jungle filled the air.

The memory, because that's what it had to be, fast forwarded to the bedroom. Bobby was miserable, waiting on the chair while Asri showered. She was terrified, angry with herself, and they were now late to pick me up and get to the airport. She was scrubbing with peppermint soap to try to erase the scent of their sex. He could smell it. Bobby knew he should, as well. He knew he must—for a thousand reasons, none of which made much sense to him at the moment.

He heard the water turn off and movement as

she stepped out of the shower and shut the curtain. He steeled himself and walked in the bathroom to take his turn with the peppermint soap. Asri had just finished combing her hair and she turned suddenly. She didn't notice him in the doorway. She hit him full in the chest with a grunt. The moment froze as their startled eyes met at the same moment their naked bodies did. Then the sheer power of physical need hit him once more and there was no thought, no words. He only remembered touching her waist with his hands, and then she was in his arms again. Her mouth found his. It was hot and hungry, taking his tongue inside and biting lightly. He lifted her up onto the countertop and was inside her before he could think, his arm . . ."

". . . *arm*, Giambrocco. LET GO OF MY ARM!"

Bobby's voice filtered through the haze in my mind, shredding it into curled ribbons of sound and motion that fell away slowly.

I heard Lucas speak. "We're going to have to break the fingers if we can't bring him to, Bobby. You're losing circulation in that hand."

I was back in the car, which was now stopped at the edge of a park. Bobby was trying to pry open my grip, and Lucas was helping from over the seat. They were as surprised as me that it hadn't worked so far.

I was very glad that Asri was busy holding onto whatever necklace she had under her shirt and sitting as far away from me as she could with wide eyes. She was crammed between the steering wheel and the door. Her knees were on the driver's seat and her back was pressed against the instrument panel. I really didn't want to touch her—ever. I *so* didn't want to see that same scene from the other side. Her eyes were wide, as though she was thinking the same thing. I would never look at those eyes the same way again, and it pissed me off. I let go of Bobby's hand like it burned me. I knew my eyes were wide and a little panicked.

The entire car reeked of hot and sour soup. My breath was coming in short gasps anyway from the . . . whatever the hell it had been, but the smell didn't help any.

"You had a vision, didn't you, Tony?" Lucas's voice was calm, but Bobby reared back so fast he hit his head on the car window.

I shook my head, trying to get the images out of my mind. "I really don't want to talk about it."

I turned my head as Asri was muttering something over and over. She was shaking her head with tiny little movements. Her eyes showed too much white.

"Dukun santet!" She said it louder this time while staring right at me. I knew an accusation when I heard it. I just didn't know the language.

Lucas shot an angry look at her. "Stop it." he snarled. The sound echoed through the car. Asri's mouth closed, but the fear didn't go away. Lucas closed his eyes briefly and when he spoke again, his voice was gentler. "He's not a black magician, Asri. Tony is an *attack victim*—that's all. His talents are probably just now becoming apparent. We already know he has second sight, so it *shouldn't* be any surprise to us that he could have foresight or some other gift—*should* it?"

Asri stopped her muttering and released the object under her shirt. She looked at me suspiciously, but her scent was the thick antifreeze of curiosity. "So you are saying he is a seer—a mystic?"

I winced, because a lot of things suddenly made sense. I prayed that Lucas would say no. I don't want to be some sort of freak.

Lucas sighed. "It looks like it. Sorry, Tony. I know it's hard to accept, but you've had a ton of magic thrown at you in the past few days. I guess whatever latent abilities you had decided to come out all at once. Maybe psychics run in your family. Either way, I'd say you're stuck with it."

"Is there any way to make it stop?" I was afraid I already knew the answer, but what the hell . . . it couldn't hurt to ask.

The three of them looked at me with something approaching pity, which didn't make me feel any better. I was also starting to realize that some of what the Duchess predicted was already happening. Just frigging *wonderful*.

Lucas took a deep breath. "There are people that can help you *control* the visions. But stop them?" He shook his head. Then he looked at me very seriously, with an edge of danger as though he knew just what I was thinking. "I'm going to send someone to see you in the next few days to start your training. Don't even *think* about ditching them or skipping town."

Damn. That was *just* what I had been thinking.

"Try not to touch anyone until then. You could be a danger to people until you get a handle on this. Don't worry about Sue, though. Oh, and don't tell anyone about the subject of the vision until you talk to one of the other seers. Just know that if you saw something that is yet to happen, the future is fluid. Sometimes things happen the way you see, and sometimes they don't. But people get weird, and there's no need to worry them unnecessarily." He turned and looked strongly at Bobby and Asri. "As for you two— *don't touch him* for the rest of the night, and keep him protected from other people for a few days."

"I think you can count on that," said Bobby, who was staring at his hand. It was still a little off-color from the rest of his arm. Asri only nodded.

"But . . . ," said Lucas, turning around in his seat and opening the door. "We have other things to do right now. Moonlight's burning, folks. Let's put on the feed bag. Bobby, Asri, see if you can take down an extra deer. I need a tribute for Nikoli. We'll put it in the trunk."

Asri turned to him and said indignantly. "You will do no such thing! I will *not* have blood soaked into my carpeting. The stain would never come out."

Again, Lucas's voice lowered to a deep rumble and he stared at Asri through narrowed eyes. A flow of magic headed Asri's way. It stopped right at the edge of her own aura. She couldn't help but feel it hovering. The hairs on her visible skin raised and the whites of her eyes showed once more. "You will do what you are *told*. I don't have time to argue with you. If you don't want to help Bobby hunt, you can wait in the car until we arrive with the game. I know that your people don't have to feed during the moon."

Asri forced her way past her fear of both Lucas and me and held up her chin. "If you hunt—I hunt. We must be quick, though. The snake and I do have certain *physical* limitations in the snow."

Oh, so now he's *the snake*. Guess they had a spat sometime before they got to my place. Or maybe I imagined the whole thing. Yeah right.

Asri left our group and found an ancient pine tree with boughs that draped to the ground. She parted the branches and stepped inside to undress. Good plan. I never again wanted to see her naked. I noticed that Bobby was staring after her longingly. I almost told him to go ahead and follow, but that would reveal what I had seen. I wasn't sure how he would handle knowing.

I had barely removed my socks and tucked them in my shoes when I heard a noise behind me. Lucas had already changed into a wolf. I was a little amazed that a four-year-old Sue had no fear of this animal. He was indeed pure white with blue eyes, but he would have towered over her. He stood to *my* waist.

"Were you even *wearing* clothes?" I held up my hand before he could respond. "No. Don't tell me. I don't want to know. Let's just get this over with. This has been a really bad day and I want it to be finished."

He smiled, a baring of sharp white teeth and pink gums. "Don't look so dour, Tony. It's not the end of the world. Let's just forget about how we got here and run under the moon for a bit." He shook himself, and the light dusting of snow on his fur filled the air like glitter. "We both need to eat and you have to admit, it's an amazing night."

That was one thing I agreed with him about. I took a deep breath of clean, cold air. Arctic wind blew snow from the tree branches through my hair. I felt the moonlight slather over my skin like thick oil and smelled the trees and the animals that waited in their depths. A thrill of excitement made my neck hairs stand on end.

I shivered with anticipation and whispered, "Let's do it."

Lucas removed his shield with a small movement of one paw. I saw the blue-white aurora disappear from around me and then the moon ground me into the snow. My scream became a howl as fur finally erupted from my skin and magic twisted my body. I felt Sue in the back of my mind again. She was at Pamela's house, and was laughing at a joke she was telling. The rush of magic gripped her for a moment and I could feel her shudder. A moment later, the world turned into a 50's photograph as color faded from my sight. I shook my head.

A crashing of panicked animals in the undergrowth made my eyes focus and heart pound. I fought not to chase down whatever had fled in fear from the sound of my howl. Lucas was staring in the same direction. Without even realizing we had communicated, we both took off at a run toward the noise.

Are you hunting? Oh, Tony. It's beautiful!

I followed Lucas across the sparkling carpet of white. Bobby and Asri headed the other direction, on separate paths, forcibly turning away from the prey we'd all heard.

With Sue seeing through my eyes, I soared across logs and skirted trees like I had with the pack. Sue was finally running with the white wolf, so many years after they'd first met, and I could feel her joy radiate through me. It made the snow sparkle brighter, made the sound of our paws racing over the snow more intense. I called out to Lucas as we passed the blackened log where I'd waited just two nights ago. "Have you hunted here before? You seem to know the way."

He turned his head briefly so that I could hear his response. "Oh, a long time ago. It wasn't a manicured park back then, just a small forest."

I heard a scurrying sound to my left and broke off. The prey was too small for two, and I figured that Lucas was perfectly capable of finding his own dinner—protocol be damned.

A swift flash of white dove into the undergrowth and I followed. I saw that Lucas had caught his own scent and was split off in the other direction. The jackrabbit was wearing his winter coat and was nearly invisible against the snow. My nose found him anyway, and I dove straight into the brush. It darted and zigged across the landscape, but I followed effortlessly. I could have caught it with Sazi speed, but it was more fun to chase it. Sue was exhilarated even with this slow speed. I skidded and bounced off rocks and stumps, my legs barreling across the snow. When I finally caught the jackrabbit, its body was still warm from the chase, and the scent of fear, and adrenaline gripped my mind like a drug. We both struggled to suppress our human reluctance to eating raw meat that was still twitching. But once my teeth broke through the skin, there was no more thought. The smell and the taste chased away any doubts. Soon there was only a pair of ears, three feet and some various entrails left to tell the tale of the hunt. But it wasn't enough. I was still hungry. I heard a noise and smelled another wolf to my right. I thought it was Lucas, but I couldn't tell for sure with the scent of the prey still filling my brain. I growled and stood over my kill protectively.

When the white wolf appeared, he had another rabbit in his mouth—this one a brown cottontail. He tossed his head and the rabbit sailed in an arc to land at my feet.

"What's this?" I asked.

"I found a nest. Go ahead and have this one, too." I

smelled black pepper in a burst. Why would he lie about that?

"After you eat, we can start to look for a deer for Nikoli. I haven't heard the other two for some time. They're probably eating, too."

I hoped they were just eating. Maybe I should take my time with the rabbit. I concentrated on the taste, instead of just wolfing it down—pun intended. I couldn't decide which one tasted better. Probably the cottontail. Sue was loathe to admit I was right. She hadn't minded eating the jackrabbit. They're not as cute as cottontails.

"LUCAS. TONY. Are you out there?" There was concern, but not quite panic, in Bobby's voice. It sounded from up above

"This way, Bobbo," I called. Lucas turned to watch as Bobby the python dropped his narrow head down from the first branch of a spruce, which always freaks me out a little.

"Did you find a deer?" asked Lucas.

"Not exactly."

He was leaving something out. I had finished my second rabbit in as many minutes and was ready for a new adventure. I huffed out a frosty breath. "What's up? You're not saying something."

"Probably because I don't know what *to* say. Asri says she's found a body."

Lucas and I both looked at each other warily. "Live or dead?"

"Dead and buried. But I can't smell it. She says it's down over twenty feet. Can she smell that deep?"

Lucas nodded his head. "Oh, easily. Even a regular Komodo can smell over thirty feet down. God only knows how deep a Sazi can scent meat."

"It's this way," he said and slithered down the trunk. He didn't move as quickly across the snow. His bulk made a wide, deep path that we'd have to cover later or some human was going to call a zoo when they found it.

Lucas stepped in front of me to stop me. "If you don't mind, Tony, I'd like to cut you off from Sue for a bit."

I felt my front legs lower into an aggressive stance. "*Why?*"

"Two reasons. First, it's a Wolven matter, and she's a civilian . . ."

I lowered my head just a bit farther. "Yeah? So am I. Your point?"

His power burned just a bit brighter and I could smell his annoyance. "You agreed to help find Barbara Herrera. That puts you in my ballpark. Until she's found, you're Wolven."

I growled angrily. So, Bobby's been checking in with his boss. These power plays and conspiracies were getting old. "Okay, let's make this really clear, Lucas, or whoever you are—Carmine told Bobby that *I* was in charge of the hunt for Babs. I agreed to help with the understanding that I *did not* answer to Bobby. Hence, I don't answer to *you.*"

Lucas stared at me for a moment, and I could see the burning blue light behind his eyes. He ignored my statement. "Reason *two*—if there *is* a dead body, Sue doesn't need to see it. She also doesn't need to *feel* what you will want to do to it. Think about it, Tony . . . I can't even guarantee my *own* reaction after so little meat."

Shit. I hadn't considered that. I'd only had a pair of rabbits for dinner. What *would* I do if I came upon a dead body? I'd studiously avoided any Family raids since I became a wolf for just this reason. It was how I'd gotten the whole "I *vant* to be alone" reputation. Before the wolf stuff, I did hits alone, but spent most of my time with the gang at Carmine's place.

I felt Sue in the back of my mind steeling herself. I'd told her once about a time when I'd killed a person in a mindless blur of blood and screams. I never did find all the pieces. It had given me nightmares for weeks. I wasn't sure she would be able to handle it.

I didn't even check with her. "Do it."

Tony you don't have to pro—

I felt her objection cut off as a solid shield of power severed our tie. The first thing I noticed is that I couldn't see Lucas's glow as well anymore. My nose wasn't as good, either. I was back to having to work to catch a person's emotions.

"Okay, Bobby. Lead the way."

Asri was standing in a small clearing near a massive red oak with few hardy leaves still clinging to its branches.

"Tell them what you told me, Asri," Bobby said when he was close enough.

"There's little to tell. We were hunting and reached this spot. I told Bobby that there was a body buried under here, and I thought it was a Sazi."

Lucas looked a little startled. "You can tell it's one of us?"

"I *think* it's one of us. My tongue is very cold. I'm not certain of much other than it's down about twenty or twenty-five feet."

"Is it a recent death?" Lucas's face took on a wary look, even in wolf form.

Asri cocked her head and slid a forked tongue between her lips. "It's odd you should ask that. I *should* be able to tell you, but I can't. It's as though it smells both of fresh meat and old bones. I am loathe to open a grave, but . . . I am curious."

Lucas lowered his nose to the snow and sniffed around for a few seconds. "Nope. My nose isn't up to the task, so we'll have to take Asri's word for it. Well, Bobby . . . Tony. We're all here because of a missing person. I hope it's not, but this might be our girl. With the ground frozen, I guess we'll have to go back to town for shovels. It would take us all night with our claws. Unless . . . *Asri?*"

He looked at her in such a way that it made her shudder. "As I said, I am *loathe* to open a grave, Alpha Santiago."

Blue eyes stared into slitted amber ones for a moment. Lucas's scent was a mix of frustration and a healthy dose of curiosity. Asri was determined and afraid. Bobby? Well, Bobby was just flat nervous all around. I personally didn't care whether we unburied the body or not. I was afraid it might be Babs. I wasn't sure what I would tell Carmine.

I guess Lucas decided that discretion was the better part of valor. "Could you dig down to within three or four feet of the body? I don't believe that the evil spirits could infect you at that distance. Tony and I can then open the grave."

Asri started slightly at his words, and so did the rest of us. Ah. It hadn't occurred to me that Asri might have much older beliefs than held by modern society—of spirits that follow the living to infect and turn them evil. Forcing her to dig all the way would be the equivalent of rape.

Her voice was soft and grateful. Ozone and warm musty air, like from a dryer vent, filled the space around her. She bowed her head slightly. "I will take you as far as I feel I can safely go. I thank you for your tolerance, Alpha Santiago." She turned before he could reply and flicked her tongue over the ground carefully. She nodded once as she found her spot and started to dig with amazing speed and strength. We moved back from the quickly growing hole that only moments before was clean white snow. Soon she was lost from sight. Only a tall plume of dirt told us of her progress.

I felt a warm flush race through me and Sue appeared in my head briefly. The steak had satisfied her and made her think of the perfect gift. Bright colors danced in my head and stained the darkness as she laughed with her friend. I never wanted to be without this connection ever again.

When Asri finally crawled out of the diagonal burrow, she was covered with a fine coating of rich brown earth. We all chuckled when she said, "Well, at least I'm finally warm—not as good as a long swim, but it will do."

I glanced into the dark hole as Lucas asked, "How much farther?"

Asri shook her body to remove some of dust, but then nestled into the large pile of warm earth when the wind started to howl. "The bones smell very decayed. There is little threat of spirits, so I was able to get you within a foot or two. The body will be straight ahead, so dig cautiously. Perhaps you won't have to completely disturb the person's final rest."

Lucas and I descended single file into the black pit. The path was an easy slope, and tall enough for our wolf bodies to stand upright.

"A light would be nice," I commented as we were swallowed by blackness.

"That's what you have a nose for. You need to learn to use it. But, if you think it will help . . ." He turn up his power until blue-white light chased away the black. There wasn't much to see, but I felt a little less claustrophobic.

"Much better," I said.

"We're close. Even I can smell it now." When he said it, I sniffed the air. I understood what he meant. There was a smell of death in the air. Asri had been correct. There was no meat, decayed or otherwise. Only the scent of bones remained. It didn't even make me salivate.

"So, I guess it's not Babs."

"Probably not," he acknowledged. "But it's a Sazi, so we still need to find out why he or she is here."

"How can you tell it's a Sazi? All I can smell is bones."

"As I said earlier, Tony, you need to start using your nose. Close your eyes and tell me what you smell."

I did as instructed. I'd been avoiding learning how to use my animal senses. It's always been a reminder that I'm not human anymore. But if I was going to be living here, with a pack, I suppose I need to start to use my nose and ears to keep myself out of trouble.

I closed my eyes and took a deep, slow breath. Then another set of short inhales as I moved my head from side to side. Lucas waited tolerantly while I oriented myself.

"Well, the bones seem . . ."

The big white wolf shook his head. "Don't focus on the body, Tony. Just tell me *everything* you smell. There's soil, isn't there? Rotting leaves?"

Oh. Maybe that's been my problem all along—I'm trying to focus and keep missing things. "Okay. Well, there's soil—but it's not just dirt." I opened my eyes and tried to concentrate on the individual wisps of color that rose from a thousand tiny points. It was a kaleidoscope of watercolors in the blackness.

"Go on," urged Lucas.

"Asri ate some bugs and worms along the way. I can tell where there was an insect that was removed as she dug. I can smell her spit."

"Good. Keep going."

I closed my eyes again. It was harder to scent things without Sue in my head. I hadn't realized how much being connected with her had helped my nose. "There are tree roots all around us—lots of pine and oak. There's . . ."

"Can you smell me or you?" Lucas interrupted.

"Well, of course," I snarled.

His shoulder moved in a version of a shrug. "You didn't say so."

I shook my head in exasperation. "Fine, you smell like watermelon and grass . . ."

His teeth appeared in a burst of white in the darkness. "Close, but no cigar. Not watermelon and not just grass. My scent is cactus tunas and buffalo grass."

"Cactus *what?*"

"Tunas. The fruit of a prickly pear cactus is called a *tuna.* They do smell a lot like watermelon, I admit, but it's the fine distinctions that are important in our world, Tony. If you need to compare scents to something your human mind can grasp, that's fine—for awhile. But if that's how you want to cope, then you need to get a better range of scents in your head for comparison. It might be important someday when you least expect it. You'll find that many females smell like flowers, and males like grasses or trees."

I huffed a bit of breath in a chuckle. "And then there are the three hundred pound bald guys with Uzis that smell like cherry limeade."

Lucas gave a short bark, and his tailed wagged for a moment. "There *are* those. But really, Tony, as you live years, or decades, longer than humans, you'll need to start to recognize scents before faces. We Sazi change faces all the time to avoid discovery. But if you can't tell the difference between watermelon and cactus tunas, you'll be easy prey for your enemies. Trust me when I say that you *will* have enemies. It's inevitable. Now, what can you smell about the body, without digging any closer?"

I closed my eyes once more and followed the scent of bones. I dismissed from my mind the trees, the bugs, the rich black humus and found the thin thread of scent to the bones of . . ."

"Wait. Those are *animal* bones." I took another sniff. "No, then again . . ."

"Ah, you got it at last," Lucas said with a satisfied nod of his head. *"That's* how you know it's a Sazi. We smell of both animal and human after we die. This is why the depth of the burial is important. Someone *knew* they were burying a Sazi and put it at a depth that most other Sazi couldn't scent the very obvious difference. Which leaves the question—why bury someone this deep unless you don't want it found? Without Asri's tongue, we *wouldn't* have found it. That makes me suspicious enough to keep digging. You're learning one of the primary tools of an investigator."

I started at his phrasing because it was something that was nibbling at the back of my mind. Why would he care if I learned these things? I had no plans to become an investigator.

"But just because it's a Sazi doesn't mean that it's something recent or has anything to do with Babs."

"Could have been here for centuries." Bobby's voice surprised me enough that I banged my head on the roof of the cave. I was concentrating on the bones so I hadn't noticed him slip down the hole. He noticed us both jump and flicked his tongue. "I got tired of waiting for you guys out in the snow. At least it's warm down here."

I could see Lucas shake his head. "Not centuries. It's not *that* old."

"And I suppose you've smelled centuries-dead Sazis before?"

This time, both Lucas and Bobby laughed—a staccato bark and a rich, throaty hiss. "Hell, I've danced on the graves of centuries-dead Sazi, Tony." Lucas exclaimed. "I've outlived an awful lot of our kind. Yeah, I know the difference. Someday you will too."

I decided not to dwell on that bit of knowledge. "I would think that it would have to be hand buried. Heavy equipment would be too noticeable in the park. How many people would it take? Or are there other good diggers, like Asri, among the Sazi?"

Bobby's voice was thoughtful. The laughter and citrus in the air was suddenly gone, replaced by determination's hot metal. "Wolves could—but it would take a pack a day or more to dig and then cover it. Again, too noticeable."

"Asri's the only monitor lizard, to my knowledge," said Lucas, who also now smelled serious and determined. "There are the badgers, but Nigel's the last, and he's never been to America. *I've never forgiven the colonies for their treachery, old boy. I am and will remain a loyal subject.*" He did a great impression of a snooty British royalist.

Bobby laughed. "That's Nigel, all right. No, he'd never sully his honor by digging on American soil."

I stared at the wall of dirt and roots in front of us. "Bears? Do they dig?"

"They *can.*" Lucas mused. "But Nikoli would know if there was a bear in his territory. I don't suppose he mentioned any visitors to you, Bobby?"

I think the hiss behind me was supposed to be laughter. His scent was bitter oranges. "Hardly. You know Nikoli—cards always close to his ever-present vest. But I haven't smelled any since I've been here."

I stepped forward, squeezing my way past Lucas. I started to dig sideways to open the space more so that all of us could stand, albeit closely. "Okay, for the moment, let's leave the *how* alone. Maybe uncovering the body will give us the *who* and the *why.*"

Lucas nodded and likewise starting his front feet moving to open more territory. Dirt flew between our legs to disappear behind.

"Watch it, people." exclaimed Bobby. I heard him spitting. "Some of us are at ground level here."

"Maybe you should wait outside until we clear more space."

"Nah, I've got a better idea." I saw a flash of green from the corner of my eye. I turned my head to see that Bobby was back in human form. His dark skin blended almost perfectly with the rich earth. He moved his upper body forward so that he was between me and Lucas. He was very careful not to touch me at all, which made him crowd the big white wolf. "I'll start to uncover the body. It'll be faster."

By working together, we opened a much larger space. Bobby could now kneel easily without touching us. He had succeeded in carefully removing dirt around the body. Actually, it was a skeleton, and badly desiccated.

Bobby's eyes worked really well in the dark. "Look at these bones. They're almost dust. It's *got* to have been here a couple of centuries, at least, I think your nose needs a tune-up, Boss." He reached forward and pressed on a portion of the skull. It cracked easily and a few small pieces fell to the dirt underfoot.

I eased forward and used the light radiating from he and Lucas to look more closely. "Nope. I have to agree with Lucas." I knew they wouldn't be able to see it, but I could. "The dirt is still loose and fluffy inside the rib cage. It's not compacted as though it's been here years. And feel how easy it's been to open this hole? It should be tearing up your fingernails. This has been dug up recently. I won't say that the *skeleton's* not old, though."

"Hey! I just found something." Bobby said. His finger pulled back sharply. Lucas stopped digging and we both came over to watch.

"I can't see a damn thing down here. It smells like silver, though." Lucas complained. "Tony, what is it?"

I reached my nose forward and stared at the object Bobby had uncovered. It was a small medallion on a chain. It was around the skeleton's neck and was buried slightly in the soil between the ribs. I nudged it with my nose and jerked back when the metal burned. It must be why Bobby pulled back, too.

"Ow. It *is* silver. Bobby, if you reach forward and down, you can unhook the chain without touching the medallion. The chain's just regular steel. Let's get a better look at it. It looks like there's a symbol or letter on it. I'm not up on Russian, but it looks Cyrillic."

Bobby hesitated. He smelled nervous. "I don't like this, guys. Grave robbing isn't a very reputable activity in my culture, either."

"This is a *murder* investigation, gentlemen." Lucas's voice was firm. "Let's just do our job and try to be as respectful as possible."

He was right. I moved closer. "We'll have to get the body fully out if we're going to see what it died of. We can't even tell if it's male or female yet. There might be other clues, as well. Look, Bobby, if you don't want to, I'll do it. I don't have any particular religious convictions. Someone will have to turn me back human, though, if that's possible."

Lucas shook his head. "I don't recommend the process. You'd be regretting it for days. No, I think that we should get the medallion out for Asri to look at. She might be able to get a scent from the chain or metal. She's been with Nikoli over fifty years. She should recognize a scent if the person was a local."

Bobby reluctantly allowed me to guide him to the necklace clasp. As we opened the body, I started to notice a growing odor in the cave.

"Do you smell that? Bobby, isn't that—"

He sneezed at the same moment. "Aw, man. That's that

same scent from Carmine's house. Man, that's nasty. Let's not dig in any further unless we *have* to."

Lucas's face took on a wary look, but he smelled confused. "You smelled *this* scent at Carmine's?"

"Yeah." I had to turn my nose away from the hole. "God, what *is* that stuff?"

Lucas's eyes narrowed and he stared at the hole while sniffing the air. "Something about that scent . . ."

"You recognize it?" Bobby asked with interest.

"It's . . . Where *did* I smell it? And under what circumstance?" He shook his head in annoyance. "I'll have to work on it. All I remember is that it was a *long* time ago."

It took a little tugging, but finally the medallion dropped to the floor of the cave.

"It's encased in leather," I commented. "The whole back side of the silver is covered."

"If a Sazi wore it as a necklace, that would make sense," Lucas replied. "Do you get anything off it now that it's out of the ground?"

Bobby picked up the necklace easily. I guess once it was out of the grave, he had no problems. I saw a small wisp of smoke and a hissing sound as he touched one finger to the metal front. "Definitely silver—nearly pure."

"So, what? You can tell the silver content somehow?"

He shrugged dismissively. "Sure. It's like telling whether you're eating a bell pepper or a habanero. How bad it burns tells you how potent it is." He turned over the necklace and reached out his tongue. "I almost hate to do this. The taste of that stuff is worse than the smell. But . . . that's the life of a Wolven agent." He touched his tongue repeatedly to the dirt-encrusted leather backing in tiny little movements. He did the whole swaying thing with his upper body again—like a cobra in front of the flute. "Definitely female. Wolf. Long hair."

"Whoa, whoa." laughed Lucas. "You can tell the *hair length* from your tongue? Give me a break, Bobby."

Bobby gave him a withering look. "No, I can tell the hair length because one caught in the chain got wrapped around my tongue."

He reached up to remove it when Lucas nudged him with his head. "Hang on to it, Bobby. It might not be the *victim's* hair."

Bobby stopped short and carefully unwound the hair from his tongue. He gripped it tight in his hand. "Let's get topside so I can see what we've got."

Lucas and I headed back up the path, single-file, with Bobby taking the rear. He had to remain in human form to hold the necklace, so it took many minutes for him to wiggle his way up without using his hands. By the time he was out in the cold with us, he was moving *really* slow. Each step seemed an effort. Asri had dug into her pile of dirt but poked out her head enough to see us exit the hole. Lucas turned human in a flash of blue-white light and took the chain and hair from Bobby.

"Go get dressed, Agent. You need to warm up." Bobby nodded slowly, like cold molasses pouring. He was even too cold to shiver. His skin had a faint blue hue that was even darker than normal. He needed to warm up pretty quick, all right.

He held out the medallion to Asri. "Do you recognize this?"

She was moving nearly as slowly as he was. The flashes of her tongue only came about once every half minute. She moved her head a little further out of her burrow and stared at the necklace. A burst of fear accompanied her frenzied flight out of the hole. She turned human in a flash and stood naked in the cold. She didn't seem to notice it. She had grabbed the necklace from Lucas's hand and was staring at in horror. Fear approaching panic, along with a sudden burst of anger, made the air heavy with scent.

"But this . . . it's not *possible!*"

"You recognize it, then?"

She ignored his question that darted into the sloping

hole. When she returned to the surface, she was pale and shaking. No more burnt coffee. There was only ammonia-laden hot and sour soup drifting from her.

"Do you recognize the body, Asri?" Lucas had taken the opportunity to step behind a tree and slip into the illusion of a pair of jeans and a sweater. Or maybe there was one hidden back there. I wasn't about to go up and check to see if there was cloth between my nose and his skin. Lucas asked the question to the shaken woman very slowly.

"It's *Mila*," she whispered. "But it *can't* be Mila. She's only been gone—what is it, Tony? Less than two weeks?" She turned to me for confirmation, but I didn't know what she meant.

Then something sparked my memory. The first day I'd arrived, Nikoli was saying his good-byes to a lovely woman with long black hair who was, if I remember, leaving to visit family in Russia. Was her name Mila?

"Was she the woman I met when I was just arriving? Nikoli's wife?"

"Mistress," corrected Asri, "But yes—Ludmila Symslova was the woman you probably met. She went to visit her family outside of Murmansk. She can't have wound up as a crumbling skeleton in the woods in two weeks!" She looked to Lucas with a frantic plea. "Can she?"

Chapter 13

IT WAS NEARLY dawn when we arrived back at my apartment building. Asri had been forced to go sit in the running car with Bobby while Lucas and I had re-buried the body. Fortunately, it started to snow hard about half way through, so any sign of our presence was erased by the time we left.

All four of us were exhausted, but none more than Bobby. He was sacked out in the back seat by the time we'd gotten to the car. I wasn't surprised. He'd used a lot of juice on me at Carmine's and had been going all day long. I had just hopped in the seat when I suddenly changed back to human form. It was a little early—being before dawn, but the rules seem to be different every month. I gratefully put on my clothes.

I couldn't even wake Bobby up to put on his seatbelt, so I did it for him. Icy roads with no seat belts might test even a Sazi's ability to heal.

"Alpha Santiago," Asri asked as we approached the stockyards, "Will you be accompanying me back to the hotel to meet with Nikoli?" She was slurring her words slightly, and her face was drawn with exhaustion. She must be beat from all the digging and the stress of knowing the deceased.

Lucas had been sitting quietly for most of the trip. He

occasionally tapped his finger on the dashboard or made small hand gestures that told me he was thinking hard. The hot metal smell of determination drifted over the seat with the warm air from the heater. He shook his head. "I think we'd all better get some rest first. Nikoli will want answers, and I don't have any yet. I also don't have a tribute, which won't be appreciated. If you would be so kind, Ms. Kho, please give my apologies to Nikoli and tell him that I will come by in the late morning."

She double-parked the car at the curb by the door to my apartment. Both Lucas and I had to help Bobby up the steps. I hadn't realized that the cold made him this bad, but Lucas didn't seem alarmed, so I guess it was normal.

Sue opened the door when she saw us coming. She waved as Asri drove away, but I don't think the dragon noticed.

"I'm so glad you're home. I was getting worried. The weatherman said we're in for a bad storm." She looked at Bobby closely. "Is he okay? He looks sick."

"Just cold. He's a reptile—cold weather doesn't agree with him," said Lucas. We moved Bobby to the couch and put his legs up. He mumbled his thanks and turned to face the wall. He was snoring before Sue found a blanket to cover him.

Lucas had collapsed into the chair where I normally sit, so I pulled up a kitchen chair and gathered Sue into my lap to snuggle. I raised my head because a delightful odor was wafting from the kitchen. "Do I smell frying eggs?"

"I was starting some breakfast. I got a call from Nikoli while you were gone. He's sending a car to pick me up at seven o'clock so I can interview for the job at his restaurant."

It occurred to me that the shield was still in place. I should have known about the interview. "Lucas? Would you mind?"

I saw him open his eyes briefly and see me point at my own head. "Oh. Sure, sorry." He flipped a finger, and my mind was suddenly awash with colors and sound and motion. I smiled tiredly as I felt Sue's happiness and nervousness about the interview.

"You'll do fine." I pulled her close against me. Her hair tickled my nose.

She looked at me and smiled. "You always have faith in me. How do you do that?"

Lucas's nose suddenly raised as though he had just come to. "Did you say *food*?" He looked at Sue pathetically. "Is there any chance . . . ? I haven't had a bite since yesterday."

Okay, now I knew that he lied about the rabbit "nest." But why would he give me his dinner?

He owed you damages, Tony. I furrowed my brow at Sue's mental comment and glanced at her. *He didn't realize he hurt you holding back the moon. The rabbit was an apology. Don't make a big deal about it, though.*

Ah, I understood pride. I stood. "Let's see if we can't find you some dinner."

Sue stood up and ran a slow finger down my cheek. The wash of warmth and pleasure made me gasp and fight not to pull her back into my arms. She jerked back her hand when she felt the same thing.

"No. You just sit, Tony. I've got just the *perfect* thing for Lucas."

She returned in a moment. A dinner plate covered with foil was in her hands. On top was a sandwich on white bread. She put a finger to her lips when I shot her a questioning look. With a flourish, she held the sandwich over Lucas's shoulder so it was in front of his face.

His nose found it first, and his eyes opened slowly. A smile and a chuckle followed, and he reached out a hand to grab the sandwich.

"Bologna on white bread with ketchup. You remembered." He sank his teeth into the thick sandwich happily. It must have been the entire package for as much meat as there was. If he had still been a wolf, he would be wagging. Sue was grinning from ear to ear. The room was suddenly rife with with oranges and tangerines. Citrus and bologna. Weird.

"I can't believe you *like* bologna," I commented with a grimace. "Yecch."

"Acquired taste." He licked the ketchup from his fingers. "It's amazing what you'll eat when you're starved. Sometimes it sticks with you."

He turned and looked up at Sue warmly. "You're a doll, Sue. Got another under that foil?"

"Actually," she said with chagrin. "The sandwich was sort of a joke. I just picked up one pack to be funny. I figured you'd laugh and then I'd throw it out." She held out the plate covered with foil. "*This* is actually your dinner. I didn't have any gift wrap to make it an actual present. I only found out you'd be coming before most of the shops closed."

He took the plate from her curiously and thick antifreeze joined the citrus. He lifted up one corner of the foil and sniffed delicately. His face took on an enraptured look and something close to lust filled the air.

"Ohhhh," he said huskily, "Is this what I think it is?"

Sue nodded happily. "Buffalo rump roast. I remember someone in Boulder saying it was your favorite. I had to go to four meat stores before I found one. Is it okay? I left it out so it would be at room temperature, but I can toss it in the oven if you want."

He held up one hand sharply. "No. This is fine. This is *wonderful!*" He stood in one fluid movement and folded the foil back under. "But I'd better eat it at the table. If I open it now, I'd get blood all over your furniture. Care to join me, Tony? Ever had buffalo?"

I shook my head and stood to follow. I leaned over Bobby to ask if he wanted to join us, but he was out cold. Well, maybe later.

Lucas was already digging in when I swung open the door to the kitchen. He was using a large carving knife to cut massive slices from the roast. Then he used the same knife to cut the meat into strips before plopping them in his mouth with the fork. He chewed slowly, savoring the meat.

I sat down and Sue grabbed another plate and a fork. I'd reached across to stab one of the slices when a low growl stopped me. I looked across to see Lucas's eyes glazed slightly. His teeth bared in a an angry snarl and magic filled the room. Sue gasped and I froze in place. I could feel my heart slow and my breath still as I waited. I'd been in this situation plenty of times—where a dangerous person hovers on the brink of being *deadly*. His scent turned to burning coffee and adrenaline. I continued to stare calmly, but all the while planning what I would do if he pounced. I understood blood lust. It was *his* kill and he'd fight to keep it. Been there, done that. I guess sometimes even the big dogs can't fight down the animal inside.

We stared at each other for what seemed like an hour, but was probably only a few seconds. Then Lucas shook his head as if to clear it, and closed his eyes. When he opened them again, the glow was gone and he seemed in control. He shivered involuntarily and took another bite of buffalo. Ozone filled the air to blend with the blood on the plate.

"Wow. Sorry, guys. It's been awhile since *that's* happened. Guess I'm a little more stressed than I thought."

I slowly moved back my hand, leaving the fork in the meat on his plate. I tried to act nonchalant, but it was a lie. I wasn't up to a battle with this guy without some major weaponry, and I knew it.

"No problem. It happens to the best of us," I said quietly.

He glanced down to see that I had left the slice on his plate, and gave an exasperated sigh. "I *invited* you to join me, Tony—the moon notwithstanding." He picked up the fork, still stabbed in the meat, and put the slice on my plate.

I eyed the bleeding meat hungrily but warily. "You're *sure*? You're not going to go all wolf and pounce on me when I take a bite, are you? 'Cause I can eat something else."

He waved off my objections and shook his head, but didn't respond because he was chewing.

I decided to take him at his word. I picked up the whole slice and rolled it into a tube before biting into it. Oh, man. Now I understood why he'd growled.

The taste was heavy and gamey, but sweet and sultry all at once. I chewed with the same rapture as Lucas, while Sue looked on with a smile. I licked off my fingers and hoped I could steal another bite.

"I take it that I should add buffalo to our menu options?" she asked with a wry smile "It's pretty pricey."

"Oh, stock up on this all right. Cost be damned."

Lucas held up a piece on his fork before sticking it in his mouth. "It used to be that you could hunt down one big bull and have it feed the whole pack for all three days of the moon. But they're federally protected now, so we switched to deer and elk. Pity—you should taste the wild ones. It's like night and day. But this is good, don't get me wrong."

He glanced at my raised brows and hopeful expression, and nodded. "Go ahead and have another bite. I get the rest, though. You already had a couple of rabbits, remember?"

I glanced at the rapidly diminishing roast. *Discretion, Tony,* I ordered myself. I shook my head. "Nah. But Bobby should try this. Let me go drag his lazy ass off the couch."

Lucas nodded. "I'll save him a slice—for a few minutes. If he snoozes too long, though . . ."

I walked into the next room. Bobby hadn't moved from where he lay, facing the wall. I slowed as I reached him, listening. I couldn't hear him snoring. Hell, I couldn't even hear him breathing, and his scent was all wrong. What the—?

I took the last two steps at high speed, and turned him over. His eyes were closed, and his jaw slack. I put a finger on the artery in his neck. He barely had a pulse. I opened one eyelid to find that his pupil was fully dilated, and it wasn't the contact lens. Shit!

"Lucas!" I yelled. "We've got trouble!"

Lucas came racing from the kitchen, with Sue on his heels. He was still wearing a napkin tucked into the front of his sweater. I guess there really were clothes on him.

"What's up?" he asked.

"Something's wrong with Bobby. He's barely breathing."

He moved closer to the couch and I let him take my place. He did all the same things, except he also opened his mouth to reveal a swollen and black tongue.

"What the hell did *that?*" I exclaimed.

"Must be whatever was on that medallion. Where is it, anyway?"

I checked my pockets and then Bobby's coat. "Still in the car, I guess. Is it some sort of poison?"

Lucas shook his head. His frustration and fear beat at my nose. "Poison has no effect on Bobby. He's immune to practically everything."

"Not this," I said wryly. "Should I call the lair? Lelya helped heal Sue earlier today."

"Nikoli's mother? No. She's not up to this sort of thing. We need a real healer." He snapped his fingers suddenly. "My wife is going to be at a medical conference downtown." He checked his watch. "They should just be sitting down to the opening breakfast. It's at the McCormick Place Conference Center. Do you know how to get there, Tony?"

I furrowed my brow. "Why send *me*? I've never even met your wife."

"Because I have to stay here with Bobby. I'm not a healer, but I've got a lot of power. I can feed some magic into him to keep him alive for a bit. You can't." He removed his wallet from a back pocket and withdrew a photo. A stunning woman in her twenties stared out at me. Her silver-blonde hair was long and loose and the blue eyes were sultry. A cupid's bow mouth smiled warmly out from her slender face. While her features were similar to

Linda, she looked nothing like her. This was a woman who was supermodel quality. Either Lucas was robbing the cradle, or the picture was decades old. It was useless.

He must have caught my disbelieving look, or maybe my scent. I can't smell my own emotions worth a damn. I could smell his, however. He smelled of cinnamon and baking bread, along with oranges. It was obvious he was smitten with her, and was amused by my reaction.

"This is Tatya—*Dr.* Tatiana Santiago. No, it's not an old picture. She really *is* still this gorgeous after thirty years and a half dozen children. She'll be easy to spot— especially for *you*."

"You've only been married for thirty years, and you're *how* old?"

He chortled. "None of your damn business. I wasn't the marrying kind, but you don't get much of a choice when you meet your mate. *Do you?*"

I grinned. Yep, he had me there. I looked at the picture, memorizing the face. I wondered about the "especially for you" comment, until it occurred to me that she was Sazi. I would be able to see her glow. There couldn't be many glowing women at a medical conference. He was right that he needed to stay here with Bobby, and Sue had her interview to attend.

I'm not leaving Bobby. I heard Sue exclaim in my head.

"You have to, Sue," I replied out loud. Lucas seemed to know what was being discussed, so he ignored us. "There's nothing you can do here, and we don't want to piss off Nikoli again, do we?"

I looked at her strongly, willing her to remember the events of just a day ago. She started and then stared at me with understanding.

She paled slightly and her reply was quiet. "No, we don't. I think I should probably keep my appointment after all."

She pulled her purse from a dining room chair and removed a set of keys. She wound off a pair of car keys from the ring. "There's a white Honda out front. It's old, but it runs. Alena dropped it by while you were out. She said it was a gift from the parents of the kids for taking advantage of me. I tried to object, but she insisted. She said Nikoli ordered them to give it to me. I guess I'm stuck with it."

A Honda. Gee, how . . . *suburban.* Oh, well. Any car was better than none. But I would be buying something more suitable with the gold very soon. I glanced at my watch. It was almost seven. "You need to get ready, Sue. The car will be here for you soon. Sure you don't need anything, Lucas?"

He shook his head. He'd gotten a washcloth from the bathroom and was wiping Bobby's face down with steaming hot water. The water, and the massive surge of power that lit up the whole side of the room, seemed to be helping a bit. Bobby was moving now, writhing in obvious pain, but even that was better than comatose. "No, just hurry back with Tatya. I have it on reliable authority that she has a green aura."

On the way out the door, I spotted a small object on the table. I picked up the cell phone and tucked it in my pocket. The drive would give me a chance to get another problem out of the way.

Once I was stopped at the next light, I turned on the cell and glanced at the screen as the phone number of the unit flashed. I wrote down the area code and prefix on a scrap of paper from my wallet. Scotty had already given me the last four on his note.

The phone rang only once. "Hello?" The voice was quick and high, a sign that he'd been waiting on pins and needles for my call.

"What in the hell do you think you're doing, kid?" I kept my voice low and menacing. We'd talk about breaking into my house when I saw him face to face.

The voice dropped from nervous to sullen. I guess he

didn't expect an immediate reprimand. "You promised to train me. That guy Leone put me with is *useless.*"

That surprised me. Joey isn't up to my level, but he's an excellent shot. I kept my mouth shut, though, trying to draw him out.

"I mean—all he's had me doing is cleaning guns for the past three weeks. We've only gone out to the range *once* since you left. I cleaned his clock on all of the targets. I think it pissed him off. So, I decided to find you. I knew that they wouldn't be able to take *you* out, Mr. G. You had to have gone underground. All I had to do was wait around Leone's fortress long enough, and you'd show up or some-one would lead me to you."

I was impressed in spite of my self. If Scotty had managed to hang around Carmine's for seven weeks without being caught he had to have *some* talent in camouflage.

That's not what I said, though. "If you don't get the hell out of Chicago, I'll track you down and *remove* you myself." I couldn't afford for him to stay here. I wouldn't be surprised if Sommers was keeping an eye on the kid. It might be known that we'd met with him before the Prezza hit. That would paint a pretty target on his back for surveillance.

His next words surprised me. His voice was a little nervous, but grew in confidence as he spoke. "No you won't. I've got you by the balls, man. This time, you're going to do what *I* want."

I chuckled darkly as I drove slowly down the busy city street. Traffic was a mess with the snowfall. "Big words, kid. Why do you think *that?*"

I could suddenly feel Sue in the back of my mind. I was blocking her a bit because I knew she wouldn't want to hear Scotty's voice again. But I could feel that she had gotten the job. It was a bookkeeping job, all right—at a fast food restaurant just down the block. She could walk to work if she wanted. She was to start the next day at eight o'clock sharp. She was back at the house, and Bobby wasn't looking good.

I could hear her whisper in my head. *Lucas says to hurry.*

I was hurrying as fast as I could through rush hour traffic, at about the pace of a three-legged turtle. Fortunately, I could see the conference center up ahead.

Scotty was stalling, trying to decide whether to ante up. When he finally spoke his words made me swear internally. "I've got pictures. I've been following you for days. You at some hotel by the stockyards. You and that black guy in Leone's library. The prints are dated and timed by the camera. I gave them to a friend for safekeeping."

I suspected that I knew who that *friend* was. I decided to string him along; make him think didn't mean anything to me.

"I suppose that if you don't call her in twenty-four hours, or something like that, she's got orders to take them to the cops. And you think they'll lock me up for years. Is that the best you can do?"

He was taken aback, but recovered quickly. "It's pretty damn good, and you know it! All you have to do for the negatives to disappear is teach me stuff—*useful* stuff. It's no skin off your nose."

He was right. It wasn't any trouble, and I would be willing to do it under normal circumstances. But not by blackmail. "Okay, kid. Let me think about it for a bit. I'm on my way to pick up someone downtown." I glanced at my watch. It was nearly eight o'clock, so I had to hurry. "I'll call you back between one and two this afternoon to tell you my decision." I didn't wait for a reply. I hit the disconnect button, and immediately dialed another number. Hey, might as well use the minutes that he'd so kindly paid for.

"Go ahead," said a familiar baritone. That's Carmine. No time, or inclination, for pleasantries.

"We've got a body up here," I told him. "Same M.O. as Babs, with the smell and all. No sign of our girl yet, good or bad. But Bobby's down. Something weird, and I mean *weird*— even for these guys. I'm on my way to get a special doctor. I'm still on top of things, though. Wanted you to know."

"Good. Keep me informed. Anything else?"

"Yeah. I need a favor. Remember the girl—Sally?"

I knew he'd remember. He'd met with her a couple of times during the plans for the hit on the player from Atlantic City.

"Yeah? So?"

"Pick her up and hold her. Nice and safe; not a scratch. But search her and her place."

His voice grew shrewd. He knows that I don't ask things without a purpose. "What are we looking for?"

"Photos. Of me. With *you*."

"Dated?"

I didn't bother to reply. The silence said it all.

"Fuck!" He spit the word. He doesn't swear unless he's really irritated. He couldn't afford those photos any more than I could.

"Exactly. But I need it done before noon."

"Who's holding the reins? Why don't we just take her out?"

I shrugged my shoulder up to hold the phone so I could park in a space that conveniently opened right in front of the front door. I had to wait while the other driver took three tries to get into traffic. His tires kept slipping in the slush.

"Don't know if she has the *only* negatives. The kid's here in Chicago. Apparently, Joey didn't treat him right. Had him doing clean-up instead of shooting. The kid swears he's already better than Joey and Joey got pissy about it."

Carmine's voice lowered thoughtfully. "I wondered about that. Mike mentioned that the kid was really good, but Joey said he was crap. It might be time to remind Joey of his place and what happens when pride gets in the way of following orders. You might also get your wish about taking care of the kid, Tony. It's a bad precedent."

"Yeah, maybe. But I think he's still salvageable. It sounds like he could be my replacement if he learns some respect. So, you'll take care of it?"

"Yeah. I'll take care of it." I could tell by his voice that he wasn't happy: with Joey, and with Scotty. In this mood he was even more dangerous than usual.

"Call me when it's done." I gave him the number and waited while he wrote it down.

"She'll be picked up right now. I'll get on the horn with Marvin. He's wandering around down there anyway."

"*Carmine,*" I said warningly. The only reason Marvin would be *wandering* was if Carmine hadn't stopped looking for the kidnapper.

His voice was placating. "Just a precaution. It's not active, just defensive. If they can take Babs, we need to keep our nose to the ground."

Uh, huh. Right. But that reminded me, "Hey, once Bobby is up and around, I'm going to send him over with a woman who's got some *special* talents. She's got a nose that won't quit. Found the body up here by scent alone over twenty feet down."

His voice sounded startled. "Well, hell. Send her over. Maybe she can find something everyone else has missed. You'll vouch for her?"

I growled slightly as I turned off the ignition and pocketed the keys. "I don't *like* her, but she's good. Name's Asri Kho—Indonesian. She's meaner than hell, so don't piss her off. I don't know that she won't consider your guys expendable. Hey, I've got to go before I miss my contact."

"I'll call you back in a few minutes when we have the girl."

It was three minutes to eight by my watch as I bolted through the front door to the convention center. A sign directed me to the early-bird breakfast. The first speaker was to start in an adjoining room in a few minutes.

I walked in the dining room. Most of the tables were full of talking men and women. A few stray people were still filling plates at a long buffet at the front of the room. I scanned the crowd, looking for the gorgeous blonde, to no avail. So, I concentrated with my—what did he call it?—oh, yeah, *second sight*. A warm golden blur appeared at a table in the far corner, but I couldn't see the person. He or she was shorter than the others at the table. And, hadn't Lucas said Tatya's aura was green?

I glanced up as an announcement came over the speaker in the corner. "Will the attendees for *Advancements in Mitochondrial DNA in Criminal Law Enforcement* please report to the Sierra Room. That's *Mitochondrial DNA* on the Atrium Level—Sierra Room. Thank you."

People began to stand and gather their belongings. My Sazi was one of them. It was a woman, but not the one in the photo. This one was very short, probably not up to my collarbone. She was a stocky sort of slender. Her short blonde hair framed a round face that was very no-nonsense and obviously middle-aged. But when she smiled and laughed with her companions, she seemed very young. Which one was the illusion?

She headed my way and I ducked behind a plastic plant and appeared to be looking for something in my pockets. It was too crowded to approach her. I'd have to wait until she was by herself. I followed at a distance, but even then, she stopped to look around her suspiciously. Her nostrils flared briefly and she excused herself from her companions to head down the hallway to the women's bathroom. I waited until she was completely inside before I followed.

A few moments later, I heard a familiar roaring sound, followed by water running in the sink. I reached for my weapon. I'd left the gun in the car. I'd been right that they would wand for metal. But they hadn't found the ceramic knife with deer antler hilt tucked into a pocket inside my boot. I removed it. I hoped she would come peacefully, but she *would* come. Bobby's life might depend on it.

She stepped out of the room, apparently knowing that someone would be waiting for her. I was surprised for only a millisecond when she raced a fist toward my face with Sazi speed. I grabbed the hand, stopping it cold, and then the world disappeared again.

The flickering gas lamps on the wall held the darkness of the powder room at bay. I opened the door and exited the room, and looked up into the smiling face of my companion.

"Are you recovered then, Madame?"

My words were heavily accented French. "Just a bit faint. Eet is zees . . . zees corset. Mon dieu! Why do your American women allow such discomfort?"

The gentleman seemed surprised by the strength of her comment. "But they are high fashion, are they not, Madame, even in France?"

She let out a shallow, exasperated breath and tugged on the whalebone and wire contraption once more. The wire bit painfully into the skin that I shared with her. "Perhaps in the salons of Paris, Monsieur, but not in the countryside, where I make my home. Eet does not allow even for a decent meal, Monsieur. They should be banned."

The man raised his brows, but smiled as well. "You certainly speak your mind, Madame."

"Oui. I have no doubt they are responsible for zees vapors spells I hear of in America, Monsieur Doctor. Vapors, indeed! No air—that ees my opinion. There ees no room to expand the lungs. Surely your good wife has mentioned her distress?"

He held out a crooked arm. "I am a single man, Madame. But it is an interesting theory you raise. They are starting the exhibits soon. I understand that one of your countrymen, Dr. Laennec, has devised a method to listen to the workings inside a patient's chest. Are you familiar with his research, Madame?"

I felt myself smile brightly. "Oui, I am indeed, Monsieur Doctor Alvers. Eet was one of my purposes for attending. I hope I will be allowed to attend the discussions."

The reply was a blustering of protest. "But of

course you must attend, Madame. Your country is well known for their fine women healers. I am pleased to have met you to share in your wealth of knowledge." He patted her hand as it lay on his arm. *"And I admit that your lovely visage is a delightful change from the soured old men who usually attend these conferences."*

I looked up and smiled. "You are too kind, Monsieur Doctor."

He returned the smile and leaned a bit closer. "Perhaps we could discuss your corset theory later . . . over dinner, *Madame? Being in a strange city so far from home must be difficult without your husband."*

I smiled a second time, but this smile had a warmer touch. I could tell that she hadn't been thinking of romance, but it might be useful. She had merely said she was married to prevent being questioned about attending alone. As head of the conference, Dr. Alvers might be able to get her in to see the file she needed to remove. "You may call me Yvette, Monsieur Doctor."

He bowed slightly from the neck and raised her hand to his lips. "And I am Jonathan."

A gentle kiss on her knuckles got the appropriate reply. "Oh . . ."

"Oh! You're one of *them*," came a very American voice from behind the hand I held. The vision faded slowly away, but the voice remained. The same, but without a trace of accent. "I don't even want to *know* what you saw. I really hate seers."

"You and me both, lady." I shook my head. I really *had* to stop touching people. Gloves, maybe gloves would help. I touched the knife to her ribs, just enough for her to feel the point through her expensive black blazer. It seemed fitting to place it right where the corset stay would have been. She flinched and tried to look down to see what I held, but

I didn't give her the chance. "You need to come with me. I don't have time for you to argue."

Her face took on a bemused expression. She smelled of ripe grapes, with fur that wasn't a wolf. The scent was sharp and a little sour, but not unpleasant. Maybe a cat?

"Are you *abducting* me? How quaint."

My eyes narrowed. "Look, Yvette—or whoever you are, I've got a friend who needs a doctor. You're Sazi, you're at a medical conference, so you win the prize. I'd rather not have to force you."

She didn't even flinch at the name. She smirked. "I highly doubt you *could.* But you *are* very fast. You might surprise me." She took a long sniff toward me. "I don't know you. But I do smell Lucas and—what's wrong with *Bobby?*" She took another sniff of my hand. I remembered I had checked his pulse with that hand. "My Lord, we have to hurry."

She pulled away from me and headed toward the front door, leaving me standing somewhat slack jawed. "Well?" she demanded as she turned her head. "What are you waiting for? Let's go!"

I hadn't expected it to be quite this easy, but I headed toward the door with her hot on my heels. She stopped for a moment to grab the arm of one of her table companions. "Oh, Robert. Could you grab an extra set of materials for this conference? Something urgent has come up and I have to leave for a bit. I should be back before lunch." She didn't give him a chance to reply before she was once more leading me out the door. "Thanks!" she called over her shoulder.

She scanned the line of cars, and sniffed her way to the Honda. I opened the door for her and she dove inside, somewhat breathless. I shook my head and went around to the driver's side. Well, I *had* wanted speed.

"This car smells of Nikoli's pack. Are you a new turn?"

I shook my head. "A new member, but I've been turned for over a year."

She looked at me again strongly, and her scent was a thick antifreeze, mingled with the soured milk smell of disbelief. "But I don't know you. And I know *everyone.*"

"Live and learn," was all I would say. She could tell I wasn't lying.

A ringing made us both reach for our cell phones. It was mine. "Yeah?"

"Done and done," said Carmine's voice and I smiled. "Stupid kid hadn't even told her to *hide* them. They were right there on the table, in the original processing envelope. I'm pretty sure we have everything."

"She's okay?"

"Fine. A little scared, but not a mark. You go ahead and ruin the kid's day and then we'll cut her loose. It was a nice try, but he needs more experience. Someone *should* train him before he does something really stupid." Carmine's voice was a warning growl. Couldn't say as disagreed, either.

I smiled again and hung up the phone without a reply. I glanced over to see the woman staring at me curiously.

"Is there anything I should know?" Her voice sounded very much like a cop.

I smiled and glanced in the rearview mirror before making a lane change. "Nothing that concerns you. A little case of foiling a blackmail."

"Ah." A nice noncommitted answer.

We got back to the house in record time. Most everyone who had to go out in the weather had arrived at their destination. The side streets were thankfully bare of traffic. I hurried up the steps with Yvette hot on my heels. I heard Sue tell Lucas, "They're here. But it's not your wife with him."

Lucas met us just inside the door. He stared at the woman in shock. "Amber? What are *you* doing here?"

She didn't bother with pleasantries. She was already taking off her coat and following her nose to her patient. She cocked a thumb my way. "Ask him." But then she smiled brightly and told him anyway. "I was *abducted!* Nobody has ever dared to put a knife to my ribs to force me to come with them, Lucas. It was . . . fun."

I shook my head in annoyance. Wonderful—I was *fun*. She's a real ego-builder, that one. Sue had gone to the kitchen to start some coffee. I could use some. I was thankful I had gotten a couple hours of sleep before they'd arrived yesterday, but I was beat.

Lucas turned to me with shock plain on his face, and in his scent. "You *kidnapped Amber Monier*? Are you *insane*? Where's Tatya?"

"Dunno. She wasn't there. But you said Sazi and doctor, that's what I got. Is she not a good one?"

The woman—Yvette or Amber—raised her brows in amusement, waiting for Lucas's reply. She was already pouring green magic into Bobby. I could see the swelling in his tongue start to diminish, but it wasn't turning back to pink.

Lucas didn't even glance her way. He clapped me lightly on the shoulder. "You did fine. Amber's not a good one— she's the *best* one. She's the healer for all of Wolven and the Sazi council. If she can't fix it, nobody can."

Her face had taken on a concerned look. "Don't flatter me too soon, Lucas. I don't know what's wrong with him. He should be healing by now. There's something in him, some sort of drug or toxin. I can *feel* it, but I can't seem to counteract it. It's paralyzing his body. It should have already stopped his heart. I don't know why it hasn't."

I remembered Sue's heart stopping and how I had kept it beating. I knew from my experience inside Bobby, whether in the past or future, that he and Asri were mated. "Could his mate be helping to keep him alive?"

Lucas looked at me in shock once more. "*Mate?* Bobby's not mated."

The doctor was staring at Bobby and nodding her head. "That could be the exact reason. I didn't *think* Bobby was mated either, but it's the only explanation, Lucas."

He turned to me sharply, and hot metal filled the air. "Do you know this *mate*? Has he ever mentioned her name? Have you ever met her?"

"You've met her too," I replied. "I should have spotted it when Asri was slurring her words. We should probably check in with Nikoli and see if she's in the same shape."

"*Asri?* No wonder!" He sniffed in amusement, probably realizing why they didn't want to sit together in the car. "You're right that we need to see Nikoli, but I still don't have a tribute. He'll make my life *hell* if I don't show up with something impressive for keeping him waiting this long."

Amber spoke up. "You haven't *spoken* to Nikoli since you arrived, Lucas? Do you think that's wise? The weather is going to start getting really nasty in a day or so." The way she said it made the words seem very important.

Ah. I watched horror slide across Lucas's face. My bet was that he'd forgotten all about whatever conference was to happen here.

He slapped his forehead sharply, just as Sue arrived back in the room with steaming mugs of coffee. The doctor accepted one gratefully. "The council meeting. How could I have forgotten?"

"A touch Freudian, I think," I said lightly, and the doctor grinned. "Ever meet him, Yvette, or Amber, or whoever?"

"Amber—for this lifetime. And yes, Sigmund was a perfectly lovely, albeit slightly neurotic, man. We had some wonderful talks. I agree with this interesting new agent of yours, Lucas, although I haven't had the pleasure of being introduced."

"Joe Giambrocco," I said while Lucas was stammering and swearing. "But you can call me Tony. The lovely lady with the coffee is Sue, my wife."

"Charmed." Amber's voice was frisky and her eyes twinkled through the steam rising from her mug.

Lucas ran his fingers through his hair and removed his wallet to look inside. "I *can't* show up without a tribute. Especially with what all I have to discuss."

"You're a council member, Lucas," Amber replied calmly. "You can do whatever you want."

"It's precisely *because* I'm a council member that I can't, Amber, and you know it. You know that Ahmad would find some way to make my life hell for not abiding by the very rule that I sponsored."

Sue spoke up for the first time. She winced a bit when she first thought it, but I approved and urged her to speak. "Would a painting do? I just bought this lovely print in Boulder. It's very masculine."

She pointed to the picture of the ducks. Lucas glanced at it, pursed his lips in thought, grasping at straws, but then shook his head. "No, it needs to be flashy or shiny. Something with obvious value that's not tied to current trends."

Shiny? I immediately thought of Linda. "Would gold make a good gift? I just happen to have a nice stack of Kruggerands."

Sue tried to stop me. "Tony, I used most . . ."

I shook my head. "Not those coins, Sue. I've got a *bunch* more." Her eyes widened, because she hadn't known.

"Gold's good," nodded Lucas. "Kruggerands can't be traced and gold has value in all times. Gems would be better, mind you."

"Oh, really?" I walked back to the entryway where the file box from earlier still sat. I opened it and grabbed three batteries. I shook each one until I was satisfied and returned to the room. I tossed one of the batteries to Lucas. "Open that. It should do."

He gave me a withering look, but Amber seemed interested. "I don't think Nikoli will be impressed with a Duracell, Tony."

"I said *open* it. Take off the wrapper. It's not a battery."

He raised his brows, and the thick anti-freeze of curiosity rose from all three of the other people in the room.

He used his thumbnail to slice open the outer foil. The gold coins gleamed in the sunlight through the open blinds. "Nice. Very nice. Hell, maybe I *should* give him the battery. He'd enjoy the ingenuity."

"Open the spacer at the top." He did so, revealing a small cache of brilliant cut gemstones resting inside a couple of cotton balls—diamonds, rubies and emeralds. I tried not to go for anything gaudy when I was buying, nothing over two carats. Small stones are easier to peddle on the black market.

"Stellar. These will be perfect. How much do I owe you?"

"Normally, I'd say market, but you've done a lot for us. Either the stones or the gold, gratis. If you need both, *then* it'll cost you."

"I'll go with the gems. Nikoli always has his eye out for stones to make jewelry for his ladies. He always goes for flashy when he's wooing."

"Oh, I wouldn't say *flashy*," Amber commented quietly. "Nikoli really has very traditional taste." Lucas stared incredulously, but Amber just smiled sweetly and changed direction. "Well, as much fun as this conversation is, it's not healing Bobby. I've got him stabilized, but he needs to be healed. The last time I saw something like this was in the jungle in Africa. Could it be an endemic poison? You know . . . something from his home that's getting an allergic reaction?"

Lucas got a strange look on his face and headed toward the phone on the table. "*Jungle* . . . you might have something there, Amber. I'll pay for the toll charges, Tony."

He picked up the receiver while the rest of us shrugged at each other. He turned his back while he dialed, so we couldn't see his face.

I heard a muffled voice over the line, but couldn't make it out. "Senator Simpson, please," Lucas said calmly.

Amber gasped and stood in a rush. Lucas turned and shot her a dark look and then motioned his head for her to leave. She grabbed both of our arms and pulled us through the kitchen door. She hissed in my ear as she tugged. "It's not worth your life to have heard that."

Well, hell! Until then, I was just going to ignore the call.

Now I *had* to listen. Sue was curious as well and, frankly, so was Amber. We all stood by the door, *not* listening intently.

"Then tell him to finish his meeting and take this call. Tell him it's urgent that *Inteque* speak to him. He *will* take the call." There was a pause. "Yes, I'll wait."

Amber whispered to us, so quiet it was barely audible. "You two did *not* hear this. But let me know if I miss anything. My ears are horrible."

A deep, angry baritone came over the wire. This voice I could hear with no trouble. "Who *dares* to invoke the name of a friend who is long dead to me! Answer me!"

"I invoke my own name, Colecos," Lucas said quietly.

"We didn't hear that either, I presume," I whispered to Amber. She shushed me with a finger to her lips and put her ear back to the door.

The anger faded slightly, and the voice took on haughty tone. A sharp sniff of dark amusement reached my ears. "And why do you call me now, Inteque—after all these years as enemies?"

"I've got a man down. It's Bobby Mbutu."

The reply was cautious. "I know him. He was one of mine . . . before."

"He's been poisoned. I've seen it, but I can't remember the cure. It was in *your* jungle, long ago, Colecos. His tongue is black and swollen, his eyes are dilated and his skin is cold and clammy. Do you remember the girl? The one in the village when you ruled Mayapán? We discovered the cause, but how was she healed? Amber has been working on him, but he's dying, Jack. He *will* die if it's the same poison. You know it."

Another pause, this one longer. Amber had her ear pressed so tight to the wooden slats of the swinging door that she was either going to have an impression on the side of her face or fall through the doorway.

I thought about what Lucas said. If I remembered my geography, Mayapán was one of the ancient capital cities of the Mayans. Okay, that's *old*. I was listening to a couple of the *really* ancient Sazi.

The voice deepened, became richer and rolling. The words were harsh and final. "The swelling salt from the sacred caves. It is the *only* cure."

Shit! There was no time to go on a jungle expedition before Bobby died. The Senator must have heard Lucas's defeated sigh, because he laughed heartily.

"Do you remember, Inteque? How powerful the magic in the swelling salt—in the *sodium bicarbonate?*" He laughed again and Lucas turned to stare at Bobby. Then he laughed as well.

"Baking soda. Plain old ordinary soda. It'll neutralize the acid! Thank you Jack." Lucas's voice lowered and became warmer. "*Thank you*—old friend."

"It's been good to talk of days when life was simpler, Lucas. But times have changed. Go save your agent. I wouldn't suggest you mention who saved him, unless the fair Amber is nearby to treat his heart attack. My regards to her and her sister." He hung up during his own bitter laughter.

Sue was already rummaging in the cupboards. She whispered frantically. "We don't have any baking soda, Tony."

Not true. I moved Amber back a pace. She had winced once during the end of the conversation and a strong scent of embarrassment drifted to me. It had been just about the time he said, "her and her sister." She was now silently musing, her brow wrinkled into deep furrows. I opened the refrigerator door. All the way in back was an open box of baking soda. God only knew how long it had been there. It was already open and damp when I'd moved in, but it might be enough.

"Baking sod—." Lucas exclaimed as he burst through the kitchen door, nearly beaning Amber in the face. I handed him the box before he could finish the word. He looked at the three of us suspiciously, but let it go.

It was only a few minutes after stuffing Bobby's mouth with soda and pouring a drizzle of water onto his tongue to dissolve it, that he was sitting up and spewing it across the room.

"What the hell kind of witches brew are you feeding me?" He retched and spit into a cooking pan that Sue had brought with the glass of water. He reeked of anger's burning coffee. "Decayed vegetables, rotten meat, spoiled milk. Jeez, guys!"

Amber just watched him swear and sputter with a smile, because his tongue was already pink and his breathing was back to normal. The bright citrus of her pleased satisfaction muted the caramelized coffee.

He got up shakily and headed to the bathroom. "I'll buy you a new toothbrush, Tony, but I've *got* to get this taste out of my mouth!"

"Okay." Lucas exclaimed while Bobby was brushing his tongue. He grabbed his overcoat and started to slide his arms in the sleeves. "Now that he's a little better, I need to see Nikoli. Let's go, Tony."

I held up my hands in protest. My eyelids were so heavy they drooped and my arms felt like lead weights. "Whoa, whoa. Why do you need *me* to go with you?" I pointed to the northwest wall. "The lair is that way, about six blocks down, in the Volkdom Hotel. I need to get some *sleep,* which I might mention I've only had two hours of in the past thirty. Go see Nikoli. Have fun—bye."

Sue came over to stand by me, in full agreement. I slid an arm around her shoulder and glared at the frustrated Latino man.

"He's right," Amber said quietly. "I can tell he's a three-day, Lucas. As the Wolven physician, I would recommend . . ."

"He's *going,*" Lucas said sharply. He stared at Amber, but glanced at me and Sue from time to time. "We've got a full council meeting to be held in Nikoli's hotel in four days. It's filled with three-day dogs and has *no* security system. Need I say more, Dr. Monier?"

Amber's eyes widened. "Nikoli doesn't have a security system in the building? Not at all?"

Ah. I was starting to see my part in this. If Lucas had done as much research on me as I thought he had, he knew about my former career. I got the feeling it was going to be a busy few days. I heard the water shut off in the bath and Bobby appeared in the doorway, looking shaky but standing on his own feet.

Amber stared at me closely and stood. She walked over to me and looked in my eyes from different angles, being careful not to touch me. Then she did the same to Sue, who was a little taken aback. Amber growled, a high-pitched, rolling *rrrow* that made the hairs on the back of my neck stand on end. She ended it in a quiet hiss, directed right at Lucas. Her scent was boiling coffee in a metal pot.

"Fine, then, Lucas. But *you're* going to pony up the power for him to do it. And Sue needs to go to bed right now to rest up. I'm sure that Nikoli will find things for her to do in the next few days, as well, and she's only human." I watched a thread of green magic appear at her fingertip. She touched Sue's forehead lightly and I felt a rolling eddy of warmth fill me. I fought to keep my eyes open.

"That's not helping me stay awake," I whispered, as Sue slumped against me gently with a sigh. I caught her weight with effort because I was fighting not to fall to the floor beside her.

"Put her to bed for a bit so she can sleep," Amber said briskly.

"It's not that easy," I complained as I picked her up in my arms and held her close to me. I shook my head to try to clear the cobwebs. No good. "I haven't tried to cut off the magic since we've been fully bound. I don't know that I *can*. I'm barely able to keep my eyes open from whatever you just did."

Amber seemed surprised. Even the penetrating scent of her confusion and curiosity couldn't wake me. "This . . . this is a mating—a *double* mating? But she's *human*."

I yawned long and wide. "That's me," I said sleepily as I carried Sue to the bedroom. "Breaking all the rules."

Bobby gave way for me to get through the doorway. I carried her down the short hall to the bedroom. Every step was an effort and the cool darkness of the curtained room called to me. Sleep lapped at my consciousness even as I struggled against it. I laid Sue down on the bed and then couldn't fight it any more. I collapsed beside her.

Chapter 14

I HEARD MOVEMENT in the darkness and I opened my eyes. I knew it was important I be conscious and alert, but I couldn't seem to remember why. I could smell Sue beside me, so I reached out and pulled her closer. She sighed and turned so I could drape an arm over her side. I closed my eyes contentedly.

Another noise—the creaking of wood and the rustling of fabric from the corner. My eyes shot open. I concentrated on the input into my nose and ears and tried to focus my eyes in the dark. I turned over casually, as though I was still asleep and then I saw a weak glow from someone sitting in the corner of the room. I inhaled deeply. It was that guy from the forest . . . Yurgi. What the hell?

Now that my senses were functioning, I noticed other things. The darkened room wasn't my bedroom. The smells were wrong. This room smelled of dust, stale air, but with overtones of Nikoli's pack. I also felt something else—an *aloneness* that transcended the two people in the room. I reached out to try to touch Sue with my mind, but she wasn't there. It wasn't the fur covered wall that I was accustomed to when I'd been cut off from her before. This was a black box that closed around my mind like a tomb. Beyond the edges of my head was despair and death.

I shook off the momentary panic. Sue was right here beside me, warm; alive. This mental shield was just a new kind. That's what I kept repeating to myself, but I wasn't believing me. I shivered the darkness. I might as well get up and see where I was and what was happening.

I gently moved away from Sue and slid my feet out from under the covers until I was sitting. Again I had to fight the panic of solitude. My breathing increased and my heart quickened. I reached behind me and found Sue's warm form. I removed my hand. Just a touch seemed to be enough to fight the eerie sense of dread.

What the hell was happening to me? I shook my head.

A whisper came from the darkness. "Ah. You wake, Tony. Is good. Come, they wait for you. We must let your mate sleep, but you are needed."

Was it important that Sue stay asleep? I didn't know. I decided to be quiet, as well, just in case.

"What's been happening, Yurgi? Where am I?" I glanced behind me to see that Sue was oblivious to the noise. She was still nestled in a deep, penetrating sleep.

Sounds and motion flooded my ears and eyes as Yurgi stood. The birch bark scent became stronger as he stepped forward. He leaned down close to my ear. "You remember my name. Is good. It has been most busy since you arrived, Tony. Is very important that Nikoli see you right away."

"So I'm at pack headquarters?" He nodded in the darkness. I could see his glowing head move up and down.

"They brought you to the den—the hotel—until all is done. The powerful Councilman who is nearly legend among my people in Siberia was carrying you. The snake who smelled sick is in the next room, also sleeping. The healer, who I am told is a bobcat on the moon, she is like the nervous hen. She runs back and forth often to be sure that you are both becoming better. I was told to stay with you, to be certain you slept and then woke safely, because she had to go back to the healer meeting."

I yawned and stretched, and was a little weirded out when I had to—*had to*—touch Sue once again. It was a disturbing trend.

I was stalling leaving the bed, and I knew it. I just couldn't seem to help it. "Why has it been busy around here, Yurgi?"

"The *meeting!*" he exclaimed quietly, with surprise in his voice and his scent. Then he slapped his forehead lightly. "But yes, how could you know?"

I smiled in the darkness, knowing he couldn't see. How indeed? I figured he'd smell the curiosity, which was fine.

"Our pack has been very honored, Tony. All of the most powerful Sazi leaders will meet in *our den,* right downstairs. But is much trouble to make the hotel ready. Soon guests will arrive and everything must be just so. My Pamela, she is in charge of the decorations—honoring the holy days from around the world: the Christmas, Hanukkah, Kwanzaa . . ."

I smiled at his obvious pride in his wife. So, the meeting was on. I wished I could have seen Nikoli's face when Lucas told him. "Anything else I should know?"

"Yes. Our most gracious Alpha has been *further* honored. He will *represent* all of the wolves of the world at the council meeting."

I pursed my lips. That *was* news.

"Is very humbling, Tony, to meet these great ones and to know that *our* pack leader is so respected as to sit at the same table, protecting the thousands of wolves in the world. The different species, they fight and fight for dominance always. But our Alpha is strong. He will protect us from the other Sazi. Never have I met the leaders of the other Sazi—the great cats, and raptors and snakes. Is a very exciting time, even if frightening."

I furrowed my brow in the darkness and could even smell my own curiosity. "Why is it frightening?"

"Have you not felt it—the magic that makes the skin

crawl? But no, perhaps you are powerful enough. Even when Alpha Santiago and the healer try to be careful, it hurts to be near them. Is making the rest of the pack afraid; the stronger wolves snap and growl at the lesser ones. Not even the children are spared their anger. I worry of our pack mates' reaction when the other council members arrive. Only a few hours, and *already* the children hide and cry. I am accustomed to the pain of being near powerful wolves. *Everyone* is more powerful than Yurgi. But to have so many so strong, all here at once—is a worry for those unprepared. Nikoli is so involved with preparing as he has not noticed."

That was a good point. I'd have to bring it up to Nikoli and Lucas. Most of the members of the pack aren't much more powerful than me. Only Lelya and Nikoli are alphic. We wouldn't want the security risk of someone going nuts because they couldn't handle being around the big dogs, whatever the species. Frightened people make mistakes, sometimes deadly ones.

I took a deep breath and let it out slow. Okay, time to go face the dragon—which reminded me. "How's Asri? Is she recovering from her . . . illness?"

Yurgi's voice was a little surprised. "I am surprised you know of our enforcer. She dropped to the floor while speaking to Nikoli downstairs last night. I was probably not supposed to see, but she was pale and writhing in pain. Nikoli, he was very worried. We were fortunate to have a great healer visiting the Duchess—the wife of Alpha Santiago. She was able to heal Mistress Asri so that she is better now."

So *that's* where Tatya was this morning . . . keeping Asri alive and kicking. The things you learn when you ask questions.

Another deep breath was called for. I stood up and reached out for the bedside lamp. A soft glow lit the room when I clicked the first setting. We were in a two-room, impressively ornate suite, not just a simple hotel room. I wondered what I did right to rate the royal treatment.

Yurgi was horrified. "But *no*. We must not wake your mate. The healer, she was most firm." He started to reach out for the lamp to turn it off, but I stopped him by grabbing his arm. Thankfully, nothing happened.

I turned my head to glance at Sue. There was no movement. "It's okay, Yurgi. She's in a *magical* sleep. She'll only wake up when Amber wants her to."

Yurgi looked skeptical for a moment. Then he glanced at Sue to see that she was out cold. "Perhaps you are right, Tony. She sleeps even still. But come, let us hurry. Nikoli and the others wait."

It only took a few minutes to dress, and run a comb through my hair. They hadn't brought my toothbrush but, frankly, I wouldn't want it anyway after Bobby used it. There was one of the trial sizes of mouthwash, though, so I used that.

I noticed that Lucas and the others had provided a clean change of clothes, folded neatly on a turn of the century rosewood wing chair. My favorite Taurus, from the box that Carmine gave me, was resting on top of the clothes in the well-used inner pants holster. I opened the cylinder and removed a shell. Now, why had someone loaded it with the silver bullets? The rounds were definitely the ones I'd made. I couldn't see Amber taking the effort. Bobby might, if it occurred to him. Would Lucas?

Regardless, I strapped it on and then zipped my pants.

"Ah! Tony, I forget," Yurgi said quietly. "Nikoli ask me to give you knife from battle as reward." He reached in his pocket and handed me a nylon sheath containing the silver push knife. I removed it from the nylon. It would fit in my boot. I put ceramic knife on the dresser.

I glanced once more at Sue's sleeping form, and fought the urge to touch her. Another deep breath, filled this time with Yurgi's birch bark scent and his growing impatience. I closed my hands into fists and squeezed tight for a moment. I'd been through worse. I'd get through this. But I would be back to hold her very soon.

"Let's go." My words were slightly above a snarl, even though I hadn't intended to. But Yurgi stepped back a pace.

"You see?" He said quietly. "Even you are affected."

"It's not the magic, Yurgi. It's . . ." Actually, he could be right. I don't know anything about the magic that was cutting me off from Sue. "Never mind. Let's go find Nikoli."

I flicked off the bedside light and wound my way through the furniture to the door. As I got closer, I realized why we had been put in a suite. The heavier door muffled the yelling and pounding feet in the hallway. While most of the swearing was in Russian, some phrases were English, and quite colorful.

I opened the door with Yurgi tight to my heels. I backed up quickly, bumping into him. A small Latina human, her arms loaded with fluffy white towels, dashed by at high speed. I'd nearly creamed her.

I turned and apologized to Yurgi, who was rubbing his nose. "Sorry."

"Is all right," he replied. He sighed. "Will be more bumps soon. Yurgi was glad to sit by the bed of Tony and his mate. Was peaceful."

The strong scents of ammonia, bleach and vinegar filled the air and made me sneeze repeatedly. Not emotions this time—cleaning solutions. My eye caught movement and sound as I stood erect after my sneezing fit. Suddenly, an armful of sheets flew by us, tossed off the landing above into the central lobby. I walked the few paces to the ornate wrought iron railing. Sheets and towels were flying down from every level, and the children I'd met at the apartment were scrambling to pick them up and stuff them into large cloth bags.

Yurgi spoke into my ear quietly. "You see? Is *chaos*. We've never guests here. There are many tasks, and we know little of making hotel ready."

He was right. I watched as the woman with the towels was directed to another task by Boris, an old wolf just barely above Yurgi in the pack. She put down the towels on the floor on the other side of the circular hallway. Moments after she left, a voice screamed, "Celia! Where are those towels?"

Alena poked her head out of a doorway further down and yelled her name, as well. Celia stopped and turned, while Boris called for her to follow him. She looked back and forth as the three continued to call. Then she burst into tears and sat down on the floor right where she'd stood.

"This is ridiculous." I glanced over at Yurgi, who was nodding.

"I would go back to watch over your mate if you ordered," he said somewhat wistfully. His eyes were a little wide. I think he was hoping I would do just that.

A rustling sound took my attention away from the drama on the other side of the hotel. I glanced to my left. The leaves of a large potted plant were moving slightly. I backed up and lowered my head so I could see better. A pair of panicked blue eyes appeared through the leafy green and a burst of hot and sour soup filled my nose over the strong chemicals. I recognized those eyes. Yurgi did, as well.

"What are you doing here, Denis?" Yurgi's voice was slightly stern. "You are to be helping your *braht,* Alek, gather beddings for laundry."

His voice was a whisper. I had to struggle to hear him over the yelling that was echoing off the high ceiling. "I made Sergei mad. Alek told me to hide. Please don't let him find me."

I knew that Sergei had a bad temper. It probably hadn't improved with the silver bullet I'd put in his arm.

I shook my head. I remembered when I was growing up, having to hide from trigger-tempered adults. I've never liked it much that people yell at little kids. I reached out to grasp his arm. "Let's go find your mother, Denis. Sergei will be able to see you through the railing."

Denis turned his head and blanched. The hot and sour turned to ammonia panic. The logic had escaped him that if he could see out, others could see in.

He flinched and whimpered when my hand closed around his arm. He pulled back sharply when I started to tug him out from behind the plant. He smelled of Worcestershire sauce, the scent of pain. It mingled with the hot and sour soup and made my jaw tight. I furrowed my brow in concern as my nostrils flared to catch more of the scent. Yurgi likewise knelt by the boy's side. I raised the sleeve on his thin arm. There was a deep black bruise that hadn't been there the other day. "What happened to your arm?"

Denis's eyes dropped to the floor. "I made Sergei mad. He tripped over me when his arms were full of glasses. Some of them broke. I got away because he still was holding one tray and couldn't get a better grip on me with his hurt arm. But now he's looking. I think he'll hit me if he finds me."

I was betting he was right. This might not be the *reason* they gave me my gun, but it would be handy. I *really* don't like people *hurting* kids.

I reached behind me and removed the Taurus. I held it out for Denis to look at. "See this? If Sergei tries to hurt you, I'll shoot his *other* arm." I smiled darkly at the boy. I looked into his eyes and could see a trembling hope replace the fear. I flipped open the cylinder and removed one bullet. I held it out for him to touch. His tentative finger pulled back when the silver burned him just a bit. His eyes went wide as he looked at the tiny blister forming. I put the bullet back in the chamber and closed the action. I spoke as I was returning the Taurus to the holster.

"It's *me* he's mad at, Denis. But *he's* mad because *he's* afraid. Get it?" I held out my hand to help the boy off the floor. Yurgi was looking at me with something approaching wonder. The clove scent of pride reached my nose, and blended in nicely with the bright citrus happiness that burst from Denis. He grabbed my hand with his good arm and rose. He stayed close by me with his head high and a smile on his face. He didn't even glance around him as we walked the hallway.

I wished I could have said the same. The further I got from the room—and Sue—the more tense I felt. The black glove of solitude made my throat tight. Is this what Lelya had meant? That I would be "very alone" in my task? I could feel my fingers trembling slightly, but neither Yurgi nor Denis seemed to notice. But one thing *I* noticed was that when I was dealing with Denis, I hadn't felt the solitude. I guess that meant I needed to stay busy—keep my mind occupied.

"Let's go find Nikoli." Yurgi nodded and Denis reached over and clutched my hand tight.

I heard the sound of breaking crystal when we were halfway down the stairs. Lelya's horrified voice soon followed. "What is going *on* out here?"

One of the children was picking up the remains of a shattered vase that had been knocked over by a flying bundle of sheets. Another was holding a broom and dustpan.

Nikoli strutted by the staircase, looking quite pleased with the chaos surrounding him. "I have instructed that all the beds be stripped and the linens sent out for cleaning. It progresses nicely, yes?"

My eyebrows raised a bit when Lelya strode out from behind the front desk. She was wearing a pair of black denim jeans and a colorful sweater that showed off her figure—interesting, but it wasn't the impressive part. Her hair was darker, the lines in her face less and her whole manner was confident and proud. She had transformed from an aging Queen Mother into the *Queen*.

She stood with hands on her hips, inches from Nikoli. He seemed a little taken aback. "It progresses—*NO!* I would like to speak to you privately, oh great and glorious pack leader!"

She took his arm and pulled him, his face still in a state of shock, into a room and closed the door without completely shutting it. I got the feeling she *wanted* people to hear. And they were certainly listening, sidling up to the wrought iron railing and tipping eager ears toward the door crack.

"Niki, if you strip *all* of the beds, what will the guests who arrive tonight sleep on? The laundry told you that the sheets could not be back before late tomorrow. The sheets on the second floor, which you have already managed to strip, were only placed there three days ago. They were perfectly clean. You strut like a peacock, Niki, with no cause. There is no planning, no order! I will take care of this."

The door opened so suddenly that no one had time to step away. She glanced around with fury in her gaze, ignoring the startled but annoyed look from "Niki," who remained in the room briefly before following his mother almost meekly. Her eyes lighted on the three of us. She tipped her head to me briskly, and then stared at Yurgi. She pointed at him. "You—you there. What is your name again?"

Yurgi paled slightly behind his dark beard. His voice quavered a bit when he replied. "Yurgi, Duchess. Yurgi Kroutikhin."

Lelya raised her brows and pursed her lips. "Ah, yes. The husband of Pamela. Well? Come down here, young one. I won't bite."

Yurgi glanced at me fearfully, but I could only raise my eyebrows and shrug my shoulders. Neither of us was quite sure that she *wouldn't* bite.

He positively scampered down the stairs. He bowed his head when he reached her. Nikoli was huffing into his beard, but Lelya didn't notice—or didn't care. She put a hand on Yurgi's shoulder, who flinched visibly. "You will go to the mall, Yurgi. You know where that is? Good! You will buy sheets for king size beds. All white, all excellent quality." She turned to Nikoli. "*You* will give him money." She stared at him until he removed his wallet and pulled out a number of large denomination bills and held them out. She took them, and then turned back to Yurgi. "Also buy a steam iron and board so we may press the factory wrinkles from them." She handed him the bills. Yurgi stuffed them in his pocket but looked around uncertainly.

She shook her head in annoyance and turned away from Yurgi. "We must make do with what we have, I suppose." Then she looked back, to see Yurgi still standing immobile. "Well? Go!"

Nikoli's eyes grew dark. He was being usurped in front of his own pack. He stepped forward as if to stop Yurgi from bolting out the door to obey. "Mother, I really think you should . . ."

She turned to him with one brow raised. She started to glow with a blinding light. He stepped back, almost involuntarily, before the storm. Once again, Yurgi flinched and tried to step away, but Lelya's hand moved to rest firmly on his shoulder. I could see Yurgi wince from pain.

"You think I should *what*, Niki? You have owned this hotel for years, but have never trained your pack members to properly run it. Who is in charge of housekeeping? Of reservations? Of the kitchen?" She shook her head at his blank expression.

"You have never planned a council meeting. *I* have, at least, *attended* a council meeting, long before you were born. *I* have hosted a gathering of kings before I left Court in Russia. *I* worked as a hotel maid while you were a baby. I really think *you* should step aside and allow me to plan this gathering so that it will honor our pack. We decided last night that we will rule together, did we not?"

Nikoli's mouth was moving, but no sound was coming out. I noted that all activity had stopped in the hotel. People were standing at the railings of all four floors, staring down at the scene.

"Besides, you have no time to organize this meeting. You will be a *council member,* Niki. You must study the issues that affect the wolves—research how it will impact the Sazi of Chicago. And of Boulder. *And* of mother Russia." She waited for a reaction, but Nikoli was a little shell-shocked. "Well? Shoo!"

A bit of movement caught my eye. I glanced to my left. Lucas was leaning in the doorway of the big conference room, looking amused. His arms were crossed over his chest and a small smile played on his face. I was too far away to catch any scent other than Lelya's thick boiling coffee and Nikoli's burned metal frustration.

She looked up and around, and then clapped her hands. Yurgi scampered away as soon as the restraining hand moved. People flinched as the sound echoed through the lobby. "The rest of you—come down here. We must meet."

Nikoli started to mutter under his breath and moved to step past Lelya. In a movement so sudden that it made him start abruptly, she reached out and threw her arms around him. She hugged him close for a moment. Oranges and cloves burst into my nose, along with the brief scent of deep, foggy sorrow. I could just make out the whisper in his ear. "I am so sorry about Mila, my son. I know you loved her deeply. And I am *very proud,* Niki. You honor us all with your standing, *Councilman* Nikoli Gregorovich Molotov!" She held him at arm's length briefly and moved forward to kiss each of his cheeks soundly.

Nikoli's eyes glistened sadly for a moment. But then a slow smile stretched his beard and he nodded once. He pulled her close, and gave her a quick squeeze before stepping back. He was suddenly a little less angry and once again standing erect.

He waved his hand imperiously to the waiting pack members. "Well, you heard your Alpha Female! Do as she says! You will report to her until the council meeting is over." He took a deep breath and then glanced at Lelya. He winked. "*I* have important documents to review."

The moment he walked away and Lelya glanced up once more with a raised brow, there was a thundering of sound as people literally *ran* to obey. I was one of the "rest of you", so I stepped down the few remaining stairs.

Lelya nodded to me warmly. "It is good to see you again, Tony. The wheels turn, do they not?"

"Not always in the directions we planned." I shivered as another burst of black despair flowed over me.

She nodded understandingly as she saw the shudder. "The trials are always more difficult for the strong."

Then she squatted down next to Denis, who was still holding my hand, and fixed him with twinkling gaze and bright smile. "And who is this handsome young man?"

I was starting to get the hint that the Duchess had kept to herself so much that she didn't even know the members of her own pack. I also realized that was about to change.

Denis lowered his gaze, but smiled shyly. "I'm Denis Siska, Alpha." He flinched a bit when Lelya's power flowed over his skin. It must have hurt his bruised arm, because he rubbed it unconsciously.

Lelya sniffed carefully around him, zeroing in on the sleeve over the bruise. Her eyes darkened for a moment, but then cleared. She nodded to herself and stood.

The rest of the pack had gathered in a circle around her. She looked them over carefully and noted which ones were flinching. She knocked her power down until there was barely any glow around her.

Her words were quiet, but we could all hear her just fine. "This will be a difficult time for you all. The men and women who will attend this conference are the best and brightest—and the most powerful—of all the Sazi. While they all will do their best to hold their power in check, it will be a time of high emotions. The power will sting your skin. I will try to keep the lesser wolves from direct contact as much as possible. If at any time one of you hurts too much to function, come see me. I will help to dampen the power as much as I can." She noted a few disbelieving looks and looked at each of them strongly, willing them to believe. "We are Sazi—we are *pack*. I *will* protect you."

There were a few scattered smiles and smattering of applause. She turned to me.

"Tony, you will head security with Asri. I am told by Lucas you install security systems. Wolven has a standard system that will be adapted to our hotel. Lucas has arranged for the materials to be delivered in a few minutes. Please be sure that the system is adequate for the meeting, but still keeps the warmth and flavor of our *home*. I am sure that based on your past history, which Lucas has also advised me of, you have arranged for meetings such as this."

I nodded without speaking. Yeah, I'd set up security for more than one meeting of family *patrones*.

"Asri will attend to traffic control and weather crisis management when she returns."

Huh? "*Weather* management? Asri can control the weather?"

Lelya chuckled. "No. But the others can—and do— *affect* the weather. The magical energy from a single council member can cause darkening skies when clear weather was forecast. Each time a councilman arrives, the weather will worsen. During the meeting, it will be a full fledged blizzard." She rolled her eyes expressively. "Why in heaven's name they chose Chicago in mid-winter is beyond me! The winter meetings are usually in the southern latitudes. But, it is what it is. Our plan to manage the meeting is to ensure that the delegates stagger their arrivals and methods of transportation so that there is time for the streets to be cleared and the planes de-iced before the next arrives. Do you understand? Asri's duties are critical for the humans of Illinois and Indiana to survive this meeting, so you will have to bear the burden of installing the system alone."

Wow! That someone could be powerful enough to

change the weather was a new concept. Was that why it was storming when Lucas arrived and got worse when he was irritated in the woods? I'd never thought to tie the two together. Maybe they need to consider teleconferencing.

Then something she said clicked. "Alone?" I crossed my arms over my chest and settled my stance. "In four days?" I shook my head. "It can't be done, Lelya. I've got to have at least one person. I can't string wire in the walls over four floors by myself."

She nodded her head, I guess pleased that I was thinking logically. A few people dropped their jaws when I called their Alpha by a familiar name—and she let me.

She swept her hand around the circle. "Fine. Choose a person to assist you from among those here."

"Actually, I'd prefer Yurgi." He follows orders well, and I would bet that he had a lot of practice doing grunt work.

She nodded once more. "When he returns with the sheets, he will assist you. As soon as we're done here, please report to Lucas." Then she turned to the rest of the people. "Which of you has experience cooking? For a large group?"

Alena tentatively raised her hand. "I went to school to become a Sous Chef. I was nearly graduated when I became pregnant with Alek and had to drop out. Then Denis came and . . ."

Lelya dropped her head briskly. "Good. You are in charge of food service. You will choose two to help you. The children can help you as well." Alena looked pleased. She smiled at her boys.

Then the queen wolf looked around again. "Who has worked in housekeeping?"

No hands raised. Her scent grew angry and her glow increased a bit. "I *said*—who has cleaned before? State your name and your ability."

The little Latina, Celia, raised her hand. Boris winced just the tiniest bit. "I'm Celia Golubev, Boris's wife. I was working in housekeeping for a ski resort when I met Boris, Madam Alpha. I worked there for many years. I was a supervisor."

Lelya smiled brightly. "*Excellent*! Why would you be afraid to speak of it? You should be proud. You are in charge of housekeeping, Celia. Choose four to help you." Then Lelya turned and stared at the glowering man with one arm in a sling. "Sergei, you will be in charge of janitorial, and will report to Celia."

The words dropped like a chunk of lead. Shock appeared on the faces of Celia and Boris. Sergei went from surprised to angry to livid in a matter of seconds. He sputtered for a moment before he could come up with a *barely* polite reply.

"Forgive me, Alpha, but she is *human*. It is beneath my station to answer to a human woman—the wife of one of the lowest pack members. *I* should be in charge of housekeeping and she report to me."

Lelya looked at him for a moment and then glanced around at the other pack members. They were all curious to see how she would respond.

"There are no pack stations until this council meeting is over. We must all serve in the capacity we are best able. You are injured, Sergei, and cannot clean a room. I was offering some way you could serve." Her words were quiet, but I knew the tone. It's one Carmine uses a lot—offering rope for the person to hang themselves. "Are you refusing the janitorial supervisor position?"

He thought for a moment, and apparently wasn't bright enough to see the trap. He nodded, believing he'd won. "I am. I should be housekeeping supervisor, Alpha."

She nodded for a moment, thinking. "Ah. Tony, shoot him."

I was happy to comply. He was an annoying little shit. I pulled my Taurus before he could even react and fired a silver bullet through his good arm. He shrieked and fell to the floor. Eyes went wide around the room and people backed up to avoid him. I caught Denis smiling. I glanced at Lelya to see her staring at me.

I shrugged. "You didn't say *kill him*, and I hated to waste a perfectly good sling." I figured if she'd meant for me to kill him, she would have said so.

"Actually," she said with a small smile, as she stalked toward the bleeding man on the floor, "that was *exactly* what I expected you to do. I think we'll work together fine." She leaned down over Sergei and stared into his pain-ridden face. "You will be the *doorman*. Your left arm is healed enough for that task. Each time you open the door, you will be reminded that it is wise to do as you are instructed." She leaned a little closer, and I saw a whip of energy slash across his body until he screamed again. Her voice became a weighty snarl of power. "And, in the future, you will *keep your hands off* the cubs of this pack. You will learn to control your temper, or you will die. Do I make myself clear?"

He nodded slowly with fear radiating from every pore. The Queen had spoken.

Chapter 15

THE REST OF the morning went by in a blur of activity, interspersed with stops in to check on Sue. When she finally woke up she was well rested and seemed in good spirits. Whatever Amber had done didn't seem to bother her. Wish I could have said the same. Every moment that I wasn't touching her made me break out in a cold sweat. I stayed by her bedside until she decided to get up, and then followed her into the kitchenette to help her cook. I couldn't seem to help it. I needed to be near her—touching her, holding her.

She laughingly threw a loofah at me when I was sitting watching her bathe, and told me to get out. Her scent didn't match the laugh. The burned metal and hot coffee gave her away, so I left. When she took Pamela up on an offer to help with decorations, I was a little annoyed. It was okay so long as she was in sight. Between them and the other pack members, the hotel was being transformed. The atrium sparkled with holiday decorations from around the world. The scent of cleaning fluids was replaced by the sharp tang from the pine boughs and the scent of fine foods being cooked in the hotel kitchen.

One of the people taken by Alena was the cook from the fast food restaurant where Sue was to begin work. Lelya had announced that all pack businesses would close until the end of the conference, with all people getting pay. It had won her friends. Sue was very pleased, because it would allow her time to go through the books privately, without new daily reports coming in or having to deal with the employees. But after throwing up for the third time in an hour, I had to wonder if I could afford to let her work.

I was sitting in the room, fighting through the latest round of muscle spasms when Sue appeared, after I'd searched the entire hotel for almost an hour. "Where have you been?" I fought not to scream the words.

She was taken aback. "I went out for a walk with Pamela. We went down to the drug store for more garland. You were busy working. What's wrong?"

I took a deep, shaky breath. "I really need you to tell me if you have to leave right now. I can't afford to have you too far away."

"It was *twenty minutes,* Tony."

"No. It was well over an hour. You can't be gone that long! You've got to understand that whatever Amber did is making me sick." I stood and walked over to her. My fingers ran through my hair and I wanted to rip it out to get rid of the pain. "Please, Sue. This is really important to me. I've got a job to do and I can't do it if you're somewhere else. I know—you can help me install the system!"

She looked frustrated and hurt. "*I've* got things to do, too, Tony."

I held out my hand to show her. She watched with wide eyes as it trembled. "Look at this! I can't even hold a fucking *screwdriver,* Sue. You *have* to stay nearby."

"Um, I don't know what to say. What did she do to you?"

The headache started again and dropped me to my knees. I alternately ground my teeth and swore. I was panting by the time the sparkles left my vision. Sue was looking down at me in shock, but the hot and sour soup told me that she was afraid to touch me. "Tony, this isn't normal. You need to get some help. Maybe Lelya . . ."

"Can't do a frigging thing," I snapped. "Already tried it.

Whatever Amber did, only she can undo. But no one can find her."

"Wait!" she exclaimed. "I have an idea!"

She bolted out the door before I could stop her. I tried to stand, and it took three attempts. She returned in a few minutes, dragging Lucas along into the darkened room. He took one look at me and cursed in three languages. He threw a wave of blue-white power directly at me. It hit me in the chest and turned the room blue. The black depression and pain faded into the background. I could finally think again for the first time in half a day.

"You're pining, Tony, and you've got it bad. I've been in the same spot. I'll send someone out to find Amber. This will take care of it for a bit. But Sue needs to get out of here. The closer she is, when you can't touch her, the worse it will get. Trust me on this."

I quickly moved forward and put my arms around Sue. The pain subsided completely. "No, goddamn it! You're wrong. It's *better* when I touch her. You have to be able to smell the difference. You've got it backwards."

He crossed his arms over his chest. "I do *not* have it backwards. Sue needs to leave. In fact, I'll make sure of it. Then you need to get back to the installation. If you keep your mind and hands occupied, it's not so bad. Feeding the addiction is the worst thing you can do while you're separated like this."

The rotten bastard froze me in place while he took Sue downstairs. Nikoli offered to let her in the restaurant to start to work. She accepted—more eagerly than I liked. My hands shook every time I thought about her absence and I hated it. But Lucas had been right. By the time she was gone for a bit, the pain subsided. But then the depression set in.

"Are you well, Tony?" Yurgi's voice sliced past my thoughts of Sue. I shook my head to come back to reality. It was the fourth time in an hour that I'd blacked out like that.

I'd apparently been holding the screwdriver to the wall long enough without moving that my fingers were white from blood loss. I shook them until they were pink, and then finished tightening up the molly that would hold the fourth camera in place. Most of the walls in the hotel were plaster and lathe, which were not conducive to installing wiring, so I'd had to adapt the plans Lucas made to only install fixtures into drywalled sections.

"Yeah, sorry, Yurgi. I'm fine. I'll need to go up into the ceiling here to run the wiring from the second floor. Run downstairs and grab the electrical tester. Remember? It's the yellow box with black and red wires coming out the front."

"Ah, yes, I remember. Is in conference room. I will be back quick like the bunny."

I climbed the wooden ladder next to me and lifted the ceiling tile out of the brackets. There wasn't much room between the bottom of the upper floor and the tiles, so I had to wiggle along the metal bracing. Fortunately, it was an older style drop ceiling, and pretty sturdy.

I was busily pulling wire down from the second floor when I heard quiet voices down the next hallway.

"Asri, would you *please* talk to me?" Bobby's voice was a harsh whisper.

"There is nothing to say, Robart. We have already discussed it. My decision is made."

A rush of heavy feet stopped abruptly, along with the lighter patter of shoes. Bobby's words were a hiss that sounded wounded and fearful. I couldn't smell a thing from this far away. "You *can't* tell me that you love him."

Asri's voice quavered just a bit. "Love has little to do with this, Robart, although—if you must know, yes, I do care for him. I have already explained it. Mila is dead, and the position of favorite is empty. I intend to fill it, the mistake of the last two days notwithstanding."

Bobby sniffed lightly. "Hardly *a* mistake. How many times, Asri? Ten, twelve? You can't say it—that *I*—mean *nothing* to you."

Asri started to walk again. Her voice was impatient, annoyed. "You are a Wolven agent, Robart. I have status in this pack. I have *purpose*. Before Nikoli accepted me, I had nothing. No family, no future. *This* is my home. What do you want me to say? That I will mate with you—be the good wife while you come and go on your errands of mercy and punishment? That is not the life I choose."

Couldn't say I blamed her. Bobby rushed to keep up with her clipped steps. "And what of the joy when we touch? The ache when we're apart? I could barely stand it when you were hurting here at the hotel, knowing that *he* was who you turned to. How often did we stop to touch on the way to Carmine's? How many times did we share ourselves with each other? I was so *proud* when you found the body of the man, hidden deep under the snow. Does my pride have no value? Does my love not touch you?"

I knew that Asri had found Sammy's body—this time, almost thirty feet down. Carmine had to call in heavy equipment to fill the hole because Asri had been exhausted after excavating him. Sammy had been dead for several days. We were definitely dealing with a shape-shifter who could cast illusion, and was one hell of a digger. It reminded me that I needed to finish up the security system and get my butt back to finding Babs's kidnapper. Every minute away was a minute more for the scent to grow cold—and increased the likelihood that Carmine would give up waiting.

There was quiet sobbing now in the hallway, and I couldn't help but listen again. Asri's voice caught when she spoke, and her words were harsh. "Yes . . . it *touches me*. Is that what you want to hear, Robart? But it doesn't change our lives. We can be mated and be apart. It is hard, but others have done it. We must each live out our own destiny— follow our own path."

Boy, I wouldn't recommended the "mated and apart" thing. I wasn't liking it very much. There was determination and passion in Bobby's reply. "My path is to bring you joy, Asri. Everything—and everyone—else be *damned!*" There was a shuffling and the sound of whispering cloth. I knew they were kissing. I heard the sound of a lock unlatch and then the door of the nearest room close quietly. The voices disappeared into groans and sighs. I needed to get out of the ceiling before I heard anything else. I can't say I was any different when Sue and I first got together. It's even worse now, but not just for sex. I felt the black glove settle over me again and fought to shake it off long enough to climb down the ladder.

By the time I got down the five steps, I was annoyed. Anger seemed to beat back the depression. *Great!* They were going to be useless now. I could go break it up, but then they'd be even more distracted. As if I didn't have *enough* to think about. I was probably going to have to add Asri's duties to my list, if I expected them to get done. I knew the little soap opera wasn't going to be played out anytime soon—certainly not before the council meeting was over. How long had it taken me to admit I couldn't fight the feelings for Sue? A month? Two? And, Bobby was my friend. He'd covered my ass twice already, so I guess it was my turn.

I returned to attaching wiring and fighting to ignore what was going on just down the hall. I was having a hard time concentrating. If Sue didn't get home soon, I was going to be a basket case.

"Damn it!" I exclaimed after I accidently snipped off the wire I was trying to strip. The shaking was getting worse and depression was threatening to rip out my gut. I was torn between pulling my Taurus and shooting up the place, or turning it to my own temple.

"Tony?" Yurgi's voice was tentative. He could hear me snarl under my breath.

I forced myself to stop. "Yeah, Yurgi? Did you find the tester?"

He shook his head. His bushy eyebrows dropped as his brow furrowed in resignation. "The Alpha and the Duchess, they are in the room. They talk angrily. I think is trouble for us." His scent became odd. I didn't quite know what it was.

"Trouble *for* us?"

He nodded vigorously. "The Duchess, she says that room must be for the banquet. Nikoli, he says is for meeting. Cannot use for both at same time."

I let out an exasperated breath. "Nikoli, Lucas and I already agreed that the conference room would be used for the meeting. It's already set up with recorders and security galore. You don't need as much security for the banquet. The banquet will be in the ballroom on the second floor."

Yurgi shrugged his shoulders. "I only say what Duchess says, Tony. The banquet must be near kitchen. She is not want the live mice to sit next to the venison for whole dinner. Is not enough space in ballroom for all dining tables and food tables. I think the Duchess, she will win."

Live mice? Eww. Must be for the birds. Then, as if by magic, I heard Nikoli's bellow from downstairs. "Tony! I need to see you."

Wonderful. Just wonderful. I stood and dusted the residue from the ceiling from my pants.

"Tony, before you go . . ." I turned and stared at him, waiting.

He opened his mouth again, but I held up a hand to stop him as Nikoli called a second time. "Let me finish with the boss first." I called toward the lobby below. "Be down in a second, Nikoli."

"Take your time, Tony," Lelya yelled back with fire in her voice. "I don't believe that Nikoli and I are *ready* for you yet."

"Yes, we are!" came his snarl again. I'd bet the strong scent of boiling coffee wasn't coming from the kitchen.

Lelya's voice was bordering on deadly. "No, we are *not.*" Then the doors slammed closed once more.

Okay, *that* settled it. I was going to wait for awhile. I turned my full attention back to Yurgi, happy to be out of the loop for a moment. "What did you want to say?"

"I forget, but remembered when I was downstairs. My

lovely *Pamela,* she has tickets. I would ask you—and your wife, to accompany us, if you please?"

"Tickets? To what?"

Yurgi slapped his forehead lightly and the dry heat of embarrassment rose from him. He was also nervous, but I didn't know why.

"Is true. My Pamela, she speaks to your Jessica, but you do not yet speak to *her.* You are very busy. You rise in rank so quickly. The others are impressed, and worried. You make the dragon bow and take Sergei from the air yesterday, and then again today you shoot him before he can strike. I hear of it." He brought up his hands into shooting position and mimicked me shooting Sergei. Then he smiled again. "Is no surprise you defeat *me.*"

I struggled not to show my frustration. I guess I was flattered, but was there going to be a point to this conversation? I glanced at my watch. I hated doing detail work on a time schedule and they were going to be yelling for me again soon.

"Okay, so I'm glad I impressed you. But what tickets are you talking about?" I tried hard not to sound condescending. English seems to be hard for him. I can't say that Russian is any better for me.

"Is to your American game—the *football.* The proud Bears battle the team from the Bay. I watch some of these games on television, but have never before attended."

He had my attention now. "The Bears and the Packers? That game's been sold out for a week."

He nodded hurriedly and smiled again. "Is true. My Pamela, she gets tickets on telephone, from radio. Four tickets. She is very excited—they are near field on center line."

Center? My eyes grew wide. "You have four tickets on the *fifty yard line?* Are you kidding?"

His face and scent grew grave. "No kid. My Pamela, she is wonderous. She puts her name on pieces of papers and sends them in mail to big companies. They mail back gifts.

Shirts and shoes and hats to wear. Once we received fancy music player—with speakers and places to play tapes *and* CDs. It fits on a shelf, but with such big sound."

Ah, It was the *pieces of paper* that gave it away. "You mean she enters *sweepstakes.*"

"Yes. That is the word—*Seepstaks.* She wins many things. Is how we met."

"You met in a sweepstakes?" Okay, that had me a little confused.

"No, I do not say right. She wins *trip*—to Moscow. She goes to nightclub and I see her. The others in our pack, they think she is plain and tiny. A little mouse. They say to me, 'Do not bother with her, Yurgi. She has no fire.' They think women must be like flames in hearth, wild and hot." He put a finger up to his temple and tapped. "But no. My Pamela. she is like *stove.* It warms as good, but fire is hidden inside, not for all to see."

Okay, so his wife is quiet on the outside, but strong. She and Sue probably were hitting it off.

"So, you're asking me and Sue to go to the game with you and Pamela?" I didn't know if Sue liked football, but I sure as hell did. "Hey, I'd be happy to go with you, but are you sure you don't want to ask any of your friends from the pack?"

His face fell a bit and his scent was the wet mist of sadness. "I am *Omega,* Tony. Beneath notice to pack. You are only person to treat me kindly." The sadness faded, left behind by the warm dryer vent smell of gratitude.

He thought that *I* treated him kindly? After I'd nearly snapped his arm off and left him to bury deer carcasses, and was now bossing him all over the hotel? Okay, that made me feel a little uneasy. What do the *others* do?

"Are these guys taking advantage of you, Yurgi? You don't have to put up with their shit. I can teach you to shoot. Then they'll treat you with the same respect as me."

He reached out to grasp my arm, but then pulled his

hand back hurriedly. I guess word had gotten around not to touch me. "No, Tony. Is okay to be Omega. Is *much* better than Siberia. Nikoli is good pack leader. I do small things, not like hard work in Russia. Only a few days a month do I have chores for pack, instead of every day, early to late. I have apartment with Pamela, a job, food on a table that belongs to *me* instead of pack. All because of gracious Alpha. They pay me American money for every hour I work—so much money. Is good life. I am happy here. There is *future.* You understand? Nikoli, he honors effort. He allows one such as me even to *breed,* if I am able."

I'd never really thought about things like that. Okay, so maybe Chicago isn't too bad, after all. I'll be keeping Siberia off my list of places to visit. It made me realize that maybe I didn't understand Nikoli, after all. He'd won a few points just now.

"So you and Pamela got married in Russia and then moved here?"

His eyes grew wide and the clove scent of pride burst into the air. "No. Not in Russia. Pamela was only for short time in Moscow, as was I. We spent time together while we could. I was bold enough to tell her my secret, because I hoped she could stay with me. But she could not. When she returned to America, she sends me letters. I learned much English from her letters, with help of friend. I learned she loved me. She could accept me."

His scent suddenly returned to embarrassment, but anger rode over the top. "My Alpha, he sees me reading letter when I should be working. He is ready to kill me, but decides to exile me instead. Is hard for low wolf to be in wild, Tony. I will not survive without pack to provide for me."

Okay, now *that* I didn't understand. Even a human can survive in the wild. It made no sense. I didn't get a chance to ask about it, though, because he continued.

"I write to Pamela one last time. I tell her I am exiled and will never see her again. But she is brave, my Pamela.

She lives in Chicago. She searches for Sazi, asking in dark places where she should not be. She is taken to Nikoli and asks for his help to bring me to America. She promises to work hard for the pack if he will bring lowly Yurgi to be with her." His face showed surprise and his scent was once again cloves and cinnamon. "My Alpha, he calls me to him once more before I am taken to deep forest. He is surprised. The great Nikoli has asked for me. He offers passage to America—to Chicago, for a lowly Omega. He makes passport and obtains visa. I do not forget his kindness, Tony. I have Pamela and if God is willing, we will have children. She is human, so it is possible. All is possible in United States."

"Even football," I said with a small smile. Despite the waves of depression fighting to take control of my mind, it was hard not to feel better with the scent of oranges and cinnamon and other happy spices filling the air.

"Yes. Even football. You will go with us? It would please me to share my fortune with one who avenges the small ones. Denis and Alek are most humble to you."

I glanced to my side when I saw Lelya walking down the hallway toward us. "Sure, Yurgi, I'd be glad to. We'll work it out later." I turned my attention to the Duchess. "So? Who won the battle?"

An amused but annoyed scent rolled off her and she glanced at Yurgi sharply. He lowered his head, and absolutely reeked of the dusty heat of shame and embarrassment.

"The banquet will be held in the conference room. You will provide two additional cameras for the ballroom on the second floor. Wolven will provide extra agents for guarding the room. It has no windows, so there should be little to delay your schedule."

I closed my mouth when I realized it was open and rubbed the bridge of my nose to ease the tension. Windows. Shit, that's right. I'd forgotten all about the windows. We needed to get bars installed, or . . .

I looked at the Duchess. "Since it's winter anyway,

would it be okay to use nails or wood screws to secure the windows to the frame and then putty and paint over them? We can pull them out afterward, and I can't imagine any-one who would need them open. That way I wouldn't have to install bars. It would save time—give me the extra time to work on the ballroom."

Yurgi almost slapped my shoulder, but stopped short a second time. "Yes. Is *good* idea. Would save much time."

Lelya glanced up to something behind me. I turned my head. Asri was walking down the hallway, pulling her long hair out from inside her shirt. The necklace she always clutched finally appeared for a moment before she tucked it back inside. It looked like a carved piece of bamboo on a chain, but it was solid, not hollow. Some sort of charm, I guess.

The smell of peppermint preceded her by about a mile. Does she carry the stuff *with* her now? I decided I didn't want to know.

The Duchess noticed the scent, as well. Her brows raised delicately. "Peppermint Castile is a new scent for you, Asri."

Asri's face went stony and blank after a brief moment of surprise at Lelya's new, improved appearance. "It was a gift."

Lelya's face was a mix between stern and amused. "Ah. I've always thought it better in tea or candy than disrupting scents. Don't you agree?"

The face and scent gave nothing away, but Asri's hands were trembling a bit. "If it disturbs you, my Alpha . . ."

Lelya flipped her hand gracefully. "No, no. But I don't believe it is one of *Nikoli*'s favorite scents. Yes, I think pep-permint is better in tea. I don't believe we have had tea to-gether in a number of years, Asri. Why don't you join me?"

Asri's eyes grew wide and panicked and her mouth opened just a bit. She closed it abruptly and glanced around her frantically. "I'm afraid that I will have to decline, Duchess. There is much to do, after all, and I have little free time."

My smile was both malicious and impish. "Oh, go ahead, Asri. Yurgi and I can take up the slack for a few *more* minutes."

She turned to me and the shock of surprise, combined with hot and sour soup, rode over the peppermint in a burst.

Lelya stepped forward and put an arm around Asri's shoulders to lead her away. "Yes, but I *insist*. Tony seems quite competent." She turned to me for a moment. "I believe your idea about the windows is a good one. You may proceed." I nodded, and then she turned back to the wide dark eyes framed by a curtain of shimmering black hair. "And we've much to talk about, you and I, Asri—with the meeting here so soon. I will tell you many things, of people and personalities. The past and the *future*."

Asri stepped quickly to keep pace with the older woman, but she wasn't walking smoothly. She turned her head often, looking for some way out of the situation. Oooh, boy, was *she* in for it. I still remembered my own tea party.

"Have fun." I called as they walked the hallway to disappear down the stairs. If Asri shot me a dirty look, I didn't see it.

I would like to say that Yurgi and I worked as a well-oiled team until afternoon, but it would be a lie. He was having a hard time grasping the necessary detail work involved for a good security system to function smoothly. I did find out that he was pretty good with a solder iron and could climb into tight spaces like a monkey. But I also knew that I would be installing and programming the computers alone if I didn't get more help.

Lucas strode up as I was explaining—for the third time—why we had to move the cameras again so that the coverage overlapped. The information just wasn't sinking in.

"How's it going, guys? You holding up okay, Tony? Will we be done in time?"

I looked around at the stacks of boxes and wires that I hoped to turn into a control room soon and sighed. "I sure hope so. I can think a little better thanks to you. I've got to run back into town to get two more cameras and a bunch more wire, though. The Duchess apparently has decided that the conference room will house the banquet, so we'll need to get some video coverage outside the ballroom on the second floor."

Lucas swore under the breath. "I was afraid Lelya was going to win that argument. I just hope Nikoli holds up under pressure better in the council chambers, or the wolves are in for a rough ride until I'm back in the saddle." He shook his head and I could smell the burnt metal frustration envelop him like a cloud. "Go ahead and get whatever you need. The budget's out the window anyway."

"Any chance you can work with Yurgi getting the computers set up while I'm gone? It would really speed the process along."

He looked around at the room, with wires sticking out the walls at odd angles. "I'm not good with electronics, Tony. But, I do have someone coming in later who's a whiz at this system. I'm sure he wouldn't mind helping out."

I didn't bother to keep the eagerness from my voice. "When does this *whiz* arrive?"

"His name is Raven Ramirez. He's second in command at Wolven. His is one of the jobs I'm watching at the moment while he's on mandatory leave." He shook his head angrily and clenched large fists. Boiling coffee rode the air and made Yurgi sneeze so hard and fast that he had to leave to find tissues.

"It's ridiculous for the council to require both Fiona and Raven to be on leave at the same time! Mind you, neither of them had a break for years, but I'm only one person! The desk in Paris is a disaster."

Ah. So Wolven is based in France. I'd wondered. "How'd you get him to work the meeting if he's on vacation? And when does he get here?"

Lucas grinned and raised his thick brows. His eyes twinkled with dark humor. "He was already stateside visiting his father. His *grandfather* is Chief Justice of the council. They haven't seen each other in over a year. He's allowed to visit *family,* after all. If he happens to wander around the hallways during the meeting when his grandfather is tied up, who's to stop him?"

Rationalization at its finest. It didn't fool me, and it wouldn't fool the council. But that wasn't my problem. The security system was.

"He should arrive by early evening, depending on how the flights between here and Denver are running."

Great—I could get the cameras and install the components, and then have help hooking them all together! I glanced at my watch and swore under my breath. I was already twenty minutes late for a call to a certain little blackmailer.

Lucas took my swearing to mean that time was slipping by, which it was. "Why don't you go ahead and get the cameras. The address and phone of the supplier are on the invoice downstairs. I can at least help Yurgi finish installing the cameras on the walls, and leave the final hook-ups for you." He glanced across the center opening to focus on the cameras already installed on the opposite side. "They look like they're about ten feet apart, right?"

"Eleven feet, two. You can go ten feet if you want, though. It might be better to have a tighter sweep close to the front door." I finished dusting off my jeans and checking my pockets for the keys to the, ugh, *Honda.*

By the time I'd gotten to the electronics store, I'd made two extra stops, and a major discovery. Sometimes, it's when your mind is occupied that weird things pop into your head. I'd remembered Scotty saying that he had photos of me and Bobby *at the hotel.* I wanted to find out where he'd been that he could take photos. Carmine hadn't mentioned finding any special camera equipment, and I was supposed to be foiling assassination attempts of council members. A rifle has a lot longer range than a camera.

Carmine had gone through the two envelopes of prints

carefully. He'd found three of me and Bobby—taken from *inside* the hotel, just before my session with Asri. We had a *big* security breach! I mulled the possibilities and problems that bombshell raised.

"The kid was looking down at you guys," Carmine had said. "There's a bit of a metal railing at the bottom of one pic, and—*yeah*—a little more railing at the top of this other print. I'd say he was on the second floor. No higher than that, and directly opposite the front door. From the green that pokes up in the corners, I'd say he was behind a potted plant."

I admit to being preoccupied when I got to the hotel, but the twenty other people who *lived* there should have noticed a teenager skulking around. It's not like the place is an actual hotel, with strangers wandering around.

I thanked Carmine, and ensured again that Sally was still healthy, if not happy. We talked a bit about the investigation. Fortunately, even though I hadn't gotten much done today he'd been pleased by Asri's efforts. He felt that finding Sammy, and eliminating him as a suspect, was real progress. It had settled him down, bought me a little more time.

He and Asri hadn't become best buddies. "That broad's got a major chip on her shoulder, Tony. She didn't have much nice to say about Barbara, which set Linda off. I had to have the guys pull Lin out of the room before she pounced and ripped out all that black hair."

The image his description provoked made me smile— delicate little Linda turned into a snarling animal, while the real animal calmly raised a brow and ignored her. Yeah, I could see it pretty clearly in my head. I wondered briefly how Bobby had reacted. He and Linda have always been pretty tight, and Linda's pretty good at noticing who's sleeping with who.

After ending that call, I'd set up a meeting with the kid. He was annoyed that I hadn't called when I'd promised. I didn't want to spoil my surprise, so I'd actually played sorry. I wanted to see his face when I blew his scheme out of the water.

I was waiting across the parking lot, hidden behind the Honda, when I saw Scotty arrive on a skateboard. Pretty impressive with a half foot of snow covering most of the sidewalk. He waited outside, checking his watch often. I focused in on him with my wolf eyes and felt a calmness flow through me as I raised the weapon to my shoulder and steadied it on the hood of the car. I put the sight on his neck—a pumpkin on a fencepost. His hair was still cut the same way, long in the front so it almost covered his eyes, and shaved in the back. Seconds ticked by as I waited until there were no shoppers. I'd already made an excessively large donation to the bell ringer with the kettle to get him to take a second lunch.

I got lucky when a fire truck roared by. The sirens and horns would muffle the explosion. A quick exhale of breath was followed by a squeeze of the trigger, and I watched him stagger back and drop on his butt into the snow.

I slid the weapon under a shelf of snow that I'd previously prepared beneath the car, and was standing next to him with Sazi speed before he could extricate himself. He was staring at the smear of pink paint on his hand. The gelatinous goop was running down his face from the splat directly between his eyes.

I tossed a handful of crumpled paper towels on his chest and knelt down next to him. I was feeling that black depression again, so I turned it into cold anger. I lowered my voice to a dangerous hiss. "Next time you break into my house, kid, you won't be wiping off paint."

He was outraged, rather than frightened. "That was low, man! I'm going to have a welt there all day!" He tried to get his balance enough to stand up, but his hands kept burying deeper into the wet pile of snow. I wasn't intending to help him. Instead, I used the cell phone to make a call.

He finally managed to turn himself over and push backwards to get out of the bank. Even turned slightly away from him I saw the knife come out of his pocket and slice at me.

I knocked it out of his hand so easily it appeared casual. I didn't even move the phone. The thin stiletto blade stuck in the wooden facade. I held the phone to my ear with my shoulder as it rang, and grabbed the knife quick enough to make his jaw drop. I snapped the blade in two, just as casually, raising my brows with a bored look.

Now he was starting to look afraid. "I've got pho—"

I shook my head, the phone once again in my left hand. "You've got nothing, kid," I snarled, letting a thick Italian accent play across the words.

I heard Carmine pick up and speak. I replied into the speaker, "I'll let you do the honors."

I handed the kid the phone. He took it warily, his face and blond bangs still smeared with pink. "Yeah?" His voice was angry, but cautious.

I listened to his heart pound and his mustard scent blend with the thick hot and sour soup. His sweat beaded to the surface of his skin, and I had to shake my head to remove the thoughts of ripping out his tender young throat.

"I want to talk to her." His voice was trembling a little. Ah, he was starting to get attached to that one.

I could hear the tearful girl sob her apologies into the phone. He made careful noises, but I could tell he was angry with her for getting caught. The anger couldn't erase the fear though. My jaw was clenching. I'd forgotten to eat, and the moon was still close enough to full that it was a problem. Not eating was becoming a bad habit. I certainly know better.

I stepped away from him, turning my face into the wind to lessen the tantalizing scents. As I leaned against one of the building pillars I listened to both sides of the brief conversation. Scotty's face moved from cautious to afraid, to angry, to resigned—all in the matter of less than a minute.

He sighed and I started forward again until I was standing next to him. "Yeah, sure—I mean, *yes sir,* Mr. Leone.

I'll head back today." He shook his head and turned off the phone, and then handed it back to me.

"Man, you guys are *good*." He glanced at me with something approaching wonder. "You could have offed me just now and Sally would be dead, too. Nobody would miss two kids like us. Why didn't you?"

I put a hand on his shoulder and then squeezed his neck in a firm grip. I did it by instinct, but then panicked for a second. I waited to get sucked away into another place and time, but nothing happened. I was grateful and relieved. Maybe that shield was good for something, after all.

"You've got raw talent, kid, but no finesse. The threat was good until you *completely* gave away your hand. This business takes smarts as well as balls. Carmine's willing to teach you the smarts *if* you play by his rules." I smiled at him, a flash of bared teeth and watched him shiver. "Besides, *I* have plans for you."

I pulled him until he was walking beside me, my hand still tight enough on his neck that he winced. He used the towels to mop the partially frozen paint from his face, dropping the paper into the waste can outside the door to the store. The hair would be stained until he washed it, but the color wasn't much different than I've seen on other kids.

I ignored the sound of canned Christmas carols playing of the loud speakers inside the store, but the music reminded me. I'd need to pick up something special for Sue—soon. It would be our first Christmas together. The warmth of the thought was cut off by the cold black shield that kept me from reaching her mind-to-mind.

"Tell me about your visit to the hotel." I ordered, my voice more husky and harsh than usual.

Scotty's eyes went a little wide over the top of the box he was carrying. When he answered his voice was nervous. "Uh, yeah. I almost got caught by that Chinese chick," he said ruefully. "It was almost like she could *smell* me or something. But then you guys showed up and she took off down the back stairs."

"How did you get in to begin with?" I piled another large box, containing twin cameras, into his outstretched arms.

He juggled until he could peek around the cameras, boxes of coaxial wire and Romex electrical cable.

"Piece of cake. I waited until dark and climbed up the fire escape to the second floor. I used a glass cutter on the window—just a little hole so I could nudge the latch open. It's an old hotel—just a single swing lock, and the window slid right up. *Man!* That place, like, *never* has customers! I was in and out of that room for, like, three days. I had to wait until everyone was downstairs, but then *boom,* you showed up and the rest is history."

I pulled him by his shirt sleeve into a corner near the swinging doors to the stock room. I listened closely. No-body was around. "*Ancient* history, kid. As far as you're concerned, from now on—I'm *dead,* just like the papers say. I'll make sure you get trained up right, but *not* by me!"

I moved my face close to his. "You fucked up royally, kiddo. You'd be missing some key body parts right now if I didn't have a use for you." The thick, heady scent of his fear rode the air. "Lucky for you, I've got one last job for you before you leave town. But then you *go,* and you don't come back unless you're called. *Capisce?*"

He nodded, a bit frantically. I had to catch the pile as it threatened to topple onto the floor. "Yeah—yeah, I get it, Mr. G. I'm out of my league. But I'll get better, you'll see. I'll be as good as you some day. I'll be a pro."

Part of me was pleased, because I knew he might finally start to get his shit together. But part of me was worried, be-cause he might be right. "Only if you learn *respect*, kid. Re-spect for the Family, respect for a cop's brain, respect for a client's probable stupidity, and respect for the mark's sur-vival instinct. You show respect—you get respected. *Then* you'll be as good. After that, if you *survive*, you'll be a pro."

Chapter 16

SERGEI THE DOORMAN blocked open the entrance to the hotel while I unloaded the back seat of the Honda. I could smell fear and anger as I walked by him. I shot him a dangerous look so he would keep his mouth shut. He was wearing a full-length red overcoat with shiny gold buttons and appliqués and looked absolutely miserable. His newly injured right arm was in a sling, and the left one was obviously still painful. I hoped it was as painful as Denis's arm.

I glanced around, expecting to see the same level of activity as before. "Where is everyone? This place is a tomb."

I'd forgotten how deep his voice is. It's a rich, rolling bass with a slight Russian accent that matches the untamed black beard perfectly. "Our Alphas prepare to greet guests. Alpha Santiago, Lady Asri, and the snake meet with Wolven agents who have just arrived. Your mate waits upstairs, and others eat evening supper."

Yeah, supper sounded good, but so did seeing Sue. I could feel some of the blackness and despair lessen just at the thought of touching her. To hell with what Lucas thought. "What's for dinner tonight?"

His jaw set and I could hear his teeth grind, but he answered civilly. "I am instructed to remain at door. Our Alpha Female will only allow me to eat when the others have finished. I do not know."

Oooh, that's a hard blow—being as he was formerly first in command under Nikoli. I didn't comment on the punishment. It wasn't my place.

I took my supplies and headed to the second floor. It looked like Lucas and Yurgi had been busy. All of the cameras were in place, and the boxes were unpacked in the control room. The monitors were connected to each other and the server and the clutter removed. I said a silent thank you.

As I was rounding the corner to our suite, Yurgi stepped out of the ballroom, licking his fingers. I could smell what seemed to be wild meat with a variety of spices.

"Good dinner?" I asked across the atrium.

"Is venison, Tony!" He kissed the tips of his fingers and rolled his eyes. "Is *heaven*. The Duchess, she hunt and bring home deer. I not know she hunt, Tony! She never do this before." He held out his hands to either side of his head, about two feet out. "Is big buck with antlers out to *here!* Alena, she cook with spices, but is still red and warm. I hope Alena, she always cook! She has gift. You must try some before all gone."

I smiled when he mentioned Lelya, and wondered how Nikoli was taking the changes in his mother. None of my business, I reminded myself.

Dinner *did* sound good . . . But no—I wanted to see Sue. I'd been able to smell her summer forest since I walked in the door. "Maybe in a bit. Thanks!" He waved and kept walking toward the stairs. I heard her voice before I opened the door to the suite. My brow furrowed a bit. "Yes, I know, Dr. Corbin. I'm trying to be understanding." I heard John-Boy's voice in the background, but couldn't make out the words. "Dr. Perdue said this could happen. But I didn't expect Tony . . . I mean, it's *Tony*. It's not like him. I just wasn't *prepared*. With the news about my family, and Tony acting like Mom . . ."

I dropped my hand from the knob and stepped back from the door. Acting like her *mom?* What the hell did that mean? *What* news about her family? Wow, the things that happen when I leave for an hour or two!

Sue's mom is a raving, manipulative, drug-addicted bitch—not to put too fine a point on it. What traits did Sue think I had in common with that old bat?

I trusted John-Boy—Dr. John Walton Corbin, M.D., Ph.D., life-long friend and former Mafia family member, *and* Sue's psychiatrist, to look out for my interests, whatever the current crisis.

How was I acting like her mom?

I turned on my heel, walking away from the room. I needed to think. As I headed to the ballroom I mulled over the events of the past two days. I might as well eat if Sue was going to do a psychiatric therapy session on the phone. Interrupting the call would be counterproductive. Besides, I wasn't sure I wanted to hear what she had to say. Not right now.

The succulent scent of roast meat wafted from the door as I walked toward the room. Most of the pack members had come and gone, probably to rest up before the big push of guests. Boris was cutting a thick slice of deer from a rapidly diminishing roast as I walked in. There was a smudge of dark sauce clinging to his white chin hairs.

"Ah! Come, come, Tony! See what our gracious Alpha Female has hunted for us!"

I glanced around the table and felt my stomach rumble impatiently. The scent of deer and blood and a dozen spices filled the air. Roast venison, ground venison lasagne, venison tenderloin medallions in a thick brown sauce. My jaw clenched from the scents. There were also bowls of rice and noodles, fruit salad and thick red beet borsch. One long glass casserole dish was completely empty except for scraps. It was shredded venison in some sort of cream sauce.

"The food is very good, Tony," said Celia in the corner. I'd never met her formally, but she certainly knew me after the incident in the lobby. Hell, everybody knew *me* now. "Please join us. Boris, tell him the joke you just told me."

I quickly filled a china dinner plate from each prepared dish, including the shredded scraps. I skipped the borsch—it's an acquired taste that I've never acquired—and sat down next to the ancient wolf. He stabbed the whole slice of roast with his fork and ripped off a piece with his teeth. No knife for this old boy.

"Why did the wolf cross the road?" He asked with twinkling eyes and a full mouth.

"I don't know," I replied before stuffing a wonderfully pungent medallion into my mouth.

"He was chasing the chicken!" He guffawed noisily at his own punch line, and slapped his thigh. "My grandson told me this joke! It's good, yes?"

I chuckled. "Yeah, that's pretty good."

"You missed Celia's dish." He looked again at my plate. "No, it looks like you got the last of it, after all." He slapped my shoulder hard enough that I almost spit out the second piece of tenderloin I'd put in my mouth. "My Celia, she made venison enchiladas with chile cream." I raised my brows and took a bite of the scraps of shredded meat when I'd swallowed the other. I knew immediately why it had disappeared so fast. Cumin and jalapeños blended with a bunch of other seasonings to create a taste so savory that it just about threw my tongue to the ground.

"Wow, Celia! That's really good. You should make sure they serve this at the banquet for the dignitaries! And write down the recipe for the rest of us." She blushed quietly and nodded. She smelled of cloves and the dry heat of embarrassment. They both picked up their plates and put them in the bussing tub before leaving.

It took third helpings before my raging hunger was quelled. I took my time eating, still thinking about what

Sue said. I knew she had triggers about her family, and it might take years to find them all. I didn't want her hurt, but I wasn't going to change who I was.

I made a plate for her, in case she hadn't eaten. I heard her snuffling and blowing her nose as I approached the door. *Acting like her mom?* I almost opened it, but then hesitated, and knocked. I could feel a knot in my stomach. "Sue? Can I come in?"

Her hurried footsteps sounded and the door opened. She smiled, but it was obvious from her face and scent that she'd been crying since I went down to dinner. "Of course. You live here, too. At least, until the conference is done."

I held out the plate. "They had a buffet in the ballroom. Lelya brought home a deer. I thought you might not have eaten."

She sniffed the plate delicately and smiled—this time for real. "Oh! I heard she was going hunting! Nikoli was so surprised he could hardly speak when she announced it earlier." She put the plate on the coffee table and sat down in one of the wing chairs. I sat down in the one next to her and rested a hand on her knee. She laughed as she started to cut a piece. "It was great, Tony! She was a hoot." She used thick accents to imitated Nikoli and Lelya: 'Are you sure you're strong enough, mother?' *Yes, Niki, I took down moose and reindeer in my youth. I think I can still manage a whitetail deer.* 'How will you get it home, mother? You have no driver.' *I can drive, too, son. We have cars.* 'The antlers will stick out of a trunk, mother.' *Niki use your head! It's hunting season! Nobody will notice. But fine, if it will make you happier, I will have it appear to be a Christmas tree.*" Sue laughed brightly. "It was priceless!"

She raised her brows in appreciation of the roast. I'd poured some of the chile cream over it. "Wow! This sauce is *wonderful!*"

"Celia made it. I asked her for the recipe. But Alena made the rest."

Sue nodded and kept eating. She took a sip of soda from

a beer mug already on the table. I watched her and realized that I was happy. I was warm and content just sitting here with her, touching her. I didn't ever want to be apart from her again. I felt myself smiling broadly.

Wait. I should be concerned and worried. That puzzled me and made me realize that there *was* something wrong. More than just having the shakes and a headache. This was deeper and was affecting my whole mind—my whole personality.

She took another sip. The flash of memory struck me like a brick. I abruptly knew *exactly* what was wrong. Seeing her sipping the drink from the bar mug had done it. The recollection was as clear as a bell.

We were sitting in another suite, of another hotel. It was the first day we'd met, and Sue had paid me a thousand bucks to sit and listen to her sorry tale about why she wanted to die, and why I was supposed to kill her. She was getting drunk on Morgan and Diets from a beer mug just like this one, and had just started to talk about her mother. I remember being amazed at the weirdness of the woman.

"After I won the money," I recall Sue saying, "I bought a big house, way larger than I needed. I figured that Mom could have space and I would have a room or two where I could be alone. I've always liked being alone. But Mom can't be alone. Actually *can't*. It drives her nuts. I sit down to take a bath and she's knocking on the door, wanting to come in to talk. It drives me insane."

I remembered how odd it had seemed, because I also liked to be alone. But now I didn't. It all clicked—the trembling when we were apart, the desperate need to touch her, and the black despair when I couldn't. Shit! No wonder she nearly bolted out the door. I *was* becoming her mom, and I didn't know how to stop it!

She was almost finished with the plate, eating and swallowing the deer as fast as she could. If she stopped to think about it, she would probably get weird, so I didn't mention it. What I did do was stand and walk to the wet bar. I opened two of the shot-sized bottles of Seagrams and poured them into a whiskey glass. I prefer Maker's Mark, but any port in a storm.

Once again, the past seemed very close as I watched her image split into fragments of color and movement through the cut crystal. The wet fog of sorrow still filled the air and her tears pained me almost more than I could bear. I shook off the feeling and swallowed the whiskey, feeling it burn its way down to my stomach. I took a deep breath.

"I overheard a bit of your conversation with John-boy earlier."

She froze in place, the fork nearly to her mouth. She glanced at me with panicked eyes, and put down the bite of deer. The scent of her ammonia laced fear hit me in the chest. I turned back to the bar for another shot. "Tony, I—"

I waved off her objection as I slugged down another bottle without bothering to pour. "No, you were right to call him. I thought about it, and I know what's wrong. I *am* acting just like Myra, and damned if I know why. The thought of it is making me sick to my stomach, but I can't seem to help myself."

I rested my hands on the padded edge and then pounded a fist on the bar in frustration. The whole works shuddered. I could see her flinch in the mirror behind the bar. "Just so you know, the offer still holds." I turned to her and felt the clawing of bats in my gut. "I don't know if I can stop whatever's causing me to be so clingy and weird. If you can't handle it, you can leave."

Time reversed once more. I watched her body language close down like a vault. Her ankles crossed, then her fingers interlaced and she slumped. Her eyes took on a haunted look while she twisted and clutched her fingers. "It's not your fault—I know that. Really!" She looked up at me with pleading eyes. "Dr. Perdue told me that wolves are very pack-oriented. It was only because you weren't *in* a pack that you had been a loner. But she said that once you bonded to a pack, you wouldn't be able to exist any other way. The pack would be your whole world. I know now what she meant."

Her eyes filled with tears and her scent tore at me. "I don't want to leave you, Tony. I know you're not like Mom. You're not doing this to manipulate me. You just can't help it. If I hadn't gotten the tape today, I probably wouldn't have even noticed it. Dr. Corbin says that he can help me disable the trigger. It will take time, but I don't want to slip back into my own depression, either. I need to be a whole person; have friends and a job and hobbies that don't involve you or the pack. Like a normal person. I want to be someone you're proud to have as a wife."

I frowned and held up a hand to stop her. "Wait. Back up a couple of sentences. *What* tape?"

Her hand flew to her mouth. "That's right! You don't even know!" She stood up and walked toward a cabinet across from the couch. She opened the doors to reveal a large television and VCR.

"It should have rewound itself." She patted the couch. "Come sit next to me. I want you to see this."

I walked toward the couch with a furrowed brow and sat next to her. She picked up the remote and pressed the red button. The television came on. Two more clicks and the VCR started whirring.

Linda's face came on the screen. She was wearing a black, wide-brimmed hat with a veil over a sleek and sexy black silk pantsuit. I heard giggling and rustling from behind the camera.

"Okay, am I in focus?"

I heard Babs voice. "You're on!"

Linda waved. "Hi, Sue! I know we're not supposed to talk to you, but we decided to risk it for this." She made pulling motions with her hand. "Barbara. Come say hi to Sue."

I saw Babs's red hair and a close-up of her nose appear

on the screen. "Hi, Sue!" She giggled again and moved to sit next to Linda on the bed. They held hands and Linda kissed the twined knuckles gently. I wasn't sure I wanted to know what was coming up.

Babs was also wearing a hat with a veil, and her eyes were swollen and red. But it seemed to be from laughing, rather than crying.

Linda spoke again. "Okay, so you've probably already read the article we're including with the tape." Sue pressed the pause button and held out a small piece of newspaper.

"I'll give you a second while you read this." Equal measures of anger and hurt played in her voice.

I glanced down at the article. Even in the dim light from the television, I could read just fine. I raised my brows at the headline:

LOTTO WINNER BODY FOUND! AP WIRE— Authorities today offered conclusive proof that a badly burned body found buried about ten miles from the old airport is indeed the remains of millionaire Suzi Quentin. DNA tests performed on samples of skin and hair obtained from Ms. Quentin's family matched that of the charred corpse discovered by construction workers late Tuesday. The Quentin family, through their attorney, has declined to talk with the press. However, a prepared press release was distributed by Marcus Thompson, attorney for the Quentin family: "The Quentin family has requested privacy to deal with the loss of their beloved Suzi. They will have a simple, closed funeral as soon as the remains are released, and then begin to deal with disposition of Ms. Quentin's estate."

"What the hell?" I said with amazement.
Sue punched the Play button once again. "It gets better."
Linda came back on the screen. What she had to say sur-

prised even *me*. "We had Camine do some checking. Apparently, your wonderful relatives either had some poor girl iced, or found a convenient Jane Doe, and fried her up. *But,* not until they spent a couple of days brushing her hair and dressing her up like a doll in your clothes so they would have matching DNA samples! Somehow, the blood samples from when you were shot *disappeared* from evidence, so they had to go to the family. It took Carmine days of asking around to find all this out. They hired some scumbag from out of town, I guess, but by the time we knew, Barbara and I had gotten a call from the attorney. We just got back from the will reading."

Babs burst into laughter once more, so hard and fast that after a moment, she couldn't breathe. She waved her hand in front of her face, and held up a finger. Then she disappeared off-screen.

I knew I had an astounded look on my face. I could see the reflection in the television screen.

I heard Babs from off-camera before she walked back into the picture, carrying some tissues and a glass of water. "I wish I could have taken pictures! I thought your sister was going to have a heart attack when the lawyer read the will." Babs took a sip of water and dabbed at her leaking eyes with the tissue. "Oh, by the way, thanks for the ten grand. It was sweet."

Linda spoke up. "And I don't need the money, of course, so I donated my hundred grand to that animal shelter group you like, in your name. Wrote them a check on the spot. They were ecstatic! So was the representative from the Wildlife Service—one hundred forty million added to their budget and all they have to do is build a lake where your house is and install goose nests."

Babs took over. "Carmine found out that the family offered a cool million to anyone for enough evidence to get their inheritance. No big deal to them, it was nothing compared to the whole. They didn't even bitch at your gifts to us. Get this—your mom patted Linda's hand to offer her congratulations!" She guffawed again. "Of course, that all changed after you cut them out. *Then* they started screaming bloody murder. Your attorney was smart, though. He knew there would be objections and has already filed all of the notes and video tapes from your office visits with him with the Court. They've scheduled a validity hearing on the twentieth—just in time for Christmas."

Sue was near tears. Her voice was a pained whisper over the laughter on the tape.

"They'll get their million. I left life insurance of that much." She snuffled and stared at me.

I felt completely helpless. I couldn't fix what they'd done. What little self-esteem she'd managed to gain over the past few months was gone—destroyed by the knowledge that money had meant more to those fucking vultures than their own flesh and blood. I hoped they couldn't pay their assassin on time and wound up in the same condition as the corpse. Hell, I'd have liked to kill them myself. Damn it!

And now she thought I was acting just like them. That would change—right now, no matter what the cost to me.

I pulled Sue into my arms and she burst into full-fledged tears. Sobs wracked her body. I patted her back and closed my eyes. I was grateful that I couldn't feel the pain she did. "Let it go, Sue. You're dead to them now. Let them be dead to you. You have a new family—this pack—and you're wanted and loved."

She pulled back and shook her head. "I don't know about that. I don't think that the pack is going to want me much after I tell Nikoli what I found out at the restaurant. I'm not even sure I *should* tell him."

I gave her my full attention. "What did you find? Were there accounting errors? I'm not even positive what he hired you to do."

She lowered her voice and moved very close to me. "He

told me he was losing money in one particular restaurant, but spies he'd put in couldn't see anyone stealing. But they are! They're robbing him blind, Tony. It took me hours to figure out what happened, but I finally did."

I rolled my hand for her to continue. She'd caught my interest. I couldn't imagine that Nikoli wouldn't know exactly what was happening in any of his businesses.

"See, each of the register drawers opens when a sale is made. Of course, in a fast food restaurant, people change their orders all the time. Sometimes, even after a sale is complete, the customer will change their mind or not have enough money. I worked at one for over a year, so I know it happens. But these kids have a *very* profitable scheme going. Fortunately, they didn't realize there was a way to figure it out."

"Oh, no! You don't get to skip straight to the end. First, what's the scam?"

She nodded and then leaned over to whisper in my ear. "After a customer orders, the employee hits the total button, enters the amount tendered and opens the drawer. Then they pass back the change, just like they're supposed to. But before they close the drawer, which completes the order, they're voiding each item from the screen and pocketing the money. *Then* they close the drawer to a voided sale. No transaction will appear on their register tape and the money loss will never show—or so they *thought!*"

I smiled and kissed her hair. I was a little taken aback when she flinched again, but continued smoothly. "That's my girl! How'd you figure it out?"

She smiled up at me, but it was shaky. "They apparently don't know there's a *master* register tape under the counter that records *all* of the transactions on all of the registers. I knew it, because I worked with the same system before. In a chain restaurant, that tape would go to the district office to be kept for a period of years. But since Nikoli owns the place, he just had his manager keep it in the safe, which I had access to. I was looking for discrepancies and found all of these voided sales. It didn't happen every shift, or even every day. So I checked the voids with the employee calendar and the voids all seemed to come from about four employees, about once a week for over two years. I have their names and amounts of voids. Some of them are in the tens of thousands, Tony! No *wonder* Nikoli is hurting there. A few of the voided transactions *might* be valid . . ." She raised her brows and looked cynical. "But I wonder if some of these teenagers are living a little beyond their means. I'm sure Nikoli could find out. But, I'm afraid he might kill them, or tell them where he got the information and they'll hunt me down."

Nobody hunts my mate. I stood up in a burst, and stared at her with cold death in my gaze. She flinched and shivered. She hadn't seen my mercenary look for awhile. "*No one* will hunt you down, Sue—*ever*. They'd never got within ten feet of you before I made sure they got a ticket to their own private highway to hell."

She shook her head and moved back further on the couch. She squared her shoulders and drew a deep breath. "No, Tony. That's not the way it can happen. You heard what Lelya said. I have to fight my own battles. I have to face the danger from people who hate me. And . . . I *need* to fight them, even if I am scared." She chuckled, but it was tinged with tears. "I finally got to where I *don't* want to die, so now this is tossed at me. Figures." She shivered, and her scent became thick and penetrating Chinese soup.

Sue was right. I hated it, but she was right. It was time to fight off the wolf instincts and follow those that I'd developed over the rest of my life. She was a big girl. I had to let *her* protect her.

I stood up and walked over to the banker's box that Lucas had delivered along with our unconscious bodies. He'd removed the Taurus to put with my clothes, but all the rest was here, too.

There was no reason I couldn't help her in the training

process. She had never developed any fighting skills. "But she also said that you should be cautious, and carry teeth and claws, Sue—because you don't have any."

I reached into the box and extracted a switchblade made of silver. I'd had it made shortly after I became a wolf—when I'd learned that the part about silver wasn't a myth.

I'd originally intended to use the knife to kill Babs—but then she'd taken up with Carmine and Linda. Had to wonder if she'd done that deliberately. She was smart enough. Which reminded me again that I needed to find her. Carmine loved her. Hell, from the look of that tape Linda loved her.

I tossed the knife to Sue and she caught it. She pressed the button and jumped a foot when the slender blade extended to the full four inches. It was plenty long to reach a brain or heart if the need arose.

"Keep this with you from now on. It's silver. Have Asri teach you to use it. I'd teach you myself, but Betty told me once that I *can't* hurt you. It's psychologically impossible for a wolf to intentionally hurt his mate—and you have to learn to use a knife by getting some bumps and cuts." I stared at her hard and long and felt the calm emptiness fill me. She shivered involuntarily. "Don't play around with this, Sue. If you have to fight, aim to kill. Because remember, if you die—I die, too. You'll be fighting for us both. So fight to *win*."

Chapter 17

A THICK BRITISH accent made me stop cold for a second. "I'm sorry to make you go to this trouble, old boy."

He actually did smell sorry. I flipped my head forward to lower the welding hood in front of my eyes. "It's not a problem, Ivan. It's only two rooms." I fought to keep my eyes open as I welded the last steel bar to a frame that would be installed over the massive Siberian bear's window. I'd forgotten just how bright the arc is with wolf eyes, even wearing a hood. My eyes were watering, but at least the final weld was complete.

I stood up, leaving the grate to cool. It wasn't pretty, but it was functional. We'd used rebar scraps from the basement, but I didn't have a grinder. We could replace it later when we did the rest of the windows, which *would* get done come spring.

I stripped off the hood and thick leather gloves. Then I unplugged the little squirt welder from the outlet before wiping the sweat from my eyes with the back of my sleeve. "It never occurred to me that bears sleep with the windows open. I would have thought you guys hibernated."

The big, bald man towering over me chuckled and the scent of oranges burst from him and blended nicely with his normal scent of cranberry cocktail. He and two other

Wolven agents had arrived overnight and we had all been working furiously to finish the security system.

I was more than happy to be occupied. Sue had slept in a different room last night, until she could "get a handle" on her reaction to the *pining*. There was still no word on Amber, and everyone was getting a bit worried, with the exception of Lucas. He said that even without her around, it can be handled successfully on both sides, but we have to limit contact. Unfortunately, that meant that Sue was afraid to touch me at all, and I didn't dare open my mouth around her. The last few things I'd said had been sarcastic and biting. It was the pining talking, but I knew it still hurt.

I brought myself back to the balcony when Ivan spoke. "Even real bears don't sleep *all* winter, old chap. I usually get my twelve hours. That's all I need. I believe Charles sleeps even less than that. He's a polar bear, and they spend *most* of their time in the dark."

A second man, also huge, walked toward us. His waist length black hair fell loose around his shoulders. "How are you guys doing over here?"

"Almost finished, Raven," I said. I stood up and immediately felt somewhat . . . inadequate. Raven is a solid 6'6", and Ivan even bigger. Jocko is the only man I know big as these guys. But Lucas had been right. They were perfect for guarding the place. They were huge, menacing, and had brains to match the brawn.

Raven nodded. "The control center is all done—nice design, by the way. I'll have to steal it for my other systems. I've showed Yurgi how to watch the screens and gave him a radio. That will allow the rest of us to wander around during the meeting. We'll keep in constant contact with each other. Emma is already perched on the roof—doing what she does."

Ivan shrugged. "She's an owl. She flies. She eats. That's about it."

Raven smiled. "You forgot, she *kills*. That's why she's here." He shook his head. "She's been a hard one to tame—no self control."

Ivan slapped his shoulder. "You've done quite well, Raven. We would have been forced to put her down if you hadn't offered to train her for Wolven."

"This is her first real assignment. I know she's skilled. I just don't know if she's *ready*. I wished we had some way to test her—test this whole damn system before the delegates get here. Ahmad's entourage is due to arrive soon."

I couldn't stop the smile and it made the two agents stare at me suspiciously. "I've already arranged for a little test. But you'll have to bear with me a bit."

I explained about Scotty's visit to the hotel and that I had instructed him to try to get in again. But this time, there would be cameras and people watching for him.

"We'll all stay in the control room, and see how the rest of the staff does. We can't be everywhere all the time, and the others should be our extra eyes and noses. We'll cut Yurgi loose to mingle with the pack. Scotty is smart and good—understand that. He looks like a kid, but he's got a dozen assassinations under his belt. He only has one assignment: sneak in to the hotel, find Nikoli and Lelya and shoot them both twice in the chest with paint balls. He knows I've installed a system, but not the details. I gave him photos of the marks and told him when to be here. Nikoli and Lelya know the hit will happen, so that they could wear old clothes. But they don't know *when* or *where*."

Raven looked dubious. His scent bordered on angry, but he was curious as well. "I don't know, Tony. Can you trust this kid? Can he be bought?"

I shrugged. "Can I trust him? No. Can he be bought? Sure—that's what he *does*." I chuckled darkly. "Don't think he's doing it for free! Although, the challenge of the job did appeal to him. No, he's getting well paid—three grand in gold coins. Plus, the death threat if he *didn't* do it also helped. He'll stay loyal for a bit."

I heard Lucas's voice behind me. "What's the scoop, guys? You look *way* too serious all of a sudden. Where's Emma?" His scent took on a sharp edge that I didn't recognize.

Ivan looked amused. "It's not Emma, Lucas. Your new acquisition has arranged for a unique system test. I think the idea is smashing!"

A few minutes later, Raven, Ivan and I were all squeezed tightly into the tiny control room. Lucas agreed to stay out among the pack in case any of them found Scotty. They wouldn't know it was only a drill, and Lucas would keep them from killing the kid.

I'd considered telling Asri about the test, but didn't. Hell, she'd been so preoccupied since her meeting with Lelya that I'd had to make the arrangements for the staggered arrivals myself. Sue had tried to talk to her twice about knife training, but all Asri did was walk the halls, muttering to herself. It was annoying as hell, but I sort of understood.

I caught her staring at herself in the mirror at the top of the stairs once this morning. She was standing sideways and kept pressing her stomach. When I combined it with the conversation I'd accidentally overheard between Lelya and Lucas, it made sense.

"No, Lelya! Absolutely not! I need every agent I've got for the meeting. We're short-handed enough as it is."

Lelya had sighed. "Yes, I understand that, Inte . . . I mean, Lucas. But *you* must understand that Nikoli doesn't know. I'm uncertain what his reaction will be if he finds out and Robart is within striking distance. At the very least, the meeting will be disrupted. I just thought that if Robart were to drive the limo for the delegates, he could be both useful and . . . distant."

Lucas sighed. "Do you think it's that bad?"

"He's already lost Mila, Lucas—and now *this*. I don't believe Niki will dance in the streets. But he might be willing to dance on Robart's *grave*."

So, Bobby was relegated to chauffeur while the rest of us prepared to be boarded. I tried not to think about Sue. She had decided to talk to Lelya about her findings at the restaurant, on the premise that Nikoli was busy with the meeting. I hoped it was going okay. I wished I could tell— but that damned black wall was still in my head and Amber hadn't shown her face since we'd arrived.

We watched people moving from place to place in the hotel. The decorations sparkled, and floors and brass fittings gleamed with fresh polish. The pack members all had uniforms now and looked like a proper hotel staff. Boris looked proud as Celia ordered her staff around. She was inspecting each room and sending people scampering when she found dust or trash.

The cameras covering the conference—now banquet— room were working perfectly. We'd stolen the signal from Nikoli's computers and added it into our system.

"Hey! Look at that!" Raven was pointing to a camera from the basement. We'd only had time to add a couple. A smiling Scotty was giving a thumbs-up to the camera. Then he melted into the darkness.

"How in *bloody hell* did he get in?" Ivan was livid. He was responsible for securing the basement accesses. He started for the door and I grabbed his shirt sleeve. I made sure not to touch skin.

"Don't, Ivan. We'll ask him when we see him. We'll still have time to close up the hole. Let's see how far he gets."

Ivan nodded grudgingly. He muttered under his breath as we continued to watch. "I've been head of security for the Chief Justice for a hundred years! *Nobody* gets through my perimeter."

Raven raised his brows and a shock of amusement swept

the room. His laughter was similar to Sue's, a tangerine-y sort of scent. "Well, unless he's a bird and flew down there, someone did." He stopped at stared at me in shock for a second. "*Is* he a bird?"

I shook my head. "He's human, and he doesn't even know Sazi exist. I told you—he's *good*. Not as good as I am, mind you, but good. I would have been in before now. I would have cased the place as soon as I got the job."

Raven looked at me askance. "What—do you break into buildings to shoot people often?"

I turned to him in surprise. "You mean Lucas didn't tell you?" When he shook his head, I laughed. "I'm an assassin, Ramirez. I'm one of the bad guys. It's why I design such kick-ass security systems. I've seen 'em all, I've beat 'em all. *Nothing* is fool-proof. We're just trying to make it tough enough that the other bad guys go next door instead."

Ivan and Raven gave each other significant looks over my head. I ignored them, keeping my eyes flowing across the screens. "Heads up! He's on the Main Level, Camera Two. Where are our marks?"

Their attention returned to the task at hand. Ivan replied. "The targets are stationary. Level Two, Camera Four. They're together, talking."

Okay, outside of the ballroom. One floor to go, kid.

"Wait! What was *that?*" Raven pointed to the roof camera. A flash of white had hit the lens, causing the whole thing to jiggle and veer off angle.

"A pigeon?" I offered. "Looked like a bird hitting the lens."

Ivan started to zip up his coat. "It looked like an *owl*. Emma doesn't hit cameras unless she's thrown into them. I'm going up."

Another flash on the camera was thin and brown and moving fast. An ear-splitting screech found our ears, which was a concern, since the cameras don't pick up sound.

"We're *all* going up!" Raven commanded. "She needs help."

We left the door to the control room hanging open as we bolted up the stairs at Sazi speed. I think that both Ivan and Raven were surprised that I not only kept up with them, but I had my gun in my hand before they did.

The sounds of a furious battle raged. Powerful flapping and shuddering thumps urged us on. We'd just reached the roof access door when a blood-curdling, ear-splitting screech cut the air. Then there was silence. Raven tried the door, but it was locked. He raised a foot and kicked it open. Snow was falling lightly onto the rooftop. The wind sent flakes swirling around a fallen figure in white. Raven and Ivan walked carefully toward the white bird, as big as a full grown eagle. One wing was at a wrong angle and a patch of red stained the fluffy feathers.

"Ah, Emma," Raven said sadly. "What did this to you?" I had stayed near the door to watch our backs, but now moved forward. The bright yellow beak was open slightly under wide eyes that stared into nothing. I could see now that the head was completely separated from the body, and a neat hole was carved in her chest. I felt nothing in particular at the woman's death, but it was obvious that both Ivan and Raven were grieving.

I started to look around the roof before the increasing snow buried the clues. "It's getting worse out here. Take her inside, Ramirez. Ivan and I will see if we can find the killer."

I took a deep breath. The scent of blood was on the wind, but there was something else, too. "I'll be damned!" I exclaimed. "It's that same nasty scent. The third time now."

Ivan raised his big head and took a deep breath. "It's ruddy powerful. But I don't recognize the smell. What about you, Raven? Raven?"

The dark-haired man was smoothing feathers on the still-warm body and putting a wing gently back into place. I couldn't smell anything over that awful odor, but his eyes were wet, and I didn't think it was from the snow. "Huh?

I'm sorry, guys. I need . . . to take her inside. We'll call off the test. I'll get Lucas."

He carried the bird carefully, putting the head on top of the chest. When he'd disappeared into the hotel, Ivan shook his head. "I told him not to get attached to that one. But he's just like his father—always putting his heart before his head."

"We might as well go back inside, too. There's not much to see out here. It looks like the whole battle was in the air. The only prints are ours. Could it have been another bird?"

Ivan sighed angrily and shrugged. "It could be a personal vendetta. Emma had a lot of enemies."

"Maybe. Or the killer could be targeting other Sazi. Nikoli is a delegate, and Lucas *was* one." I took a deep sniff and, predictably, sneezed. "The scent is identical and . . ." I reached up and pulled a small piece of fabric off an overhead line that just caught my eye. "This looks like raw silk. It's the same stuff as when Babs disappeared."

Ivan's face was shocked. "Babs Herrera? I didn't know she was missing! When did that happen?"

"Only a couple of days ago. It's how Lucas managed to drag me into this mess. Babs is the one who turned me."

His face set into a knowing look. "Oh! You're *that* one! I've been looking for you! Charles says you've got an interesting future ahead of you."

I snorted and dropped the silk into my pocket until Bobby could inspect it. "Like he would know."

Ivan grabbed the back of my coat before I reached the door, being very careful not to touch me. He stepped forward and nodded his head. "He *would* know, Giambrocco. Our Chief Justice is also our most powerful seer. He told me that you're going to be one, too. I was instructed to make sure that you stay alive until the meeting. But he didn't tell me your name. I've just been looking for a dark-haired wolf." He snorted. "There are a lot of them here."

I furrowed my brow, but I had an uneasy feeling. "You're supposed to guard *me?* Why?"

Ivan snorted and returned his big Baretta semi-auto to the holster. "Don't you understand? It's why they've all come to Chicago—why we're going to all this trouble. The council wants to meet *you*."

Chapter 18

I DIDN'T HAVE much time to dwell on Ivan's statement because of the commotion going on in the main lobby. Raven and Emma's remains were nowhere to be found, but Scotty had apparently arrived, if the shouts and screams were any indication.

We sprinted down to the second floor and caught the tail end of the incident. Lelya was wiping pink paint from one arm and the side of her neck. There was a bit of pink on a nearby lampshade. Not bad, but not enough for the prize. He hadn't tagged the artery.

Nikoli was untouched, but . . . Yurgi was being helped from the floor, and had two neat splats of pink right over his heart. The rest of the pack had gathered in a circle around the three.

I could hear the shock in his voice as he looked at his shirt. "Is . . . is *paint?*" He touched the pink and looked at Nikoli in surprise. The pack leader was chuckling. "It is game being played?"

I realized what had happened. Scotty had gotten Nikoli in his sights, but Yurgi saw. He jumped in front of Nikoli as the shots were fired. Scotty had managed to get off two more shots at Lelya, but missed the kill, before he was jumped. I glanced across the lobby to see that Lucas was helping Scotty to his feet. Boris and Celia had apparently taken

Scotty down. The kid was lucky that Lucas *had* been nearby. Boris looked furious.

Nikoli's face moved from amused to surprised. Then it softened for a moment—became serious, because he suddenly realized the import of what had just happened. Yurgi hadn't known it was a drill. I couldn't smell it from my position, but the looks between Nikoli and Lelya said a lot. They were proud and pleased.

Nikoli straightened his back and approached the stunned Omega. He put a firm and warm hand on Yurgi's shoulder. "Yurgi Stefanovich Kroutikhin—you have saved my life and that of my mother this day. You are Omega no more, my . . ." He glanced at Scotty, who was watching with interest. I knew he had been planning to say "my wolf," but the presence of a human changed that.

"My . . . *friend.* Come, we will discuss your prize, and clean you before the guests arrive." He walked by Lucas and raised his brows. "Quite an impressive display. You are correct that we have been lax. I will discuss this with my people and we will be more prepared by nightfall."

Lucas nodded upward in my direction. "Thank Tony. It was his idea."

Nikoli glanced at me and Ivan and nodded thoughtfully. Then he wrapped an arm around Yurgi's shoulders and led him away.

Lelya clapped her hands sharply. "Let's go, people! Celia, have this lampshade replaced. The rest of you—straighten the carpet and look for any more paint. We have guests arriving soon, and I want this place clean and ready. And . . ." she said, staring at each person in turn, including the children. "We will be keeping a closer watch for strangers, correct? Use your eyes, your ears, even . . ." She shot a significant look at Scotty, "Your . . . *noses* to check for anything out of the ordinary."

She walked over to Scotty and Lucas. She gave Scotty a stern look. "You really should cut back on the cologne or use unscented soap, young man. It's quite strong. I knew you were in the room somewhere. You're just *asking* to be caught."

Scotty's eyes stared into the older woman's and he suddenly realized that she wasn't a sweet, fluffy sort of mother. She was quite serious. Scotty lifted his arm to his nose and sniffed. Apparently, it *was* strongly scented, because he swore and muttered. He nodded and dropped his head. Lucas chuckled and led the kid over to where Ivan and I were descending the stairs.

He was whining before he even reached us, and Lelya was right. The soap was one of the "fresh scent" varieties and damned powerful, even if I'd still had a human nose.

"You didn't tell me you were going to have *heroes*, Mr. G. It was a good hit! And I wouldn't have missed the old lad . . . *her*, if I hadn't gotten jumped."

I shook my head and let my face go cold. "No excuses. The job is the job, and you know it. See? It's not so easy playing with guns, is it? You've got to plan for stuff like this and be ready. You need training."

His face fell and the burnt metal scent of frustration blended with the wet fog of sorrow. "Ah, man! I don't get the gold, do I?"

Ivan was staring at the negotiations and shaking his massive head in disbelief. I waggled my hand for a moment and then decided. "Okay, you *might* have clipped the artery on the mom. And depending on the bullets you used, you might have still wounded the first mark through the hero." I held out my hand. "I'll give you half. Deal?"

He sighed and shook my hand. "Deal, I guess. Do I *gotta* go back to Carmine's and hook up with Mr. Karasiuk again? He's got it in for me."

"No. I made a few calls." I reached into my pocket and extracted the sum we'd agreed on. "Joey won't be able to pull a trigger for a few months. You'll be working with a new guy. He's coming in special to train you."

I'd scored some points when I made that call yesterday. Dad had still thought I was dead. I used a payphone just outside the city and called his boccie club. They've got a switchboard, so it's a lot tougher to trace. I convinced him to fly back and stay for a while to train the kid. He's pretty good, after all—he trained *me*. Carmine's pretty happy with the deal, too. He'd get a fifth for poker for a time. My chair hadn't been filled. I'll probably still never see Dad again, but he understands. It's how the game is played.

Scotty's face brightened, and he looked like a regular kid again, instead of an assassin in training. "Cool! I've already got my bus ticket, about an hour from now. Can someone give me a lift?"

I glanced around the room. I really couldn't leave. Lucas raised his head. "I'll get him there." He put an arm around the kid's shoulders and tightened it until a light scent of fear rose from him. "I want to have a little *chat* about staying out of Chicago from now on."

Fair enough—it saved me the trouble. I nodded and stepped sideways when little Alek rushed by with a replacement lamp shade.

I thought of something suddenly and sprinted after them as they stepped out of the building. "By the way, kid, how *did* you get in?" I'd almost forgotten to ask.

He turned his head and flipped the hair out of his eyes. "Laundry delivery, man. You ought to post a guard on the basement door. Your people unlocked it and left. The company driver got a bag from the truck and took it inside. The door stood wide open until they came back to get another one. It was easy."

I gave Ivan a significant look before calling after Lucas' retreating form. "Raven tell you about Emma, Lucas?"

The older man took a deep breath, let it out slow, and then closed his eyes for a second and nodded. "Yeah. We'll talk later."

I returned the nod. I turned back to go inside when a bright quad of headlights appeared out of the swirl of snow. The massive black beast of a vehicle stopped in front of the hotel. I realized what it was as soon as it came fully into view—a Hummer limo. They're powerful, extremely surefooted in snow and ice, but *ugly as sin.*

I watched as Bobby jumped out of the driver's seat and sprinted around the vehicle to open the doors. He was in full chauffeur's gear, including the grey brimmed hat.

Sergei peeked out and I heard him yell backwards that guests were arriving. I stood off to the side, just guarding. I slipped my Taurus from the holster and held it loosely behind my back, watching for any movement on the street.

A slender Middle Eastern man stepped out of the Hummer. I could barely see him through the blinding red aura that blazed around him. It made my eyes hurt. He eyed the snowy sidewalk with disapproval. Yeah, I guess we should have shoveled the walk. I'd mention it to Lelya. Sergei certainly couldn't handle a shovel and I didn't know where they were.

The man had a thin, long face that frowned more often than smiled. He nodded to Bobby. "My thanks, Agent Mbutu, for your driving talents. I'm not often in snowy climates." The words didn't sound very thankful. They hissed and rolled angrily.

Bobby dropped his head slightly. Either he didn't take offense, or he hid it well. "My pleasure, Councilman Al Narmer. I believe your rooms are ready and there is a buffet available for appetizers before dinner. Your bags will be brought up." Sergei rushed out to bring a gold plated cart for the luggage before returning to the door.

The man nodded imperiously and stepped into the carpet of white. He shook his foot each time it sank into the snow. God forbid that his expensive pants might get wet. Still, he was a guest. I'd met worse. He barely glanced my way as he walked through the door that Sergei held open, but his entourage did. Eight similarly slender men with cold, cruel faces exited the Hummer behind the councilman. They stared at me long and hard, deciding whether I was a threat. I nodded my head and let my face drop into its mercenary best. One of the olive-skinned men approached me. He didn't glow as bright as his employer, but it was still impressive. He smelled of desert trees and brush. It was a sharp unpleasant smell.

"You're Wolven? I don't know you."

I shook my head. "I'm part of Councilman Molotov's security team. There are Wolven members inside."

"I would have thought that our arrival would merit better security than a simple *wolf* guarding the entrance."

I raised my brows. I thought about shooting him, just for fun. But it would probably be taken badly. I didn't respond to the dig. I stared into his eyes and let the silence stretch until he started to shiver. He turned in a huff and walked back to his group. They entered the building, totally ignoring the pile of bags that Bobby was unloading from the rear of the limo. I walked up to him and could smell that he was seething.

"Great guys, Bobbo! Are they typical of the other council members?"

"Thank God, no! That's Ahmad—he's a king cobra, representing the snakes. He's dangerous as hell, and don't forget it."

No wonder Bobby was deferential to the guy. "So he's *your* representative on the council?"

Bobby removed the last bag from the trunk and loaded it on top of the others on the cart. He rolled his eyes. "Don't remind me. But, he is good at his job for what it's worth."

He was just starting to move it toward the front door when Boris appeared at the entrance. He tugged at his uniform, which was stretched tight over his barrel chest. He was shaking his head and muttering under his breath.

"If our gracious Alpha did not insist on clean language, I would devise a proper curse for that . . . that *kham*."

I knew enough Russian *mat* to know that it was a mild curse, calling a person rude or unmannered. I chuckled. "Yeah, I could think of a few choice phrases myself. I take it he's being a pain in the ass?"

Boris tugged the cart through the slush. He glanced

down. "I will call the children to remove the snow. But yes, Tony. He is, as you say, a pain in *osiól*. Already he has made demands: 'My room is not clean enough.' 'Why am I placed on second floor, like a common beggar?' 'These mice look like laboratory culls. Can no one find healthy wild mice in this city?' *S'blood!* He is . . ." He struggled to find an appropriate word, but eventually gave up and just threw up his hands.

Bobby snorted. "That's Ahmad, all right. I'm surprised that someone hasn't already killed him. Well, I better get this rig back to the airport. Someone else should be arriving soon." He glanced around, looking for someone.

Boris gave Bobby a final clap on the back.

"You are lucky man! Everyone talks of the event." Ah, man. I'd already heard the rumors. I had hoped that nobody would mention it. I hate gossip.

He stared at Boris in confusion. "What are you talking about?"

Yep, I was afraid of that! Nobody had bothered to tell him, and he's been doing other stuff. That pisses me off. He has the right to know if he's going to be a father. It's his life, too.

I debated on whether to say anything more, but I didn't get the chance. Boris's voice lowered to a slightly less than shouting whisper. "You do not know yet, my friend? S'blood! No! This is *wrong.* You must make plans with Lady Asri and how can you do this without knowing?"

Bobby was staring at the big man frantically. The strong scent of fear and frustration beat at me across the short distance.

"C'mon, Boris. Spit it out."

He stepped closer to Bobby and lowered his voice even more while I shook my head. Stuff like this is how people get a bullet in the brain. "I have overheard our lady Duchess and the councilman talking. They say that you must be on driving duty because if Nikoli *finds out,* you would suffer. And then my Maria, she saw Lady Asri staring at herself in the mirror and pressing on her stomach.

Lady Asri has been crying much and speaks in harsh tones, even at Nikoli! It is clear, is it not, my friend?" He raised his eyebrows significantly and then made a big show out of zipping his fingers across his lips before turning and pushing his cart back to the entrance.

Bobby's mouth opened slightly and his eyes darted from side to side. He looked down and a slow smile spread his lips. "Tony, do you really think Asri could be pregnant?" I shrugged.

He reached out to grab my shoulders but then stopped short like a dog on a rope. Good thing. I had no desire to see his latest escapade with the dragon. He lowered his hands but kept the smile. "If there's even a chance, Tony! That's . . . it's . . . *amazing!* We're both the last, Tony! If she could have children like even *one* of us . . ."

I raised my brows. "But we *are* talking about Asri, Bobby. God knows what her plans are. It could be significant that she hasn't mentioned it to you."

"It's all the peppermint we've been wearing. Maybe *she* doesn't even know!"

A sharp laugh erupted. "You're not making sense, Bobby. Women know that shit about themselves."

A noise made me turn. A sleek silver sedan was pulling up to the hotel. Bobby didn't notice. "Well, I'll just confront her! I mean, a *child!* It'll be . . ."

"*Interesting,*" I completed. The sedan stopped and Bobby finally turned. The man who exited was as wide across as a building, but not more than 6'1." he barely had a glow about him. He was wearing a London Fog trench coat over a *really* expensively tailored grey wool suit. But his most striking features were his large nose under tiny little brown eyes. It made his face seem out of proportion. Bobby was struck dumb at his appearance, but finally recovered as the man walked up to him with raised brows.

"Chief Justice Wingate, *sir!* You drove yourself? Where are your guards?"

The man spoke with a thick, refined British accent. His

voice boomed, even when he was trying to be quiet. He waved his hand airily. "I left them at the hotel. I grew weary of them fussing about." He lowered his head as Bobby sputtered. "I *can* take care of myself, you know."

"Oh, of course you can sir. It's just that . . ."

"*Chief Justice!*" exclaimed Ivan, who was tearing out the door. "Where are John and Bruce?"

"I . . . oh, what is that phrase?" He raised his finger in the air and smiled. "Ah, yes! I *ditched* them, Ivan. I was in a bit of a rush to get here, and they were dallying." He raised his nose and sniffed slightly. He sighed and smelled annoyed. "But I see I'm too late. *Dash it!* I had hoped to get here before Ahmad arrived. Has he killed any of the staff yet, Ivan?"

Ivan also sighed in a manner very similar to his employer. "Not yet, thankfully. He's too busy berating them about the buffet." He smiled and nudged the older man in the shoulder. "It's *excellent,* by the way, sir! Venison with berries, wild pig and . . ." He winked. "The Duchess Olga's famous borscht!"

The Chief Justice's face absolutely glowed. "You mean that I will at last have a meal at a council meeting that doesn't give me indigestion? A meal without thick French sauces and pastries everywhere? Heaven be praised!" He rubbed his hands together in anticipation and turned toward the door—and me. He nodded his head. "I see you've found our new seer, Ivan. Good job. It's a pleasure to meet you, Joseph Giambrocco. While the council members are a bloody imperious lot, the seers are *not.* I am *Charles.* I would offer to shake your hand," he said, and then looked suddenly serious, "But I don't think either of us would enjoy it."

After my recent experiences, I agreed. He seemed like a nice enough guy. It made me wonder why everyone was afraid of him. But then something occurred to me—hadn't Bobby said that the Chief Justice rescinded my execution? Then why couldn't he give Ivan my name? I furrowed my brow lightly. "No problem. Consider us shaked, Charles."

He raised a finger. "But not stirred." He laughed at his own joke. "Has anyone explained your new talents to you yet? We seers will be meeting with you when the others arrive."

I nodded slightly and crossed my arms. "The second sight is seeing colored auras, right?" The seeing backwards— what was it, *hindsight?* That's a little too strange for me to wrap my head around so far. Oh, and please call me Tony. Joseph was my father."

He growled lightly, and it made the hairs on the back of my neck prickle. "I'd rather you not muddy your present life with the past too much, but I *suppose* it will be all right. We did use Anthony for a middle name." Yep, he knew me all right. Just another plan within a plan for me to discover.

He nodded. "Very well, Tony. Apparently someone has explained second sight to you—probably Lucas. His Second, Raphael, has the same gift. Good. Your other gift is very rare. There is only one other living seer who shares your talent. You have the ability to see the recent, as well as the ancient, past. Most likely, you will pick up images that are important to the person you are reading at that precise moment."

Ah! Finally something made sense. Bobby was thinking about Asri—naturally, Lucas about why he was in Chicago, and Amber was experiencing a bit of *déjà vu* at the conference.

"So I'm not going to see planes crashing and people dying and stuff like that when I touch someone?" That was a *huge* relief.

The Chief Justice shook his head. "No. You're quite fortunate, old boy. As seer gifts go, yours is distinctly less . . . *messy.* You will never get images off objects, because they don't think or feel. But you will pick up strong images from people. It will be worse when that person is in a crisis. You will need to learn to control the images. That is why I have invited the other seer who shares your talent to this meeting."

Bobby dropped the bag he was holding, and Ivan paled visibly before stammering. "Are you sure that was *wise,* sir?" Hot and sour soup and ammonia panic filled the air between the two of them enough to make me sneeze.

Charles raised his brows at the scents floating into his twitching nostrils. "It would be distinctly *less* wise to allow Tony to wander around untrained, Ivan. Wouldn't you *agree?*" The words lowered to a dangerous growl. He glared at the large bear and then turned to the snake. "Bobby, would you please park my car? I circled, but couldn't find the entrance to the garage. The keys are in it."

Ivan shut his open jaw and nodded mutely. Bobby did the same.

"Good," Charles said. "We'll talk more later, Tony. But right now, I need to get inside and undo whatever damage Ahmad has caused." With a brief nod of acknowledgement he passed inside, with Ivan at his heels. Bobby had gone to park the car.

I stayed where I was. Someone needed to watch the front. A sudden, strong north wind threatened to knock me over. I had to lean against the nearest light pole to remain standing. Soon, even the Hummer began to shake. I watched a whirlwind of snow appear a block away, and stared in fascination as it slowly moved toward me. The wind began to howl and tear at my jacket. The whirlwind became a tornado and seemed to be lighted from within, like there was a beacon inside it. I heard faint voices over the wind. They grew louder as the swirling snow got closer.

"I suppose the food will be Russian?" I recognized the voice, but couldn't quite place it. Pleasantly male and ever so slightly disdainful, with just a trace of a French accent.

I heard Lucas's reply, even though I couldn't see him through the blowing snow. "It'll be a nice change from Fiona's dishes, won't it?"

There was a light, distinctly male laugh. "My sister is an adequate cook, I suppose. But I agree that her dishes are a bit heavy with sauces. You'd think the woman had never seen a vegetable. We *are* omnivores, after all. At least part of the time."

The whirlwind lessened to reveal the older wolf, accompanied by a tall, slender blond man with a neatly trimmed blond goatee, who was wearing an ankle length white fox coat. I could barely see him through the intense white light that surrounded the pair. But I *knew* him! His face was plastered on billboards all over the country. He was Antoine Monier, a circus performer who had gone big time, like Siegfried and Roy. Now he traveled the country with his cats and entourage, entertaining for extravagant ticket prices. It would never have occurred to me that he was *Sazi*.

The wind lessened even more, and the thick braid of long hair settled against the coat.

"Oh, before I forget, Antoine," Lucas said, "You'll be acting as a *seer* for this meeting."

Another burst of light made me close my eyes for a moment. My headache was getting worse. "Then who will represent the cats? I was not informed of this change, Lucas."

"Fiona will represent the cats. I tried to reach you all last week, but you didn't return my calls. You have an amended agenda in your room."

"I was on tour, as you well know. And last I heard my twin was on forced leave." His geen eyes narrowed to slits, and his voice trailed off into a hiss. "You're *up to something*, Lucas."

Lucas put a hand on his chest and raised his brows. "*Moi?* Never, Antoine. You will sit with the seers, your twin will represent the cats, and Amber will represent the physicians."

Antoine gave a harsh laugh as they finally reached the doors of the hotel. "You are putting Amber and Fiona in the same room? And there will be *three* Monier siblings in the same room as Ahmad? How *fascinating!* And how unfortunate—I suppose one of us will be ruining a number of tables at this meeting. Would you care to flip a coin to see who pays for the furniture this time?"

Lucas smiled. "Actually, since I'm representing Wolven I won't be in the room for most of the meeting. Still, you might want to split the bill with your sisters—*four* ways."

Antoine stopped and staggered a bit. "What do you mean—*four* ways? You can't be implying . . . *Mon Dieu!*"

Lucas nodded his head. "Charles invited her to meet our new seer. Have you met Tony yet?" He motioned to me, and I tipped my chin in greeting.

Antoine stared into space for a moment before he could focus on me. When he did finally look at me, he started as though he remembered something. He raised a finger into the air and swung an expensive leather backpack from his shoulder. He unzipped it and rummaged around for a moment before removing a box. He held it out to me, being careful to remove his hand just as I touched it. "For you, *mon ami*. You will find them useful this meeting. Welcome to our humble and insane ranks." Then he stepped toward the door, swearing in French. He glanced at Lucas and shook his head. "You will be the death of me, Lucas! Had you reached me last week, I would have declined to attend. To see Josette after all these years! *MON DIEU!*"

"*Aspen*, Antoine. She is called Aspen now."

He continued to mutter and swear in French as Lucas held the door to the hotel open. A cab arrived as I opened the small box. Inside was a pair of expensive sunglasses, similar to mine, but with a price tag at least two hundred dollars more. I slipped them on and found that the bright light emanating from Antoine and Lucas diminished greatly and my head stopped throbbing. Cool.

A woman exited the taxi carefully. She looked around, taking every single thing in with a glance. She wasn't a pretty woman, but she was incredibly striking. Long legs, long arms, about a size four body, with a chest worthy of Penthouse. Her face was sharply angular, with high cheekbones and a hawk-ish nose under dark brown hair with pale highlights. I was thankful for the sunglasses as she let loose a burst of radiant yellow light. She pointed at me and spoke with a French, bordering on Belgian, accent.

"You! You, there! Take my bags inside and pay *zee* man." I raised my brows and almost winced. Her voice was a high pitched squeak. It was sharp, penetrating and painfully similar to fingernails on a chalkboard.

Then she called out to Lucas, who was still standing by the door. "Lucas! What has happened to *zee* protocol? My plane was not met, I had to *gather my own bags!* Surely *you* see that this *iz* unacceptable! Who *iz* responsible?" She stepped forward quickly.

Lucas bowed from his neck briefly. "I am sorry if your car was delayed. We have many flights, and only one driver, Angelique. You understand that Wolven's resources are stretched thin at the moment."

Her voice rose even higher. "You see? Unacceptable, Lucas!" She pounded one tiny fist into her other hand. "This *iz* why the meetings should not moved to *zis* place and *zat*."

"You will have to speak to Charles about that, Angelique. He and the other seers chose the location." She flounced through the open door, leaving Lucas shaking his head.

"Who was *that?*" I asked in awe.

Lucas let go of the door and walked toward me, removing his wallet from his back pocket. He whispered as he passed, "Angelique Calibria, representative for the raptors. You might guess that she's friends with Ahmad."

He removed several bills and paid the taxi driver, who was busily removing bags and cases from the tightly packed trunk. He was dropping them unceremoniously into the snow. "Glad to have that broad out of my cab. Her voice could shatter glass, and she won't shut her trap! I ought to charge double for not dumping her in the lake."

Lucas started picking up bags and replied to the driver. "It wouldn't do any good. People have tried. She just won't *die.*" The driver burst out laughing and tried to give Lucas his change.

He waved his hand dismissively. "Keep it. You deserve it."

There were too many bags for Lucas, so I picked up a few as well. It looked like she was planning to stay for a month.

Boris met us at the door with a second wheeled luggage cart. Lucas excused himself to go talk to the Chief Justice. I heard Sue's voice and turned to see her and another woman walking toward the entrance. The woman was about Sue's size and shape, but with pale blonde hair and penetrating brown eyes.

Sue stepped closer to me and started to reach out, but then pulled back and lowered her hand, clenched into a fist. *She still can't touch me. Great.* I felt a little stab in my chest. I shook it off and smiled instead. I had to give her space, and I hated every single, solitary moment.

"Hi, Sue. Going out?"

She smiled in return, and I could tell she was grateful that I wasn't going to bring up a tense subject. "Hi, sweetie. Yeah. This is Pamela, Yurgi's wife. We're going to go for a walk and then grab some dinner, since you and Yurgi are going to be busy for a few hours."

I nodded to the woman, who was holding out her hand. I raised my brows at Sue, and she gasped. She reached out and pushed Pamela's hand down and gave her a *reminding* look. God forbid someone should touch me right now. Emotions were *way* too high for that. Pamela's face flushed lightly and she hurbled an and apology. The dry heat of embarrassment blended badly with her natural spearmint scent.

"Gosh, I'm really sorry! I've just never met a *seer* before."

I let out a short snort of air. "Me neither." I glanced upstairs to see Yurgi motioning to me. I stepped into Sue and gave her a quick kiss on the cheek before she could pull back. "Well, I'll let you girls get to your walking. Have fun!"

I sprinted up the stairs. *Keep the mind occupied, Tony.* But the ache and trembling wouldn't listen to my head. I clenched my hands into tight fists and felt a shudder pass through me before I got to the control room entrance. "What's up, Yurgi?"

"I see shadow on screen, Tony! It moves very fast! Is more test?"

"No, Yurgi. There is no other test." I walked toward the bank of computer screens. "Show me where. What did it look like?"

He pointe⅃ to the camera on the alley behind the hotel. "Looks like . . ." he raised his hands in frustration. "Like . . . *shadow!* It moved quickly—like Sazi, but not shadow I recognize."

If I stopped the camera to rewind the tape, I'd lose current input. Damn it! That's a system flaw I hadn't anticipated. "Where's Bobby? Have you called him to check it out?"

Yurgi looked suddenly uncomfortable. "Yes, I call. He tell me . . . well, he tell me too busy and not bother him."

I growled in annoyance. I glanced around the various cameras and finally saw one corner of his arm. I moved the camera until it was fully on him . . . and *Asri.* Damn it! They were in the parking garage, arguing—and I bet I knew about *what.* The camera didn't pick up sound, but it was obvious that the argument would go on for some time. I was sorry to interrupt, but security comes first and he damn well knew it!

I picked up the nearest radio and punched the call button. "Tony to Bobby."

I watched him raise his hand to stop Asri's next comment. She crossed her arms and started to storm off. He grabbed her arm to stop her and then took a deep breath. A crackle and a cheep came over my set. "Go ahead."

I decided to let him hang himself. "How's the perimeter?"

Yurgi shook his head and pointed to the image again. I nodded and waved him off.

"Perimeter looks good. No action."

Uh-huh.

"*Bullshit.* Bobby! I've been watching your little spat.

Wave to the pretty camera!" Bobby and Asri both got panicked looks and turned in a circle. I obliged by moving the camera from side to side with the joystick until they saw it. I watched him swear, and this time Asri did step out of view.

"Get your ass back to work, Mbutu! We had a contact on Camera Seven, in the alley. Yurgi said it was just a shadow, but it was moving fast."

I saw him move his head in frustration and put the radio in front of his mouth. "I've got to settle this, Tony! I need more time. Can't someone else look for the bogie?"

I shook my head and flicked the button again. "You've got your priorities whacked, Bobbo! You and your girlfriend have got nine months to settle *that* problem, but we've got a house full of delegates *now*!"

Yurgi opened his mouth and a shock of surprised scent gripped my nose. I guess I shouldn't have mentioned the *nine months* part. Oops.

"*Seven* months, but that's not the point. C'mon, Tony! Just ten minutes. Then I *swear* I'll take care of it. *Please!*"

I remembered trying to concentrate on anything else when I first mated to Sue. I sighed. "*Five* minutes, Bobbo. Then I send *Lucas* to get you."

He didn't reply, but wore a startled look. He stuffed the radio back in his pocket and sprinted out of camera range. Great! Raven and Ivan were busy keeping the delegates from slaughtering each other, and Lucas was meeting with Charles. That left *me* to go searching. I stuffed the radio in my pocket and turned on a second one for Yurgi. I pulled my Taurus from the holster and checked the chamber. I turned to Yurgi as I was sliding it back into the leather and walking out the door.

"If I don't contact you in five minutes, send Lucas to get Bobby and get Raven or Ivan outside to pick up my corpse."

Yurgi took a surprised breath and stood up. "I go with you!"

I took a step back and put a firm hand on his shoulder to press him down. I was again thankful that nothing happened. "No, Yurgi. I need you here to watch the screens. Call me on the radio if you see anything on the cameras— and be *precise*. If you see something show up, give me a play by play." When he looked confused, I amended. "Like the television football, when the voice tells you what's happening."

His face showed his understanding. "Ah! I see! Yes, I will do this for you, Tony!" I started to walk away, then he stopped me. "Oh! And I forget! I will *miss* the football game, with the tickets. Nikoli is pleased with Yurgi for being brave. He buys for me and Pamela a *house!* We must go to sign papers night of game."

Nikoli was buying them a *house* for taking a paint ball? Then again, Yurgi hadn't known it was a drill. He'd been ready to take a bullet for his Alpha. It made me think better of Nikoli. "Cool! No problem on the game. It'll be on TV, unless they black it out."

"But I choose to remain Omega, Tony. Pamela, she is angry with me, but I am happy in position. Is it wrong to be—what is word—uh, *content?*"

I shrugged my shoulders. "I wouldn't think so. It's your life in the pack, not her's. You don't always have to make your choices to please other people. But I've got to get outside, Yurgi." I stepped out, shut the door, and shook my head. Bobby and Asri, Yurgi and Pamela. How do I keep turning into the therapist of the group?

I walked toward the entrance wincing at the noise from the banquet room. The shrieks, hisses and snarls made the place sound like a zoo. As I started to open the door, I noted that the kids shoveled the walk. Or so I thought. A blast of warm air greeted me as I stepped into the night. I've heard of chinook winds in winter, but this was ridiculous! It must be seventy degrees outside! The sky was clear and stars twinkled and the sound of running water greeted my ears. A glance down showed why. The melted snow was running down the gutter to exit into street drains. A slim, compact woman walked toward me. I recognized her.

"Hi, Amber! I see you made it in time for the meeting."

The woman smiled and I suddenly realized it *wasn't* Amber. Her hair was a shade lighter, and freckles were scattered across her tanned nose. Her scent was sort of like candle wax with red hot candies, and her voice was a bit more musical when she spoke, "A pleasure to see you again, Tony." She furrowed her brow lightly and cocked her head. "Oh, but this is the *first* time, isn't it? In that case, a pleasure to *meet* you."

"And you are . . ."

"Aspen Monier. I'm Amber's twin sister."

Okay, now I was confused. *This* is the woman who has everyone terrified? She seems a little flaky, but not particularly *dangerous*.

Another woman suddenly appeared. And I mean *suddenly*—she wasn't there, and then she was. I recognized her too, but from a dream. It was the old woman from the vision in Lucas's head. She looked just the same, but now I caught the scent of sweet yucca flowers. I must have started, because she spoke.

"Yes, that's right. You've already seen me. I'm Nana, the seer for the Boulder pack. I've seen you, too. A dozen times, in a thousand scenarios where you should die, but *don't*. So refreshing, your ingenuity." She turned to Aspen. "And so wonderful to see *you* again, my dear. I waited to come until you cleared the weather. Thank you. These old bones, you know . . ."

Aspen smiled brightly. "Always happy to oblige, Nana. I've never liked the cold. It's why I live in the desert. I thought I would bring a little warmth with me this time, but you knew that."

Nana nodded and I could only shake my head at the bizarre conversation. This one could actually *control* the weather, not just affect it? And the other one expected it and waited until it happened? This was just *so* weird.

Another flash of despair gripped me briefly and I shuddered. Both women glanced at me.

"Ah! That's right!" exclaimed Aspen, and a burst of citrus filled the warm air. "I remember now why I came *to-night!* My sister is a wonderful healer, but quite heavy-handed." Nana nodded, and Aspen touched my forehead before I could react.

The blackness in my head disappeared, and warm sunlight replaced it. *See? Isn't that better?* I heard the voice, but couldn't place it. Then I saw Aspen step into the bright light. *You only need control, young wolf. Mating should be a joyous exchange of lives, not bogged down in darkness.* An object appeared at her feet and she picked it up and turned it in her hands so I could see it. It was a square block of glass. She put it down and another appeared. She stacked it on top of the first. More glass bricks appeared and she stacked them with blinding speed until they created a wall. The sunlight through the glass sent swirls of rainbows across my mind. With a swish of her hand, an old-fashioned screen door appeared in the wall of glass. A warm breeze flowed across me so that I shivered. But the warmth carried the scent of the summer forest, with ripe fruit and rich earth. I heard a heartbeat and quiet female conversation that didn't overwhelm me or suck me inside.

Sue? The word echoed in my head and I felt her react. I could see her in a restaurant with Pamela. I walked to the screen door and could see the inside of a bistro, along with the waiter bringing plates to the table where Sue sat. When I stepped back, the scene disappeared. Just that easy. Aspen smiled in my mind.

You see how simple it is when someone shows you how? You may open the screen when you love, and close it to be within yourself. Or, put on storm windows during a crisis. There are always options in our world, Tony. Then she disappeared.

I came to myself, standing in front of Nana and Aspen.

My head was still filled with rainbows and sunlight and I felt like myself for the first time in days. "Uh, thank you, I guess. I'm not sure *what* you did, though."

Aspen shrugged. "You already knew how to shield, this was just a . . . *refinement*. We'll need to meet more, of course, to train your other gift. You are so *lucky* to only have hindsight."

Nana nodded. "And we'll meet, as well, so you can learn the benefits of second sight. It's not just seeing colors, you know. Although I hear they're quite pretty."

Lucas came out of the hotel just then, giving me a reprieve on responding. I didn't know quite what to say to these women.

"Nana! I'm glad you made it just when we're ready for you."

She laughed brightly. "Why would I show up *before* you were ready?"

Lucas chuckled and then smiled warmly. He embraced the old woman. Then he did the same to Aspen. "I haven't seen you in *centuries*. Your siblings are looking forward to seeing you."

Even *I* could smell the black pepper from that statement. Aspen laughed lightly. "I highly doubt that, Lucas. It's not yet the time for forgiveness from my brother, or my sisters."

Nana looked at her with interest, and the thick antifreeze of curiosity rose from her. "Odd you should mention that. I notice you haven't asked me the date or time since I arrived."

A bright smile lit Aspen's face. "That's right!" She grabbed Nana's arm in delight. "I'm only in Chicago *once*, in my whole life! I know *exactly* when I am! And," she said confidentially, leaning close to the old Sazi woman, "I meet *him* today! I remember he was so handsome at this age!"

I was getting a little lost in the flurry of speech tenses, and I could tell that Lucas was, too. But Nana returned the bright smile, showing yellowed, but straight teeth. "Well, that *is* a cause for celebration, isn't it? Let's go inside and see if Lelya has some champagne!"

Aspen snorted. "Well, of course she does! Unfortunately, we won't get to drink it, will we?"

Nana sighed. "No, I'm afraid not. But we should *try*. Maybe things will be different this time." They both laughed at a private joke, and walked arm and arm into the hotel. Lucas shook his head in frustration as we trailed slightly behind.

"Did you catch any of that?" I asked quietly.

Lucas shook his head. "I never do. Seers drive me insane! I wish they would talk about things in one tense. The back and forth makes me nuts."

I'd almost forgotten why I was out here, with the ladies arriving. I caught motion from my right side, and turned to see Bobby walking toward us. He glanced at me angrily, apparently deciding that I had told Lucas. He waited with a set jaw in front of the older wolf, who looked at him curiously.

"Is there something wrong, Agent?" Lucas asked after a second. Bobby's startled look said it all. He looked at me again and I shook my head lightly. I hadn't ratted him out.

He recovered a bit. "Uh, no, sir. Nothing's wrong." Then he moved his eyebrows slightly. "Unless you want to count inviting the entire Monier clan to a reunion. Lucas, we don't have enough agents here—hell, we don't have enough agents in the *world*—for that sort of fallout! We're standing at ground zero of a disaster."

"I didn't invite them, Bobby. Charles did. But we'll have to make do. If he says he can handle it, I have to believe him. I don't like it any more than you do. We've got one agent down already, so I'll be patrolling the roof myself. I've already informed Charles of the change."

Bobby looked absolutely terrified, and I knew he wasn't faking. His scent was strong ammonia that even his cologne couldn't block. "But I'm just one little snake, Lucas—the last of my kind. Isn't this considered *genocide?*"

Lucas looked askance at him and his voice was thick with sarcasm. "You're hardly *little.*"

"And apparently not the last of your kind any more, either." The words slipped out of my mouth before I could stop them. I absolutely knew better, and normally have better control. Damn it!

Lucas closed his dropped jaw, but didn't get a chance to say anything. Bobby didn't seem to mind at all. All of us turned to the sharp sound of breaking glass and hissing from inside the hotel. "Great!" he snarled. "That's *all* we need right now!"

A scream followed, but wasn't from inside the hotel. I turned toward the garage and started to move. A shadow . . . well, sort of *scuttled*, down the street at blinding speed. I stopped and tried to focus on it to see what it was. But there was no time to dwell on *that*, either, because I felt something heavy hit my back. I moved aside, but then had to catch Bobby's unconscious body with one arm before he landed face first on the pavement. As soon as my bare hand hit his dark skin, the street dissolved to blackness. *Damn it!* I definitely need to buy some gloves. . . .

Something new happened, but it was sort of familiar. I was inside the snake, who was inside the dragon. I'd been in two places at one time before, but it was really strange to be a third party observer.

I was walking across the cement floor of the parking garage. I'd just left Robart, and was angry, but also afraid. Too many things were happening. The life I'd planned was being torn asunder. A child—for so long dreamt of, and to actually have one, or more . . . But how would Nikoli react? I'd never been his favorite, but if I could give him a child, which no other of his mistresses had . . .

And what of Robart? He's a proud man—strong and fierce. Unlike the black wolf, it would be match that my father would have approved of.

They would have fought for my hand, and father might have let him win—even if he is a python. He is Wolven, and those who serve all Sazi have long been revered among my people. But, no. Robart is too controlling for this country, for this time. He would try to run my life, and I've run my own for too long.

A sound from ahead stops me, and the lights go out. I call into the darkness. "Robart?" There is no answer. A familiar scent slips by me and it chills my blood—the pungent odor of the killer of Mila and of the human at the estate.

I've been careless. I'm in an unprotected area, and no one knows I am here. I would be stronger if I changed forms, but I'm more agile in this one. I glance up as the sound moves overhead, but I cannot see. I was foolish not to carry a flashlight!

Now the sound is to my left, so I move right, but bump into a car. My heart pounds and I can feel a cold sweat on my brow. No more of this foolishness! I close my eyes, as I have done a thousand times in exercises and focus on the scent. I flick my tongue out repeatedly. The scent is to the left. No, now overhead. Now behind. What is this thing?

I'm near the garage entrance. I will not play into the fear the thing is attempting to instill. I will go for assistance. The wolves are better suited to the dark, and Tony has second sight.

I move quickly, but am not fast enough. Still, I am near the entrance. I only need to reach the outsi . . .

The thing drops down in front of me just before the opening, a black silhouette against the light of the street lamps. The shape is wrong . . . there are too many appendages . . . it cannot be what I am seeing, or think I see.

*"I've been waiting for you," it says in a voice
that is both hiss and trill.*

*I move quickly, darting around it with all of my
speed, but it moves in a blur that the eye cannot
follow. I am trapped. Before I can blink, I am
caught. I struggle with all of my might, but I feel a
sudden stabbing pain in my chest. I thrash as
something starts to spread in me. It hurts like fire
and I scream.* Robart, where are you?

Oh, very good, said another voice inside my head. *Let's
back that up a bit.* I saw Aspen walk into the scene, and the
image of Asri screaming froze in time.

What are you talking about? I hear myself ask. *How are
you here with me?*

*You have hindsight. Tony. It is a memory you see, not vi-
sions of the future to be trapped in until it ends.* Aspen
stepped up to Asri and put a hand right through. *They are
not real in the here and now, and you can take what information you require and then leave.* She raised her hand and
pulled, like opening a curtain. *Like so.* The image blurred
and changed. The scene reversed in time until it was just
before Asri spotted the entrance.

Now, Aspen continued, *Let's see what she saw.* She
moved her hand forward just a bit and the movements
slowly progressed, as though it was a frame-by-frame fast
forward on a video. She looked at me and smiled. *Yes! Precisely! I should have thought of that explanation. It's much
better than mine. It is like a movie video.*

I felt myself start. *You can hear my thoughts?*

She put hands on her hips, while the image stood still,
waiting. *Well, of course. If you'd just step out here, we
could stand together and watch this. It's your mind, Tony.
You can picture yourself inside.*

Okay, let's give it a try. I thought of myself standing
next to Aspen, and poof! There I was. The image of Asri
grew until it was the size of a theater screen. I reached out
my hand to push it back a little, like stepping back a few

rows of seats, and the picture shrunk. Now, this is just *too cool!*

Yes! Aspen exclaimed. *You're getting it. But we don't have much time, so you'll have to practice on your own when there aren't lives at stake.*

She moved her hand again and the scene replayed. When the shadow dropped at the entrance, she froze the vision. *What is that? I've never seen anything like that before.*

I shook my head and shrugged. *Got me. It just looks like a blob. There's not enough light. Can we add some?*

Unfortunately, no. The vision is what it is. You can only view what the person remembers seeing.

Not true! I thought instantly. *When I was in Leyla's past, I saw the scene played out in third person. I saw things happen after she left the scene.*

Aspen smiled in my head. *Of course you did. You weren't seeing Lelya's experiences at sixteen—you were seeing her* vision *of her sixteen-year-old self, when she was* eight. *It's a common problem with catching the thoughts of a seer. But no more instruction—we need help here. Let me get Lucas.*

I didn't even have time to respond to the concept of a vision within a vision, before I felt unearthly power slide across my mind. Aspen reappeared and pointed to the black blob. *There! You've been around the longest of us all. What is that?*

There was suddenly lights and motion and I struggled to breathe. The image exploded into a thousand sharp fragments and then I was awake again, inside the hotel on the couch. Bobby was next to me, and Nana was removing my shaking hand from his neck. My face was covered in sweat and I couldn't seem to warm myself. I felt Sue shuddering in the background, despite the warmth of the restaurant.

A chirping sound reached my ears and I fought to move my eyes toward the sound. Lucas's cell phone was ringing. He looked pale and drawn, somehow years older than just a few minutes before.

"Santiago," he said tersely.

"Lucas! Thank the gods I reached you in time." It was the voice of Jack, or Colecos, or whatever the hell name he was using. The voice rushed on. "I *remembered* what the poison was. But, I'm almost afraid to say it out loud."

All the sound and motion in the room had stopped. Faces were turned to Lucas and the effect was sort of like that old television commercial about the stock broker, E. F. Hutton.

Lucas fought to ignore them by keeping his eyes fixed firmly on the plush oriental rug. "You don't have to say it, Jack. I've seen it—it really is here."

"But . . . we *killed* them all! I know we did!"

Lucas uttered a short bark of a laugh. "Ever hear of a double recessive gene?"

There was a long pause where there was only breathing in the room. A glance around showed a wide variety of expressions. Ivan and Nikoli were in a state of shock, with open mouths and wide eyes. Charles looked positively furious, as did a couple of the council members. Aspen was nowhere to be seen, and Raven and Nana managed to ignore the conversation by continuing to work on healing Bobby from *whatever* had attacked Asri. I hadn't realized that Raven was a healer.

"Do I need to come?"

Lucas shook his head, even though the other man wouldn't see. "You *can't* come. You aren't welcome in this territory, Jack. The council is meeting here. You'd never make it."

The laugh that followed was bitter but amused. "I go where I please, Lucas—much as Aspen does. The council can be damned, and I hope they hear me! I can assure you all that I am better than the alternative in this case!" Another pause and the voice was suddenly deadly serious. "If you survive, call me in the next twenty-four hours. If you don't, I *do* plan to retrieve the sword from storage and visit Nikoli's territory, because I will not allow those *things* to decimate our kind. Do you have anyone there with any skill at all? You know what is required for this task."

Lucas looked up and scanned the crowd. I swore under my breath as his eyes fixed on me and he smiled. "I've got just the man for the job—a new turn. He might beat your old record on the course some day."

A burst of loud laughter made Lucas hold the phone away from his ear. "Ha! Hardly likely, Inteque, but nearly anybody is faster than *you.* Remember—twenty-four hours. Otherwise, the *esteemed* council will gaze upon my face once more."

Lucas pressed the End button on the phone and looked up into the shocked faces of the assembled crowd. He stared them all down, looking serene. He'd apparently made his decision and he would stand by it.

Charles spoke first. His voice was just short of rage. "He killed one of my best friends, Lucas, as you well know! I will remove him from the face of the earth if he shows up—file or no file!"

Lucas walked over to the old man who was trembling and red with fury. He spoke quietly, but with strength. "It's a *spider,* Charles. I will bargain with whatever devil I must. If I die—and I probably *will*—he is your only hope. No one else, including yourself, has ever fought one."

Charles's face had gone pale and he stumbled enough that he had to catch himself on a table to keep from falling. The rage had evaporated. He was still trembling, but for another reason. The scent of his fear hit everyone in the room. "But they're *extinct* . . ."

"Apparently not." Lucas's face was cold. His determination rode over the scents of fear and anger. It made him dangerous. Sort of like me.

The shrieking pitch of Angelique's voice made me shudder. "But were-spiders are merely zee *myth!* Zee story to frighten children."

Lucas turned to her and opened his mouth to reply, but Nana beat him to it. "No, they are *NOT,* you foolish bird!" She stood and the weight of years fell away from her, to reveal a shining, powerful woman in her prime. "They wiped out all but a handful of the red wolf pack, and the dragons, all of the cheetahs, the eagles, *and* most of the jaguars—until Colecos was the last. I was surprised that he didn't go insane before he *did*. They feed on *our* kind! *And* humans. *And* any other thing that lives, including their own elders when there is no other." She turned from face to startled face. "You all know me! You know that I do not suggest death lightly. But the spiders would destroy the earth as we know it if they are allowed to survive!"

Lucas nodded his head. "Right, then. Tony, we'll need every weapon in that box upstairs! You've just gotten your first Sazi assassination job! Congratul—"

I didn't hear the rest of the word, because Sue was suddenly in my head. *Tony! I just saw Asri with some woman. She looked sick. I recognized the woman and I'm afraid. She was in the mall back home—one of those perfume sprayers in the department store. She came through the whole crowd just to spray Barbara right in the face. I remember Asri complaining that someone had done the same thing to her a few days ago, but I didn't connect them. I know something's wrong. She may be the Sazi you're looking for. Pamela and I are going to follow them.*

I felt panic suffuse through me. *No, wait, Sue! You don't underst . . .*

Her voice took on a hard edge, cold and calculating, and very much like me. *I do understand, Tony. I've been listening. It's time for me to grow up and be an adult. This is the thing I have to do alone. I just know it. We'll be careful, but you need eyes and ears out here, and I'm it—for a change. I'll let you know where they end up.* She cut off contact.

I came back to myself with a shake of my head. I looked at Lucas, who had apparently just finished saying something to the crowd, because they were starting to scurry about. "Sue saw Asri with a woman. She and Pamela are going to follow at a distance and tell us where they land. I told her it was a bad idea, but . . ."

Lucas was checking the edge on a sword that had appeared from somewhere and he swore furiously. Nikoli was standing by, looking concerned. Lucas took a deep breath. "No, actually, Tony, it's a good idea. I'd hate for anything to happen to Sue, but this is more important than any one person. I know it's dangerous, but if they keep a distance, they should be fine."

He glanced at the couch, where Bobby was breathing shallowly. Both Nana and Raven were feeding power into him, but it was just barely keeping him alive. "I hope I can say the same about Bobby."

Nikoli approached carrying a sword that he handed hilt first to Lucas. "No, Nikoli, this has been a wall decoration too long. Get someone to sharpen it. If we don't come back—Jack, Raven and Ivan are the next line of defense. You, Charles and the cats are after them. Find as many swords and weapons as you can. I pray that there is only the *one,* and that she hasn't laid eggs."

Nikoli nodded and left. He was putting his pride aside and taking orders from the older wolf with an ease that surprised me.

I found Yurgi, who broke into a cold sweat at the news that Pamela and Sue were out tracking the thing that had everyone panicked. He wanted desperately to come with us, but he would only be a liability.

I decided to give him something else to think about, so I asked him to run a very special errand for me—to buy a Christmas present for Sue. I had something special in mind. I told him where the case of batteries was in the apartment and gave him a key. I told him to take as many as he needed. As a bonus for helping, he could get something for Pamela with the gold, too for *when we got back*. My confidence made him feel better. If he noticed the black pepper, he didn't mention it.

Lucas tapped me on the shoulder as I was finishing my instructions. "How did I get elected to go with you?" I asked as we bolted up the stairs to my suite, and the weapons. "There are ten other people downstairs with more power."

I swung open the door to the room and Lucas grabbed the box from the floor and opened it. "And they all offered to come, while you were talking to Sue. But I've watched you, Tony. Power means nothing against the spiders. Speed and accuracy are what count. It'll take us both, with everything we've got, to bring this lady down." He shuddered and drew a deep breath. "I've got to tell you—there's a good chance we won't walk away from this."

I shrugged. Death holds little horror for me. I've faced it too often. "Yeah? So what's new? In case you didn't notice, I'm pretty stubborn about holding onto life."

A tired smile and a shake of his head were my reply.

Chapter 19

THE WAREHOUSE WHERE Sue directed us to go was only a few blocks from the hotel. We were moving slower than usual because of the sheer volume of weapons we carried. All of my guns—minus the .17 HMR, which was too small for the task—along with a wide variety of weapons from Nikoli's arsenal in a canvas duffel bag. We had a stock of both silver and lead ammo, and some bowie knives long enough they nearly *were* swords.

I see her, Tony! Babs is still alive—but she looks bad. She and Asri have been put in some sort of . . . well, web, and are suspended from the ceiling about . . . wow, it must be forty feet high. There's no way I can free them.

I related the message to Lucas quietly, and he nodded.

We heard a scream in the distance. I started to bolt forward, but Lucas held me back. "That's just what she *wants*, Tony. Hang back and see if you can reach Sue."

Sue? What's happening?

It got Pamela, Tony! Oh, God, it was awful! It's HUGE and incredibly fast. It took her inside with the others.

Are you okay?

I felt her take a deep breath. *It's harder than I thought to be a grown-up. But I'll be fine.*

That thing will be back, Sue! Stay out of sight, but look around for a window. I want to see that monster.

I threw open the screen in my mind and was suddenly inside of Sue—seeing through her eyes, feeling her heart pound. I tried to slow her breathing, struggled to focus her mind. The first thing I noticed was a strange sound. It was a half-sentient wailing trill that made the hair on Sue's neck stand on end.

I tried to describe it to Lucas, who was waiting patiently for some word. "It's making some sort of weird sound— like a hundred crickets on angel dust. It's got Pamela now, and the others are in some sort of webbing near the ceiling."

Lucas went even paler. His skin had lost most of its natural tan. "It's the nesting song. It *is* ready to lay eggs. The women are sacrifices for the children to feed on when they hatch. They'll be alive, but paralyzed. *That's* the connection we all missed. The ladies must *all* be pregnant. It's the preferred food for the young ones and probably why Mila was killed, too; for her enzymes. The female spiders don't need a male to breed if they can take the fluids of a pregnant Sazi.

No wonder Nikoli was so broken up. I remember Yurgi mentioning that Nikoli didn't have any children.

"We can't wait any more. We have to *move*."

This time I held *him* back. "Just a second. Let's see if we can find out more about it. Do you remember what they look like? Let's make sure we're dealing with the same baddie."

He nodded. "The ones I fought stood about three foot high, but they're about four foot around. Pale brown to yellow. Eight slender legs without hair, and armor plated body. The eyes are multi-faceted. Same one?"

I slid back into Sue's mind. She was watching the spider inject Pamela with something from a fang. She screamed once and Sue started to cry. I pushed through her pain. *Focus, Sue! We'll get them. Lucas says they'll stay alive until the eggs hatch, so we've got a little time. Just give me your senses so we know what we're dealing with.*

Sue closed her eyes briefly and then calmed a tiny bit.

When she opened her eyes, we watched the spider move, as it wrapped Pamela in the same webbing as the others. Yep, pale brown, no hair—this was our baby. It glowed with an unearthly silver-grey light that fluxed and roiled. It wasn't a color I'd ever encountered. The whole scene was something out of a particularly bad nightmare, or an H.P. Love-craft story. This particular Sazi was *definitely* Cthulu mythos fodder. It made me wonder just how much *fiction* some fiction is.

"It's the same one," I replied to Lucas. "It's wrapped Pamela in webbing."

"Get Sue out of there. It'll be back for her once the other is secure. It can smell a human at close to a mile. It won't allow any witnesses to live."

Get away from there, Sue. Lucas says it'll be back for you.

Her voice in my head was calm, but determined. *I won't hide, Tony. I won't leave Barbara, Asri and Pamela to that . . . thing.*

It can smell you, Sue! You have to leave!

I felt her move toward the purse on her shoulder, as though I could see her. *No, it can't smell me. I sort of . . . well, borrowed Bobby's cologne yesterday—it's a form of teeth, like Lelya said. But I forgot to spray Pamela. That was stupid of me! No, I'll stay here to watch until you get here. I'll keep out of sight.* She cut off contact, slamming the screen door in my face.

"She's being stubborn," I whispered. "She used some of the Wolven cologne and is keeping out of sight, but she won't leave until we get there."

Lucas pursed his lips and started forward again. "It might work. Jack and I hadn't developed the cologne when we fought them. It shouldn't recognize the smell. I hope she didn't use it all. We'll put on some, as well, when we get to her."

We moved in shadows, keeping to the darkest black as we skirted ancient, decaying edifices that rose to greet a pale, unfeeling moon. Jeez—now I was *thinking* in Lovecraft-ese, not exactly confidence inspiring. Enough of *that*.

I listened for any sound as we slipped silently forward. We'd taken a few minutes back at the hotel to get ready. Now we were both wearing black, face camo and gloves. We moved silently as shadows. Lucas let me lead the way, following Sue's direction and scent. I watched him move with lethal ease. Eyes and ears took in everything—even the scurrying of rodents didn't escape his notice. He'd lowered his inner light until it was non-existent and had lessened his breathing until it was barely audible. I watched his nostrils flare for any hint of danger as the breeze drifted by us, pushing our scents back behind.

We both stopped at the sing-song rise and fall of the spider's trill. The sound and the horrible smell made me shiver, and once again the terrors of forbidden, ancient gods tickled my mind. Natural instinct made me want to bolt and run. I struggled against the urge to leave. I couldn't imagine what would it have been like to go into a spider den—to confront dozens, or hundreds, of these things who were eating your people alive and I wasn't about to touch Lucas to find out.

He lifted one hand the slightest bit and jerked a finger to our right. I moved across the alley without a sound. Sue was hiding behind a dumpster near the window. I raised my head a bit to catch Lucas's eye and moved my head and eyes toward the dilapidated metal box. He gave a short nod and then we moved forward together until we reached her side.

"Anything new?" Lucas whispered so low that I could barely hear.

Sue had taken the hint, and shook her head mutely. She spoke directly into my mind. *It's been spinning a lot of silk since it hung Pamela on the ceiling, but it doesn't seem to be sticky. It's been fluffing it in the corner near that balcony. I think it's some sort of nest.*

I nodded and relayed the information to Lucas, close to

his ear. He looked up and around. He raised up a finger and moved it back and forth. Sue didn't understand the question, but I did.

How did the spider get inside, Sue? Did it go through a door or the roof, or what?

She opened her mouth and raised her brows in understanding. *There's a hole in the wall in back. I saw it when I followed the spider after she took Pamela. It's pretty small. The spider had to squeeze to go through and then reach back to take Pamela through. But by then she was paralyzed. I might have saved her if not for that.*

I put a hand on her shoulder and winked. *Don't beat yourself up. This thing has taken down the best of the best. The fact that you're still alive is pretty damn good.*

She smiled and nodded. Lucas let out a small annoyed breath. Oops! I forgot to bring him up to date.

I leaned close. "There's a hole in the back wall, but Sue says it's pretty small. One at a time, I think, with Sue keeping watch on the mark?"

He blinked his eyes in agreement. He pointed to me and then to himself. He winked at Sue and squeezed her shoulder lightly, and then touched her nose. He pointed a finger at her and then at the window and then leaned close to her ear. "Keep in touch with Tony. If you see the spider leave, for *any* reason, let him know."

As we were walking to the back of the building, I heard a noise to our left. I touched Lucas's shoulder, but he'd heard it too. We split and dropped into the shadows, our weapons cocked and ready.

I smelled thick jungle vines and pain before I saw shadowy movement next to the building across the alley.

"What are you doing here, Agent?"

"We're mated, Lucas. She's in my head all the time now. I'd tried to ignore it, but I can't. I know where she is and I know the trouble they're in. I couldn't just keep driving a frigging limo while she's in danger!"

Even though Lucas gave him a disgusted look, his scent was pleased. Bobby noticed. It reminded me that we'd forgotten to spray ourselves. Lucas apparently recognized Bobby's scent as well. I turned my hand inward and moved my finger up and down to imitate spraying. He shook his head in annoyance. He'd forgotten, too.

Lucas moved close to Bobby and we all returned to Sue's side. She shook her head. *No change. She's still building the nest.*

I opened my palm and moved my fingers in and out several times. *Cologne? Did you use it all?*

She shook her head and opened her purse. She handed me the small bottle. There was still plenty for us all. After I'd sprayed myself, I handed it to Bobby. He looked at the bottle and glanced at Sue with raised brows and annoyance before passing it to Lucas.

She had the good grace to blush.

Lucas sprayed himself and then grabbed my chin. Before I could react, he tilted my head and spritzed some of the fluid directly up my nose. I struggled not to cough and sneeze.

Lucas held my nose closed and put his other hand over my mouth. I shuddered and tried to remove his hands so I could breathe. He leaned close and hissed into my ear. "Leave it! As we get closer to the spider, the scent can get too strong. The odor will disorient you. This will last about an hour. If we haven't killed it by then, we're out of luck anyway. It'll have laid the eggs and we'll be spider food."

I held my breath for a second and the stinging from the cologne abated. When Lucas removed his pinching fingers, I could breathe again. I watched he and Bobby do the same thing to themselves with the bottle. I suddenly couldn't smell a damn thing, as though I had a head cold. I rubbed my nose on my sleeve to remove the remaining liquid, and blinked wetness from my eyes.

I stared at Bobby for a moment. His normally ebony skin was like coffee with two creams. He swayed twice and had to catch his balance on the side of the building. Lucas shook his head angrily. "Mbutu, you're in no condition to fight." Lucas's nearly silent words were terse. "Go home. We'll manage."

Bobby took a deep breath. He looked pale and wan, but determined. "I can't, Lucas. I really *can't.* Think what you would do if it was Tatya up there. I have to try to save her."

Lucas shook his head. "They're over forty feet up, suspended from a rafter by webbing. We'll have to wait until we bring down the spider to get them."

Bobby shook his head but smiled. He'd apparently already planned this out. I'd bet Asri's predicament, along with a possible solution, was being projected into his head. Asri's no slouch in tactics. "You forget, boss, I'm from a long line of a tree climbers, and nearly forty feet long myself. You get the spider—I'll get the ladies. They're all tiny. I can change forms, slither up, and tear apart the support webbing with my teeth. Then I'll lower them down with my tail, change back, and bring them all out. Of course, you'll have to keep it *busy.*"

Sue's voice sounded pleased in my head. *And I can use my silver knife to cut the silk. Then we can take them back to the healers. I bet it will work.*

I shrugged my shoulders. It sounded like a good plan to me. Sue nodded as well. Lucas sighed. He knew he was outnumbered. He threw up his hands and shouldered his AR-15, filled with silver bullets that Nikoli just *happened* to have on hand. Oh, yeah—silver is a *big* affront!

Lucas pointed at Bobby with narrowed eyes and hissed, "Do *not* get in our way, Bobby. I won't risk this thing getting out of the building to find another nest. I don't want to, but I *will* put you down. Do I make myself clear?"

Bobby got a surprised look, but it hardened. He nodded once curtly. "Eminently. We're all expendable—I get it."

Sue's face was likewise shocked. Her fearful eyes turned

to me and I could feel her panic pound my heart. I pushed it aside coldly and shook my head.

He's right, Sue. Learn this now—everybody is expendable when the prize is big enough. I accepted it a long time ago. The more useful you are, the longer you'll live. But if you cause trouble, you won't last. I would suggest you keep your head down. Don't doubt that Lucas will put you down, too, if you get in the way. He's already admitted he doesn't expect himself to survive.

Sue glanced at Lucas, who had picked up the duffel and was taking a deep breath with closed eyes. He was centering himself. I do it, too. She turned her eyes to me and nodded more confidently than she felt in my head. I smiled and winked.

It's okay to be scared, Sue, as long as you keep moving. It takes a lot of practice to go where only fools dare to tread.

She shook her head as I stood and moved to crouch next to Lucas. *Not practice. It takes a lot of skill, Tony.*

That too, love. That too.

I couldn't resist anymore, and I knew the other two would do the same thing if they could. I grabbed her and held her close for a moment and kissed her slowly. I ignored the grumbles from the other two as I let my body soak in warmth and sunshine and the intense physical pleasure that rode over my skin and tore the breath from my chest.

She didn't want to let go, but I finally pushed her back to arm's length.

"But Tony," she whispered, "What if . . ."

I smiled. "Then we had everything that most people can only dream of. Promise me that if anything happens to us in there, you'll keep going. Start a new life far away from the pack and be just as strong and capable and happy as I know you can be. I *want* you to be a whole person, Sue. I want you to be my equal, and more. I'm sorry for everything I've put you through, and don't want you to think I really meant the things I said last night. I didn't. I swear."

She threw herself back into my arms for a moment and I held her close. When we finally broke apart, there were tears in her eyes and a few stray ones had managed to find their way into mine, too.

The keening was growing faster. It was time to go. I nodded and gave the thumbs up sign to Lucas just before I put on the storm windows to close down the connection with Sue. I'd have to trust that she would be safe. I couldn't afford to be two places at once.

Lucas and I moved toward the back of the building, leaving Bobby to find his own entrance in the front. When we reached the hole in the wall, I stopped Lucas, and threw open the screen door so that I could watch the spider through Sue's eyes. It was still nest building, oblivious to our presence. That bothered me. I had to assume that there was a reason it was so confident in a location so close to wolf headquarters.

"We'll move slow. Something about this set-up smells bad."

Lucas nodded and responded in a similar whisper. "I was thinking the same thing. It's too confident. Either it's stupid—which I doubt—or it's booby-trapped the place."

I raised my brows. "Or there are more of them than we think. There could be guards."

I could see Lucas shudder and take a deep breath. "I would rather not believe that. But let's load up every spare pocket with ammo, just to be safe."

I wish we would have had the time to go back to the apartment for my military camo. The pants have pockets all down the legs. They're incredibly useful. But the jeans were what I was wearing, so they would have to do.

I had Lucas hold onto my legs so I could stick my head inside and recon the place before we crawled inside. He could pull me back out quickly if there were problems. It looked clear, which—again—bothered me. I tapped my left foot twice, which was the signal that everything was okay. He let go of my legs and I shimmied inside the building, slow and silent. The interior was pitch black, but we couldn't afford a light. Once I was standing, I listened for any movement, but there was only the sing-song wailing in the next room. I stuck a hand outside the wall and gave the thumbs-up. Lucas pushed in the duffel and then slowly worked his way inside until he was standing beside me.

We couldn't afford to speak, so I was surprised to hear his voice. But then I realized it was all in my mind—literally. I winced a bit, because his intrusion into my head was painful.

I don't do this often, Tony, but it's an ability that most pack leaders have. It's part of the package. You won't be able to answer back, though. Let's move to where there's a little more light so we can see hand motions.

I nodded and stepped forward, but then stopped suddenly and put a strong arm across Lucas's chest to halt him in his tracks.

He put a hand on my shoulder. *What is it? Did you hear something?*

I shook my head. It wasn't something I heard, it was something I *saw*—or sort of saw. I tried to focus my eyes as I peered into the darkness.

Yep, there it was again—glowing fragments; ribbons of something pale and silver right in front of us. I took a deep whiff before I remembered it was useless.

I took Lucas's hand off my shoulder and put mine on his. I pressed down, which is the universal signal for "stay down." I moved forward an inch, and then slid sideways along the faintly glittering line of luminescence.

When I got to the adjoining wall, I swore silently. It was a goddamned *web!* It covered the whole room from wall to wall. Now that I was looking at it from an angle, the glowing ribbons formed a pattern I recognized. I reached down carefully and felt along the floor until my fingers found about half of a brick. I pressed it against one of the radiating strands. It stuck to it and I couldn't pull it away. Nor would the webbing budge from the wall, even when I pulled sideways on the brick with all my strength. Just fucking wonderful! No wonder she could be confident— and we'd nearly walked right into it. I was starting to be grateful for my second sight.

I returned to Lucas, who was standing right where I left him. I had no choice—I leaned over and whispered into his ear. "It's a web, right in front of us. You've dealt with them before. Is there any way past?"

The hiss of air from him told me he was swearing internally. I heard him reply in my head and I winced again. *No, damn it! I should have remembered! It was how they caught all the eagles. These are Sazi webs, meant for Sazis. Once you're stuck, there's no escape. I hope Bobby isn't already trapped.*

Something clicked in my head. If it was a *Sazi* web . . .

I leaned and cupped my hand to his ear once more. "Would *silver* cut the strands? I've still got Nikoli's push knife."

Lucas started. *I don't know. We never had any in the jungle. But you'll have to try it. I can't see the damn thing. And, be careful. They usually had noisemakers attached, like bells or hollow sticks to tell the spider when the web was full.*

I nodded and removed the silver push knife from the boot sheath. I inched along with my back to the wall once more, being *really* careful not to touch the thing. When I got to the right angle, I eased the knife in front of my face and pressed it against the glowing strand just under where the brick was stuck. There was a hiss and a small wisp of smoke floated up. The strand released from the wall and the web sagged a bit. There was a small sound above— probably the noisemaker Lucas had mentioned, but it wasn't loud enough to be noticed over the spider's trill. Unfortunately, the smell might bring the spider just as quickly as noise would. I knew what burning silk smelled like. I used the knife to release two more strands along the wall and a couple on the floor, so that one corner was free, but the integrity of the web remained. Still, there was no way we could get under the web without being trapped, unless . . .

I moved back to Lucas and leaned close. "Pick a long gun you can do without."

Why? His voice sounded suspicious in my head.

"We'll have to lift the web to go under it. She'll be able to smell it if I do any more."

He sighed and handed me his AR-15. *I hate to do this, but we have handguns that will do the same thing. I hope you know what you're doing. It'll be a lot slower to kill her.*

I shrugged. "If we don't *reach* her, we can't kill her at all."

Lucas nodded. I took the rifle and eased back to the corner of the room. I held onto the sling and swung the rifle the tiniest bit along the floor, until it touched the loose strands. It stuck like it was bonded with super glue. Then I pulled on the sling and damned if the whole corner didn't move up and out. But then I had a problem. If I tried to attach the web to itself to hold open the hole, the swivels on the sling would shift and I'd get caught, too. If I threw the rifle against the web to attach it, the bell would sound. Nope—we'd have to do it the old fashioned way. I put the rifle on the floor with the sling safely away from the webbing and returned to Lucas.

"You'll have to trust me on this," I whispered in his ear. "You can't see the web, so when you reach the adjoining wall, go on your belly and keep your face in the dirt to go under. Keep going until I tell you to stop."

My eye twitched when his voice seared across my brain. *I really don't like this.*

"Yeah? Well, get over your control issues," I hissed. "Because we've got work to do. I'll slide through the duffel and then figure out how to get myself through when you're past."

There was barely enough room for one, so getting me to hold the web and Lucas to crawl along the floor, avoiding something he couldn't see or smell, was quite the trick. I had to step over him repeatedly in a little dance until he was face first to go under, with his legs rising up the wall at my back. I straddled him and used my feet, kicking his legs lightly to tell him the direction to move. He would slide an inch, stop and wait for me to direct him another inch. God, I hoped this was the only web we had to deal with. It was a pain in the ass.

Once he was through, I kicked the duffel forward until it was completely on the other side. Now, for me . . .

I looked the whole scene over while Lucas stood frozen, waiting for me on the other side. We didn't know if there were any more webs, and I couldn't see past this one to tell him.

I looked carefully at the rifle, to see *exactly* where it was attached. Okay, it was mostly the top of the barrel and receiver. With one hand holding the rifle taut by the sling, I gripped the trigger guard and took the weight onto my other hand. I released the sling and transferred it to the bottom of the stock and pressed the whole works forward lightly. The rifle stuck to the webbing just as planned, but when I let my fingers loose, my right thumb remained firmly attached to the web. Shit!

What's wrong?

My hiss of a response sounded annoyed, even to me. "I'm caught. Give me a second."

Lucas started to reply in my head, because I felt a flash of power. But he changed his mind and kept silent.

Oh, this was going to be a joy! The whole right thumb was attached, down to the palm. And to top it off, the frigging silver knife was in my *right* boot! This was a test of balance I hadn't anticipated. I lifted my right foot and crossed it over my knee. It threatened to touch the web. Then I tried to slide it backward and around my left leg, but met the wall. Nope, I couldn't reach the knife while my thumb was attached without making the situation worse.

But if a silver *knife* can cut it . . .

I pulled my Taurus from the back of my pants and

thumbed the chamber release with my left hand—not *easy*, but doable. I flipped the wheel sideways and used my fore-finger to pull the cartridge release backward a bit and then pulled a bullet out with my teeth. Then I reversed the pro-cess until the revolver was safely in the holster and the bul-let was still between my lips.

I held onto the bullet by the brass and eased it forward—no sense ruining *both* hands. I pulled backward on my thumb until it was taut, and steeled myself.

The silver bullet seared both flesh and silk and I gritted my teeth against the pain. I don't know which one gave out first, but the two separated. I was glad that Sue was safely behind the storm doors.

That hissing sounded painful.

I belly-crawled under the web and stood beside the old wolf. I whispered tersely while my thumb pounded. "I'll heal, but I'm glad I'm ambidextrous. Let's get moving."

We'd only gone a few feet when the singing stopped. I felt Sue blast through the storm windows. *Tony! She heard you, or smelled you or something. But she's moving your way. Get out!*

No doubt she smelled me burning my own flesh! But there *was* no getting out. I pushed aside her fear and closed the door again, gently shutting her out.

"It's coming," I said quietly to Lucas. He tensed and nodded.

I kept my eyes trained on the darkness while Lucas un-loaded the duffel. He handed me weapons, and I didn't even bother to figure out what they were before I slid them into pockets and my waistband. I'd know them by feel when I drew them to fire.

I told Lucas that there were no other webs as far as I could tell, and fortunately we couldn't smell the reeking stench of the spider as we neared the door to the main warehouse. I looked up and could see the three cocoons near the ceiling. Bobby was nowhere to be found. I could only hope for the best.

We decided silently to take the high ground and each climbed opposite staircases to balconies that overlooked the main floor. There was no movement, but there was sound—the whisper of wind through broken panes of glass near the roof, dripping water from somewhere in the depths of the basement, and a ticking, scuttling sound of movement to my left. No, now overhead. I looked around me frantically and caught sight of a blur of light as it raced across the ceiling, toward—

"LUCAS! Look out!"

He turned and saw the spider just as she pounced from an overhead beam. He dropped and rolled, while I bolted down my stairs and raced across to climb his. He moved fast, but not fast enough. One fang caught him in the upper thigh. A brilliant flow of raw white light exploded and the spider was pushed back, but only briefly. I pulled two handguns at random and was pleased they were both semi-autos. I ignored the pain in my thumb and I emptied them both in the spider's direction. The silver bullets caught her in the chest and cut one leg off at the knee. She fell backward off the balcony. The resulting crash told me she hit hard. But when I glanced over the balcony, she had disappeared. But, at least she was wounded for the moment.

I raced over to Lucas, who was gritting his teeth in pain. The leg was already swollen and the entry point of the fang was black.

"Are you going to be all right?"

He chuckled a bit, but it was a raw, bitter sound. "No."

"So you'll go paralyzed like the girls?"

The bitter laugh turned sharper, like jagged, broken glass. "Don't I wish! Nope. Different venoms for different uses. She used the good stuff on me." I knew what that meant. It was only a matter of time.

He pulled out a pocket knife and cut off the pant leg just above the wound, and then used the cloth to tie a tourniquet around his upper leg at the joint. "And I gotta tell you—it really screws up my plan to kill her. I won't be able to walk any second now, so you'll have to do the hard part. I hope you're as fast as Jack."

"Tell me what I have to do." The words were cold and sure, because he was right. This thing couldn't be allowed to live, much less *breed*. "I don't know how fast I am. I've never put it to the test."

He explained his plan, and by the time he was done, my eyebrows had nearly raised right off my forehead. "You have *got* to be kidding!"

"It's the only way, Tony. It has to be heart and then head."

I looked at him incredulously before glancing around again to watch for the spider. "You're expecting me to go find this thing, let it chase me, get it to this balcony, and then somehow get *behind* it, slide underneath it while firing my weapons at her heart while you're firing *through* it—toward *me*, I might add, while your hands are shaking like crazy—to cut off the head. Is that about it?"

Lucas nodded, satisfied. "That's about it."

I shook my head. "You're *insane*. Did your buddy, Jack, ever tell you *that?*"

He actually smiled for a moment, even through the pale skin and sweating. "Frequently. But it works—as long as you're fast enough. You've seen it, Tony. You'll have to push yourself to your absolute limit to beat her. But for the record, I managed to cut off the head *last* time after getting bit. I can do it this time, too."

"You got bit last time, too? Jeez, Jack was right—you really *are* slow!"

He flipped me his middle finger in response. He got himself to a standing position. I didn't help, because he needed to be able to do it himself if this was going to work. He started pulling the weapons out of his waistband and placed them in a row on the balcony ledge. "Just get her to me and take out the heart. I'll handle the rest."

I turned to leave, but had to ask, since it might come up in my future, too. "How'd you survive the bite last time?"

He shook his head, understanding the implication. "Not an option this time, sorry. There was an antidote waiting for us back in Jack's village. Just try not to get hit." I nodded, but didn't leave. I could tell from his face and posture that there was more to be said.

He didn't look at me. He just kept repositioning the weapons on the ledge. "If you end up going back alone, I'd like to be buried near Mesa Verde in Colorado. It's where my pack lived when I was young. And tell my wife I really did love her . . . despite . . . well, a lot of things."

I nodded once and descended the stairs to the sound of him violently jacking rounds into the chambers of the semi-autos. He really *didn't* think he'd survive and, unfortunately, I couldn't disagree. Most of his thigh had turned black and the wound had started to ooze a pus-like fluid just in the time we'd been talking.

When I got to the bottom of the stairs, I stopped and tried to remember what I knew about spiders. It was obvious that this one could climb any surface and liked to attack from above. I glanced up and around. The three cocoons were still in sight, but no Bobby. *Stop it, Giodone*, I commanded myself. He isn't my problem right now.

I took a deep breath and looked all around again. Back to spiders—they usually keep to dark places. So, I had to *look* in dark places. Wish I'd thought to bring a flashlight. Even my Sazi eyes need *some* light. Instead, I used my ears. I'd heard it move before, and now it *should be* wounded, depending on how fast it could heal.

A second later I stopped and stared at my feet—or at least, at the floor, which was now covered with a light mist, like fog rolling. Okay, now that's just *creepy*.

I heard a faint sound and the twin Barettas rose and pointed before I had my head fully turned. There was nothing there but . . . one of the cocoons was missing! That was either a really good thing, or a bad one. Was the spider already moving her nest? I needed to speed up this process.

I took another step cautiously. The mist was up to my knees now. I wished I could smell enough to decide whether this was something natural that was going to kill me, like some sort of chemical leak, or something *unnatural* that was going to kill me instead. I calculated in my head as I stalked the edges of the room—if the spider is three feet high standing, how high does the mist need to be before the spider can just hunker down and lie in wait right in front of me? Oh, about knee high. *Just frigging wonderful!*

I felt Lucas's intrusion into my head before I heard his voice. *The mist is the spider's scent, Tony! They did this in the jungle, too. I'm starting to get my nose back. Hurry and find something to stuff up your nostrils, or you won't be able to think any second now. I cut a couple pieces of cloth for mine.*

Shit! I found a wall to put my back against for a moment. He could have mentioned this *before!* I pulled the silver knife from my boot and cut a couple of squares from my jeans and stuffed them up my nose, adjusting them like ear plugs until there was no air intake. Fortunately, I didn't have my sense of smell back yet. I hoped to continue that trend. But breathing was going to be a pain in the ass.

I heard a shuffling sound as I stepped away from the wall, along with a scraping thump. Hmm. That might just be the sound an eight legged creature would make when using *seven* legs. The sound still moved too quickly for my taste, but it wasn't the blur of sound from before. I glanced up again and swore under my breath. Now there was only one cocoon remaining! I didn't even care whether it was Bobby or the spider—I should be noticing this stuff! I'm letting my nerves get the best of me. I closed my eyes for a brief moment and focused.

When I opened them, I'd switched sides. I wasn't on the defensive anymore. I was the hunter, and the mark would go down, even though I hadn't quite worked out how I was going to lead it and follow it at the same time.

The screen door ripped open in my mind. *You're not going to lead it! I hope you're ready, because here we come!*

I looked up and across the vast length of the room. Sue was running with the speed of an Olympic sprinter toward the balcony where Lucas stood. But she wasn't going to be fast enough to stay in the lead much longer. I took off at a diagonal angle toward the pair.

How did you get her to follow you? I asked as I raced toward them.

Her voice was breathless in my head. *Hit her in the eye with a brick! I played softball in high school.*

Yeah, that would do it.

But I'm having a hard time thinking, Tony. That mist is making me dizzy. She shook her head as I watched.

The creature started gaining on Sue, despite the strange way it was running. I saw why—I'd cut off one front leg, and the one behind it must have broken in the fall and was healing badly. The spider was moving in an ambling, twitchy kind of shuffle that made it seem even more monstrous and unnatural.

I heard that same hissing trill as I'd heard in Asri's memory. "I won't save you for my children, woman! You'll satisfy my hunger *now!*" The spider's fangs reached out and forward with a lurch, snagged on Sue's jacket, and started to drag her to a stop.

Lose the jacket, Sue! I pushed myself out and forward through the open screen, until I was inside Sue's body. She was right, the smell was awful. I fought to focus enough to take action. The next few seconds slowed to a snail's pace.

I threw back her arms, and she let me. The coat slipped off her, pausing only briefly as one cuff caught on her watch, before she was racing forward toward the balcony once more. The spider didn't even break stride. It increased its speed, and I did the same for Sue. I struggled to keep her mind on running. But her body was only human and it was wearing down. I pushed more magic into her and hoped the cost to her wouldn't be too high. Faster and faster I forced her to race forward as I increased my own speed to intercept them.

My arms were pumping hard and I was struggling to take in enough air as I pushed my body to go even faster. I reached them just as they passed, and then turned to follow.

"Get ready!" I shouted, even though I couldn't see Lucas behind the wall. I hoped he was still conscious, or this would end badly. The sound echoed off the high ceiling. It blended and split into a thousand voices that surrounded us and encouraged me, pushing me to my limit.

"MOVE !" I ordered Sue as I leapt into the air toward the spider. Sue turned at high speed toward the spider's right— and the wounded legs. The spider couldn't pivot quickly enough to grab Sue, but it saw me coming and kept running forward. It wouldn't be fast enough to escape its fate.

I was suddenly under it, firing bullets the full length of the spider's body. The ancient wood floor underneath creaked and groaned as I slid. Splinters and chunks of wood embedded themselves in my back, legs and scalp, while blood and stinging fluid covered my exposed face from the bullet wounds.

When the guns were empty, I dropped them in full slide, pulled a second pair from my waist band at lightning speed and unloaded them into the spider's chest as I passed under. I heard the explosions echo and then split as they were joined by more shots from above. I twisted and turned as bullets rained down on me. One piece of spent silver bounced off a nail, and slashed a burning line across my cheek. Another caught me in the bicep.

I'd done my job. I could only hope that Lucas had good aim. I crossed my arms over my chest and face and let my momentum take me out from underneath the spider just as she dropped into the mist. I spun out of control and hit a huge pile of rusting equipment and crates against the wall. I lost track of the number of cuts, bruises and punctures I collected as I came to a screaming, crashing halt. Thankfully, mercifully, I blacked out.

Chapter 20

I woke to pain. I heard movement, felt the debris shift as someone dug through it towards me. I panicked. Was it the spider? I couldn't smell anything and couldn't move no matter how hard I tried. I couldn't seem to wake up completely.

Bobby's voice made me let loose a breath I hadn't even known I was holding. "Hang on, Tony! We'll get you out of there."

Grunting with strain he managed to move a chunk of metal the size of a car that was holding down my right arm. Sue was helping him move smaller pieces away. I could feel cuts healing and bones mending like time-lapse.

She touched my face with cool dusty fingers. It felt nice and I leaned into her touch. I would have done more, but my head was all I could move presently.

"Tony! Oh thank God, I was so worried! Lucas kept shooting and the bullets kept hitting you! I was terrified I was going to lose you. I don't care if you want to watch me cook, or sit in the bath, or want me around every minute of the day! Tony? Tony! Please say something!"

They redoubled their speed in moving metal and wood off of me. I'd been in this bad a shape once or twice in my life and survived—eventually. We may have won, but not without cost.

I could taste blood and too many body parts didn't have enough feeling. I opened my eyes slowly and saw Sue's worried face brighten. "How's Lucas?" I rasped, and then burst into a fit of coughing. I immediately regretted it since I seemed to have broken most of my ribs.

Bobby glanced around. "I don't know. Where is he?"

I pointed up to the balcony. "He got bit by the spider. He might not have made it."

Bobby swore and bolted for the stairs. Sue helped me carefully to my feet. We staggering behind him with all the speed of a three-legged turtle. I couldn't share her thoughts—she'd shut me out to protect herself from my injuries, but there was no mistaking her sob of anguish when she first caught sight of the fallen man.

Lucas looked a lot worse than when I left him, but he was still breathing. The black had spread to his chest and arm, and a line of black was even crawling up his jaw.

"We have to get him out of here," Bobby said with feeling. "The girls are already in the van."

It *had* been Bobby moving the cocoons. That explained the sticky webbing that covered most of his battered body.

I flinched first when I tried to bend over—and again after I reached under Lucas's legs. The flesh on the wounded one was squishy, like holding a plastic sandwich bag full of mush. Bobby had a similar reaction when he grasped his shoulders. I raised my brows significantly. "Do you think we *can* move him?"

Bobby took a deep breath, looked again at his boss and friend, and nodded his head. "We have to get him to the healers—or at least *try*."

"Fine," I turned to Sue. "See if you can find something we can use to carry him." She nodded and limped off, slow but steady, leaving me and Bobby with Lucas.

"Are you going to be able to lift him?" Bobby asked. "I can hear you wheezing from here. You've broken some ribs. I'd heal you—but I don't have the juice."

"You worry about your end. I'll manage mine."

Sue came back dragging part of a wooden crate. Between the three of us we managed to get Lucas onto our makeshift stretcher. With Bobby holding one end, and Sue and I the other, we made our way downstairs.

The fog had dissipated. A woman's petite body lay in the middle of the dark-stained wooden floor. Her head was neatly severed. I might have to come back to get it—if Babs didn't make it. If not, I'd just leave it to be disposed of by Wolven.

We walked out of the warehouse into a winter dawn, our footsteps muffled by the thick layer of snow as we fought to keep our footing on the slippery asphalt.

Asri was pale, and moving slowly, but she held open the rear doors so we could get the old wolf into the back. I winced when I looked inside. Babs was already there, looking just as bad as Lucas, if not worse. Pamela wasn't much better. I didn't know what the hell that stuff was that the spider injected, but it was going to kill them all if we didn't get help. I was amazed it hadn't already. There wasn't one of us that wouldn't need the healers. Sue was in the best shape and she'd screwed her leg up badly in that forced run.

Bobby ignored all of his fears about driving in weather as he raced back to the hotel, taking his attention away only long enough to check on Asri in the mirror every few seconds. She saw him watching once and smiled tiredly. I saw him tap his fingers impatiently on the wheel as we rounded the corner and skidded to a sideways stop at the hotel's curb.

In a blur of motion Ivan, Amber, Charles and Raven moved to the rear of the van. The second the doors were open, Amber began barking orders.

Bobby and Asri held open the hotel doors as Raven and Charles took the stretcher with Lucas into the hotel. Sue and I were still staggering toward the entrance when they rushed back for Babs. Both stretchers were immediately surrounded by healers. I recognized the new one from Lucas's photo. Tatyana had finally arrived.

With tears streaming down her face she poured a tube of viscous, foul smelling fluid down his throat while whispering. "Don't you *dare* die on me, Lucas. Don't you *dare*." She was glowing too brightly for me to look directly at them as she flooded magical energy into his still form.

Amber poured a similar tube of fluid down Babs throat before lighting up like a Christmas tree. In the distance, I watched Pamela stagger into Yurgi's arms. Raven handed her a tube of the same medicine, then left the two of them to join the group that was forming around me.

"Did you get the spider, or did it get away?" Raven spoke softly, his voice calm but worried.

I turned to him, looked up into his dark eyes and nodded. "It's done. You can go collect the body if you want. We left her at the warehouse."

Ivan was horrified. "You left a dissected, giant *spider* where humans could find it?"

I thought about it. Would a swarm of police be descending on the warehouse from a "shots fired" call? I doubted it. It was a fairly secluded area. Most of the warehouses had been deserted. It had been the middle of the night. There might have been a couple of bums—but they wouldn't exactly have cell phones, and weren't likely to call the cops anyway.

"She wasn't a spider when we left, she was a woman. But you should probably go pick her up."

Raven and Ivan looked at each other and then at me with a significance I didn't understand. "Did she turn back before she died?"

I shrugged. "Don't know. I was busy getting shot and colliding with a wall at the time."

Raven stopped and apparently just saw my wide variety of slowly healing wounds. He walked slowly around me.

When he saw my back he gave a low whistle. "I'll need to put you under to get some of those out."

"I need to deal with a couple of things first," I answered. "Why don't you take care of Sue's leg."

I left him doing just that and made my way to the lobby telephone.

I shook my head and dialed Carmine's number from memory. I wasn't surprised when he was wide awake and answered on the first ring. "Talk to me."

"I've got Babs, but she's in bad shape. They're working on her now, but she may not make it."

Carmine's breath came out in a rush that wasn't quite a sob. "And the other thing?"

"It's done."

"Where are you? I . . . *we* . . . want to see her."

"No visitors for now." It wasn't quite a lie. Having Carmine and Linda here wouldn't do her any good—and there was no way the Sazi would let them come anyway. "I'll call you as soon as I know more."

"Do it."

"*Now* will you let me take care of that back?" Raven asked as I placed the phone back in its cradle and felt my legs go to rubber under me. I sank unceremoniously to the floor.

Must be in worse shape than I thought. "Right. Probably a good idea."

His hand shot out in a blur of movement and the world went black.

I woke lying on my stomach in the middle of the lobby floor. Hearing came back first.

Lucas had apparently come to. He was utterly astonished at being alive and was patiently listening to his wife tell him that she had never in her life wanted or expected to be grateful to Jack Simpson for *anything*, but that she'd almost be willing to *kiss* the old bastard for sending that antidote. And *furthermore,* that if Lucas *ever* pulled another stunt like this she'd kill him herself and save Jack and everyone else the bother!

Then she burst into tears.

I heard a soft chuckle far above my head. I cracked my eyes open in time to see Charles squat down beside me. "I'm pleased to see you came through this relatively un-scathed. It bodes well for your future with us. I've tem-porarily reinstated Raven so that he can handle the security for the remainder of the meeting. *You're* going to be busy. We only have two weeks to get you trained to use your gifts."

I started to open my mouth to ask what he meant, but he silenced me with an impatient gesture. He looked like he had been through a wringer, so I kept silent. He sighed. "It's unfortunate that we moved this meeting to Chicago and invited the seers in order to get to know you, only to have the plan completely upended. For now, Ivan will debrief you. Then you can return to your apartment. Aspen will come by there in the morning to begin your lessons."

He was gone before I could comment, but I had to won-der what was happening in two weeks. I would have to find him and ask—just as soon as I could stand.

A moment later, Sue knelt beside me. Her eyes widened as she watched another drama unfolding a few feet away.

"I'm fine!" Asri hissed. "The healers are needed for the sick and injured. I'm neither!"

Bobby's face was tight and fearful. "But you were in-jected with the venom—in the *stomach* . . . How do you know what damage it might do?"

"I would *know*, Robart. It is *my* body! I am not some *mammal* . . ."

She was so intent on the conversation that she didn't see Nikoli walk up. "Have you been checked by a healer, Asri?"

She turned in shock and he raised bushy eyebrows.

"Alpha . . . it's . . . I'm *fine*. Truly I am."

Nikoli snorted into his beard. "And you have suddenly

transformed into a healer in these past hours? I think not!"
He pointed to Raven. "You will go to the wolf and be
checked. You must be *certain* there is no damage to the
children. You must not *guess*."

Asri's jaw dropped open and Bobby moved back from
them, a bit flinchy. I raised my brows and held a finger up
to stop Sue from speaking. She'd noticed I was awake and
her lips had opened a bit.

I needed to hear this conversation. I hoped that Nikoli
wouldn't go off the deep end, but it might get rough.

Nikoli didn't wait for words to come out of Asri's moving but silent jaws. His brow furrowed and his eyes flashed.
"I have a nose, Asri. I occasionally use it, even when I
might not *seem* to." His voice wavered for a moment at the
end. But then he cleared his throat and straightened his
back. "If for no other reason than the fact that I have protected you and housed you all of these years, you will tell
me the truth now. Do you love him?"

Asri glanced at Bobby and looked lost for a moment.
But then she turned back to Nikoli. "I am *yours* to command, Alpha."

I watched Bobby's eyes close and his big hands clench
into fists. Nikoli noticed. He crossed his arms over his
chest firmly and he settled his stance. "Then I *command*
you, Asri—reveal your heart. Do you *love him*?"

Asri looked at Nikoli for a long moment with tears
sparkling in her eyes, but finally dropped her head.

Nikoli nodded slowly. His voice cracked a bit. "And of
course he loves you. He would be a fool not to. Agent
Mbutu is many things, but he is not a *fool*."

Asri reached up and put a hand on his jacket. "Nikoli . . .
I . . ."

He looked at her and his face softened. He turned his
eyes to Bobby, who was trying hard to stay neutral, but
wasn't succeeding well. Nikoli uncrossed his arms and
pointed at the dark man. "You will be *good* to her, and the
children. Or you will answer to *me*."

Bobby got over his initial shock, and nodded strongly.

Asri looked at the pair with panic. "But my home is *here*. I cannot leave! Who will enforce the rules? Who will you confide in?"

Nikoli shook his head and put his large hands on her trembling shoulders. "You must do what is best for your children, Asri. I can enforce my own rules for a time and keep my own confidences. But your little ones will not be able to abide the cold. Go back to Komodo for now, be with your mate and raise your children. You may return whenever you wish. You will always have a home in this pack."

He turned and walked away from them. Bobby hesitated for a moment as Asri watched Nikoli leave, but he finally rested a soft hand on her shoulder. She twisted her head with tears rolling and then turned and threw herself against him, sobbing. He held her close and let her cry.

Yurgi walked up to me, smiling. "You have saved my Pamela, Tony! I have no way to repay you for this gift to me." He reached down to shake my hand, but instead pressed a small red velvet box into my hand without Sue noticing. "Is very nice," he whispered. "I have friend at shop downtown and he gives me good price."

I smiled and nodded as he walked away.

Sue turned to me, trying to allow Bobby and Asri as much privacy as the lobby would afford. Her voice was soft, timid, but she held her head high as she spoke. "Are you mad at me?"

I tried to look stern, but probably failed. "You mean for leaving your cover? For playing bait to that . . . *thing* and scaring the living daylights out of me?"

She nodded with her head lowered. "Yes, that." Sue looked up at me with determination in her face. "But you couldn't have done it, Tony! Not by yourself. I want to be more to you than just something else you have to protect. I'm going to be your *partner*."

I raised my brows.

Her face got a startled expression, as though she just realized what she'd demanded. "I mean . . . if . . . if that's *okay*. You said an equal."

I couldn't hold up the act. I laughed and pulled her into my arms. "Hell yes, it's okay! It's what I've always wanted you to be—smart and sexy and a *very* dangerous woman. We'll just have to toughen you up a bit. Do you have any idea how *proud* I am of you? Any idea at all?"

I grabbed her hand and put the small box into it. "Merry Christmas, Sue. I know it's early, but it seems the right time. It's not everything I want to give you, but it's all I have for now."

I was leaning in to kiss her when I heard Lucas's voice behind me.

"About that, Tony . . ."

I stared up in shock. I couldn't believe he was actually upright. He wasn't whole and perfect, by any means, but his skin was back to a normal color and he was only a little saggy around the original wound. He was aiming a little point and shoot digital camera at the ceiling and wearing an impish grin.

Why in the hell was he taking pictures of the ceiling.

I let go of Sue, rolled onto my back and looked up. Sue did, as well, forgetting about the box in her hand. "Oh my." I stared, wide-eyed for a second before turning to Lucas. "Can I have a copy?"

It was worth a shot. Hell, he might make a small fortune selling copies to Nikoli's pack members. A certain annoying councilman, along with four men and three huge snakes, were plastered against the ceiling, four stories up.

"What happened at the meeting?"

I hadn't noticed Nikoli standing behind the couch until Lucas said something.

He paused and looked at the old wolf, waiting until he had turned his attention from the ceiling. "The Minnesota pack will be split in half. They have been offered an alternate territory in Quebec, but it's far from prime land. It was either that or Alaska, and there's the whole oil drilling debate up there." He paused. "I wish there was a better time or place to tell you all this, Lucas. But there isn't a private spot anywhere in the hotel. The meeting will begin again in the morning, and Charles mentioned you have to be elsewhere."

Lucas nodded for him to continue.

"The cats will be allowed to remain as they are without grouping into prides."

Lucas laughed. "I'm sure the Monier family had something to do with that!"

"Oddly, it was Ahmad's idea." Lucas looked suspicious, but Nikoli continued. "Angelique's raptors lost a parcel of hunting land in California where the humans have reestablished the condor."

Nikoli's face fell. "And, I hate to tell you—I did my best, Lucas, but the council granted Catherine Turner part of your territory. I *was* able to hold them to only the part she'd purchased. Ahmad wanted to make an example of your wife and Dr. Perdue by exiling the entire pack hierarchy, but Charles finally agreed that it seemed too extreme for breach of doctor/patient confidentiality. It was a close vote. Fortunately, I was able to sway Angelique by voting her way on the California land. You seem to have made a few enemies on the council, Lucas."

Lucas took a deep breath and nodded. "I was afraid of that. But the odds were stacked against me. I should have stepped in myself long before now, but I truly thought that Jack could get control of his madness. He's killed too many people without regard for our law, but attacking *Charles's godchild?* Slaughtering his best friends? That was finally too much. He'll have to be put down, at long last. I presume they signed the warrant?"

A deep slow breath made Lucas look at Nikoli. "It's still

in discussion. There are those who believe he can be saved, because of his efforts tonight. And there is the matter of the file . . ."

His voice cut off as one of the pack members rushed by, bringing a pot of hot water from the kitchen. Obviously, this *file* was something that wasn't to be discussed in public, but they didn't seem to notice me and Sue, so I let them continue.

"As for my wife . . . well, that's been a long time coming too. I love her, but I can't protect her anymore." Then he returned to clicking pictures. But I could smell his anger, and his fear.

"Still, I am sorry. You may have to split the Boulder pack if you can't find more hunting territory."

Lucas put up a hand to stop Nikoli. "Let me savor this sight for a moment longer before I have to return to reality, please, Nikoli."

It seemed that they were finished, so I decided to indulge my curiosity.

"How? . . ." I asked toward the pair, as though I hadn't heard a thing. I gestured toward the ceiling.

They both looked up again. "Ah, yes. Ahmad said something . . . *unfortunate* to Aspen." Someone else caught Nikoli's eye and he moved off. "She lit up like the sun and he and all of his guards ended up there. Then she left and said he could find his own way down."

"She can *do* that?" I was impressed. I could *see* the brilliant glow of power the snakes were expending, trying to get down. It was making the Christmas lights and massive chandelier seem positively *dim*—it wasn't even making a dent in their condition.

"He's lucky that's *all* she did." Lucas snarled. "Then again, for Ahmad the humiliation may just be *worse* than death."

Bobby strode up, his expression fierce. "Lucas, I have to talk to you."

"As soon as I'm finis—"

Bobby shook his head and kept speaking. "No, I have to say this before I lose my nerve. I want every person here to know this, so that there are no questions or suppositions. I'm leaving Wolven. Asri and I are going to move south to Komodo and be wed in her old village."

Lucas held up his hand and I saw a flash of power hit Bobby in the chest. It froze him in place. "Would you *stop* for a minute, Agent! I already anticipated this, when I found out that Asri was pregnant. But you also have a number of months before you are a father. If you insist on leaving Wolven, you will *at least* train your replacement."

He released his hold on Bobby, but Raven had heard his words and was walking quickly our way. "Lucas," Raven said warningly. "We're dangerously low on agents . . . Fiona won't . . ."

Lucas turned to him with flashing eyes. "*Fiona* is not presently in charge of Wolven, Raven. *I* am. I will be returning to the field myself, and will be recalling some retired agents to pick up the slack until the case load is whittled down some. We can't be positive that only one spider was born this generation. And Jack's warrant has finally been issued."

Raven looked startled and fell silent.

Lucas smiled. "As I was saying before I was so *rudely* interrupted, Bobby will be training his replacement." He turned to me. "That would be *you*, Agent Giambrocco."

Sue gave a little yip of happiness and started grinning broadly. I held up my hands. "Whoa! We have *never* discussed this. I don't want to be a cop."

Raven and Bobby both wore the same shocked expression as me. Lucas raised his brows, and lowered his voice to a threatening rumble. "I didn't *ask*."

"Lucas," Bobby stammered, "He doesn't have enough power. He's a three-day, for God's sake!"

The older man turned and stood to his full height. "Then we'll give him a powerful partner—perhaps Ivan." He held up a firm hand to both my and Raven's objections. "Tony is fast, he's smart, he's an excellent shot and, most importantly for the jobs I have in mind, he has *hindsight*. Think about it, gentlemen. How many cases are unsolved? One touch from him and *bingo!* Done and gone, case closed. And he has no messy *morals* to get in the way of proper punishment. We'll be busy with new cases. He'll handle the old ones."

Raven and Bobby stared at me with something approaching wonder. It made my skin crawl.

"Excuse me!" I interrupted with annoyance. "I don't like being talked about in the third person while I'm standing in the room. I'm one of the *bad guys*."

Lucas turned back to me and raised his brows. "And you're for *sale*, just like always. I merely have to make sure that I'm the highest bidder. For the right price, I think you'll play by my rules. We also might have a very *lucrative* position for Jessica." He turned to Raven. "She's a professional *bookkeeper*."

Raven's dropped jaw closed and his lips parted in a broad smile. "All of those acres and acres of paper on Fiona's desk! My God! I'll *take* the assassin as long as the wife comes with!"

I shook my head. I wasn't sure I liked how this was turning out. But Sue was practically beaming.

"Please, Tony? I'd really like to have a useful job, and we could stay near each other, at least most of the time. You'd like that! And," she said with a finger pointed at me, "Who better to train me to be tougher?"

I turned back to Lucas with a sigh, but he was back to taking photos of the snakes on the ceiling. I suppose I could be a cop for a little while, if it would make Sue happy. I would probably hate it, though.

Sue had taken the few moments while I contemplated to

open the velvet box. Since I hadn't seen what Yurgi had bought either, I glanced over. The light overhead caught the flurry of gemstones in the ring and made them sparkle like fire. Sue gasped. A swirl of white gold was covered in diamonds, sapphires and rubies. They framed and enhanced a full-carat brilliant round diamond. Impressive, and a little scary. I winced when I thought about how many batteries were probably gone. I wondered just what a *good price* ended up costing me.

Then I chuckled to myself. It didn't matter. No price could be too high.

I reached over and kissed Sue lightly on the lips. "Merry Christmas, Sue. I hope you'll be my wife for a long time to come. I think we should have a real wedding, instead of just names on paper. What do you think? Will you marry me, for real this time?"

She was awestruck, staring at the ring. I finally had to remove it from the box, and put it on her finger. It was a perfect fit. Another point for Yurgi. Tears rolled down her face, and she nodded her agreement. The scents of her happiness were almost overwhelming.

Bobby glanced at the ring when he caught her scent, and nodded his approval. Then he turned his attention to Lucas. Like me before, his eyes slowly followed the path to the ceiling. His jaw dropped as he finally noticed the ornaments four floors high. "Oh my God!" he whispered, but with humor in his voice. "Who are the pictures for, Lucas?"

Lucas answered without moving his lips. "Jack would lick dirt off a hyena to get a copy of these!"

Bobby's face grew startled. *"Jack?* Jack Simpson?"

That's right! He'd been out of the picture both times. "The one and only," I replied, just as quietly. I didn't want to risk the councilman's wrath if he heard us. "He saved your tail when he gave us the antidote to the spider paralyzing venom back at the apartment."

The startled expression turned to absolute horror. *"Jack*

Simpson saved my life?" He grew silent for a moment and all that moved were his eyes, which showed too much white.

Then he snorted abruptly. "Figures! I still haven't gotten that taste out of my mouth!"